God Knows No Heroes

God Knows No Heroes

Norman Shabel

To Brian — Best. Look forward to your next ...

Chateau Publishing House, Inc.
New York

FIRST EDITION

Library of Congress Control Number: 2001092359

ISBN 0-9712710-0-3

To my mother, who taught me . . ."to survive is to win."

Acknowledgments

To Arleen, my wife and partner for almost four decades, who has tortured, demolished, and lovingly resurrected my ego and writing from the dead, time and time again. Without her intense dedication to accuracy, this book would not be a reality today.

To Lexie, a daughter who has shown me what true grit really is. She has refused to follow any path that she has not plowed herself. She eternally surprises me with her ability to be loved by all and yet not succumb to the desire to be loved by all.

To Daniel, a son who has picked himself up from the debris of an insane relationship with his father, to eventually become his own man.

To Steve Batterman, a friend and advisor who has aided me in presenting an accurate forensic scenario for this book.

To Mary Morris who has shown irrational faith in my writing ability well beyond the parameters of our in-law relationship.

To Harold Morris, a man who has grown from the depths of insensitivity to a bright, caring, wise old man.

To the thousands of young and old writers, filmmakers, painters, and artists in general who have been destroyed by rejection, frustrating anonymity, and the years of seeming failure . . . plod on because you may yet be recognized by the world for the genius that lies so fallow within.

God Knows
No Heroes

PROLOGUE

The hot August sun beat down on suburban Larchmont Hills.

The residents had escaped from the town to enjoy the white sands of the Atlantic Ocean beaches.

Eleanore Rubin swerved her white Jaguar into the circle drive of her white colonial house. Quickly she alighted from the car, holding a bank deposit bag under her arm. In her late fifties, Eleanore strode toward the front door as if she were gliding across the American Ballet Theater stage in New York. Trained religiously as a ballerina by an overzealous Jewish mother who envisioned her daughter as the next Pavlova, Eleanore's body seemed to float as she walked.

She opened her front door, patched in the burglar alarm numbers and then moved quickly to the kitchen area, located in the back of the house.

The answering machine beeped incessantly. She dropped the bank deposit bag on the black granite counter and impatiently hit the answering machine button.

"Mama," the voice sang out. "It's Lilli. When are you coming over for dinner? You know it's your 27th? Is Dad home? I have been trying to reach him all day at the synagogue . . . but they say he is in a meeting and he can't be disturbed. Call me. Please."

"Carl," Eleanore shouted through the first level of the house. She fast-forwarded the answering machine, hearing bits and pieces of messages, then, as if she was not happy with what she heard, she angrily pushed the delete button on the machine. "Where is he?" she murmured to herself.

As she absentmindedly stared out the panoramic kitchen window, her eyes rested on the sculptured greenery of the manicured back yard. The phone ringing brought her mind sharply back to reality.

She abruptly picked up the phone, and in an almost shrill voice, said, "Yes . . . Oh . . . It's you, Lilli. No, I don't know where your father is. I'm very angry with him. It's our 27th, and he disappears. Well, he's not supposed to be at the synagogue. It's his day off. Who knows where your father is, Lilli?" The doorbell rang suddenly. "Lilli, it's the doorbell. Maybe it's your father. Why would he ring the doorbell? Maybe he lost his key. I don't know. No . . . no . . . it looks like a delivery man. Look . . . I'll call you back. I have to run . . . Yes, we'll be there at 6 p.m. Sharp. That's if I can get your father moving. I'll call you back."

She dropped the receiver onto the cradle, and hurried toward the front door. After peering through the glass portion of the top of the front door, she opened the door.

Lilli called back one hour later and there was no answer. She called Temple Beth Shalom and the secretary said her father had left for the day. She called her parents' home again and all she heard was the answering machine recording.

Forty minutes later she let herself into her parents' house. Everything appeared normal except for a few drops of blood she found on the rear of the marble foyer leading into the kitchen. As she fearfully peered past the opening of the pocket doors leading to the kitchen, she screamed hysterically.

Eleanore Rubin's body was laying in a fetal position on the white tile kitchen floor. Her neck was partially severed from the shoulders, her eyes were wide open, disbelieving in the horror, her right hand extended, palm up . . . pleading . . .

CHAPTER ONE

It was past 6 o'clock in the afternoon and the summer heat lingered over Main Street in Bristol.

Professional Row, the residents called this side of Main Street. Mostly lawyers. Small offices in historically degenerated buildings, long in need of repair.

Joshua Ryan, feet up on his desk, his hands fumbling through the law journal, was the only human remaining on the Street, as the lawyers so affectionately called it. The exodus to the shore, situated along beaches of the Atlantic Ocean started at noon on Friday, left the surrounding towns of Philadelphia empty.

Ryan had had a good week. He had settled three personal injury cases, a record since the good old days of unrestricted personal injury practice. The only problem was that Ryan could only keep about 10 percent of what he brought in. The rest went to the bankruptcy receiver, or the IRS. That would be his financial situation for at least another year unless his luck changed.

The only redeeming virtue about Ryan's financial straits was that he could finally see the end in sight.

Joshua Ryan had just turned thirty-five. He celebrated his birthday alone, at the Washington House, across the street from his office, sucking on a straw floating in Pellegrino water, lime and a bunch of maraschino cherries. Occasionally, a fellow lawyer would pat him on the back, wish him a happy birthday and then take a place at a table filled with other lawyers. Ryan avoided his fellow lawyers. He hated them. When he had sunk to the bottom of the ethics barrel, no one cared. No one threw him a life preserver. Not even a string. They were all overjoyed. Lawyers are like that . . . when you're on top, they love you. But when you're the least bit vulnerable, they'll eat you alive. Once upon a time he had been on top. First assistant county prosecutor: the title and job meant all-consuming power. Summit County's second most important law enforcement office carried all the perks of the state attorney general. The prosecutor, Roger Leary, deferred to him on most cases. Ryan called the shots while the prosecutor was out screwing any pair of legs he could persuade to come out in his 'Vette. Ryan had to cover Leary's tracks with the local law enforcement boys because Leary was sloppy in his peccadillos. All the guys chuckled secretly in the APA's (Assistant Prosecuting Attorney's) corner of the Washington House when the prosecutor was caught with his pants down, a Puerto Rican file clerk who worked in his office blowing him; the Larchmont Hills Police Department had scared the living shit out of him with their sirens and search lights—all in the middle of the last remaining cornfield in Larchmont Hills. The pros—short for prosecutor, and how everyone in town referred to him—never forgot that incident. Any time he received a Larchmont Hills case, he was sure to take the town police department over the hurdles, bare ass and all.

Ryan, the peacemaker, had cajoled the Larchmont cops into forgetting the whole thing. He convinced them it was a mistake. Consensual adults and all. Why humiliate the pros? Who gains? And the cops deposited the report in the dead file room, yet they still prepared and filed the report, just in case.

Then the hammer suddenly fell on Ryan. His mother died of breast cancer. Without warning. The cancer was rapid and overwhelming. Her poor body was overtaken by the unrelenting cancer. After the surgery, he hated the uncaring doctors. They treated his mother like shit. No feeling. And he was treated no differently by them. They didn't care who he was. He wasn't one of *them*. Just another innocent soul caught in *their world*.

Sarah Ryan. He and his mother had a special relationship that his wife Helen could never penetrate or understand. Helen tolerated Sarah Ryan during those five years of marriage. And Helen was happy when she died. Josh and Helen fought miserably about Sarah Ryan when she was alive. Helen refused to accept Joshua placing his mother before her. Sarah Ryan had an Irish surname but she was as Jewish as a Jewish mother could be. Married to an Irishman, Michael Ryan; her family, the Wassermans, reviled her for it. A *shagetz* in the family. The Wassermans had been orthodox Jews, *Kohanim*, the high priests of Israel. His mother Sarah was the first one in her family to breach the sacrosanct rule prohibiting marrying outside of the religion. She met Michael Ryan in the Poconos. Love at first sight. Michael Ryan literally charmed her into a corner bedroom of the Mt. Airy Inn. She had been a virgin. Saving herself for the right man. Just like her mother and her sisters and her cousins and all the Wasserman women. She always blamed her indiscretion on the liquor, yet she still loved Michael Ryan, although he was a drunk, an abuser, and a womanizer. He died in a men's welfare shelter, drunk and beaten by the other more aggressive misfortunates of the Bowery in New York City. She had stopped caring about Michael. She had her son Joshua to worry about. And she took care of him. He went to college, became an upstanding citizen. A lawyer! He was the best. And yet that, too, was taken from Sarah.

After almost six years with the Summit County prosecutor's office, rising from an intern to the exalted first assistant prosecutor position, Joshua Ryan had fallen off the mountaintop. When his mother died so suddenly, his wife decided that she would assume Sarah Ryan's matriarchal role. Joshua and Helen fought. Physical battles. Helen was not shy when it came to going on the offensive. She pulled Joshua's .357 magnum from the top of the armoire where he hid it and threatened to blow his brains out if he ever tried to stop her unrestrained lifestyle. No kids. She didn't want any. Not with Joshua Ryan. It got worse. They stopped sleeping together. Separate rooms. Then separate houses. Then divorce. He gave in. He just didn't care anymore. Helen took everything. Except the credit card debts. Joshua retained all her debts. Bankruptcy. Except the IRS was not exempt from the bankruptcy. You paid 'em whether you had it or not. And then the drinking. The old Irish Ryan drinking.

Alcohol became his real world. It lifted his spirits for the moment, then he would sink into long periods of depression. Lately, the ethics suspension . . . only six months. Because the Supreme Court understood alcoholism among lawyers. They forgave drunken lawyers, to a point. If he had stolen a dime from his clients, he'd lose his license for sure. At the beginning, Ryan just didn't appear in court when he should have. When he did, he was unshaven and he reeked of alcohol. The assignment judge reported Ryan's repeated shortcomings to the prosecutor, but nothing happened—until the horrible accident with the kid.

The pros had tried to overlook Ryan's problems. He needed Ryan. After a time, newspaper reporters started leaking stories. And when the drunk-driving accident happened, hitting the kid with his car, it was all over. The license suspension, the job, his world. All came down at once—and Ryan didn't care.

He left Summit County. Spent almost a year drinking wine, ouzo, or whatever alcohol he could afford while wandering through Europe. Then it happened. The beating in Hamburg. He was drunk out of his mind, wandering down on the waterfront. The gang jumped him, beat him from limb to limb, and stole his passport and money. He didn't even remember the pain. Just the hospital bed, the nurses, the doctors, and the misery. When he left the hospital, he sat by a cafe at the Hamburg waterfront, drinking coffee. He had hit bottom, just like his father. His father had died a beaten man, yet Joshua Ryan refused to die in the same way. Not like Michael Ryan. His mother, dead and all, would never stand for it. And he wouldn't either.

Back two years, October, Joshua settled into a small office, doing whatever came into the door. The power was gone but he was back.

And then suddenly it happened. Out of the blue, the phone rang one Friday night, causing Ryan to fall back in his chair against the window behind his desk. Righting himself, Ryan picked up the receiver.

"Ryan here," he bellowed into the receiver.

"Mr. Ryan, my name is Lilli O'Malley. My mother has just been found murdered!"

CHAPTER TWO

Detective Lew Mathias pushed passed a crowd of reporters up the front steps of the Rubin house. The dispatcher had called him at his Long Beach Island house just as he was ready to start the barbecue. He had fished all day with a few of the county detectives who he had invited down to the shore for the day. His head buzzed from the six or seven beers he had downed as the guys reminisced about the good old days, before *Miranda*, before *Brady*, before the Warren Supreme Court had released all the criminals onto the unsuspecting law abiding citizens of this country.

Bull-necked, a paunch growing around his middle, Mathias lumbered into the yellow taped-off foyer, showed his badge to the policeman at the door, standard procedure now even, though the policeman well knew the lieutenant detective of Larchmont Hills Police Department. Right after the Rodney King incident and the O.J. Simpson fiasco every backwater police department in the nation had attempted to tighten up its investigative procedures so that their police department wouldn't be the next LAPD clowns. The uniformed sergeant was standing over the body with the county medical examiner kneeling at the body's side. The county detective's photographer was flashing pictures from all angles and occasionally the medical examiner would instruct him to photograph certain sides of the head and body of the deceased.

"Sorry, Lew," the sergeant's gruff voice bellowed out at the Lieutenant. "I know you didn't want to be disturbed this week. But I thought this is one you should be in on from the beginning."

"Thanks Orville . . . I almost got arrested by the troopers for DUI.* They wouldn't understand why 100 miles an hour was standard operating procedures for a half drunk lieutenant on vacation."

*Driving under the influence.

"She's been dead over an hour . . . maybe longer," the gray-haired medical examiner said as he rose to his feet, pulling a cigarette out of his pocket. He lit it and sprayed the lieutenant and the sergeant with a smoky haze.

"Doc . . . you need to smoke that shit?" Lew said as he turned his head away from the smoke.

"I hate you ex-smokers," the medical examiner said as he continued to puff on his cigarette, spraying even more smoke onto the onlooking policemen.

"How can you tell so soon?" Lew queried in a suspicious tone. The county medical examiner's office was notorious for submitting quick, unsupported opinions that usually caught the prosecution by the shorthairs when the matter came to trial.

"You don't trust me, Lieutenant? How come?" He paused to puff on his cigarette. "Anyway, the temperature of the body, the state of the rigor mortis . . . and yeah . . . the watch crystal on her right wrist is busted and it stopped about 5:45 p.m."

"It looks like somebody cut her neck off, or tried to . . ." the Lieutenant said as he kneeled down at the side of the body. Mathias was surprised at the little amount of blood near the body.

"Strangulation," the examiner said. "The person was so strong, the wire, or whatever, must have cut through the neck . . . on the left side. It was like a surgical scalpel cutting through flesh . . . bad, bad boy."

"Why do you think it was a man?" Mathias queried.

"Too strong for a woman . . . unless she was a weightlifter or something," the medical examiner drawled, a bit of North Carolina seeping into his voice.

"Goddamnit, Orville!" the lieutenant said to the sergeant, pointing to the mass of reporters outside. "We don't need this shit here. God, do you see those animals out there? That's all we need . . . before you know it we'll have Court TV cameras looking up our assholes!"

"I'm trying to follow the book, Lew," the sergeant replied.

"There ain't no book anymore, Orville. Talk to Fuhrman in Idaho. He'll tell you the book was thrown out when they let the ACLU run the show!" The Lieutenant turned his gaze from the body and peered out into the greenhouse in the backyard.

"We can't find the husband, Lew," the sergeant said.

"He's the first one we have to talk to," Lew answered.

"The daughter, who found the body, says she's been trying to reach him all day. It was her parents' 27th anniversary. She looked pretty good for 27 years of marriage," the sarge remarked as he leered down at the body.

"You finished here, Doc?" Lew declared in a frustrated voice.

"A few minutes. The ambulance will be here in a couple of minutes . . . I want to make sure I got everything."

"No screw-ups, doc . . . please," Lew whined.

The medical examiner raised an eyebrow and sighed inwardly as he walked out of the kitchen.

"Lieutenant," the sergeant whispered as he walked slowly toward the side of the kitchen, "I got something to show you." Mathias followed the tall plodding sergeant, his eyes gazing suspiciously out the window of the kitchen wondering how a rabbi's family could live so well.

Opening the side kitchen door, the sergeant entered the laundry room. Mathias dutifully followed. "You see here, Lew," the sergeant said, as he pointed to the broken corner of the glass in the door leading to the outside of the house from the laundry room.

"A normal breaking and entering, Orville. What's so strange about it?" Mathias said impatiently.

"Looks like that at first sight, Lew . . . but looky here." The sergeant pointed to the jagged edges of the glass still clinging to the wood lattices of the door. "The hit was made from the inside, Lew."

Mathias bent his stocky body down to the opening in the door frame, ran his fingers along the jagged edges, and said, "Can't tell, Orville. Maybe. I'll have the state lab boys look at it. Why the hell would anyone want to break a glass from the inside?"

"To make it look like a B&E," the sergeant replied.

"Who talked to the body last?" Mathias asked.

"Her daughter, besides the killer; the daughter was on the phone with the victim when she heard a knock on the door. The victim told her daughter there was somebody at the door. Said maybe it was a delivery man." The sergeant answered quickly.

"And that was the last time the daughter talked to the victim?"

"Last anybody talked to her."

"Did you call the synagogue? Was the husband there?"

"They said he left about 5:30 or so . . . put out an APB for him. You think he'd have heard," the sergeant said, as Mathias stared at the red, bulbous nose of the wrinkled face, noticing the tiny blue veins creeping down from the sergeant's eyes.

"Why the hell would he kill his wife?" Mathias mused in a whisper.

"The rabbi's an important man, Lew. Be careful. We don't need another political blow-out like last year," the sergeant warned.

"Fuck 'em!" Mathias replied in a phlegmy growl. "If the mayor gets picked up on a DUI again, I'm gonna put her ass in jail."

"Just be careful," the sergeant reiterated.

"What does the rabbi have to do with politics?" Mathias asked, as he again examined the jagged edges of the broken door glass.

"He's a leader of the yuppie professionals. ACLU, Anti-Defamation League. All the politically correct ones. Clinton named him to be on some national committee. I heard him on television once . . . he reminded me of Jack Kennedy without the Boston accent."

"Pick him up," Mathias said angrily, "I don't give a goddamn who's covering his ass. If he killed his wife, he's like any other perp killer."

A Larchmont Hills policeman entered the kitchen as Mathias and the sergeant walked through the laundry room door into the kitchen.

"Lieutenant," the policeman said, "The daughter of the victim is here . . . in the living room."

Mathias and the sergeant walked past the policemen into the living room. The front door was ajar and all Mathias could hear was the commotion of the television cameras outside the house.

"God save us, Orville . . . you'd think it was the O.J. case all over again," Mathias said in a muffled voice.

Lilli O'Malley was seated in a silk chair next to the fireplace. She stared numbly out the living room window, her tiny hands folded childlike on her lap. Wearing jeans and a white golf shirt, she appeared to be cast in papier-mâché.

"Ma'am," Mathias said as he approached the ghost-like figure "I am Lieutenant Mathias."

Lilli didn't move. Her breathing seemed to have stopped. Just staring out the window, her eyes searching for something.

"Ma'am," Mathias repeated.

"Who could have done it?" she muttered angrily. "Nobody hated her . . . nobody."

"Where's your father, ma'am?"

"Who?" she replied as her pale oval face jerked toward Mathias. "The rabbi . . ."

"I don't know . . . I called everywhere. He was supposed to have been at my house for their 27th wedding anniversary. He never showed up."

Her small voice trembled with fear as she continued, "Maybe he's dead too . . . maybe it was the Mafia . . ."

"I'm sure your father is all right, miss."

"Mrs. Lilli Rubin-O'Malley," she replied.

Mathias's voice wavered with surprise. "I thought . . ." he said.

She stared at him and muttered, "I married out of the faith."

Mathias leaned on the fireplace mantel and tried to hide his momentary surprise.

"Can you tell me who'd want to harm your mother? Had she ever been attacked before?"

"Everybody liked her. I don't know anybody who would—" Her voice lurched into a series of uncontrollable sobs.

"Can I get you something?" Mathias offered in an ambivalent voice; he was always uncomfortable when a woman cried in front of him.

"I just can't believe it!"

"Was she carrying any money?" the sergeant asked.

"She took home the deposit from the bakery," Lilli replied.

"It wasn't more than a few hundred dollars . . . not enough to kill anybody," she continued.

"You never know," the sergeant replied. "There's a lot of druggies out there who would kill for a dollar."

"But . . . but she wouldn't have let a stranger into the house. I was on the phone with her. It must have been whoever was at the door," Lilli stammered, her voice filled with tears.

"How did your parents get along?" the sergeant asked. Orville didn't appear to be fazed by the woman's tears.

"Fine. The usual marital arguments, but fine," she paused, and then her eyes fixated on Orville's face. "What are you implying?" she continued in a demanding voice. "They got along just fine," she repeated.

"You don't know of *anyone* who would want to see your mother harmed?" Mathias repeated.

"I told you, no! She was loved by all of us. No!" she replied, as her face stared hypnotically out the picture window. "My mother was a wonderful person . . . why . . . ask anyone . . . she did voluntary teaching . . . she . . . she . . . contributed almost all the money she made to help the poor children of the community. I can't imagine why anybody would . . ."

"Thank you, ma'am," Mathias said as he caught up with the sergeant and led him out of the living room into the foyer of the house. "Find him, Orville," Mathias declared in an impatient whisper. "We need to know where the good rabbi was this afternoon. You hear me. Now! Go, go," Mathias said as he walked out the front door into the waiting cameras and microphones of the voracious media.

CHAPTER THREE

"Mr. Ryan, my name is Lilli O'Malley. My mother has just been found murdered," a hollow female voice stated. "I was referred to you by my husband, John O'Malley. He said you were against each other in a trial about a year ago."

"Yes . . . I remember John. How can I help you, Mrs. O'Malley?" Ryan answered.

"I don't know if you can . . . it's not for me. I don't know if you read the newspapers . . . about my father . . . Rabbi Carl Rubin . . . Temple Beth Shalom."

Ryan didn't reply for a moment and then said "Yes, something about a killing in Larchmont Hills. Has your father been charged?"

"Not yet. But the police say he is a suspect."

"The spouse is always a suspect in the beginning of an investigation, Mrs. O'Malley."

"They told him he couldn't leave the state . . . without permission."

"Unless they get a court order, I don't know how they can prevent him from leaving the state. But I think if you want me to help him . . . we should set up an appointment here in my office."

Never give advice over the phone, Josh thought.

"They want a statement from him," she blurted out, tears filling her voice.

"I wouldn't advise him giving any statement until he has talked to counsel, Mrs. O'Malley," Josh warned dramatically.

"Can you see him this weekend? He needs to talk to someone," she said.

"I was going into New York City this weekend," he replied as his voice trailed off.

"Please, Mr. Ryan. He needs to talk to a lawyer this weekend . . . please."

"Well," he replied, thinking how it would be great to be

involved in a capital case again, even on the other side, "if he doesn't mind seeing me on Sunday . . . in the afternoon."

"That'll be fine. The afternoon . . . about 3 or so. He's teaching Sunday school in the morning at the synagogue."

"That would be fine. Do you know where my office is?"

"We'll find it," she replied.

"By the way," Josh added quickly before she hung up, "Make sure your father doesn't talk to anyone . . . meaning police, newspapers, reporters . . . anyone at all until he sees me on Sunday."

Waiting for a reply, Josh noted the pregnant pause at the other end of the phone line. "Did you hear me?" Josh repeated in an irritated voice.

"Yes . . . yes, I did. Mr. Ryan, I think my father has already talked to the police. They took him to the station last night . . . not in handcuffs. He went voluntarily. He said he just talked to them . . . not like an arrest or anything."

Ryan ran his hands through his thick chestnut hair and then rested his right palm against his forehead as if he could stop the painful rays from spreading throughout his head. He cleared his throat, more as a time-consuming effort than physically necessary, wanting all the time to gather his thoughts and control his temper. Slowly he articulated, "Mrs. O'Malley, please. You must impress upon your father the dire necessity that he talk to *no one* . . . whatever he says. No matter how innocent it now seems. It could hurt him. *Really hurt* him," Ryan enunciated the words.

"I'll tell him, Mr. Ryan. But it's hard to keep my father from making a speech if he hasn't already."

"I'll see you Sunday, Mrs. O'Malley and one thing . . . bring any documents, statements. Whatever your father has that bear in any way on this case. Anything at all."

"Yes. I'll tell him. And thank you, Mr. Ryan for seeing us on Sunday."

Ryan put down the receiver and then leafed through his dial-a-matic phone directory located in the corner of his half moon desktop. The desk was the only thing of value he salvaged from his six years at the prosecutor's office. Something Helen had found for him at a used office supply store in Philadelphia when he graduated law school.

Stopping at the O's in the directory, he dialed the phone number listed under Olsham.

The phone rang for about ten seconds when the answering service responded with the phone number.

"Is John in?" Ryan queried.

"Sorry, Mr. Olsham is gone till Monday."

"May I leave him a message? He may call in over the weekend. Tell him Joshua Ryan called. Have him call me at home anytime over this weekend. It's important that he be in my office on Sunday afternoon at 3 p.m."

"I'll tell him . . . *if* he calls in," the answering service operator replied in a curt voice.

"You do that," Ryan said as he hung up the phone. He leaned his tall athletic frame back against the high executive chair, almost hitting the window ledge behind him. Muttering to himself, Ryan said, "Goddamn it. The prosecutor always gets a free bite at the apple. Goddamn people!"

CHAPTER FOUR

Sunday morning was hot and humid. The drive back from New York was hell for Ryan with all the late travelers attempting to leave the sweltering sidewalks of the Big Apple for a spray of polluted ocean air at the New Jersey shore.

Ryan wheeled his battered Maxima in and out of the heavy traffic on the New Jersey Turnpike, sweating profusely because his air conditioner had conked out yesterday on the way into the city. He knew then that it was going to be a lousy weekend. His then-girlfriend, an aspiring actress, who doubled as a barrista at Starbucks, complained of menstrual cramps. That erased sex for the weekend. The only redeeming benefit about being an alcoholic was his sex level had plummeted down to zero. Off the sauce, he suddenly had a sex drive again. He thought he had found a soul-mate in Philicia, someone with an unfettered libido. Ryan had met her at the Tavern on the Green bar several Saturday nights ago. She was nuts about professional men and Ryan was no exception. They spent the weekend in her apartment in the Village. Philicia had a roommate asleep in the next room. And Philicia was a screamer. Ryan had given her much to scream about. All day Sunday was the same. When Joshua left her apartment that afternoon, she made him promise he would return to her womb the next weekend. He did and every weekend thereafter for a month. Josh became addicted to the ferocity and frequency of these passionate weekend encounters.

Saturday night was different. Joshua thought Philicia had grown tired of him and therefore claimed menstrual cramps and flow as her excuse for abstinence. "The hell with her," he muttered to himself as he weaved maniacally through the heavy traffic, honking his horn in angry retaliation for his aborted sex life. When he was drinking, he could lose himself in alcoholic insularity, never giving a thought to whether he got laid or not.

He pulled off the Turnpike exit and sped down the four-lane

highway into Bristol. Pulling into the specialty coffee store recently opened in an attempt by the Township of gentrifying Bristol, he purchased a 20-ounce traveling cup of Colombian Supremo coffee and a toasted bagel loaded with cream cheese.

At the office, sipping on the hot coffee and munching on the bagel, he telephoned the Olsham number again.

It was 2 p.m., Sunday.

"Olsham here," the deep baritone voice at the other end of the line declared.

"John . . . it's Ryan."

After a respectable pause, Olsham replied, "I thought you died, Josh."

"Almost did," Josh paused and then asked, "How've you been?"

"Better than you," Olsham replied.

"You weren't such a wiseass when I was first assistant," Ryan said.

"Power spent, Joshua."

"I need you for a new case. He'll be here at 3."

"You got any cash, Josh?"

"The client does. Since when are you so hungry for the green stuff? I thought you were only concerned about the public good."

"The Prosecutor let me go when you went Josh . . . gotta make a living somehow."

"Can you be here in half an hour? We should talk before the client gets here," Ryan said, annoyed that his old chief investigator would even think about money.

"Put the coffee on," Olsham replied as he hung up the phone.

Ryan was sipping his coffee absentmindedly when Olsham strolled into the outer office of Ryan's second floor office. "In here, John," Ryan shouted, as he saw Olsham's tall, well-muscled body pass through the outer office doorway. Olsham turned slowly toward Ryan's voice, his piercing eyes covering all the corners of the dilapidated office.

"Nice window," Olsham remarked, as he walked into Ryan's office.

"Right overlooking Main Street, John. Just like the Pros' office."

"Just like it," Olsham answered with a slight smile on his angular face. Most of his corn-blonde hair had receded towards the middle of his scalp.

"It's been . . . what . . . three years, John?" Ryan said.

"A long time not to hear from a friend."

"I wasn't talking to anyone," Ryan answered, rising from the chair, extending his hand toward Olsham. Gripping the hand tightly, Olsham held it for a few seconds, staring into Ryan's face.

"You've aged, Josh," he finally said.

"I know. That's what the good life will do for you." Releasing Ryan's hand, Olsham looked around at the spartanly decorated office, his eyes fixed on the half moon desk.

"At least she gave you your desk," he said in a deep, almost whisper-like voice.

"Noble wife that she was," Ryan replied, returning to his chair. "Sit down, John. My client will be here in less than half an hour and I want to brief you on the background of the case."

"It's different being on the *other* side," Olsham declared.

"You adapt."

"Prosecuting was so easy," Olsham said, paused, then continued: "Who's the client?"

"Rabbi Carl Rubin."

"The guy who killed his wife."

"Nobody's accused him of the killing," Josh stated in an irritated voice.

"Eighty percent of the time it's the husband. He's a big shot in town, I hear."

"Do you have time to do any investigative work, John?"

"Got all the time in the world, Josh. To be honest, the legal world ain't been beating my door down since I left the Pros' office. Who the hell wants an old dog when you've got those kids in the street doing it for minimum wage?"

"If it's what I think it is," Ryan said, "political bullshit and all. . . it's going to be an uphill battle. Leary is up for reappointment this year and I know he's going to want to show the governor what an aggressive Pros he is."

"The rabbi hasn't been indicted yet . . . or am I missing something?" Olsham queried, as he slid into the ancient black leather chair located in front of the semicircular overhang of Ryan's desk.

"Not yet. Leary is waiting to complete the investigation. . .or the state police anyway. Once he's indicted, the state will have to try him within six months. You know: the speedy trial requirement and all that good stuff."

"I'll need a retainer of five big ones, Josh."

"Five hundred dollars?"

"Five thousand bucks. I ain't devoting twenty-four hours a day for the client on a five-hundred dollar retainer."

Ryan smiled, "You learn fast, John."

"The safety net is gone, you know. Ask for money or go on welfare. Anyway, like all good ex-husbands, I'm still paying my former loved one's alimony."

"I'll ask for the money."

"You do that, Josh boy." He paused and then continued, "and make sure you get a couple for yourself. There ain't no government check arriving every Thursday morning."

Olsham lifted his arms over his head, his biceps showing black-and-white US marine tattoos that had been John Olsham's identifying hallmarks at the Summit County prosecutor's office.

Ryan remembered the five years Olsham had been chief investigator at the prosecutor's office. Friends they had been. Not real close. Ryan was still first assistant and Olsham was the investigator. There was always a chasm between them. At least, Ryan mused, Olsham never lost respect for him, even after he lost the power of being the First Assistant Prosecutor.

CHAPTER FIVE

"Ryan is very resourceful, Pros," Crutchfield said anxiously to the Summit County prosecutor. They were seated in Roger Leary's sixth floor corner suite of offices in the relatively new Summit County Justice Center.

Leary had inherited the family power and prestige when his father, Senator Aloishus Leary, died under mysterious circumstances in a vehicle crash with a young high school cheerleader at the wheel. She survived but never revealed why the senator's pants were found wrapped around his ankles while his head was lodged in her lap just under the steering wheel. Captain Daniel Crutchfield, also known as Captain Crunch, the chief of Summit County detectives, squelched any desire for anything more than a perfunctory investigation by the prosecutor's office.

Roger Leary smiled. He walked around his desk and pulled on the back of his judge's chair until the back of the chair almost touched the floor. "You know," Leary announced, his eyes piercing through the captain's suspicious demeanor, "What if . . . what if . . . we got a wire order from Judge Sturmer. We wire the good rabbi's office. Maybe his house . . . and. . ." Leary's eyes appeared to crawl under his lids and then disappear, and then he continued, "and maybe even Ryan's office."

Leary paused like a little kid waiting for his third grade teacher's approval after he had just sung "The Star Spangled Banner."

"Pros," Crutchfield interjected automatically. "I don't think that is such a good idea. Besides, only an assignment judge can issue a wire tap order and . . ."

Leary interrupted, suddenly blurting out, "But the AJ* will be gone on vacation for the next two weeks and Sturmer is temporary AJ and Sturmer would do anything for me, Captain."

*Assignment Judge

"I know, Pros . . . but Ryan's office? That's violating the attorney-client privilege, Pros. Even if we got anything incriminating, a trial judge would throw it out. Besides . . ." Crutchfield started to stammer.

"Fuck the trial judge!" Leary shouted as he pulled on the judge's chair and then released it. The chair struck the edge of the desk and vibrated back and forth in a convulsive shiver. "So he throws it out. We get enough on the rabbi to hang his goddamn Jewish ass from the highest cross in the county!" Leary continued, his passion unabated.

"Pros," Crutchfield mildly objected, "there are better ways . . . I don't want to ruin a damn good case by doing something foolish. Let me handle it. . . ."

"Yeah," Leary sneered, "And the governor will throw my ass on the political dungheap."

Leary paused, with a belligerent sneer on his lips. "If I lose this case, Captain, I'll be licking envelopes at the Republican Club for the rest of my life." Leary's eyes raised to the ceiling, and then continued in a rapid staccato, "God . . . if we get a conviction. . .I'll have the state Republicans eating out of my hand. They'll nominate me to the Supreme Court!"

Crutchfield quietly watched the young man's face light up, his hands reaching to the ceiling as if he would receive his wish directly from his late father. Crutchfield was painfully aware that the boy could never touch the senator's shoelaces, no less his head.

"Hear me good, Captain," Leary whined on with a voice in cadence with his steps as he paced back and forth across the room. "Get Adrian to prepare the wiretap orders. Sturmer will be back to his office at 2 p.m. Tell the good judge to hold the orders till next week. Then have'em date them, sign them and call you—only you —to pick'em up. Then you file them with the county clerk and execute the orders with your best men. Men we can trust. Am I coming in loud and clear, Captain? Because," Leary's voice lowered dramatically to a threatening whisper, "if you fuck up . . . there ain't gonna be any retirement. Nothin'. You'll be out in the street like Olsham. Do you understand my meaning, Captain?"

Crutchfield raised his once muscular body, now degenerating into beer flab, from the armchair. Saying nothing, he turned to leave the room. Leary raised his diminutive body onto his toes and yelled, "I haven't dismissed you, Captain."

Leary strutted up to Crutchfield's face, and spewing saliva out of his thin-lipped mouth, he shouted, "Don't screw with me, Crutchfield . . . I ain't nobody to screw with!"

"Your father wouldn't do it this way, Roger."

"He's dead and I call the shots in this county," Leary's outraged voice melted into a threatening whisper, "Follow my instructions to a T, Captain. Any goddamn screw-ups we both go down the tube . . . understood?"

Without a response, Crutchfield walked out of the office.

CHAPTER SIX

The media had had a field day. Somebody had leaked the latest developments in the Rubin murder case. Ryan knew the source of the very detailed summary of the rabbi's indiscretions when it came to the public light.

As part of the rabbi's ministerial duties, Rubin offered religious counselling to grieving spouses who had recently lost their loved ones. Although small in physical stature, the rabbi, through his eloquent voice and deep religious passion—exuded a confident grandeur that befit a larger-than-life Cary Grant playing the sexy angel in *The Bishop's Wife*. Both sexes responded positively to the rabbi's compassion and seeming understanding of the surviving spouse's overwhelming grief. Unfortunately, the rabbi offered more than verbal compassion to his female parishioners. The rabbi's words often were translated into physical consolation to his more vulnerable and susceptible female followers.

Lieutenant Mathias had met with the president of Temple Beth Shalom on Wednesday evening at the man's home. His name was Norman Goldstein, a lawyer by occupation.

Over tea and rugalah, Mathias matter-of-factly asked Mr. Goldstein general questions about the rabbi and his duties at the Temple. Having met and talked to the rabbi, Mathias had long developed a gut reaction that the rabbi was motivated by not only the written word of the Talmud but perhaps by the unquestioned adulation of his listeners. The rabbi was a "toucher." His surgeon-like, almost effeminate hands, moved dramatically through the air as he spoke, occasionally touching some part of the listener's body. Nothing offensive. More in keeping with the motion of his voice and words.

Mathias had little faith in religious men. He had seen too many pious leaders in New York lead their flock into bankruptcy, either emotional or monetary—or both.

"Rabbi actually started the temple over a decade ago," Mr.

Goldstein declared. He was a tall and wiry man, his body more fitting to a long-distance runner than a sedentary middle-aged lawyer.

"I only hear good things about Rabbi Rubin," Mathias replied in a gratuitous voice.

"He's one in a million. A brilliant Talmudic scholar as well as a magnificent speaker. He lectures all over the world, not only on Judaic history but also on the general human existence," Mr. Goldstein declared solicitously. "It's more than just religion, Lieutenant. The rabbi preaches a way of life. Family values are more than words to him. It is the cornerstone of his philosophy." Goldstein sighed as his words elevated the rabbi to a cultist level of adoration.

"I presume his marriage was a happy one?" Mathias queried, his steely blue eyes focusing on the president's face for a noticeable reaction to the question. There was none.

"Mrs. Rubin would sit in the audience during Friday and Saturday services, a wide-brimmed hat atop her head, and just *kvell* over the rabbi's sermons. She was always well-dressed, sometimes setting fashion trends in the community. Everyone admired her energy. She was a businesswoman who ran a popular bakery in town . . . but was really known for the great deal of time she spent in all kinds of charity work. A real lady." He paused and smiled self-consciously. "Some of the members might have been a little envious, but most of us loved both of them for what they each brought to the temple."

"So they were happy?" Mathias impatiently reiterated.

Goldstein smiled.

"Of course, I wouldn't know what went on in the privacy of their home, Lieutenant," Goldstein admitted, "but, yes, from what I observed, they were happy."

"Did the rabbi have any outside interests that you knew about?" Mathias pressed on, his eyes more passionate than his voice.

"Well, I know the rabbi lectured at the University of Pennsylvania in archaeology. He had a master's in archaeology, y'know." Goldstein appeared boastful of the rabbi's accomplishments. "Then his writings . . . he wrote several books on the Lubavitcher movement."

"And that is?" Mathias asked.

"An eighteenth century, very orthodox sect from White Russia. You may see them in the diamond district of the city. The rabbi, at one time, long before he came to Temple Beth Shalom was one of the hierarchy around Rabbi Schneerson. Y'know about Rabbi Schneerson, Lieutenant? He's also called the Rebbe."

"Not much . . . just what I read in the papers." Mathias paused to abruptly look out the living room picture window. About 100 or so feet away, on the other side of the street, he could barely see the outline of a small dark car, the driver smoking in the front seat.

Goldstein continued in a monotone, his hand fondling a old-fashioned crystal whiskey glass, occasionally raising the glass to his lips.

"Something happened. I mean something happened to his relationship with Rabbi Schneerson. I mean . . . for whatever reason, Rabbi Rubin left the Lubavitchers in Crown Heights. . .Brooklyn. It's where they live . . . and he came south . . . to Larchmont Hills." Goldstein paused again as he drained the Scotch.

"A drink, Lieutenant? I already asked you . . . I hate to drink alone."

"I'm still on duty, Mr. Goldstein. I'll take a rain check."

Goldstein paused and then continued in almost a whisper. "So he came here. I still lived in upstate New York. But I guess in the late '70s, maybe earlier . . . I don't really know. . . . But I do know he was an instant success to the gathering Jewish community. And he preached tolerance of other religions. In fact, he was the first rabbi in the Philadelphia area to allow non-Jewish spouses to become members of the synagogue without converting."

"Did he treat all parishioners the same?" Mathias asked, his eyes sometimes darting out to the parked car on the opposite side of the street, noting the bright ash from the driver's cigarette glowing in the darkness of the moonlight.

"What do you mean, Lieutenant?" Goldstein's voice was suddenly filled with suspicion, as his eyes narrowed into pencil-line slits.

"Y'know, Mr. Goldstein . . . did he favor women over men?" Mathias's voice raised in intensity. His patience seemed to be wearing thin at Goldstein's cautious responses.

"I don't know," Goldstein hesitated as he got up from his chair and walked deliberately to the oak-paneled bar located in the corner of the living room across from the picture window. Nervously, he poured a double Chivas Regal scotch from a crystal decanter, drank about half the scotch in one gulp, then peered out the picture window.

"Y'know, Lieutenant . . . there's a car out there. Have you seen it?" Goldstein declared.

"I've noticed it . . ." Mathias replied anxiously, wanting to lead the conversation back to the rabbi.

"Looks like an old Beetle . . . the VW. Had one when I was in law school. Anyway, you were saying, Lieutenant . . ."

"Did the rabbi seem to favor women . . . y'know . . . in a more than familiar manner than he should have?" Mathias stammered, knowing that he was now getting close to what he came for, and yet not wanting the lawyer to suspect.

"No more so than any other man . . . y'know, somebody in his position always attracts the females. He wasn't a ladies' man, if that's what you mean. The ladies liked him . . . we all did. He is a dynamic leader. Part of his job is to console the members who are suffering. When the husband dies the rabbi is always there to talk to the survivor. Nothing unusual," Goldberg paused, his eyes widened as if he had suddenly realized the import of the Lieutenant's question.

"You don't suspect?" Goldstein blurted out, before gulping down the remainder of his scotch.

"No, I don't, Mr. Goldstein. . . we have to ask these questions about anybody who might be remotely connected to this crime. Nobody suspects the rabbi," Mathias repeated, his voice belying his sincerity.

"Well, Lieutenant," Goldstein said with an undercurrent of antagonism, "I have to be in court early tomorrow. If I can be of any further help, please call on me. But if you think—" he raised his voice shortly—". . . that the rabbi . . . well, I think you're barking up the wrong tree."

Goldstein paused, and with a voice filled with open hostility, continued, "With all those dope addicts out there, I would hope that our police force wouldn't waste our valuable tax dollars chasing after a man as respected as the rabbi."

Mathias wearily lifted his pear-shaped body out of the arm chair, walked over to Goldstein and handed him his business card.

"Look," Mathias explained amicably, "We have to talk to everybody. I've been in Larchmont Hills for almost 20 years. We don't usually have murders . . . especially the murder of a prominent citizen's wife. I wouldn't be earning my pay if I didn't ask questions."

Mathias shook hands with Goldstein, whose initial friendly attitude had changed dramatically. Mathias walked slowly out the front door, pulled his pipe from his pants pocket and extracted a leather tobacco pouch. Tapping the tobacco down into the bowl of the pipe with a tamper, he lit the pipe with his cheap Bic lighter and puffed languorously, as his eyes surveyed the parked car up the street. He couldn't see the head of the driver but he confirmed Goldstein's observation that it was an old VW.

As he stepped down from the porch steps onto the concrete path and then onto the sidewalk, Mathias heard the dissonant motor sounds of the VW starting up. When Mathias stepped off the curb into the street, the VW shot out like a misdirected cannonball from the other side of the street and headed directly towards Mathias. With an agility unexpected of a middle-aged man not used to daily exercise, Mathias jumped out of the street gutter just as the VW hurtled past his legs, the heat of the speeding vehicle filling the void.

Mathias stood dumbfounded on the sidewalk, pipe smoke rising into the hot, muggy August night air.

Mathias's Skytel beeper emitted a sound on his hip. He looked at the numbers recorded on the picture side of the beeper and then walked to his unmarked police car. He sat in his car for several minutes, his body sweating profusely before he started the ignition and pulled out into the silent street.

CHAPTER SEVEN

Seated in the booth at the far end of a dimly lit bar, Mathias and Crutchfield sat silently drinking the beer from frosted steins placed in front of them by the waitress.

The bar was a hangout for local police and state troopers stationed at the Fort Dix state police barracks about a mile out of Wrightstown. With the standard neon roadside sign blinking erratically BUZZIES on the disintegrating pylon, the yellow lights on the sign gave the rectangular building an eerie fog-like luminescence. Except for a half-dozen private vehicles and two state police sedans, the immense parking lot surrounding the decaying red brick building was virtually empty.

For half a minute they said nothing The only sounds you could hear were that of the two men hoisting beer mugs. Mathias slowly looked up at his drinking partner. His eyes adjusted to the glare of the single light bulb dangling over the booth.

Then he asked in a dry monotone, "Where did you get the information, Captain?"

Crutchfield's eyes stared into the froth of his beer glass and said without looking up, "a tap."

"Whose phone?"

"What does it matter, Matt?" Crutchfield said, murmuring under his breath.

"It matters to me."

"We have an order . . . signed by Judge Sturmer. It's all legitimate, Matt."

"I don't trust your boss, Captain. He's fucked up too many of my cases."

"He's young, Matt. He's trying to fill his father's shoes," Crutchfield admitted.

"Whose phone?" Mathias reiterated, demandingly.

"The tap is on the rabbi's home phone. He got several calls from members of his synagogue. Female members, mostly . . ."

"So?"

"The calls were more than condolence calls, Matt."

"Tell me, already. I have a feeling you're holding something back, Captain." Mathias smiled a crooked smile that compressed his eyes into irregular slits.

"Two of the ladies seems to know the rabbi real well. More than the usual church talk. He arranged meetings with them. Not together, mind you. Alone . . . with the rabbi."

"And so . . . what's so unusual, Dan?" Mathias calling Crutchfield by his given name.

"Their meetings were scheduled at the Larchmont Hills Hyatt," Crutchfield declared, lifting his eyes up from the beer stein, focusing directly into Mathias's face.

"That's it?" Mathias's voice demanded more.

"The women . . . I checked with the rabbi's secretary. They were surviving spouses who were supposed to be seeing the rabbi for grief consolation. . . ." Crutchfield paused with a leering smile on his face. "There's more. He called his lawyer's office . . . Ryan. He used to be our first assistant. His daughter called him and they talked . . ."

"How did you get that info, Captain?" Mathias asked suspiciously.

"We got taps on all the rabbi's phones."

"That's his lawyer's phone," Mathias declared, his hand grasping the stein of beer in front of him, lifting it, and then swallowing the beer that was left in the bottom half of the glass in one gulp.

"Leary wanted Ryan's phone tapped. Sturmer signed the order . . ."

"Yeah," Mathias replied cynically, "Sturmer would sign anything Leary placed in front of him. Everybody knows that. What the hell is that going to do to our case if we present it to a jury . . . Captain?" Mathias paused, his face etched with deep concern, and then he continued, "You don't win cases like that. You know . . . Captain . . . Even if we win in the lower court, you lose on appeal. Any patrol cop knows that. Why screw up a good case? There's better ways to catch the guy." He paused, then continued, "I don't know, Captain." Mathias paused again and then shook his head from side to side in apparent disagreement.

"You can't stop Leary when he goes off the deep end, Matt. He wants . . . no, he says *he needs* this conviction. He's up for reappointment and he thinks putting the rabbi away for life will guarantee that reappointment."

"You should have stopped him, Captain. You know better than that. We've lost more cases because the prosecutor gets too anxious. If you want the conviction that bad, you get blown away by a good defense lawyer . . . and I hear Ryan's a good lawyer." Mathias sighed, removed his pipe from his shirt pocket and lit up. Puffing on the pipe nervously, he continued, "What was the conversation all about . . . the rabbi and the women . . ."

"One of 'em was a bawler . . . cried throughout the entire conversation. The rabbi was good. Never got angry. Just stroked her head with his voice."

"So what makes you think they were intimate?" Mathias asked.

"Love talk . . . I love you, do you love me? You know . . . like in one of those romance novels. If they weren't intimate, Matt, he's one helluva of a consoler."

"Maybe that's his way," Mathias objected, weakly.

"Well, if it was," Crutchfield confessed, "then we'll have to wait until the tapes come in from Ryan's office." He paused and then continued, "And we also wired that Hyatt room."

"That tap in Ryan's office, Captain. We don't need it. It could really screw up the whole case,"Mathias said in pleading tone.

"It's done already. Leary would go bananas if I pulled it, Matt. I got two years to go . . . two and out, and I'm not fucking up my retirement for some lousy tap. It'll be Leary's ass, not mine."

"Why do you stay with that son-of-a-bitch?"

"I'd stay with Hitler to retire with a full pension, Matt. I put my life in this job and I'm not going to let some punk kid ruin it for me." Crutchfield paused and then drank slowly from the warm beer in front of him.

Mathias rose abruptly from the booth. Looking at his watch, Mathias said with a sigh, "I have to go, Captain. My wife closes the door at midnight and then I have to sleep in the storage shed. Anyway . . . be careful out there. . . I almost got blown away by a VW . . . the Bug . . . whatever the kids call it. Black and some insignia I couldn't make out on the hood of the rear motor."

"Probably some mistake. Who the hell would try to kill a police officer . . . just for kicks? Who knows, you get some crazies out there . . . And I thought LA was nuts. Listen, I'll call you at the end of the week. Maybe meet for dinner or something. No reason why we have to be at each other's throats . . . let the politicians shoot themselves in the foot. Just stay out of the line of fire . . ."

"That's how you survive, Captain . . ." Mathias said in a half question, half statement reply.

"It's still easier than LA," Crutchfield replied.

"You and Chief Wilson. He says the same thing."

"We served together, y'know . . . He left before me. Funny how we both wound up in Summit County," Crutchfield said in a low whisper.

"The minor leagues for old cops, I guess," Mathias replied. "Call me Friday, Captain, and we'll exchange notes."

"Just be careful. I mean Leary is more dangerous than that VW driver. Watch him. Carefully. . . ."

Mathias waved to the dumpy, short-skirted waitress as he left the bar. As he approached his car parked in the rear of the parking lot, he suddenly heard that familiar VW motor engine, as if the driver was purposely revving up the tiny souped-up engine to threaten Mathias.

Mathias couldn't see the car, but the growling sounds of its motor filled the dark, empty parking lot. And then the sounds stopped.

Mathias entered his car and sat there for a moment puffing on his pipe. Waiting. And nothing happened.

Resolutely, he turned on the key of his car, waited for the sound of the ignition and then threw the shift into gear. As he exited the lot on to the highway, he saw a vehicle with two headlight beams nestled against the trees, also waiting. Mathias shook his head in disgust and accelerated his vehicle up the deserted highway.

CHAPTER EIGHT

"May I smoke?" the rabbi asked, his eyes nervously circling the room. He was seated in the black leather armchair in front of Ryan's desk. He seemed at ease. It was the first meeting between Ryan and Rabbi Carl Rubin. Ryan had already had an initial meeting with Lilli O'Malley, the rabbi's daughter, that previous Sunday afternoon, with John Olsham present. Her father couldn't make it, she had said. It totally surprised Ryan and Olsham.

"Your daughter's not coming?" Ryan asked, as he lodged uncomfortably in his chair.

"No," the rabbi continued, his voice deep and pleasant to the ear. "She's devoted enough time to my . . ." he paused, and then whispered, ". . . situation."

The rabbi was dressed in a fashionable pinstriped suit, with a handkerchief smartly tucked in his breast pocket. Cutting the musty smell of dead files strewn around Ryan's office and desk, the rabbi's cologne was like a burst of springtime in the decaying, unkempt office. Ryan had received a preliminary report from his investigator, Olsham, on the background of the rabbi, his deceased wife and a short summary of what Olsham thought the Prosecutor's office had in evidence and witness statements.

As usual, the Prosecutor's office was noncooperative with the defense in revealing damaging evidence against the defendant. Under state and federal law, within a limited period of time after indictment, the state is compelled to reveal all relevant evidence, along with names and statements of witnesses and generally anything else the state will disclose at trial against the defendant. The rule was meant to be broken.

The gritty pieces of incriminating evidence were usually held till the eve of trial under the guise that whatever evidence was withheld, had been newly discovered. The unwary defendant usually has no time to refute the damaging evidence by the trial date and is forced to request an adjournment of the trial, which may not be granted by the trial judge. Although the prosecutor is the accusatory arm of the people of the state, he is sworn to play even-handed with criminal defendants who are constitutionally presumed to be innocent but are always treated as guilty after indictment. Prosecution zeal is frowned upon by most appellate courts who appear to be insulated from the realities of the criminal justice system. The prosecutor views his job a bit differently than the appellate courts do. Winning is justice to him. Once the State railroads an indictment through the grand jury against the defendant, the sworn oath of the prosecutor to seek justice for all is washed away in the sea of political reality. Losing prosecutors rarely make it to the second round. And with the almost unlimited resources of the taxpayer's money, the state can overwhelm the lowly defendant with sheer muscle power. Rarely can a defendant fund a thorough but high-priced private investigator, no less retain the services of a defense lawyer who can pointedly destroy the state's case. Poverty means guilt.

"Did you receive my check, Mr. Ryan?" the rabbi asked in a patronizing voice.

Ryan hated to discuss fees with clients. He felt his role as an attorney should be treated with the same sacred respect that doctors received. Doctors never asked for money from patients; their underlings did. Ryan learned soon after his submergence into private practice that the lawyer who shunts the money issue aside files bankruptcy within the year. And after the client has been served, satisfactorily or inadequately, most lawyers have to surgically remove the unpaid fees from the client's intestinal tract.

"Thank you, Rabbi," Ryan replied sheepishly, not wanting to appear as if the money meant anything in their relationship.

"We sent $15,000; $5,000 for your investigator," the rabbi continued, as if he sensed Ryan's discomfort in discussing money with clients.

"Yes . . . yes . . . we deposited the money in escrow until the work is actually done, Rabbi. We'll bill periodically," Ryan added.

"I'm sure you'll be fair, Mr. Ryan."

Ryan was aware of the intent of the rabbi's inquiry concerning the retainer. "I'm the hired hand and he's the master controlling the servant," Ryan thought as his hand clenched into an angry ball fighting off the urge to tell the rabbi to get another lackey.

"I was disappointed you couldn't make last Sunday's meeting . . . when I met with your daughter," Ryan said, regaining control of his turbulent feelings against the rabbi.

The rabbi took a deep breath and then, in a clear, low voice, said, "Before I came to you, I had my people run a complete background check on you, Mr. Ryan."

"And what did you find?" Ryan asked, his anger rising again from his stomach to his eyes.

"You're a fighter . . . but you've had your problems," the rabbi replied, his voice measured and controlled.

"What problems?" Ryan asked innocently.

"Let's not play games, Mr. Ryan," the rabbi interjected brusquely. "We both know you're a reformed alcoholic. That you were suspended from the bar for almost killing a child . . . while drunk."

Ryan jumped up from his seat and walked past the rabbi's chair to the doorway of his office. Standing there, his eyes burning with anger, Ryan said, his voice even and low, "Rabbi, I appreciate your thinking of me . . . but I'd rather return your retainer and ask you to get another whipping boy to represent you. . . ."

The rabbi turned his body toward Ryan without leaving his chair. A smile curled around the corners of his wide, thin-lipped mouth, barely showing his large white teeth.

"You're very sensitive, Mr. Ryan," the rabbi declared.

"I don't like being manipulated, Rabbi."

"And you think I've manipulated you?"

"You know you're trying to, sir. It's enough to battle the prosecutor. When I have to watch my back against my client, I don't need the case."

"I just want you to be sure we understand each other, Mr. Ryan. Whoever represents me has my life in their hands . . . I just want to be sure." He paused, taking a deep breath, almost a sigh, and then continued in a deep, convincing voice, "I had my choice of some very celebrated lawyers, Mr. Ryan. Please," the rabbi extended his hand in an attempt to restrain Ryan from opening the door of the office, "please . . . sit down . . . I don't mean to offend you. I have enough enemies as it is right now . . . please . . . ." Ryan reluctantly resumed his seat, his hands folded tent like on his desk in front of him. "My son-in-law, John O'Malley, as you know, is a prominent defense trial lawyer . . . You know who he is, Mr. Ryan?"

"Yes. I've had several cases . . . some trials with him."

"Well," the rabbi continued, "he said you were the best trial lawyer he has ever been against when you were First Assistant Prosecutor. Then you disappeared. No one thought you would ever return, but you did. Well, John thought . . . please . . . don't repeat what I say to John."

"I understand."

"Well, anyway, John says very few lawyers come back after, you know . . . suspension or whatever . . . and more so with your . . . "

"Alcohol problems . . . ," Ryan interrupted with emotion.

"Yes . . . that . . . well, anyway, John said and he's been a lawyer for a long time . . . he didn't expect anything from you when you returned." The rabbi paused again, uncomfortably placing his hand through his delicately coiffed mane of hair.

"You tried a complex civil case against John last year. He thought it would be a run over . . . With you . . . Anyway . . . He was unpleasantly surprised that you had not lost your . . . what is it lawyers call it . . . magic . . . charm . . . jury appeal . . . anyway, he said you were better than ever. I guess . . . he said . . . the pain . . . whatever, your involuntary retirement, certainly has matured you. And then . . . that rape trial last month . . . the one all over the papers . . . "

"The Salerno case . . . , " Ryan interjected.

"Everybody was surprised that he was acquitted. John said you really were . . . anyway, John said that it was you more than your client's innocence that won the acquittal." The rabbi paused again and smiled, "Anyway, Mr. Ryan, I'm here . . . Again, and I know that I am repeating myself, Mr. Ryan, but I am putting my life in your hands."

Ryan leaned back in his chair and said, "Well, I understand, Rabbi, you're not the first client to bring my . . . whatever . . . to my attention . . . but let's get over that. I presume you want me to represent you."

The rabbi nodded in the affirmative.

"Well, than, let's get down to your defense."

The rabbi adjusted the silk handkerchief in his breast pocket and then nonchalantly blurted out, "I have been having an affair with two women. Members of the synagogue. . . ." the rabbi confessed.

Ryan's face grimaced, reflecting his disappointment in the rabbi and thought, "the unprepared defendant is a convicted defendant," Sam Levine, his mentor would repeat and repeat. "Control the client and the facts and you win. No matter how guilty your client is. . . ." Sam would preach.

"Somebody's already leaked general information about other women to the media, Rabbi. I wish you had informed me about the women when we first spoke on the telephone," Ryan replied.

"Who knows about the details of these affairs . . . besides the women, I mean?"

"We were always discreet."

"Leary . . . the prosecutor . . . knows, I bet. That's the only source who would leak it to the press," Ryan stated absent mindedly. "You know what this does to your defense, Rabbi?" Ryan added.

"It has nothing to do with my wife's murder, Mr. Ryan. We had been having marital troubles for some time. But it had nothing to do with Eleanore's murder."

"Is there anything else I should know, Rabbi. *Anything* at all?" Ryan's manner was curt and demanding.

"Nothing. Except . . . that we had taken life insurance policies out on each other's life. About a year ago . . . on the advice of our tax attorney. Something to do with estate taxes."

"What was the face amount of the policy?" Ryan's mind echoed as to what he thought the prosecutor's opening chant to the jury would be: "Extramarital affairs and a giant life insurance policy . . ." A deadly combination that could certainly hang the rabbi.

"I think it was a million dollars or so . . . for each of us."

"And you were the beneficiary on her policy, I presume," Ryan shot back.

"Of course . . . as she was on mine."

"Have you filed for the proceeds yet?"

"I have . . . but the insurance company has delayed payment until the prosecutor takes me off the list."

"Have you been informed by the prosecutor's office that you're a target of any investigation in your wife's murder?"

"Not officially. But a Lieutenant Mathias told me not to leave town. That I could be called before a grand jury . . . something like that . . ."

"Do you plan to leave town, Rabbi?"

"In the near future, yes. I have several speaking engagements scheduled in Israel."

"Cancel them, Rabbi. Whether you're indicted or not. If you dare to leave the country, that could be construed as an admission of guilt," Ryan instructed.

"They can't be canceled, Mr. Ryan. Some of the speeches deal with the coming elections in Israel."

For a moment, Ryan said nothing. His eyes locked into the rabbi's seamless face. Not one worry line invaded the handsome face of the rabbi.

Ryan's mind wandered back to the days right after his car accident. He couldn't drink enough alcohol to blot out the vision of the child striking the front grill of his Lexus and then watching the tiny body hurtling across the front hood onto the windshield. The vision of the agonizing face and body of the child sprawled across the windshield bombarded his brain day and night for months after his release from the hospital. The aftermath was even more excruciating than the tragedy itself. Newspapers and television reporters hounded him, his telephone rang constantly with pleas for interviews. And then the crank calls and letters came. In raucous avalanches, the public outrage was voiced. Only because of the intervention of Sam Levine, his legal mentor, peacefully enjoying his retirement in Aventura, Florida, did Ryan emerge from this daily torment. Leary supposedly helped. Ryan doubted it. He was no use to Leary now. Leary helped only those who could serve him. Quid pro quo. Dollar for dollar. Scratch my back . . . and I'll scratch yours.

The indictment against him caught Ryan in the depths of alcoholic depression. He could sink no lower. In his own eyes or in the public's perception. Suicide was easier, Ryan mused as he stood by the 20th floor window of the Philadelphia defense lawyer's office Levine had chosen to represent him. Political connections, Levine advised.

"Why Philadelphia?" Ryan had queried. Levine just smiled

an owlish, knowing smile. He was right. Campaign contributions during a general election in the state brought leniency. Even in a foreign state. The indictment was dismissed and it was downgraded to a disorderly persons offense by the state attorney general's office. No felony. No record. Just perpetual public shame. The bar suspension proceedings were not as kind. Ryan's mind reached up through the depressive haze, beyond the shame, beyond the self flagellation, and most of all searing through the alcoholic fog destroying his sanity. He stopped. One day he stopped drinking. Die or continue sopping up the booze. Ryan didn't want to die. Not now. He didn't want to jump out of that 20th-floor window either. Life was all there was. That's what his mother always said. She survived the cancer, the chemo, the pain, until God refused to listen to her pleas anymore. The daily abuse of his drunken father had only hardened him. He would never give up. That's what made him Ryan. The tragedy only made him stronger.

And he could feel the client's pain. When he wanted to. Yet Ryan marveled at the equanimity shown by the rabbi. No fear. Confidence without apprehension. Was it all true? Was he innocent? Ryan thought. Was he?

It didn't matter to Ryan. Or did it? Was there a streak of morality coursing through Ryan's being, absorbed during the years of living with his mother? She played it straight and narrow. Supported him with those torn fingers spent sewing in the Philadelphia sweatshops.

She could have applied for welfare but she refused. She cut no corners. And Ryan didn't either.

"Once the prosecution latches onto those two women, Rabbi, and if you try to leave the country, the prosecutor may be forced to seek an immediate indictment. Do you understand that?" Ryan declared and paused. "Does anyone know the names of the women?" Ryan added quickly.

"I have already written to the board of directors of the Temple revealing my transgressions. Moral transgressions that I am deeply ashamed of. . . . I have not revealed the names of the women . . . for their sake."

"As your attorney, Rabbi," Ryan's voice deepened in a pedantic manner, "I must advise you to cancel your trip to Israel . . . *now*! Any attempt to leave the country would be construed as flight from prosecution and may be allowed into evidence at trial. In simpler terms," Ryan paused, " it could hang you, Rabbi."

Ryan's eyes searched the rabbi's face for understanding. Seeing none, he continued acidly, "Do I make myself clear, Rabbi?"

"There is no evidence against me, Mr. Ryan. None whatsoever," the rabbi replied flatly.

"We don't know that, sir. Since we don't have discovery yet from the state, we don't have the evidence they have. Besides, sometimes circumstantial evidence is the strongest type of evidence. The affairs. The life insurance policy. Rabbi . . . combined with a misunderstood attempt to leave the jurisdiction. The county. Well, sir, in Summit County it's enough to convict."

The rabbi rose from his chair, smiled in a confident manner, held his hand out to Ryan and then said in his professional voice, "Mr. Ryan, I have great faith in you as an attorney. But I am a man of God. I trust my life to God. Whatever will be, will be. Please . . ." The rabbi extended the palm of his hand so Ryan would not leave his chair. "I'll let myself out, Mr. Ryan. Please keep me—or my daughter Lilli—informed of any development in the case. Thank you again for your kindness."

The rabbi's compact body turned quickly and ambled out of the office.

Ryan shook his head from side to side. He knew he was going to earn his fee defending this client.

CHAPTER NINE

"What should I do?" Mathias pleaded as his large head sank into the foam pillow.

"What can you do, Lew?" his wife Joanna asked, her back against the bedboard, her worried eyes focused on her husband.

"Go to the AG's office," Lew replied dubiously. He ran his hand brusquely through his salt-and-pepper hair.

"Leary would crucify you. . . ."

"Maybe . . . but it ain't right what they're doing, Jo. It ain't right. I need a drink," the words barely audible as he rushed out of the bed. Angrily he bolted out of the bedroom and headed downstairs to the living room.

Joanne waited, barely breathing, until her husband returned with a glass of Jim Beam whiskey. He only drank when the tension became overwhelming.

"The doctor said you should stay off the booze, Lew," Joanne warned, her Philadelphia accent flavoring her words.

"He doesn't have Leary to fuck up your case."

"It's a job, Lew. You told me it's only a job . . . why get so worked up about it? You can't control the world. That's why we left New York, Lew. For the easy life . . . now look at you . . ."

"You don't tap a lawyer's office, Jo. You just don't. Not even in New York. I told the captain . . . ah . . . what the hell . . ." he lifted the half-full glass of whiskey and let the brown liquid flow down his throat in a soundless gulp.

"Lew," Joanne said, as she turned toward her husband at her bedside, "We have two lovely kids. Good neighbors. We made a life here. Please, don't get yourself worked up like . . . y'know . . . like five years ago."

"It was only angina. It wasn't a real heart attack, Jo." Mathias stared out the second floor bedroom window onto the silent cul-de- sac.

"The next one could be more than angina, Lew. Please. Tell the chief about it. Let him handle it. It's not your job to control the prosecutor's office. Come back to bed. Please, Lew . . ." Her tense eyes filled with tears as she extended her arm toward Mathias. Draining the whiskey glass, he set it on the nightstand and reluctantly climbed into bed next to his beckoning wife.

"The chief thinks it's a political hot potato. He doesn't want to get in the middle of any political fight," he paused thoughtfully and then continued on. "Maybe I have to go to the AG's office. If Leary grabs those tapes . . . anything that comes from an illegal tap is tainted. It could taint the entire case against the guy. I know the son of a bitch killed that woman. I just know it."

"I love you, Lew . . . y'know that," his wife's voice filled with sadness. "I don't know what I'd do if anything happened to you. Please. Do what you have to do. But let it not eat you up alive, Lew . . . and kill you. It's not worth it . . . no job is."

Mathias's eyes closed and Joanne could soon hear the uneven breathing of her husband sleeping.

She tenderly kissed his grizzled face, turned over and fell into a fitful sleep.

CHAPTER TEN

"I received a strange call today, Carl," the svelte, impeccably-dressed woman declared in a lilting voice. Her sculpted chestnut-brown hair accented her delicate facial bones.

"These are strange times," the Rabbi replied, as his eyes fixed on the woman's face.

"A man named Olsham called. He said he worked for your lawyer. Some kind of private eye. He talked like Mickey Spillane. . . ." She laughed in an unrestrained manner.

"He works for Ryan . . . my lawyer . . . what did he ask?" the rabbi's eyes wandered out the picture window of the dining room. The restaurant was empty except for two well-dressed businessmen sitting at a banquette across the room from the rabbi's table. He stared meaninglessly into the late evening traffic of the Benjamin Franklin Parkway.

"About us. Y'know . . . about us."

"Did you tell him?" the rabbi's voice sounded tired, uncaring of the response. His fork poked at the tiny leaves of the mesclun salad.

"I told him to talk to you, Carl," she replied. Her slim fingers reached across the table and snuggled into the rabbi's palm.

"They'll find out eventually, Moira. I'm afraid you're in for it. Just like me." The rabbi paused as his attentive eyes stared into the woman's face.

"I'm sorry," he added.

"I'll survive, Carl. What about you? Why do they want to bother you . . . us?"

"The husband seems to always be a prime suspect."

"But," Moira's face was startled as she spoke, "You're a respected rabbi. How could anyone think that you . . . would . . ."

"Anybody is fair game. It's a feather in the prosecutor's hat. With all this publicity. On people's lives careers are built. That's the way of this world, Moira."

"You weren't even there. How can anybody believe you could have . . . I can't even say it, it's so awful."

"In a way, if you look at it intellectually . . . sure you see it. The wayward husband seeing another woman. Life insurance policy taken out shortly before the murder. You can make a case out of much less, Moira," the rabbi's voice was even and soft, his hand tightening onto her fingers.

"Did Eleanore know about us?" Moira asked in a voice filled with pain.

"Who knows what she knew? You knew Eleanore. She'd never say what was on her mind." He paused to look over at the two businessmen softly conversing over their dinner. The waiter sauntered over and the rabbi requested two orders of capons with orange-cranberry sauce—the specialty of the restaurant. The wine steward then came over and the rabbi ordered the appropriate wine.

"I hope you like the wine," the rabbi said.

"I would have committed suicide. When Morris died . . . well . . . you know what a basket case I was, Carl."

"It was my salvation also," the rabbi said.

"But people will look at it differently. Won't they, Carl?"

"Yes."

"We fell in love . . . what's so wrong with that," she said with conviction.

"My job was to console my flock . . . not to sleep with them," the rabbi replied cynically.

"You were ready to divorce Eleanore even before you met me."

"Nobody knew that . . . except Eleanore. And she can't testify on my behalf," the rabbi replied.

"What are you going to do. If they charge you, Carl?"

"What is there to do? I'm innocent . . . and I know God will protect the innocent."

"Who could have committed such an evil thing?" She paused to pull a lace handkerchief out of her small bejewelled purse and softly dabbed her eyes.

"That's the trouble. Eleanore was so careless with her money. And you know she carried hundreds of dollars home from the bakery every day. . . . Who knows?"

"Can you still leave? Your speaking engagements and all?"

"I have to . . . no matter what. Too much depends upon my going."

"Your lawyer said that it could hurt your position."

"Lawyers want a perfect world, Moira. He does not know about Israeli politics. Anyway, my life is not that important in the grand scheme of things. What will be, will be."

The wine steward arrived with the requested Sancerre white wine, showing it dramatically to the rabbi. With the rabbi's assent, he opened the bottle and poured a small amount of wine into the rabbi's wineglass. After the rabbi approved the taste, the steward expertly poured both wineglasses.

The rabbi lifted his glass, as Moira did, and he said in a loving voice, "To you . . . to us . . . May we both be here next year."

The waiter brought the hot entrees to their table and for a few minutes neither person spoke. They sat there, slowly eating.

One of the neatly dressed businessmen rose from his table. His head turned away from the rabbi as if he were searching for a rest room, and then suddenly turned toward the rabbi's table. Within seconds he was standing by the table, a rectangular white legal document in his hand thrust toward the unsuspecting rabbi.

"Carl Rubin?" the man asked in a brusque, officious manner.

The rabbi turned his head up toward the sudden intruder and replied, "Yes? Who are you?"

"I'm a county deputy sheriff and I'm serving you with a subpoena to appear before the Summit County grand jury on Wednesday, August 31st."

Tossing the subpoena on the table, the businessman turned abruptly around and left the couple, now shocked and speechless. As a cold shiver raced through his body, the rabbi realized his cloak of innocence in the murder of his wife had suddenly disappeared.

CHAPTER ELEVEN

"You know you'll have to give him immunity if you force him to testify before your grand jury, Roger."

Joshua Ryan spoke the words slowly, without any feeling, hoping that Leary would attribute the nonchalant demeanor of Ryan as confidence in his client's defense. They were seated in a wood-paneled conference room at the front of the sixth floor of the county administration building adjacent to the county prosecutor's bank of offices.

John Olsham sat to the right of Ryan and Captain Crutchfield sat at the other end of the elongated conference table, alongside Roger Leary, the county prosecutor. Leary's paunchy face was fixed with an immovable smile that showed mostly his lips and the tiny tips of his teeth.

"It's only an investigative grand jury, Josh. He's not the target. Why wouldn't he want to help us with his testimony?"

Ryan laughed without mirth, his hand tapping nervously on the tabletop.

"Yeah, and Madonna is a boy. Let's stop bullshitting, Roger. We've known each other too long to play games. If I let him testify, you have to grant him complete immunity. Not just transactional immunity. Complete immunity. No matter what. Understand, Roger?"

"I can't do that, Josh. You know that. The press would drill me a new asshole."

"Well," Ryan rose and walked slowly toward the window as he continued in a monotone, "if that's the case . . . if he's not the target, why not grant the immunity? Since when do you care what the media says about you, Roger?"

Of course, Ryan knew about Leary's vast collection of press clippings he meticulously saved whenever he or his office were featured in a daily tabloid.

"I don't care . . . but I have a public obligation to search out the truth about this vile crime," Leary replied, sounding more like Jimmy Swaggart than an objective public servant.

"You mean you're up for reappointment," Ryan replied.

"That has nothing to do with this case, Ryan," Leary angrily declared, the tenor of his voice rising with the obvious displeasure Leary held for his former first assistant.

"Anyway," Leary continued, "we know about the women. And the life insurance policy. We have enough to seek an indictment right now, Ryan." Leary's face turned florid as he tightened his lips around the threatening words.

Ryan turned toward Olsham. Olsham stared at Crutchfield and Leary. Crutchfield's eyes focused on the top of the table.

"There's something funny going on here, Leary," Ryan's eyes closed to almost knife-like slits as he spoke.

"John," Ryan said as he spoke to Olsham at his side, "Is there any way Mr. Leary or his cohort . . . the good captain here," Ryan's face pointed at Crutchfield, "could have received information about any so-called other woman or some phantasmagoric life insurance policy?"

"I don't know, Josh . . ." Olsham drawled in slow response.

"Captain," Olsham directed his words to Crutchfield, "You've always been an honorable law enforcement officer. It seems to me that the prosecutor has information that we're not privy to. And if we are, could not have been revealed to the prosecutor's office by legitimate means. Am I off-base, Captain?"

"We don't have to reveal nothing to you. Nothing till your client is indicted," Leary replied, cutting off any response from the captain.

"I'll tell you this, Mr. Prosecutor," Ryan's voice was edged with venom, "if you mess with me . . . I mean fuck with the law, Leary . . . you ain't ever going to see re-appointment. You think you stand on top of this county, all powerful, can't be touched by us mere mortals. Well, Roger baby, you ain't got your father to save your ass now. Did you get that, Roger-Dodger?"

Ryan turned his back to leave when Leary shouted across the room, "Where you going, Ryan? What . . . to down a few bottles of booze . . . you don't scare me. You never did . . . I saved your fucking ass from disbarment and this is how you repay me. Well,

Mr. Clarence Darrow, let's see who's going to win this match. I'm going to indict your fucking kike client and I'm going to convict his Jewish ass and I'm going to place him on the gurney myself so he can meet his God. And I'll tell you, I also know about this Israeli bullshit. . . . If that sucker tries to leave my jurisdiction, I'll have Judge Sturmer sign an order putting his ass in jail until I can issue the indictment. You got it, Mr. Ryan?"

"Mr. Ryan," Crutchfield said in a husky voice, his head raised to focus on Ryan. "Please, let's all keep our heads. There's a lot of shit we've all been through together. John here and I worked together for twenty years and we never had a disagreement. When you were just a young A.P . . . The prosecutor . . . and I can tell you . . . goes by the book. We all do. Any information we've come by has been gathered by the book. You have my word on that," Crutchfield's eyes were watery, almost appearing as if he were crying. He clasped his brawny hands together on the table as if he were a fourth grader waiting for the teacher to speak.

"Captain, shut up," Leary spewed the words out at the older man at his side.

"I don't have to explain my actions to these . . . these . . . fucking has-beens. Look," Leary pointed his bony forefinger at the departing body of Ryan, "You do what the fuck you want to do. Go to the AJ if you want. But you better produce that murdering client of yours when I indict his ass. I'm telling you. If he leaves this county without my prior approval, Ryan, I'm going to hold you accountable." He paused and then continued in an ominous whisper, "I might even indict you for obstruction of justice and whatever the fuck else I dream up." Leary then shouted, "You hear me, Mr. Ryan?"

Ryan wheeled around, his back to the exit doors. "Roger, just remember without me you were nothing and you still are nothing. Do what you will . . . I'll be ready."

Ryan, with Olsham directly behind him briskly left the room. Crutchfield's eyes continued to stare at the tabletop.

CHAPTER TWELVE

The night flight to Tel Aviv was late leaving the gate at Kennedy International. As usual, personnel offered no excuses for the tardy departure. El Al expected everyone to understand that El Al operated its airline under different rules then any other airline in the western world. Explanations were unnecessary.

"We are the airline of the Jewish State," they boasted to the outside world. That should be enough.

Of course, up until the late fifties or so it was the only airline that had scheduled flights to the Promised Land. Its personnel were extremely competent, its pilots having trained in mortal combat. Along with the competence came an undercurrent of surliness which can only be matched by New York City's taxicab drivers (who probably trained under El Al's instructors). Forgiving the indifferent manner of its employees, El Al offered its faithful riders a modicum of security in a world filled with madmen. Subjecting its passengers to the most rigorous of mental and physical inspections, El Al enjoyed the highest percentage of completed, unbombed or non-hijacked flights. All at a price.

After a limousine dropped him off at the El Al entrance to the airport, Rabbi Carl Rubin hurriedly kissed his daughter Lilli goodbye and said in a hushed voice, "I'll be fine, Lilli. Don't worry. Make sure you call Ryan tomorrow. Not a minute sooner. Do not use the phone or fax machine to contact me. I'll communicate with you by personal courier. If you need to contact me, here."

He slipped a small memo page to her with a phone number inscribed on it. "Just leave your name. I'll keep in touch with you."

"But Poppa, I thought—Mr. Ryan told you that leaving . . . could hurt your case. Do you have to go?" she asked in a childish, pleading voice.

"I have to go, Mommala," he replied, tears filling his eyes. "I love you, no matter what happens . . . you know that, don't you?"

He kissed her on the cheek, his mouth feeling the salty tears streaming down her face.

"Poppa . . . you didn't do it . . . did you?" she asked in a trembling voice, her eyes staring at the ground.

"I loved your mother, Lilli. But things changed as we changed. Our needs were different. No, I didn't do it. I could never hurt your mother." His voice was without passion.

Grasping her tiny face with his hands he kissed her on the eyes and nose and then quickly turned, grasped his dark leather handbag, and walked briskly to the revolving doors into the airport's ticketing area.

At the El Al ticket counter he handed his tickets to a young man dressed in jeans and an El Al shirt, a *yarmulke* perched on his prematurely balding head.

"Good morning, sir. My name is Eliyahu. I will have to ask you a few questions. Do you have your passport, sir?" The young man's eyes searched the rabbi's face as if the face would reveal some hidden evil intent of the traveler.

Retrieving the passport from the inside pocket of his sports jacket, the rabbi handed it to the security attendant. As he was leafing intently through the passport pages, the young man was joined by a tall, well-built women in her late twenties, who wore no makeup. She was similarly dressed as her male counterpart.

Peering over the male attendant's shoulder, the woman's eyes scoured the pages of the rabbi's passport.

"Is this your first trip to Israel?" she asked matter-of-factly. Her eyes stared into the rabbi's face as she asked the question.

"No, I am on official business." The rabbi smiled and then continued, "You might say that I am a guest of your government."

The young security attendants looked at each other and then the man said, "There is no official stamp on your passport, Mr. . . . ." he looked at the name in the passport and then he said, "Mr. Rubin."

"There wouldn't be. But I am . . . anyway . . . I am a rabbi. My business in Israel involves several lectures I will give at the university in Jerusalem."

"What is the subject of your lecture?" the young woman queried, her voice unimpressed.

"Politics—history—an assortment of topics. Are these questions necessary?" The rabbi said in a voice noting his growing irritation.

"We are just doing our job," she instructed.

"Unfortunately, there are people who would like to destroy our planes," and as an afterthought she added, "And you also, Mr. Rubin . . ."

"Where will you be staying in Jerusalem?" the young man asked.

"The King David Hotel."

"How long do you expect to be in Israel, Rabbi?" the woman asked.

"I do not know—I have been invited to lecture there by several members of the Likud party," the rabbi declared, hoping the mention of one of the leading political parties in the upcoming Israeli election would quash the interrogation.

"In particular, by whom were you invited?" The young woman continued to interrogate, her voice soft but husky, like a smoker's voice.

"For one . . . the candidate himself. Benjamin Netanyahu."

"Do you have a written invitation . . . something to show us?" the young man asked.

The rabbi angrily snatched a letter from his travel folder, situated in his breast pocket.

"Here," he offered, "a letter from Rabbi Mashu Lievite." The letter was on plain white paper inscribed in handwritten Hebrew.

The El Al employees held the letter between them, both studiously reading the Hebrew inscriptions.

After a few minutes passed, the young woman peered up from the letter, and in a suspicious voice declared, "I do not see Netanyahu's name mentioned in this letter, sir. Nor anybody from the Likud party. Just Rabbi . . . Lievite . . . mentioned some other party. The Shas . . . where do you see the Likud mentioned, sir?"

The rabbi's patience was apparently wearing thin as the minutes dragged into what was almost an hour of interrogation by these inscrutable young people. His primary concern was that he might be stopped in leaving the country by the messy affair he was hurriedly leaving behind.

"If you want, I will give you a number at the Israeli consulate in New York. The person whose name I will give you will vouch for me. Would that be sufficient?"

The rabbi withdrew a business card denoting a name and phone number on the back of the card and handed it to the young woman. She continued to stare at the rabbi's face as if she had recognized something familiar about the face and then quickly peered down at the business card.

"Hold him here for now, Eliyahu," she instructed her colleague, as she moved behind the El Al counter to the back room.

"I have never been subjected to such—" the rabbi complained.

"The elections . . ." the young man softly admitted. "We have to be extra careful. And the bombings."

The rabbi was aware of the recent series of catastrophic bombings that had shocked even the war-ravaged Israelis. Right in the heart of Jerusalem. At the core of daily life. The bus station surrounding Ben Yehuda Street had been destroyed, along with hundreds of unsuspecting Israelis. It was meant as a warning. The peace process was in full bloom between the Israeli liberals and the moderate Palestinians and was endangered of being destroyed by the Hezbollah suicide bombers. A fitting prologue to the contentious political battle being fought between Shimon Peres' Labor party and Benjamin Netanyahu's Likud party.

Likud and the terrorists of the Hezbollah had similar goals. Neither wanted peace between the Jews and the Palestinians. Of course, the effect of the bombing was to choke off any further movement between Israelis and Palestinians. Hatred between the age-old enemies again prevailed. The seismic vibrations of the killings travelled throughout the world. Especially to the United States.

The Clinton administration knew the road to permanent peace in the Middle East would be sidetracked if Peres lost and Netanyahu won the Israeli election. All stops were pulled out by the Clinton administration to ensure the Peres victory. The United States did not lend any support that might aid Netanyahu and the Likud. Rabbi Carl Rubin had been noted by the state department as a right-wing religious leader who had ties to the ultra-Orthodox Shas Party. Netanyahu might seek out such a pivotal small party to win a majority of the fickle Israeli electorate.

Anything was possible in Israel during the first direct election of its Prime Minister.

The rabbi anxiously eyed the large clock on the wall behind the El Al ticket counter as he waited for the young woman's return. Several people queued up behind him but the security attendant instructed them to seek other El Al ticket agents.

Briskly, the young woman returned from behind the wall and grabbed the rabbi by the arm as she picked up his leather bag.

"Please, Rabbi . . . do not say anything. Just follow me . . . quickly," she whispered into his ear as she pushed him along the airport corridor to the US customs passport control counter. From the outside of the airport came a series of police sirens as several New York squad cars converged at the curb of the terminal.

"What is happening?" the rabbi inquired as he hurried alongside the fast-stepping Israeli woman.

The woman handed the rabbi's passport to the US customs officer who stamped it perfunctorily. Waving off the El Al security guards scanning the passengers and their luggage, the woman frantically pushed the rabbi through the metal detectors into the outer corridor, leading to the El Al gates.

"An arrest warrant has been issued, Rabbi," she spoke clearly, her body propelling the rabbi along to the El Al gate.

"By whom?" the rabbi replied, knowing the answer.

"My people were informed by the person you had me call at the Israeli consulate in New York. New Jersey police have requested your arrest. I do not know anything more. Except you must be a very important person. My instructions were to get you on our plane now . . . before the US authorities pick you up."

The rabbi peered over his shoulder as he handed his first class tickets to the steward at the air corridor door. Captain Crunch had just entered the airport with three uniformed New York policemen and two plainclothesmen of questionable authority.

The captain bolted towards the El Al ticket counter then suddenly stopped in his tracks when he spotted the rabbi passing through the passport control gate. With a feverish gesture of his forefinger, he directed his frantic entourage to run through the airport after the fleeing rabbi.

The rabbi had been led aboard the plane by his newfound compatriot who ensured that she would close the plane doors as soon as she deplaned. With military efficiency, the plane embarked from the gate and backed out of the loading area.

The young security woman walked slowly down the covered passageway, toward the lounge area where Captain Crunch and his party waited with impatient urgency.

"You have to stop that plane from taking off, young lady!" Captain Crunch shouted as he pointed his finger menacingly out the airport lounge window towards the departing plane.

"I am sorry, sir. The plane is on its final takeoff and cannot be stopped." She uttered the words without emotion.

"I am a law enforcement officer with a warrant of arrest for one Carl Rubin, ma'am. I believe that he is on that plane. If you do not stop that plane . . . I'll . . ." One of the plainclothesmen stepped in front of the captain and stuck his nose directly into the face of the young woman.

"Little lady," he said in a thick New York accent, "my name is agent McGuire. I am attached to the FBI office in New York. Captain here has a federal warrant for the man's arrest and you cannot let that plane leave. It's that simple, lady."

Smiling demurely, as if she were controlling an insane audience of juvenile delinquents, the young woman declared, "Gentlemen . . . I am attached to the Mossad, the Israeli intelligence agency. I am a trained lawyer and I am telling you that the plane is going to leave. Once a passenger is on an El Al plane, you cannot interfere with his flight. You gentlemen have no jurisdiction over El Al once the plane leaves the airport and," she pointed skywards, "you can see the plane is in the air. I am sorry that I can't be of more help," she said, her voice, slightly hoarse which added to its already lusty tone. She pushed through the group of men, smiling as she disappeared into the outer corridor of the airport.

CHAPTER THIRTEEN

Ryan knew he was being followed. The tail had only started a day ago. He even thought that his phone could be tapped but he summarily discarded that notion as unduly paranoiac.

"Who the hell would tap a lawyer's phone?" he mused to himself. "Never happen. Not even Leary. He couldn't be that stupid. A tail, maybe . . . even that would be an extraordinary measure for Leary. Who would tail the defendant's lawyer?"

Ryan soon found out who and why. The newspapers seemed to be Ryan's source of reliable information about his own client. The rabbi, unbeknownst to his own lawyer, left the country just ahead of Captain Crunch's claws. Stupid thing to do. Ryan knew jurors were not sympathetic to defendants who ran from prosecution.

Lilli O'Malley had finally called him after the local news rag had blared of the rabbi's escape the night before. Great timing, Ryan had thought. How can a defendant hang himself in more ways than the rabbi is doing? And the funny thing about the whole case is that Leary had, at best, a weak circumstantial case against the rabbi.

Ryan knew that Leary would now be pushed to convene the grand jury and indict the rabbi. Who knows? Maybe Leary knows more then he is letting on. DNA, blood smears, skin deposits, fingerprints—who knows what Leary will conjure up to get a conviction. Ryan wouldn't put it past Leary to convert innocent data or exculpatory evidence found at the scene into damaging evidence against the rabbi. A means to an end. Leary would stop at nothing to get his reappointment.

Leary had threatened Ryan with possible indictment on obstruction of justice charges if the rabbi fled the jurisdiction. Well, he had. Ryan wondered if Leary would carry the game one level higher by indicting the defendant's lawyer for obstruction of justice or whatever other bullshit Leary could dream up. There was no trouble getting an indictment past the grand jury. The prosecutor only need shake his head in the affirmative and the grand jury bowed and delivered the indictment requested. In fact, the prosecutor could even bypass the grand jury and issue an accusation against the defendant that would have the same force and effect as an indictment would have had.

Normally the prosecutor would want to curry favor with the petit jury, the final arbiters of guilt or innocence of the defendant, by informing them that the grand jury had already adjudicated the defendant guilty. No matter that the standard to indict was dramatically lower then the standard to convict. Detail. Only a small detail. The prosecutor always declares in his opening statement to the petit jury that the defendant had been indicted by a grand jury. At trial, experienced defense counsel, in his opening would explain what an indictment is all about.

"It means nothing, ladies and gentlemen, a rubber stamp, a mere allegation of the prosecutor. There are no defenses for the defendant before a grand jury. That is the way of the imperfect legal world," Ryan muttered, as he entered the Philadelphia Airport for a flight to Fort Lauderdale. Sam Levine, his ailing mentor, was at the receiving end of his flight.

CHAPTER FOURTEEN

"So this is how you live, Sam?" Ryan said, smiling as he surveyed the spacious swimming pools adjacent to the Intracoastal Waterway at the Turnberry Yacht Club.

"Life is good, Josh," Sam replied as he adjusted his old wide-brimmed straw hat.

Both men were stretched out on the lounge chairs nestled under waving palm trees.

"I thought you'd blow your brains out before retiring to Florida, Sam."

"You learn to adjust," Sam's round face admitted a reluctant smile, causing creases to form on his bald head.

"Don't you miss the action?"

"What action?"

"The infighting of the courtroom—you know what I mean, Sam."

The older man methodically rubbed suntan oil over his rotund belly, up onto his shoulders and saturated his face and head with the musky liquid.

"The joy is gone, Josh. I leave the spoils of battle to the next generation."

Pushing his hat forward, Sam Levine stretched his mammoth body over the full extent of the lounge chair. He picked up a tall curved glass filled with a tropical drink and slowly sipped the straw.

"What do you think I should do?" Ryan asked.

"I would be careful."

"You don't think Leary would carry out that bullshit threat?"

"His father did it to me."

"That was different," Ryan declared, and then after a few seconds continued, "I didn't mean the senator should have indicted you. But at least there was somebody there who would sign a complaint against you. There is nothing here . . . except Leary."

"Yeah. I guess it was different." Sam flipped the straw hat back over the top of this head and stared at Ryan with rheumy, bloodshot eyes.

"As you know, Joshua my friend, Senator Leary . . . when he was the county prosecutor, persuaded my live-in woman to get her sixteen-year-old daughter to say I was fornicating with her. Ugliest kid you ever did see, Josh. But you didn't mess with the senator. Nobody did. Except me. A Jew in KKK country. In those days, Josh . . . a Jew was on the same level as a black. At least they had the benefits of a white- sheet performance before they hung'em. Me . . . the only Jew for ten miles. They didn't even bring out their white sheets. . . ."

"You were acquitted."

"Only because one juror had taken a liking to me. Or else, I would have been some anonymous number in Trenton State Prison. Writing briefs for my colleagues so that they would pass me by when the cornhole sessions were on the nightly agenda." Sam paused and grimaced, his face a mask of pain as he continued. "He almost had me, Josh. But, let me tell you. It still took its toll on me. I was never the same after that . . . took the fun out of trying cases."

Josh noted how the years in Summit County had neglected to diminish the heavy Brooklyn accent of Sam's speech. Ryan loved the accent. It reminded him of his mother's accent.

"Let me say this, Josh: if it were me. And I were a young buck like you . . . I'd tell Leary to go fuck himself. And go all out in defending my client. And I don't give a shit that your client decided to spend the summer in Tel Aviv. Just because Leary tells you to prevent your client from leaving . . . there was no obligation on your part. Or even on your client's part—to stick around. After the rabbi leaves the country, then the son of a bitch gets the indictment. Makes your guy look like a guilty man on the run . . . but, hey."

Sam motioned to the passing waitress in shorts and pointed to his glass, "Another Jamaican bomb, honey," he cried. "You okay, Josh?" he added.

"The Shirley Temple is fine."

"I forgot," Sam chuckled huskily, "you are a rummy on the wagon. You're still on the wagon, aren't you, Josh?"

"Forever and ever, big fellow," Ryan replied in a good-natured voice.

"Those mother-sucking ethics cops. That's all they are, you know. The goddamn Supreme Court has unleashed the Puritan patrol," Sam bellowed, his eyes burning with smoldering hate. He continued in a bitter voice, "Why don't those black-robed monks just declare that all lawyers are suspect and put those electronic armbands around our bodies so honest, ordinary citizens can watch out for the evil that we do?"

"You don't forget so easily, Sam. I guess I don't either. They really tried to destroy you." Ryan downed the remainder of the Shirley Temple and stood up from the lounge chair.

"That's why I'm here and they're there. Fifteen hundred miles is just far enough. Anyway, Josh, you're still young . . . you'll bounce back. This old 'cocker' . . . well, resiliency is not part of our aging makeup." He paused and held his hand out to Josh.

"Come here, my young friend. Sit at the edge of my chair. Let me give you some fatherly advice. First of all, you've got to get your fellow back here. No matter what. And before the Israelis decide to extradite his ass. Then he'll come back in chains . . . the news boys will have a field day . . . and your guy will be as good as dead. The pretrial publicity is a mountain most defendants can't climb."

"I think Leary's had me followed . . . even down here." Josh's eyes suspiciously treaded around the pool area.

"Sure, why not, it's not his money. Does he still have Captain Crunch working the bathrooms?"

"Still there. Trying to hold Leary in check. But nobody tells Leary what to do. Not since his father died."

"You got any money from your guy?" Sam said, as he slurped the remnants of his Jamaican bomb.

"Some. Not enough to track him down in the Middle East."

"Well," Sam said, "if you need a few dollars . . . I'll lend it to you. You'll pay me back when you get paid, Josh."

The hot sun bore down on the two men who appeared to be the only souls around the lush water area of the yacht club.

"His daughter is still in town," Josh replied.

"You got to get him back, Josh, without an extradition order facing you. Leary's probably sending the Texas Rangers to Israel."

"As far as I know they don't have a case unless Leary is holding some black aces to his chest."

"He's got something. Besides, the women the rabbi was making it with . . . a million-dollar life insurance policy . . . it's a damn good start, Josh. Until you get an answer to your bill of particulars . . . well . . . you'll never know what Leary is holding. He's a desperate man. And desperate men do very rash things." Sam paused and then agilely whipped his thin shapeless legs off the chaise lounge onto the colored tile walkway.

"Let's stop talking shop and go to dinner, Josh. They have a wicked Thai chef here that will blow you away. What do you say my young friend, dinner at eight?"

CHAPTER FIFTEEN

Mathias shoved his way through the young revelers crowding around Buzzies' horseshoe bar. At the far end of the bar, a three-piece band played county and western music. Occasionally a bosomy singer, wearing lizard boots up to her thighs, jumped up on the makeshift stage and sang her whiny, tragic songs.

Mathias threaded past the bar and into the far dark corner where a tall, beefy man sat alone in a booth drinking a pitcher of beer, some foam flecking his black-and gray-beard.

"Why don't you use a straw?" Mathias said as he slid into the other side of the wooden booth.

"Fuck you, Matt." The man replied without missing a gulp of beer.

"You picked the damnedest night to drink beer at Buzzies," Matt said, his hand grabbing the pitcher out of the big man's hand as he poured the beer into an empty glass sitting on the table.

"Have some beer, Matt," the man declared cynically, grabbing the pitcher away from Mathias.

"I'm here. Tell me, what do you have, Madden. You drag me out of the house on Saturday night to tell me about some big news." Mathias grimaced as he peered around the smoked-filled room. Buzzies was the biggest singles hangout in Summit County, especially on Saturday night. The locals also used it as a cheaters' hideaway. Madden seemed mesmerized by the bar activity.

"Did you see the tits on that singer, Matt? Man, I would drive to Hoboken for those tits," Madden said as his gray eyes blinked in spastic motion staring at the gyrating singer located across the room.

"What the hell do you got, Madden?" Mathias was angered that he had to leave his frosty air-conditioned family room, his recliner, and favorite Phillies game to meet the former Summit County detective called Madden.

"I can't invite you out for a beer? We go back a long way. All the way to the Big Apple. Remember the East New York narco squad in Brooklyn, Matt? We could have become millionaires if we sold the dope we glommed from those niggers. But not you. So here we are . . . in the middle of nowheresville . . ."

"You're here because they booted you off the force, Madden. It wasn't voluntary, remember." Mathias was tired of the complaining. Everywhere he went that was all he ever heard. What an imperfect world we live in, he mused.

"I want a hundred smackers for this info, Matt. It's worth more but you're my buddy . . . so for you it's only a hundred." Madden's thick lips slurred his words as the beer slogged its way from his brain to his mouth.

"How will I know it's any good," Mathias replied. Slowly sipping his beer, he wondered how a good cop like Madden could fall into the sewer. They caught him taking bribes in New York. Internal Affairs crucified him. The newspapers made him the target of a massive corruption probe that eviscerated the NYPD's narco vice squad.

Madden got off with termination. No jail time. No conviction. Drummed out of the corps without a pension to come home to and like all ex-big city cops, good and bad, he sought refuge in the 'burbs. Mathias helped him get into the Summit County detective squad. But he messed that job up also. Always on the take. Madden couldn't resist the booze and broads, and they both required money. Summit County didn't actually catch him on the take, not in so many pictures, but they had had enough of Madden. So off he went, an ex-cop looking for a buck. Mathias paid him for information Madden somehow came up with from "unidentified sources," he would brag.

"Do I get the hundred, Matt?" Madden pleaded.

"I got fifty. . .if it's even worth fifty."

"You've gotten tougher in your old age, Matt. Okay . . . Remember that wife murder in Larchmont Hills? The one where the husband took off . . . a rabbi."

Mathias showed no emotion on his face but his mind pleaded for Madden to spit out the information.

"Well," Madden continued, "your favorite prosecutor is doing the dirty deed. He's wiretapping the guy's lawyer's office. That's not all. He's trying to get the lab guys to postdate some of the blood evidence to match the murder date. And the medical examiner's autopsy report."

"How the hell do you know all this shit, Madden? I have to know your source to believe you."

Madden's joyless face turned to look behind him, and then he smiled a wide-gapped smutty grin.

"How do I know? What would you say if I told you I was getting my info from Leary's office itself. What'd you think about that, big shot?"

"You gotta tell me who, Madden. The information is too important to depend on an unidentified source."

Mathias insisted on the source because what Madden was charging the county prosecutor with could certainly land the son of a bitch in jail. Mathias didn't like Leary, but he was still the chief law enforcement officer in Summit County.

"I'm banging his secretary, that's how," Madden blurted out.

"That old bag? Why, she is over sixty, Madden," Mathias replied disbelievingly.

"That's my business," he replied angrily.

"How do I know you're telling me the truth?"

"You don't. But let me tell you buddy," Madden's small eyes shone brightly as he talked, "that ain't all I got. Your name came up in the conversation. Leary ain't too happy with your sniffing around. He thinks you're some wide-eyed liberal from the big city. Remember the Stewart case, when you questioned the state troopers that said the nigger fell down the stairs of his girlfriend's house. His white girlfriend?" Madden bit off the word white as he spoke.

"I remember the case," Mathias replied flatly.

"Well, because of you, Leary had to settle for an involuntary manslaughter plea from the coon even though he fuckin' shot her five times in the chest. The papers had a field day with that bullshit plea."

Mathias's face screwed up into an angry vise.

"They beat the shit out of him at the barracks. He didn't fall down the stairs. Listen, Leary knows I ain't turning over to get bit in the ass for nobody, especially him," Mathias replied.

"He knows that, Matt. That's why you better be careful. The

senator took no shit and his kid's no better. . . . I'd watch my ass from Captain Crunch. They have some kind of right-wing bullshit going on in the Pine Barrens."

"Hey, buy me another pitcher, Matt. Hey, honey," Madden shouted to the waitress at the bar, "bring me another pitcher."

"They got it in for the rabbi," Madden continued, as he tried to suck out the few remaining drops of beer from the empty pitcher still in front of him.

Mathias stared at the loud group of civilian-dressed, off-duty state troopers located at the middle of the bar area. He could tell they were state troopers by the way they held themselves. The crowd seemed to know that they weren't to be messed with as they cut a large swath around the group.

"I heard about their little bonfires out in the Pines." Mathias threw a five-dollar bill on the table as the waitress slid the overflowing pitcher of beer onto the table. Madden grabbed the pitcher and slogged down almost half of it before coming up for air.

"He didn't like you going to the AG's* office either," Madden added as he wiped his dripping mouth with his shirtsleeve.

"What else doesn't he like about me?" Mathias replied.

"They're afraid of you. You're a straight cop and they don't know how to deal with straight cops. This killing with a Jew . . . well, might bring a lot of shit out in the light. Leary doesn't need any bad publicity . . . not when he is up for reappointment." Madden stopped abruptly and then for almost thirty seconds stared into Mathias's face. "You've always been a good friend to me, Matt. Through all the shit, you've been good and I appreciate it."

Mathias thought for a moment that the big sallow face of the ex-cop was going to explode into tears but it didn't and Madden continued ruefully on.

"Them state troopers," Madden pointed over his shoulder to the yelling group of off-duty troopers at the bar, "Leary uses them for all his shit. Like the Stewart case. You know he didn't fall down those stairs. They took him to the Wrightstown barracks and beat the shit out of the black mother until he showed them where the

*Attorney General

- 63 -

gun was . . . except the assholes forgot they couldn't use the gun at trial. That's why Leary had to accept the bullshit plea."

"It was Ryan who got the plea," Mathias said in a low murmur.

"The rabbi's lawyer . . . yeah, that's who got it," Madden said in a high-pitched voice, "and Leary wasn't happy to see his former buddy fucking him like that. Anyway, he blames you for calling the AG's office. He'd a never told anyone about the beating."

"I know," Mathias agreed. He started to slide out from the bench seat of the booth.

"Where're you going Matt?" Madden's voice seemed almost childish in his query.

"Home. I got a good woman waiting for me, Madden." Mathias paused for a moment, then put out his hand towards Madden.

"Thanks, JC." Mathias called Madden by his first two initials as they shook hands.

"You're a good guy, Matt, I hate to see you get hurt," Madden added.

"I got out of New York in one piece; these farmers ain't going to hurt me. Anyway, here's the fifty," Mathias declared, as he threw the money onto the table.

"Get yourself some food, JC, and a haircut. You're starting to look like a dead bear."

"See you around, Matt." Madden picked his beer stein up and gulped the rest of the frothy liquid.

Mathias left the booth and pushed his way across the hot, humid, smoke-filled room. His eyes caught the laughing off-duty troopers, pushing each other in playful gestures, their shoulder holsters in plain view under their state trooper T-shirts. Mathias recognized the leader of the group, Sergeant Joe Dickson, the loudest of them all. His body virtually mauled a young woman who was trying to extricate her body from his clawing hands. Mathias walked over to the half-drunk Sergeant and placed himself between the well-muscled body of the state trooper and the girl.

"Hi, Joe," Mathias said friendly-like to the trooper. The girl had freed herself from Dickson's grasp and quickly pushed her way toward the exit door. Dickson's broad, scarred face, stared vacuously at Mathias, ready to cock his right arm back, when his glazed eyes took note of who he was ready to slug.

"Oh . . . it's you," Dickson sneered, as he grabbed a bottle of beer off the bar and poured half of it down his throat.

"You're not giving off a good image of Summit County's finest, Sergeant," Mathias chided.

"Fuck you, Mathias. You ain't one of us. What the hell are you doing out here? This ain't little Jerusalem."

"Be nice, Joe. You know how much you can hurt me if you're not nice to me." Mathias smiled as he turned to leave the bar.

"Yeah, and maybe you'll call the AG up and tell them what bad boys we are drinking up a storm."

"Maybe I will do that, Sergeant, Anyway, have a nice day." Mathias walked steadily out of the bar half expecting the crazed trooper to pull his gun and shoot him in the back.

When he opened the front door of Buzzies, the night air hit him squarely in the face, shooting gusts of cold air up through his nostrils, releasing the painful bands of tension from around his head. He stood there, unmoving, for almost five minutes, his mind racing over the events that occurred since the murder of the rabbi's wife.

As he fumbled for the key to the car door, he heard the inimitable roar of the VW engine starting up but couldn't see where the car was located. Another fun-filled night, he thought sardonically, as he drove off the gravel parking lot onto the highway.

CHAPTER SIXTEEN

Strapping himself into the business-class seat, Ryan closed his eyes in a vain attempt to block out the nightmarish illusions intermittingly flashing across his brain. Nothing seems to be easy, he thought. In the good old days when his mind seized up like it had in the past few days, he found blissful solace in the warmth of tequila and vodka. The two virgin sisters of doom. He got blinding drunk and they remained pure as snow.

Leary's angry face, small as it was, loomed menacingly in front of his closed eyes. Ryan could feel the vibrations of the massive 747 Boeing jet lifting off the ground. One of Ryan's acquaintances, since deceased, had told him that if the plane didn't get off the runway in fifty-seven seconds, he was doomed to a fiery death. Ryan subconsciously counted and when the number ran over fifty-seven he started to sweat and picture his death.

Olsham sat quietly in the window seat, slowly drinking his favorite tequila sunrises. Dressed in Bermuda shorts, T-shirt underneath a denim jacket with the Summit County PBA emblem on the breast pocket, he looked like any other vacationer searching for the famed Israeli sunshine in history.

After about ten minutes, the pilot turned off the seatbelt sign and Ryan's body relaxed. He could almost smell the tequila in Olsham's glass, which was set on the middle console between the two passenger's seats. His mouth started to water.

"A taste only," Ryan's mind said without voice, "only a taste."

"He's a piece of work, that Leary," Ryan said as he looked over at Olsham.

"The rabbi made him look like a jackass. Taking off and all."

"Threatening to put me in jail doesn't bring the rabbi back. He knows it," Ryan added.

"He's just looking for a scapegoat," Olsham replied as his eyes wondered down the aisle at the statuesque hostess making her smiling way up the aisle.

"If what Mathias told us was true, John, I could have Leary disbarred. You know that, don't you?"

"Maybe. Maybe not. Sturmer signed the original wiretap order."

"Yeah. But we all know those orders have to be reviewed every week. And when the assignment judge got back from vacation, Leary continued the tap on my office without any continuing authorization. Besides, I don't think the original order would hold up. Leary knew that. That's why he waited for the AJ to go on vacation to have his scum-bucket buddy Sturmer sign the order."

"He's used to getting his own way," Olsham absentmindedly said, as the strawberry blonde, blue-eyed stewardess lingered by their seats, offering further libations to Ryan and Olsham.

Olsham reordered his tequila sunrise and Ryan dejectedly murmured for another cherry-spiked lime drink.

Just like a real drink, he thought sarcastically.

"You think the good Captain Crunch is over there?" Ryan queried. And then added, "What jurisdiction would he have in Israel?"

"I'm sure Leary petitioned a federal judge for an arrest warrant on the rabbi. Crunch won't be alone, either. The whole thing is an embarrassment to the administration. The federal administration, I'm talking about." Olsham declared.

"Thank you," Ryan peered up to the stewardess as she placed the ice-cold can of Sprite on his tray and then reached over to place a tall glass of tequila on Olsham's tray.

Olsham openly flirted with the young stewardess.

"You know," Ryan said as he watched the brief interchange between Olsham and the young woman, "this is not a pleasure trip, John. You're going to have to keep it locked up. No nookie. If we don't stick to business, I may not have anything when I get back. You understand all that, John?"

"You're such a deadbeat since you hit the wagon, Josh." Olsham paused and then continued, "I know why we're going here. Don't worry. I got us all set up with the best guide in Israel. If anybody can find the good rabbi, its Yehuda . . ."

Ryan gulped the bubbly liquid down his throat, somehow hoping that the biting taste of tequila would miraculously appear. You never lose the desire, he thought of the words drummed into his head during those torturous and unending rehab sessions at the Parkins Center for Alcoholic Studies, the last way-station for incorrigible alcoholics.

"Leary should go on his own for a couple of years, John—after a few bangs on his head, he'd straighten out," Ryan said.

"He doesn't have to . . . the senator left him plenty. Besides money, the senator left him a legacy. If your name is Leary everybody's supposed to bow at the waist and stay out of your way."

"He's been dead for almost two years, John."

"Yeah, but his memory lives on. Everybody whose over fifty knows the power of Senator Aloishus Leary. He *was* Summit County for over forty years, Josh. Before your time I expect . . . but I remember those closed door backroom conferences he held at the Leary law offices on Main Street. Whatever he said was law . . . not just the judges. Sonofabitch, they all owed him their lives. Most of the judges were hacks, anyway. Couldn't make a goddamn living if their lives depended on it. He was the king . . . except to Roger . . . his only son." Olsham paused and gulped down his drink before continuing. "There were times I remember when the kid would actually throw tantrums on the floor in the office, right in front of everyone. And the kid was already a teenager. The senator would just smile as if he half expected the kid to do what he was doing. Shit, I'd a picked up his little ass and kicked it up Main Street. But not the senator . . . the kid was the apple of his eye."

Ryan's mind wandered back to the days at Carlisle Law School where Roger Leary stood last in Ryan's class. Sitting beside him at the bar exam, Ryan observed incredulously how Leary cheated on the exam by getting answers passed to him by his sidekick Allen, who had been well-paid for his supportive effort in getting Roger past the bar exam. Leary married soon after passing the bar. To the prettiest girl in Summit County. A Larramie. A family that farmed the lands when Summit County was a stagecoach stop on the New York–Philadelphia line in the eighteenth century. The marriage bore, unfortunately, three children, all girls, whereupon Roger became unfaithful on a grand scale. Sometimes, during some of Roger's drunken orgies, the state police would carry him out the back door of the local whorehouse just before the local media boys were scurrying up the front stairs looking for a story.

In the beginning of Roger's lustful meanderings, the newspaper publishers would, at the request and demand of the senator, squelch all denigrating stories about his son. Even the senator occasionally would deconstruct at his son's more egregious transgressions. But Roger was a Leary, and the family name was a family trust. Murder could not even be allowed to tarnish the name. All that changed with the death of the senator. Now, Roger Leary's peccadilloes sometimes became news. Like the time the Larchmont Hills cops found him drunkenly chasing three whores through the cornfield outside of town, all of them buck naked, in the middle of winter, yet. Nothing could kill *that* story. But Roger survived; he was still a Leary and there still existed a large reservoir of Summit County functionaries who were beholden to the recently departed senator.

But now, Roger Leary was at the wall. Without reappointment by the governor as prosecutor of Summit County, he would sink into oblivion. No power, no stature, nothing but a name that people were starting to forget. Everybody realized that Roger would never be the senator. A missing link somehow existed that Roger would never find. And without the exalted prosecutor's job, Roger Leary knew he would be fodder for the waiting omnivorous forces who had hated the senator and what he stood for. He knew that the conviction of a celebrated defendant like Rabbi Carl Rubin would ensure that reappointment. And he would stop at nothing to attain that goal.

Ryan thought of friendship. With Leary. Roger Dodger was the name maliciously coined by his schoolmates. Not because Roger Leary was physically fast, but more because you could never trust Leary to do the right thing. Whatever was good for Roger, at *that* time, Roger did it. Friendless, except for Ryan, Roger insulated himself by avoiding his fellow students. Carlisle, an old steel town bordering on the Monongahela River, was not Summit County. It was the real world. The senator did not run it.

Ryan closed his eyes to the sound of the humming jet engines and wondered: why had he become friends with Leary? Ryan had been an idolized football hero at Carlisle undergraduate school until he ripped all the ligaments in both his knees to shreds. After surgery, he was finished in college football. Still, no one could understand how the celebrated jock and the spoiled ne'er-do-well Leary found some misbegotten common ground that allowed them to cohabit the same room for the entire law school year. Leary was the pied piper to Ryan, leading him away from his law books to the seamier side of Carlisle.

Fortunately, the third year of law school was a gratuitous ritual. Everyone was already searching for employment, something law school does not train its students to master. How to get a job in the law profession, a forgotten science.

Leary knew where he was going. Ryan hoped that he could latch onto Leary's political coattails. Trial work was what Ryan wanted. Other than the public defender's office, which paid little and offered scant trial work because the public defender usually plead its penurious clients out before trial, Ryan knew the avenue to pursue was the state side of the criminal justice system.

His association with Leary finally paid off. After passing the Bar, both friends became interns at the Summit County prosecutor's office. Leary stuck to the administrative side while Ryan was submerged immediately into the frenzy of litigation. Supervised by Sam Levine, who had been hired on a temporary basis after old man Leary had first been voted in as state senator. The senator would never have hired Sam to the prosecutor's office but the interim prosecutor needed a trained litigator to shape the newly formed full-time Summit County prosecutor's staff. Temporary status evolved into five years of full time employment for Sam Levine; that is, until Roger Leary was qualified to assume his father's former position as prosecutor. Levine was terminated the day after Roger Leary was sworn in as prosecutor. Ryan became first assistant that same day.

Ryan slept most of the night. Olsham wandered around the first-class section of the plane, kibbitzing with the Israeli stewardesses who were enamored with his funny stories about New York City. Ryan dreamed of Helen, his ex-wife. How could a relationship so fine turn into such a nightmare?

They had met at Carlisle University. She was a year behind him. Upper middle class, worldly and nurtured by the liberal New

England Democrats. The night they met, she had dumped her lover of long standing because he was anti-abortion and thought pre-marital sex was immoral. Helen disagreed on both counts.

Between graduation from Wellesley and entering law school at Carlisle she had spent two years in Paris. Sex was fun. She was unburdened by any morality attached to casual sex. When she met Ryan at a student bar off the Carlisle campus, she immediately wanted to bed him. Older and more experienced, Helen led Ryan through their first night together. By morning, he crawled to the front door for air.

Within three months after his graduation, they were married. The flow of libertine sex suddenly terminated. Helen had lost interest. She turned to God. A reborn Christian. Ryan turned to alcohol.

In combination with the degeneration of his marriage and the cataclysmic stresses of his job as the up-and-coming trial specialist for the Summit County prosecutor's office, Ryan sank deeper and deeper into alcoholic depression.

The dependency became obvious as he would sneak nips of tequila or vodka or both during the day. Just before trial. Just before the opening to a jury. After the trial day was over, he would wind up at the Washington House, the Summit County legal bar hangout on the corner of Main Street, drinking his dinner.

At first, everybody accepted him as the life of the party. The booze loosened his tightly-wound persona, his shyness, and a built-in inferiority complex inculcated into his psyche by his abusive father who repeatedly told him he was dumb as shit. Then the accident happened. And his world ended.

Helen left him. So did Leary and all of Ryan's newly found friends who enjoyed sharing Ryan's power as first assistant prosecutor. When Ryan became a pariah, he was suddenly lost. Unprotected from the elements. Except for Sam Levine, he was alone.

Morning came with the sunny stewardess offering breakfast to Ryan. Coffee, bagels, and lox, combined with sweet Danish, were served. Olsham traipsed behind the stewardess, still drinking the tequila sunrises. Ryan marveled at Olsham's capacity to absorb alcohol. Never displaying the effects, Olsham could drink all night and still put in a day's work.

"We're two hours out of Tel Aviv, sleepyhead," Olsham instructed Ryan.

"Did you sleep at all, John?"

"Sleep is a waste. I have been entertaining our hostesses with stories of the Big Apple. We're set for female companionship . . . if you want any while we slave away in the Old City."

"I think we should discuss a plan of action before we land, John. Mrs. O'Malley's money won't last us more than a few days and if we don't find the rabbi . . . well, we're in deep shit."

The stewardess placed a white tablecloth over the extended tray tables and then gently placed the breakfast foods in front of Josh.

"Coffee or tea," she said with an enticing smile.

"Black coffee, please," Ryan replied, his body experiencing faint stirrings of sexual desire. He had been celibate for almost six months. He simply never thought about it. Except for occasional forays into New York with Philicia, the aspiring actress. No ties. No relationship aftermath. Purely physical. That's all he wanted. Ryan had no stomach for an emotional liaison. Not yet. Maybe never.

"Yehuda will pick us up at the airport. He controls a white-stretch Mercedes limo. It's all in the fee," Olsham said.

"We don't need a limo, John," Ryan chided.

"Yehuda does not go anywhere without his limo. Anyway, he gets us into places normally where tourists are prohibited to visit. Plus, a big thing in Jerusalem: he has diplomatic security clearance. Not a bad thing when you're going into an armed camp."

"I presume he knows the city."

"Like I know New York. Better. The man has lived in Jerusalem all his life."

"We need a private investigator, John . . . not a tourist guide," Ryan's voice denoted his fatigue and growing frustration. He sipped on the black coffee.

"He doubles as a secret agent," Olsham said in an attempt to get a laugh out of Ryan.

"Lilli O'Malley said her father does not want to be found."

"Yehuda will find him," Olsham replied.

"Well, he better. Before the good captain and his crew bring him back in chains to the good old USA. Then we can think about our plea for leniency at sentencing."

"Ever hear of this area called Mea Shearim?" Olsham said, reaching over to raise his window shade. The bright rays of the morning sun blasted through the airplane window sending waves of pain through Ryan's head. He grabbed the half-filled cup of black coffee, grimaced at the acidic aftertaste, and hoped that the caffeine sludge would clear his lethargic mind of unfulfilled sleep.

"Mrs. O'Malley told me it's a warren of streets where an old Eastern European sect called the Lubavitcher live. They don't talk to strangers, John."

"Well, if it's tough for us to find him, nobody else will either."

"The captain has the help of the state department," Ryan paused and continued cynically, "and we have a tourist guide to lead us around."

"Don't underestimate Yehuda. He knows every alleyway in the Old City." Olsham's weathered face opened with a craggy white-tooth smile as the blond stewardess bent over Olsham's seat to take the tray.

"Anything else I can offer you, John?" she said, her face aglow with an inviting smile.

"Thank you, no, Triana. Maybe in Tel Aviv."

She then withdrew into the front galley.

"Let me tell you this," Olsham declared, "you think those state department boys know anything?. The Israeli government doesn't know whether it wants to help find the rabbi. There is a big election coming up, you know, and the Peres government doesn't want to piss off a right-wing group like the Lubavitcher. Anyway, Yehuda is an army reserve colonel. The paratroopers . . . he's in with the Likud. Netanyahu's party. They served in the same division, the one that liberated Jerusalem in the 1967 war. Yehuda was the first Israeli into the Old City, so he is more then just a tourist guide, Josh."

"Leary sent the captain and two lead investigators from the state police."

"So?" Olsham queried. "All those guys will stand out like bull's-eyes. They don't exactly look like Israelis, y'know."

Ryan peered out the window as the plane descended over the Mediterranean, swooping down over the ship-laden port of Haifa.

"My mother would have wanted to come to Israel," Ryan said in a whispery voice. "Some of her relatives live in Haifa. The ones that managed to survive the camps. She always talked about going but something always came up . . . mostly my father . . ."

Olsham stared into the sharp-featured face of Ryan.

"I never think of you as Jewish," Olsham admitted.

"My father never did either." Ryan's voice became husky with seething emotion.

"He tried to convert her . . . to Catholicism. She never would. It was enough that her family threw her out for marrying a Irishman. An uneducated Irishman to boot. She insisted on the bar mitzvah. Me? I was satisfied throwing a football after school. But she brought in a tutor six months before my thirteenth birthday. Where she got the money to pay him God only knows. She probably stole it off my father."

Ryan paused as his eyes caught the sun reflecting off the glass spires of the modern office buildings of Tel Aviv, just coming into view.

"Well," Olsham replied as he adjusted his seatbelt for landing, "all I know is this country can't be big enough that we can't find an American rabbi on the lam."

Ryan smiled and then said drolly, "maybe not . . . maybe not." He paused and continued sarcastically, "Y'know John, we Jews all look alike. And with the rabbi's political ties . . . there's a million places he can hide. Even in a small country."

CHAPTER SEVENTEEN

Yehuda Ben-Zvi wasn't a big man. No more then five-foot seven inches, but he appeared larger then his actual physical size, Ryan thought, as he gazed into the man's sun-tanned face. It must be the posture. Straight as a ramrod, Yehuda Ben-Zvi's body formed almost a perfect T from the broad shoulders down to his rippling, striated abdomen that exploded into two stanchions resembling legs. Except for the introductory smile, Yehuda Ben-Zvi's face was a frozen mask awaiting further instructions.

Quickly moving through the passport-control booth marked FLIGHT PERSONNEL ONLY, Ben-Zvi led Ryan and Olsham through the crowded Tel Aviv airport to the side door near the baggage escalator. Within seconds, an El Al attendant brought out Ryan and Olsham's bags, and Ben-Zvi quick-stepped the group out toward the swinging doors of the milling airport into the warm Tel Aviv morning sun.

Other then desultory introductions offered by Olsham, no one said anything. Words seemed unimportant; action was the verbiage of the morning meeting.

Ryan could feel the intense Israeli sun penetrate his sports jacket while his eyes followed Ben-Zvi, who dropped the luggage at the curb and then sprinted across the noisy congestion of the airport roadway to the parking lot. Olsham stood silently next to Ryan.

"Talkative chap, isn't he?" Ryan said.

"Yehuda is not big with small talk. You spend a week with him and think you are in a John Wayne movie," Olsham replied, as he waved to the tall blond stewardess now boarding an airport bus.

"How'd you find him?" Ryan asked.

"I used him in a divorce case a few years ago. Tracked a wayward husband down. And all his assets too. The guy knows his stuff, Josh . . . in Israel anyway."

The white-stretch Mercedes limousine suddenly appeared from the adjacent parking lot.

Nimbly, Yehuda Ben-Zvi jumped out of the driver's seat and opened the back door of the immaculately groomed vehicle for Ryan and Olsham. The frigid blast of air-conditioning greeted them as they seated themselves in the posh leather seats of the limo.

Yehuda climbed into the driver's seat and then offered in a husky, gravelly voice, "Help yourself to the liquor, gentlemen."

"It's too early to drink, Yehuda," Olsham replied.

"I never know with you Americans," Yehuda replied.

With surgical agility, Yehuda maneuvered the giant caterpillar of a vehicle through the chaotic miasma of darting automobiles and unwary pedestrians hurrying out of the airport.

"Did John tell you about the rabbi?" Josh shouted across the expanse of the limousine.

"I can hear, Mr. Ryan. You don't have to shout. The acoustics in here are fine," Yehuda instructed.

"I received his summary before you landed. Yes," he added, "I know all about your rabbi. He is very important to certain people in Israel . . . especially now."

"We don't have much time, Mr. Ben-Zvi," Ryan declared.

"Call me Yehuda. Well, time is all we have in Israel, Mr. Ryan."

"I need to find him . . . Yehuda," Ryan offered, his eyes peering out of the tinted window of the limo, amazed at the speed of the giant vehicle as it snaked its path through the afternoon traffic jam.

"If he's in or near Mea Shearim," Yehuda replied. "Well . . . it all depends on how serious the Lubavitchers are in hiding the rabbi. You come at a bad time, gentlemen. This is the first election in Israel to vote directly for the prime minister." He paused.

"And after those hyenas . . . the bombings of innocent people," Yehuda's voice became angry and almost shrill.

The limousine wended its way through the suburban Tel Aviv traffic south along the Tel Aviv–Jerusalem highway. After a few miles, the volume of traffic diminished substantially. In place of buildings, Ryan could only see hills of massive rocks and high desert.

"Where are we heading now?" Ryan asked suspiciously.

"To the King David Hotel," Yehuda replied.

"Do you see those tents at the top of the hill?" Yehuda continued, "Well, those are the so-called friends of Israel, the Arabs. Living the way their forefathers have lived for thousands of years."

"Where are we now . . . this road I mean?" Ryan asked, his eyes capturing the biblical scenario of goats, bedouins, and rocky hill-tops dotting the sparsely green landscape.

"This road is on the notorious West Bank. You Americans have heard of the West Bank?" Yehuda jibed.

"Looks different than what I had imagined," Ryan replied. His eyes darted across the tented enclaves of Arabs and goats to the fenced order of covered hothouses in American-style stucco block buildings with manicured lawns. Flower beds surrounded the houses.

"That's Israeli." Yehuda pointed to the fenced-in enclaves.

"The settlements on the West Bank are the most advanced in the agricultural sciences," Yehuda continued proudly. "They grow tomatoes up there as big as your head."

"It ain't worth killing for," Olsham muttered.

Swiftly turning his head to angrily stare at Olsham, Yehuda said in a husky-impassioned voice, "Not for Americans, anyway. Land is only money to you . . . but to Israelis . . . well. . . ."

He paused to lower his voice, and then continued, "To us it means much more . . . much more. Do you read the Bible . . . the Old Testament?"

"Not lately," Olsham replied.

"No, you wouldn't. You Americans have the *New York Times*. Well, here . . . in Israel . . . the land has always been our life. From the very beginning. What is one life . . . to preserve the sanctity of God's land? They want it all. The Arabs. As if *they* were God's children. What do they know? They still sleep in camel shit."

Ryan noticed that they hadn't passed another vehicle on the road in several minutes. The landscape turned to rough-hewn high desert, as if they were passing hilltops from a Cecil B. DeMille biblical saga. Out of the distance, a military vehicle appeared with the white field of the Israeli flag fluttering in the hot desert air.

"I thought the West Bank was turned over to the Palestinians," Ryan declared.

"Most of this has," Yehuda replied, as he saluted to the oncoming Israeli military vehicle with its two soldiers seated casually in the front seat. "But we still control the highway. We'll never cede control of the highway to the Arabs. It's our lifeline."

"I presume that you're not for giving up the land?" Ryan asked innocently.

"Would you?" Yehuda shot back, his gravelly voice alternating between passion and boredom. As if he had answered these questions many times before. "My family has been here for over a hundred years. My great-grandfather walked from Kissenev. In Rumania. To the promised land . . . with nothing but the clothes on his back. He had just been bar-mitzvahed. And then his parents were trampled by the *gulyahim* . . . the Cossack sons of bitches. He took his little sister . . . my Great-Aunt Fannie . . . and they walked. In the middle of winter yet . . . to Palestine."

Yehuda peered into the rearview mirror to observe his listeners. "Why would anyone want to give up the land his forefathers worked and died for?"

"Do you have a choice?" Ryan queried, fascinated by the fiery chauvinism of the Israeli driver.

"You always have a choice, Mr. Ryan. The land will always be here. After I'm dead and buried. That's all that will ever be . . . The land. Why wouldn't I want to fight for this land?"

Suddenly the explosive sounds of rifle shots rang out across the highway. The driver instinctively tromped his foot on the accelerator, the massive limousine catapulting headlong on the two-lane highway. Olsham tried to open the back door windows to get a better view of the source of the gunshots, but Yehuda yelled to keep the windows closed.

Ryan could barely pick out the several men on horseback on top of the hills to the west of the limousine.

"Sounds like M16s," Olsham shouted.

The horsemen descended from the hilltop toward the limo as Yehuda swerved crazily from side to side to avoid the rifle shots.

"Stay down back there!" Yehuda yelled.

Suddenly the road exploded all around the careening vehicle.

"They must have a grenade launcher," Olsham muttered.

"Who the hell are they?" Ryan yelled to the front of the limo.

"Not friends," Yehuda replied softly. He swerved the limo off the road away from the cascading gunshots and explosives, onto the sparse grassy shoulder that seemed to disappear as the vehicle lurched ahead.

"Don't roll us over!" Olsham yelled.

Yehuda did not reply, his hands glued to the steering wheel, the vehicle almost perpendicular to the roadway along the precipitous embankment.

The horsemen disappeared from their view but the sounds of automatic gunfire surrounded the limo, as the spires of the Old City loomed in the far distance.

"AK-47s," Yehuda cursed under his breath. Behind the muddy escarpment near the top of the hill, Ryan could see the flashes of the automatic weapon discharges. Suddenly, several men wrapped in red-and-white striped headdresses descended from the top of the hill, towards the limo, AK-47 automatic rifles attached to their hips, belching deadly fire. The horsemen rode toward the speeding limo.

"They're in front of us also!" Olsham shouted to Yehuda, as his hand pointed towards the road in front of the vehicle. No more then a thousand feet away, they could see the blockage of old tires, wooden debris, and rusted old barrels piled chaotically in the middle of the road.

"The shoulder is too small to go around it!" Yehuda shouted.

As if dropped by helicopter, the Israeli military jeep they had passed miles before, suddenly appeared alongside the wavering limo.

From a mounted machine gun located in the back of the jeep, the Israel soldier sprayed bullets directly at the blockaded roadway.

"We'll never make it!" Olsham yelled, as the blockade loomed directly in front of the great limousine.

"I'll have to go over it, gentlemen," Yehuda said in a matter-of-fact manner.

"Hold onto the shoulder straps! God! I hope I don't damage the limo," Yehuda pleaded.

"He's worried about the goddamned limo!" Olsham chastised.

The white limousine's front wheels lifted up from the roadway as if on a great ramp, hovered at the top of the massive pile of debris, then continued in flight for almost thirty feet, before smashing onto the asphalt roadway, Ryan and Olsham holding onto the shoulder straps as if they were umbilical cords at the beginning of everlasting life.

The reverberating cacophony of automatic weapons suddenly stopped. Yehuda pulled the limo off the highway onto an extended shoulder and halted, with a repetitive pumping of the brakes of the great vehicle.

"And *that's* what I have to deal with," Yehuda murmured, as his body quivered noticeably.

"Who the fuck are they?" Olsham shouted as he abruptly recovered from the initial realization that he wasn't going to die.

"Our neighbors," Yehuda replied.

Ryan's mouth was painfully dry, and there were sharp pains coursing through his knees and back.

The Israeli soldier sauntered over to the limousine, his Uzi machine gun held above his shoulder toward the sky.

"Shalom," Yehuda said, a broad smile on his face as he shifted out of the driver's seat.

"Shalom," the young soldier replied. "This is the fourth incident today. All along this stretch of highway." His voice was high, almost effeminate, matching the soft lines of his oval, beardless face. Perched on the middle of his head was a quilted yarmulke.

"Rabin's dead and now they go crazy. Who knows from these people?" Yehuda said, as his eyes searched the near hilltop from where the attackers had descended.

"Netanyahu will show them," the young soldier replied, a broad, childish grin suddenly appearing on his face. "My family lives in Hebron . . . the settlement just outside the Tomb of the Patriarchs. Rabin was their enemy."

Ryan and Olsham got out of the limousine and walked toward the barricade. Less then a hundred feet from the side of the road lay the bloody bodies of three Arab men. Ryan approached the closest body and noticed the dead man was no more then an early teen, his face marked only with the bullets that had seared through his forehead.

"Your clients are American?" the soldier queried of Yehuda, a cigarette dangling from the corner of his young mouth.

"Nu, what else? Only Americans can afford my services," Yehuda replied with a broad grin.

"I was born there. Pittsburgh. My family made aliyah* when I was a baby," the soldier declared.

"These fellows are not here to make aliyah," Yehuda said, as he moved to the nonsmoking side of the soldier.

Ryan slowly walked by the depression on the side of the road, then towards Yehuda's position on the other side of the limousine.

"We're grateful," Ryan said, a thin smile creasing his pale face.

"It happens," the soldier replied. "I'd suggest you continue quickly into Jerusalem."

"Are they all that young?" Ryan asked of the soldier as he pointed to the dead Arab gunman closest to the side of the road.

"Some are younger. They graduate from the intifada** to automatic weapons before they can shave. We are the eternal enemies. And it will always be that way," the soldier remarked, his voice dry and steely cold.

"You don't look much older yourself," Ryan said, his hand shading his eyes from the invasive afternoon desert sun.

"This is my second tour of duty, my friend," the soldier replied, "I am old enough to have known Lebanon."

Yehuda smiled as he moved toward the back of the limo and opened the back door.

"Gentlemen, let this young man continue with his patrol. Please," as his hand pointed into the back of the limo.

Ryan and Olsham entered the limousine and Yehuda closed the door. Grasping the young soldier by the shoulders with his right hand, Yehuda whispered into the ear of the soldier. The soldier smiled and offered a respectful salute to Yehuda.

Ryan turned his head and could see the vacuous stare of the dead young gunman lying by the side of the road.

*aliyah—to settle in Israel.
**intifada—campaign of rock-throwing Arab teenagers

CHAPTER EIGHTEEN

The conversation had stilled after Yehuda quickly departed from the attack site except for Yehuda's explanation of why they had to avoid the normal east gate to the Old City. Barricades of white cement pilings had lined the eastern end of the city gate as the limo pulled to a stop at the end of a long line of vehicles stalled before the roadway entrance.

"New rules, since the bus station bombings. No Palestinians are allowed into the city without a permanent visa pass. Everyone is checked. It'll take us a half a day to get into the city," Yehuda declared, his eyes scouring the area for an alternate route.

Yehuda suddenly wheeled the great vehicle across a grass embankment onto the other side of the road and maneuvered the vehicle down to the nearest street crossing the road.

After he abruptly turned the wheel to the left, the vehicle entered a half paved street leading through an enclave of white stucco houses.

"We'll go by the Jerusalem airport. It is on the Palestinian side . . . but we have no choice. Sit back and take a drink. Shabbat will begin in a few hours."

After guiding the limo through a circuitous maze of back-alley streets, Yehuda deftly guided the limousine around the narrow circle drive leading to the King David Hotel entrance. Opening the door for Ryan and Olsham, Yehuda waited impatiently as his two passengers alighted from the backseat. The sun was setting behind the battlements of the Old City in the near distance. A chill wind blew in unexpectedly as the clouds darkened around the mount where the King David Hotel stood.

The uniformed doorman lifted the luggage out of the trunk as Yehuda led the way through the revolving door into the marble columned reception area.

"Wait here, gentlemen," Yehuda said, as he marched up to the registration desk of the hotel.

Ryan's eyes roamed around the dimly-lit lobby that led into the immense formal sitting room that appeared sheathed in dark luxurious oriental tapestries hung dramatically against the walls. Seated throughout the well-appointed room were smartly dressed men, women and children, mostly in black and white, as if they had stepped out of the Manet *Luncheon on the Grass* picnic scene. Most of the men wore either yarmulkes or wide-brimmed black hats. The women were either bareheaded or wore tailored hats. A balcony led out to a lush, multitiered garden that overlooked the Old City.

As Ryan meandered into the spacious room, he felt a gentle touch on his shoulder.

"Sir, may I check your handbag?" a short, stocky man said, referring to the shoulder bag Ryan was carrying.

Ryan looked quizzically at the square-jawed face staring into his eyes and meekly handed over his shoulder bag to the man.

"It's all right," Yehuda said, as he approached Ryan and his inquisitor. "Just security. . .the bombs y'know, Mr. Ryan. Everybody is checked. Especially foreigners."

The security man mechanically searched the bag, and without any words, handed it back to Ryan.

"You're checked into the corner suite overlooking the Old City. It's quiet," Yehuda remarked somewhat pridefully. "I know the manager."

"Any room would've done, Yehuda," Ryan replied.

"You're my guest here. My guests only stay in suites. Anything else is for peasants."

Olsham was talking quietly to the El Al stewardess who somehow appeared after they had entered the hotel.

"I see your colleague has found a friend," Yehuda said, a leering smile on his tanned, weathered face.

"John doesn't like to be alone in a strange city," Ryan replied.

"John." Ryan called out in a slightly agitated tone, "we have work to do."

Olsham kissed the tall, shapely young woman on her cheek and she tenderly brushed his face with her hand.

"Guess where she's staying, Josh?" Olsham remarked, as he approached Yehuda and Ryan.

"We don't have time to screw around, John," Ryan chided.

"There's *always* time to screw around, " Olsham replied, a broad grin etched across his hollow-cheeked face.

"Some place," Olsham added. "Last time I stayed in Jerusalem, it was a rabbit warren near the airport."

"These people . . ." Ryan pointed towards the elegantly dressed people milling around the great room.

"Shabbat is beginning," Yehuda replied. "They come to the King David for the Shabbat evening meal. Tradition."

"How do we find my client?" Ryan asked.

"Sunday. I've already made some inquiries . . . Mea Shearim is a maze. We'll find him . . . unless he's dead."

"Why would he be dead?" Ryan asked.

"He's not just a foreigner here. Mr. Rubin comes often. A fundraiser for the Likud. More importantly, he carries the word of the Rebbe . . . all the way from Brooklyn," Yehuda explained.

"He broke from the Rebbe years ago," Olsham chimed in.

"Nobody breaks from the Rebbe," Yehuda replied softly. "He is God to them . . . " pointing to the milling people in the sitting room, "and nobody stays mad at God," Yehuda added, his eyes lifted skyward.

"There are other people looking for him, y'know," Ryan warned, his eyes following the rhythmic flow of the well-dressed family members walking down the corridor to the cavernous dining room on the easterly side of the hotel lobby. As his eyes drifted back to the great room leading to the garden, he found himself staring at a portly, distinguished looking man. His face was surrounded by a neatly trimmed fiery red beard and his head was covered with a colorful, patch-quilted yarmulke. His massive hands were holding the *New York Times*. He was seated on a sofa in front of the fireplace. For some inexplicable reason, Ryan could feel the hot glare of the man's eyes on his face, although the man continued to bury his head into the extended newspaper.

Standing against the white, marble mantel, was a diminutive skinny man, impeccably dressed in a three-piece custom Saville Row suit, a gold pocketwatch stretching across his black vest. His eyes were clearly focused on Ryan and Yehuda, as they talked near the entrance to the room. The small man's eyes never wavered, even though Ryan stared directly at him.

"Yehuda," Ryan murmured, his eyes focused on the small man across the room, "why are we being watched by that fellow at the fireplace?"

"I don't know," Yehuda replied, as he eyed the observer.

"He could be Israeli security. Every foreigner is suspected of being a potential terrorist. Stay here," Yehuda said, as he confidently stepped over toward the garden French doors alongside the fireplace mantel.

For what seemed like an hour, Yehuda talked to the small well-dressed man and it appeared as if the portly reader, seated across from the fireplace, was also engaged in the conversation. Yehuda's hands moved up and down in an excited pattern as he talked to the two men, their eyes darting from the fireplace to where Ryan and Olsham were standing. Suddenly, Yehuda broke away from the twosome and quick-stepped back to Ryan and Olsham.

"They are Shin Bet . . . counterintelligence," Yehuda whispered into Ryan's ear.

"The American state department has asked the Israeli government to help find your client," Yehuda said dramatically.

"So?" Ryan asked.

"So the Israelis haven't answered formally yet. There are internal pressures from the right wing to protect Rabbi Rubin . . . from the American authorities."

"Will they help us find him? Did you explain to them I was his lawyer?" Ryan's words stumbled out in staccato fashion.

"They know. They knew who you were when you left New York. According to them," Yehuda said, as he pointed toward the now disappearing duo, "the rabbi may not want to be discovered. It's the usual government bullshit. The only help they could offer us is to warn us about a group of American policemen also looking for your client."

"The captain," Olsham said. "Will they help them?"

"The government wants to stay on the sidelines . . . until after the election on Tuesday anyway," Yehuda replied.

"Anything can happen. A thing like this that explodes here could hurt Netanyahu's chance to win. Nobody wants that," Yehuda warned, his eyes searching the lobby.

"Nothing is clean," Ryan mused. "Politics run the world. . .even back in little Summit County. Maybe more so in Summit County but no one else in the world cares about Summit County. Yet, the whole world focuses on the tiniest political disruption in the Holy Land."

Walking over to the French doors, Josh looked at the garden and noticed a light rain had started. A low bank of dark clouds hovered over the Old City like some blanket of protection from an all-caring God above. Symbolism means everything here, Ryan thought. Nothing goes unnoticed. Everything that happens in Jerusalem must have some ethereal meaning or else why would it happen? Time becomes an element that must be considered. Everything in the Holy Land is measured in time. The monumental events that occurred and the great men that had lived in places other than the Holy Land would long be forgotten blips in history. Not so in the Promised Land. These events became history as they happened. Those men's lives are immediately chronicled into history. In the Talmud, in the Bible, in the Koran, these events and lives of those great men are remembered and revered, or hated, forever, by the entire world surrounding the land of Moses and Abraham.

Ryan rubbed his eyes with the back of his hand in a vain attempt to erase the shooting pains in his forehead. The rain outside intensified. The whole world appeared dark and engulfed with some heavenly foreboding. Lightning flashed directly from the core of the dark clouds above. Even the weather has meaning, Ryan thought. Punishment from a revengeful God above for man's follies toward each other. Especially here. Arab against Jew. Brother against brother. Abraham was the father of both Isaac and Ishmael and still his sons and their sons and on and on, each successive generation of Abrahams's progeny murder each other. Unmercifully. Centuries of peaceful coexistence prevail and then suddenly, the senseless destruction of each other's way of life. No wonder God is a punishing God.

"I'm beat, Josh," Olsham reached out and touched Ryan's elbow as if to direct him towards the elevators.

"Where did Yehuda go?" Ryan asked with a note of fear in his voice.

"He'll pick us up Sunday morning," Olsham stated. "We should be fresh by then . . . once we get going."

As suddenly as the rain started, it stopped, and a bright, blazing sun emerged from the disappearing clouds. It was all so . . . Ryan thought, so . . . well . . . like somebody was manipulating the elements. A great heavenly puppeteer pulling the strings.

"I'm tired," Ryan declared as he followed Olsham toward the elevator.

CHAPTER NINETEEN

Ryan had just fallen into a deep sleep when the telephone rang, jolting him out of his hard-earned reverie. Olsham never moved from the other bed in the luxurious suite of rooms Yehuda had arranged for them. Rising in a stupor from the bed, Ryan's hand reached for the phone, knocking the phone onto the floor from the nightstand. Cursing under his breath, Ryan reached down and pulled the receiver towards his ear. He could hear Yehuda's voice blaring out of the speaker.

"Yes . . . yes," Ryan repeated angrily. "Who the hell is this?"

"Mr. Ryan," Yehuda stated matter-factly, his voice displaying no emotion. "I'm sorry to wake you, but I thought you should know immediately."

"Know what?" Ryan answered, his voice a shade above a bark.

"Those men on the highway . . . the gunmen we thought were Arabs."

"Yes . . . what?" Ryan angrily replied.

"They weren't."

"Weren't what?" Ryan answered in a petulant voice.

"Arabs. They were from a settlement outside Ramallah . . . a Jewish settlement . . ."

"Why?" Ryan shouted into the phone, waking Olsham.

"We don't know the why. We know they wanted you dead. Or at least . . . out of the way."

"How did you find out?"

"Friends of mine . . . in the Shin Bet. Rabbi Rubin has many friends in Israel, Mr. Ryan. Be careful." Yehuda added, "Good night Mr. Ryan. I'll see you Sunday."

The phone went dead. Ryan dropped it on the floor. His eyes remained open all night, staring at the coffered ceiling of the spacious suite.

CHAPTER TWENTY

The plaque on the outside of the building stated that it was the Museum of the Patriarchs. The building itself was nondescript. It was located in the middle of the Jewish Quarter, not far from the Western Wall on the Temple Mount.

On the first level, the museum had a miniature display of Jerusalem during the days of King David. Behind the sloping ramps circling the miniature buildings and walkways, three men sat in the back room around a table sipping coffee and tea, smoking withered cigarettes, gray fumes filling the stucco-walled room. There was a small barred window that was a one-way mirror, allowing the inhabitants of the room to look out onto the winding cobblestoned streets of the Quarter but allowing no one from the outside to peer into the room.

"Moishe, how can you drink that tea without burning out your throat?" The large-headed man, greatly overweight with gray hair surrounding his shoulders like a lion's mane, muttered to a tiny, hollow-chested man sitting to his side.

"Why do you care, putz?" the little man replied.

"Because you are my brother . . . and I wonder how a human being could drink such fire without a sound."

The third man at the table, his fingers yellowed from the nicotine embedded in the skin, spoke with an upper-crust English accent that belied the Arab dress wrapped around his overweight body. His name was Abraham.

"Instead of bitching at each other, let's find a way to hide him until after the election. Mea Shearim has just so many cellars we can use before somebody finds out who he is," Abraham said.

"Why is he so important?" the overweight man remarked as he lit another Turkish cigarette. He was called Pinny, the younger brother of the smaller man who was called Moishe.

"Because the Americans want him," Moishe replied. "Anyway,

who cares why they want him. We were ordered to keep him undercover until the election is over."

"Did he kill his wife?" Abraham asked in his clipped English accent.

"Who knows? Since when is killing your wife a crime?" Moishe replied.

"In America, everything is a crime," Abraham interjected sullenly.

"Only Arabs can kill their wives. They're allowed four. Who the hell can afford four wives?" Pinny said.

"A rabbi shouldn't kill his wife," Abraham said in his clipped English accent, his voice giving way to a Yiddish accent near the end of the sentence.

"He carries the word of the Rebbe with him," Moishe remarked. "We need him until after the election."

"They have American policemen looking through Mea Shearim," Pinny declared.

"They'll find nothing," Moishe replied.

"How can I not tell Yehuda?" Pinny replied while he lifted another unfiltered cigarette from the pack that lay on the table and then lit it with the remnants of the old cigarette held gingerly in his fingers.

"We served in the Palmach, then the 28th Paratroopers together. He'd kill me if he knew I knew where the rabbi was." Pinny added.

"You're not betraying Yehuda," Abraham stated. "It's his clients. We owe nothing to them."

"Yehuda is our friend," Moishe interjected.

"Orders come from the top . . . not Yehuda Ben-Zvi," the overweight man declared.

"Abraham," the small man said derisively as he coughed from the cigarette smoke, "to you it's orders . . . friendship means nothing."

"I'm a soldier . . . I take orders from the Shin Bet," Abraham replied indignantly. His head was completely bald except for dark brown sideburns that grew into muttonchops almost touching his jowls.

"We all served together," Pinny declared. "Yehuda saved my ass enough times that I owe something to him. Even against orders."

"It's not his life at stake," Abraham said. The veins in his forehead just below the widow's peak pulsated in a staccato beat as he spoke deliberately, each word uttered without passion.

"Even if we don't tell him, he'll find him. Give him enough time and Yehuda will find the good rabbi," Pinny said.

"Then it'll be too late," Abraham said. "After the election it doesn't matter. We'll hand the rabbi over to Yehuda and his clients . . . or whoever pays the highest price."

"Since when have you become such a *kurvah* (whore), Abraham?" Moishe, the small man remarked, as he drained the coffee cup in front of him.

Abraham, his English accent disappearing completely, said in a Yiddish-flecked speech pattern, while extending his right forearm, "See these numbers," he arched the hairless portion of his inner forearm toward Moishe's face, before continuing in a deliberate voice.

"I got out before my German friends murdered whatever remained in the camp . . . just ahead of the Russians." He paused and then continued, "That's another story. I walked across Poland . . . no shoes . . . in the middle of winter. Thinking about a beach. Any beach. I prayed for the sun . . . and the hot sand under my frozen feet. That's when I realized it's not enough to remain alive just to be alive. You need to be alive and feel good. Feeling good means the sun on your face and your belly *shtupped* with wonderful food . . . and your mind thinking of getting laid . . ."

"You were only a kid . . . and you were already thinking of getting laid," Pinny remarked without humor.

"Anyway," Abraham continued as if he had not been interrupted by his cynical listener, "You need shekels, drachmas . . . dollars . . . whatever buys the sun."

"You immigrants are all the same," Moishe interjected as he blew a wide swath of purple smoke into the whitewashed room. "Pinny and me were born here. No stories of camps and walking across Europe. Just fighting everyday those *momzers* (bastards). They're your friends one day and the next day, you know, they have a gun up your ass."

"Nothing is easy," Pinny said in almost a whisper. "The only thing that remains is your friends. Like Yehuda. We came through the ancient arches of the Old City together. In 1967. Before anybody . . . not even the tanks could beat us through those arches. I couldn't believe him. I said, let's wait for the others. Why get killed just to see some old stones? He wouldn't listen . . . so I *schlepped* along after him. We were the first into the Jewish Quarter . . . and we both knelt before the Wall. The first Jews in God knows how long. I understood then what he meant. Why he was in such a rush. It wasn't just a few stones that were there. It was the whole thing. The Wall rising up toward the sky. And what the Wall meant to us. No, Abraham, you can't buy time . . . and friends. He watched my back and I watched his. But anyway . . . you want to go out and get a pizza . . . they opened a new Pizza Hut near the Jewish Quarter . . . what a *shandah* (shame). A Pizza Hut near the Western Wall. It's enough to bring Abraham back from the dead."

Moishe rose from his beach chair and strode toward the window facing the square of the Jewish Quarter.

"There are so many people looking for him," Moishe said in a low voice.

"Who?" Pinny asked.

"The American rabbi. One man can't mean so much."

"Americans are funny," Abraham declared, his English accent returning in full force, "I lived there for almost ten years. I sold Jaguars. Everybody thought I was English. Anyway . . . they get something in their minds, they never let go. It's as if they have nothing better to worry about. Life is too good. So they need to create things to worry about. They turn the world over to find a philandering husband . . . if they did that in Israel we'd have time for nothing else."

"Where is the good rabbi now?" Pinny asked.

"Below the bakery on Weissman Street," Moishe replied.

CHAPTER TWENTY-ONE

The basement had the sterile white aura of a hospital ward. Adobe colored bricks dotted the windowless confines. Waves of bread smells filled the air, shrouding the hanging lightbulbs in a foglike mist.

Night covered the cobblestone streets with eerie shadows. It was dark outside, the sun soon to rise above the spires of the Old City.

The rabbi slept fitfully on the army cot lodged against the wall in the monastic cubicle at the far end of the basement. His clothes were black except for the white, crumpled shirt that fell across his waist.

Yaacov walked softly across the basement floor to the little room. The bakery operation had closed for the Sabbath and except for the security guards, also dressed in the black of the hareti orthodox, the basement was empty. Except for the sleeping rabbi.

Gently opening the metal door of the cubicle, Yaacov slid into the room, cursing as the 9mm Beretta lodged in his belt struck the edge of the metal door.

Bolting up from the cot, the bearded rabbi pulled the long barrelled 9mm revolver from under his pillow and aimed it straight at Yaacov's head. Yaacov threw his hands up into the air, his knuckles striking the green metallic shade of the hanging lightbulb. He cursed loudly.

"It's me, rabbi," Yaacov muttered in a consoling voice.

"What are you doing, climbing around in the dark?" the rabbi replied loudly.

"I didn't want to wake you. It's still dark outside. I needed the legislative proposals . . . for the council."

"You should have asked, Yaacov . . ." the rabbi declared in a more conciliatory tone. "I could've blown your head off."

"Bibi is meeting with Shas this morning. They want your plan."

"Did you bring coffee at least?" The rabbi raised himself off the cot, tucked his shirt into his pants, and pulled the bottom of the fringe down past his shirt cuffs.

"I'll put a pot on, rabbi."

Rabbi Carl Rubin swung his legs onto the floor, pulled his paunchy body upright and stretched his arms towards the ceiling.

"You would've thought they could have found a better place for me to sleep . . . than this," he murmured as his bloodshot eyes scoured the room.

"After the election, Rabbi. There are a few people looking for you . . ."

"I know," the rabbi admitted. "Did you hear the music, Yaacov?" the rabbi asked, his eyes shining with elation. "Rodrigo. Do you hear, Yaacov?"

"There is no music, Rabbi. It's the Sabbath . . . there is no music."

"I miss the music . . ." the rabbi muttered absentmindedly.

"My life was always filled with music . . . until she died," the rabbi added.

"Who?" Yaacov asked in a childish voice.

"No matter, Yaacov. What are we doing today?" the rabbi asked quickly as he strode over to the sink located in the corner of the cubicle.

"You'll want to go to shul? Won't you, Rabbi?" Yaacov added benignly.

"Shul. I haven't been to shul in a week. God forgive me. Yes . . . I'd like to go to shul, Yaacov. Is that possible?"

"Maybe. There is a small synagogue at the end of the street. It is not Hasidic," Yaacov's voice trailed off.

"I'm Reformed, Yaacov . . ."

"But I thought . . . the Rebbe . . . you know."

The rabbi smiled as he turned the faucet on in the chipped porcelain sink. Hungrily, he poured water onto his face. The sting of the cold wetness seared through his eyes into his overfatigued brain.

"Do you at least have a towel here?" he roared as the water dripped off his bearded face.

"Yes . . . yes . . . Rabbi . . . here in the closet." Yaacov rushed to open the doors of the closet, withdrew a small towel and handed it to the rabbi.

"Where are we going to meet them?" the rabbi queried, as he strenuously rubbed the skimpy towel over his face and beard. "Where's the coffee, Yaacov?" he added impatiently, his voice cracking slightly.

"I'll go now, Rabbi. . . . We have a small kitchen in the bakery."

"Where did you say the meeting is?" the rabbi asked.

"Behind the jeweler's shop. Just past the shul at the end of the street."

"A strange place to decide the fate of Israel," the rabbi said as he ran his hands through his thick dark hair, stroking his beard in a semidisorderly state.

"They have your picture in all the newspapers, Rabbi. The American police . . ."

"Yes, I know. Can we hurry . . . Yaacov . . . coffee is more important to me now then my public notices."

The rabbi followed the diminutive form of Yaacov as he limped slowly across the basement floor towards the small kitchen at the far end of the basement.

"Is there any place I can take a shower, Yaacov?" The rabbi asked in a demanding voice.

"Not here Rabbi . . . maybe after the meeting."

After gulping down the hot coffee, almost scalding the roof of his mouth, the rabbi's mind meandered through last week's events. Who'd ever thought that Eleanore would have caused me more trouble after her death then before, he mused painfully. A week of running. From basement to basement, until the election is over. Tonight and I can surface. Or can I? he thought. Everybody's afraid to offend the American authorities, even though I carry the word of the Rebbe.

"Where did you get that limp, Yaacov?" the rabbi asked in an absent-minded manner.

"*Le guerre* . . . Rabbi."

"Which one?" The rabbi smiled sympathetically.

"1948. I was sixteen. Just arrived. The war of independence. I made it through the camps all right . . . but some Arab shot me in the leg."

"No peace in the holy land," the rabbi replied in a sullen voice.

"There will never be peace here, Rabbi. Too many have suffered . . . not just Jews . . . the Arabs, too. They hate us too much."

"And then what? If there is no peace, then what's left, Yaacov?"

"The Messiah. When he comes, there will be peace, Rabbi."

"Does he want to come to this place of eternal war? He's better off where he is, Yaacov."

Yaacov emitted an innocent smile, his eyes watered with humor as he poured the rabbi another cup of coffee.

"Do you believe in the Messiah, Rabbi?" Yaacov asked as he stared into the bemused face of the rabbi who was now seated beside a wooden table sipping the hot coffee cautiously.

"What else is there to believe in, Yaacov? Peres . . . Rabin . . . even Netanyahu. Can mere mortals calm the troubled waters of five thousand years of eternal strife? The Talmud says He will come when all the Jews of the world inhabit the lands of Abraham. How are you going to get the Jews of Larchmont Hills to live in the deserts of Israel?"

"You don't believe in the coming of the Messiah, Rabbi?" Yaacov asked in a surprised voice.

"He will come when He will come. I'm not the one to decide such important things, Yaacov. I'm just an emissary from the living Messiah . . . in Brooklyn. The Rebbe will decide for me."

"Maybe he's the Messiah . . . the Rebbe."

"Maybe . . ." The rabbi quickly rose from the table and went into his cubicle to put on his disguise of a long black coat, usually worn by the hareti, and a black homburg.

"The sun is rising and I'm in need of some Talmudic enlightenment, Yaacov. Let's daven together awhile. And then I'll be ready to answer more important questions . . . such as who is going to lead Israel tomorrow."

CHAPTER TWENTY-TWO

The room was small, a skylight its sole source of light. Hidden behind a massive painting, the entrance was covered with an eighteen-inch gauge steel door that slid into the adjoining wall. Fronted by a rectangular jewelry and *tchotchke* (knicknacks, collectibles) shop, inhabited by blackdressed hareti salesmen, the back room was indiscernable, even to the knowing.

Tall, burly security guards dressed in sportswear lined the blank walls of the hidden room. Except for the bulges alongside their armpits, the guards were nondescript and blended into the sterile environment. In muted tones, four men around a table argued, their voices rising no more then the level of a whisper. A crowded glass ashtray sat in the middle of the table, ashes spilling over as the meeting intensified.

"You want to be prime minister, you have to go along with the deal." The slim young man with payes said in a demanding voice.

"He's a felon. How can I appoint a felon as my attorney general? They'll never accept it," the distinguished, almost silver gray, middle-aged man with a square jaw and fiery hazel eyes declared in the well modulated voice of a New York actor.

"He's only charged, Bibi," the young man replied emphatically.

"In Israeli politics, charged is as good as convicted, Ashov. If the Labor *momzers* ever found out, I'd lose the election," the man called Bibi stated.

"Without Bar-On as your attorney general, the Shas will stay out of the election," Ashov replied without passion.

Carl Rubin chewed on the stem of his pipe as he watched the two men grapple with their respective positions. The only other man at the table was a balding, hawk-nosed man who was probably younger than he looked. His name was Percha and he was Bibi Netanyahu's right hand man.

"The Rebbe . . . *my Rebbe*," Rubin announced, "doesn't care about Bar-On. He only wants your position on the lands. Any deviation from your public positions on the lands will change our position also."

"My position is the same . . ." Netanyahu said in a compromising voice" . . . we must show a willingness to negotiate . . . or else."

"The Americans will pull out," Rubin finished his sentence.

"Yes," Netanyahu pronounced emphatically, as he nervously ran his well-manicured fingers through his thick mane of hair.

"Get rid of the Americans . . ." Ashov warned, "You can't sit on more then one horse, Bibi. If you want to win this election . . . Bar-On must be the attorney general and the peace process must be kaput." Ashov's accent was a melange of British upper-class speech salted with Yiddish expressions. He was the dynamic leader of the Shas, a right-wing Sephardic-based religious group that had found its political strength in the last Knesset election. Since the Israeli parliament was splintered into many political parties and only the party with a majority of the voters could govern, each of the two major political parties had to have the religious fringe parties on their side, or lose the government. The Shas controlled a block of Sephardic Israelis that wanted ultra-Orthodox Talmudic principles applied to secular Israeli life, as well as the shunting aside of the Reform and Conservative movements of Israeli religious life.

"You have your own troubles too, Ashov," Netanyahu declared.

"We all do," Ashov replied as his dark eyes furtively glanced toward Rabbi Rubin.

"My problems have nothing to do with Israeli politics," Rubin replied indignantly. "I'm here as the Rebbe's emissary . . . messenger . . . whatever you want to call me."

"It's hot in here." Netanyahu directed his voice to the short, burly security guard behind him.

"There's nothing we can do, Prime Minister," Percha whispered inoffensively to his leader. He continued " . . . the skylight doesn't open," pointing his finger up to the skylight.

"Both of you could be problems for me," Netanyahu added, his finger pointed at Rubin.

"I will be leaving right after the election, Mr. Netanyahu," Rubin remarked. "My Rebbe will see that you have enough funds to continue buying up all of the Palestinian lands in the West Bank. To guarantee the Jewish settlements. He, my Rebbe . . . will never agree to any release of Talmudic designated lands anywhere in Israel."

"I can't guarantee that position," Netanyahu stated blandly.

"Then I can't guarantee the Ashkenazi orthodox vote. Nor the several million dollars that go along with that vote, sir," Rabbi Rubin stated in a voice filled with certainty.

"The Shas and the Rebbe have no choice but to support the Likud, gentlemen," Netanyahu pronounced.

"Yes, they do," Ashov quickly interjected. His face was almost hairless except for the long payes reaching down from his curly brown hair onto the sides of his face. Modern, round spectacles crossed his thin aquiline nose, and he occasionally poked his forefinger against the frames to push the glasses against his forehead. He added, "We could let Labor win and then destroy the Peres government by striking out on every bill he tries to pass in the Knesset."

"You would have anarchy," Netanyahu said, with a flourish of his hand across the room.

"Anarchy is better then surrender," Ashov said as he rose deliberately from his folding chair, almost tipping it over. The burly security guard quickly grabbed the top rung of the metal chair and placed it silently under Ashov's rising body.

"The Clinton government would withdraw its support if we reneged on the Oslo accords with the Palestinians," Netanyahu argued, his eyes glazed over with indecision.

"So what?" Ashov yelled.

"Who cares about Clinton? He has his own troubles also," Ashov continued. "We always worry about the Americans. Well," Ashov's voice lowered in a dramatic whisper, "God will provide for us . . . Bibi. Clinton is not God."

"And you, Rabbi . . . ," Netanyahu's voice was directed at Rubin. "Do you think the Shas' position . . . anarchy . . . is the future of Israel?"

"The Rebbe believes in the will of God as expressed in the Talmud, Mr. Netanyahu. If anarchy must result in order to save our land . . . well, anarchy it will be."

Netanyahu rose from the table as he said in a voice filled with concern, "Gentlemen . . . I will . . ."

The sound of his voice was deadened by a sharp, metallic sound clanging against the steel door. The explosion lifted the flimsy table from the ground and blew it against the wall. The four men were thrown to the floor, each cowering in a fetal position in a vain attempt to protect their bodies from flying shards of metal shooting through the air. The smell of acrid smoke engulfed the room as the burly security guard pushed himself up off the floor and rushed to the still form of Netanyahu. Lifting the still body of the political candidate over his shoulders, the security man pulled at a ring attached to the floor boards. Suddenly the floor opened into a flight of steps leading into a dark, cavernous tunnel. Without a moment of hesitation, the guard disappeared down the steps, the still form of the Israeli politician's body on his shoulders.

The other two security guards rose quickly from their shocked state and rushed to revive Rubin and Ashov. Percha disappeared down the tunnel steps, closing the floorboards above his head.

Police sirens and shouting voices could be heard coming from the blown-up steel entranceway to the tiny backroom of the shop. As the smoke started to clear, Rubin could see the shredded remnants of the front shop and the jagged outline of the vault- like steel door that separated the front shop and the back room.

"We must hurry, Rabbi," the tall security guard murmured to Rubin as he gently pushed the rabbi through the jagged door opening and around the bloodied forms covering the debris-strewn floor of the shop.

"Why?" the rabbi muttered as his hand felt bloodied paste on his bearded face. Ashov walked boldly past the rabbi with no help, his body concrete straight. Rubin could see that Ashov's right arm had been blown away up to the shoulder, the opening a mass of bloodied pulp. Ashov's face was smiling as his body marched out the door opening onto the street and then collapsed into the arms of the ambulance attendants.

The security guard virtually lifted the rabbi's small body off the ground as he rushed Rubin into a waiting black limousine parked at the corner of the street. Inside the sedan Ryan sat, his face a blank mask.

"Good morning, Rabbi," Ryan said as he extended his hand to help the rabbi into the backseat of the limousine.

CHAPTER TWENTY-THREE

For the entire previous week, Ryan, Olsham, and Yehuda had traversed the streets of Jerusalem as if they were conducting a guided tour for visiting American Jews. The night before the bombing in Mea Shearim they sat in Yehuda's limousine chewing on carrot sticks and fried pita slices, waiting for the rabbi to emerge from the ancient bakery located beneath the street level. Eluding the omnivorous arms of the captain was not easy. The day before, Captain Crutchfield and Ryan bumped into each other as the two groups searched the Jewish Quarter for the rabbi.

Crutchfield invited Ryan and Olsham into a small cafe overlooking the square of the Museum of the Patriarchs. Surrounded by orthodox Hasidic children playing in the sunlit square, Crutchfield sat silently.

Yehuda sat across from the cafe in the middle of the square.

They drank the strong Turkish coffee, no one speaking, all staring out into the square.

Crutchfield broke the silence as he reached into his pocket for his lighter, pulled it out and lit the Pall Mall cigarette at the corner of his mouth.

"He's mine, y'know," Crutchfield said in a benign whisper.

"You have no jurisdiction in Israel, Captain," Olsham replied.

"I have an extradition order waiting to be signed by the chief justice of the Israeli Supreme Court, Olsham," The captain declared.

"On what grounds?" Ryan asked, his eyes searching Crutchfield's sallow face for the truth.

"Fugitive from justice. Even good in Israel."

"Bullshit," Olsham declared angrily. "You got no evidence linking the rabbi with his wife's murder."

"Maybe, maybe not, John," Crutchfield admitted, his eyes staring out at Yehuda, who was kicking the soccer ball for a group of black-garbed Orthodox children milling around the fountains in the square.

"But we still indicted your client, Joshua," Crutchfield continued, a smirk quickly crossing his red-veined face.

"You can indict Mother Teresa if you want to, Captain," Ryan said in an even-tempered voice.

"There's enough on your client."

"That he's the husband of the deceased? That should be enough to convict anyone," Ryan said in a sarcastic voice.

"Doesn't matter, Joshua," Crutchfield declared in a pompous voice. "It's enough to ask the Israeli courts to extradite the good rabbi back to the hills of Summit County. That's the way it works."

"Retirement means that much to you, Captain?" Olsham interjected, his voice charged with a caffeine surge from the dark brown, Turkish coffee.

"More then anything else in the world, John. You should know what it means to be fired . . . and have to scrounge around for a meal in your old age . . ." Crutchfield smiled, his mouth showing an irregular row of teeth, ground down with age.

"I didn't think that you would be Leary's executioner, Captain," Ryan stated. "We've had our differences . . . but I always found you to be a fair man."

"Necessity, Joshua. Necessity. Roger is not an easy taskmaster, I must admit. He's all I got . . . and he calls the shots."

"After the election . . . and if Netanyahu wins . . . you'll never get the new Israeli government to extradite the rabbi," Ryan declared as his eyes scoured the square, noting the two gray-suited men leaning against the museum building directly across from the fountains.

"Well," Crutchfield puffed heavily on his cigarette, his eyes following Ryan's stare directed at the two plainclothes. "If that's the case . . ." He stopped and pointed his yellow-stained index finger toward the two gray-suited men, "You see those guys. . .You recognize them, John."

Crutchfield addressed Olsham, "They're your favorite state troopers . . . the mean ones . . . I figured if the Israelis can steal Eichmann out of Argentina . . . we can invite the rabbi to leave with us . . . friendly-like, y'know."

"That's kidnapping, Captain," Ryan remarked testily.

"Maybe. If we get stuck in Israel. Maybe . . . but once we get out of here . . . well . . . I don't think anyone is going to stop us from returning a fugitive from justice to the USA."

Crutchfield directed his forefinger to the two muscular men, who looked too formally dressed for an Israeli summer day. Briskly, the two men walked over to the cafe, just outside the entrance.

Olsham called to Yehuda, who threw the soccer ball to the milling children surrounding him. He boldly moved past the two state troopers, brushing through them instead of around them, and stopped alongside Olsham's chair.

"Yehuda . . . the captain here suggests that these two goons over there can steal the rabbi from your protection. Why don't you show him the persuasive methods you use in protecting your guest."

Without hesitation, Yehuda sidestepped the table with lightning speed, grabbed the captain's neck with his right hand, his two forefingers pressed tightly against the captain's larynx. The two men started to move, but Yehuda held his free hand out towards them in warning. Yehuda's large white teeth blazed forth into an innocent grin, his eyes fixed on the captain. The captain's arms flailed out, his hands landing on Yehuda's wrist in a vain attempt to disgorge the death strangle from his throat. The policemen again started to move. Yehuda's grip tightened.

"Gentlemen . . . I advise against any movement," Yehuda said in a soft, pleasant voice. "Any more pressure and your captain is dead."

Ryan's eyes focused disbelievingly on the guide's hand and then back to the two policemen, their hands moving into their suit jackets.

"Drop the guns on the ground, gentlemen." Yehuda said "If you don't. . ." the captain's right arm motioned to the policemen to drop their 9 millimeter guns onto the pavement. Yehuda released the captain's throat as the metallic weapons clamored onto the concrete patio outside the cafe door.

"Yehuda is a graduate of the elite Ben-Gurion Battalion of the Israeli paratroopers," Olsham bragged shamelessly.

"He can kill you in ten different ways . . . just with his hands, Captain," Olsham continued in a chuckling voice as the captain violently rubbed his neck.

Crutchfield rose excitedly from the table, the chair was knocked out from under him, his eyes a mixture of fear and anger.

"We'll still get him, Ryan . . . even if I have to break his legs. The rabbi is going back to Summit County . . . with me!" Crutchfield bellowed in uneven gasps, his body leaning threateningly over the table.

"And if you try to stop us," Crutchfield continued, his voice gaining confidence as he spoke, "we'll get you for obstruction of justice. We'll indict your ass so you can't ever show it back in the States, Ryan. D'ya hear me?" Crutchfield's voice rose almost to an hysterical pitch, his face burning with red-hot fury.

"This is not Summit County, Captain," Ryan replied. "If the rabbi returns, he comes back with me, of his own free will. Got it, Captain? You are not going to parade him around in your backyard as some lunatic murderer. He comes back with me on his own steam."

"We'll see. . ." the captain's mouth foamed with gray spittle at the edges, his right hand still massaging his finger-scarred throat. The captain wheeled from his position and stomped out of the cafe, angrily pushing the two policemen aside.

"You pissed him off, Yehuda," Olsham said in a whimsical voice.

"Was that necessary, John?" Ryan chided, his eyes following the three policemen rushing from the Square.

"We only know violence here," Yehuda said in a low voice, "Kindness is seen as as weakness."

"Crutchfield isn't an Arab terrorist," Ryan replied.

"Maybe not, Mr. Ryan," Yehuda addressed Ryan as if he were a teacher lecturing to a student. "He knows that the new government won't extradite the rabbi. So how else can he take him? Only by force. So . . . we show him that if he uses force . . . we use force. And God is on our side, Mr. Ryan."

"Let's hope we find my client before we have to test your theory out, Yehuda," Ryan declared, as he slowly rose from the table and walked out onto the square.

The young boys, their white shirts stained with sweat, were still kicking the soccer ball.

CHAPTER TWENTY-FOUR

It was night in Jerusalem and the full moon was glorious. The house sat majestically on the slope of a gently rising street overlooking a large empty tract of land dotted with stilled bulldozers.

Subtly lit with indirect lighting, the dining room in the white stucco house was surrounded by archeological artifacts. Six people sat comfortably around the glass-topped dining room table. Five sipping the Israeli red wine, no one speaking. The sixth person was a teenage girl sullenly sipping on a straw protruding from a large water glass filled with Pepsi and lemon.

"You already had enough to drink, Shula," the tall, slim woman seated at the head of the table remarked.

"One glass is not enough, Mama," the girl responded in a plaintive voice.

"When you turn sixteen you will be allowed a second glass at dinner," Yehuda interjected in a hoarse, laughing voice.

"My friends all drink at dinner," Shula continued, "You let Sosie drink when she was fourteen."

"I was sixteen when I had two glasses at dinner," the young, strikingly beautiful woman, sitting across from Shula, pedantically replied.

"You don't drink wine?" the woman at the end of the table remarked towards Ryan, who was seated to the right of the woman.

"Not for some time, Mrs. Ben-Zvi," Ryan answered in a reluctant voice.

"Call me Zeppi, Mr. Ryan."

"Her real name is Zepporah," Yehuda said.

"Everybody calls me Zeppi . . . my friends do anyway."

"I'll take another glass," Olsham gaily interjected as he reached for the glass decanter situated in the middle of the table.

"Wine thins the blood," Yehuda stated expertly.

"Too much wine kills you too, Yehuda," Zeppi remarked with a trace of a smile, making her face even prettier.

"Jews have been drinking too much wine for five thousand years, Zeppi . . . and we're still here," Yehuda added.

"We make the best wine in the world right here in Israel . . . the Galilee. Y'know the Galilee?" Yehuda asked.

"Since we're guests in your lovely home . . . please . . . Josh is my first name . . . Call me Josh. No. I didn't know about your wine. I sort of lost interest in wine some time ago . . . along with all alcohol."

"You're a recovering alcoholic!" Zeppi declared without criticizing, "I work for the Benedict Institute here in Jerusalem and we do studies on addictions. Israelis have many . . . and alcohol is one of the worst. Especially among the new immigrants . . . from Russia."

"It has been two years . . . to the day almost," Josh replied.

"Aren't you . . .?" Sosie said, her voice stopping abruptly and then continuing, as she stared directly at Ryan with her soft green eyes, "You're young to be . . ."

"You're never too young," Zeppi remarked sharply. "I see teenagers who are addicted . . . not only to drugs but to alcohol."

"That's why I can't have two glasses at dinner?" Shula asked, her hand brushing away a trace of falling blonde hair over her face.

"You can't have two glasses because I say you can't have two glasses, Shula," Zeppi said in an exasperated voice.

"This is your first visit to Israel?" Sosie asked, as her eyes looked into Ryan's face.

"Yes . . . yet it seems I've been here before," Ryan replied, his eyes digesting the sun-streaked hair and bronzed classic features of the young woman's face.

"All American Jews seem to feel the same way," Yehuda stated.

"Maybe you all have," he added philosophically.

"I was in New York when I was a teenager," Sosie remarked, as her full sensuous lips drank the last of her red wine.

"Mama won't let me go," Shula remarked soulfully.

"Sosie went with her senior class, Shula," Zeppi said, as she rose to pour coffee into the cups in front of each of the adult diners.

"Shula wants everything Sosie had . . . but sooner," Zeppi added, her illuminating smile filling her face.

"Sosie here," Yehuda proudly declared as he rose from his chair and placed his arm around Sosie's shoulder, "graduated from the same elite Ben-Gurion training course I finished thirty some years ago. Only ten percent graduate—eighteen months of hell . . . but Sosie passed. With flying colors yet."

"Young girls shouldn't learn how to kill," Zeppi said, her eyes watering slightly.

"In Israel everybody has to learn to defend themselves," Yehuda argued, as he walked to the rear of the dining room and peered out the elliptical stained-glass window facing the large construction site behind the house.

"You see that mess of dirt out there, gentlemen," Yehuda continued solemnly. "That's more housing for the rich American Jews who need to make aliyah to Israel. One-hundred thousand dollars a room it costs, but they still come. They think it is the Garden of Eden out here . . . until they hear the first bomb go off."

"Now that the election is over . . . shouldn't the bombing stop?" Ryan asked, his eyes still fixed on Sosie's face.

"It'll increase," Yehuda replied. "The Arabs know that Netanyahu won't give up the land. He can't and still remain in power. Then all hell will break loose."

"Well . . . at least the rabbi has agreed to return with us," Olsham declared, his glass refilled with red wine.

"Now . . . maybe now," Yehuda muttered, "Who knows if he will feel the same way tomorrow. You can't force him to go. Not now."

"I hoped we could leave tonight," Josh said wistfully. "The captain's not giving up so easily."

"What's the difference who brings him back?" Sosie asked.

"If we bring him back . . . he voluntarily surrenders to the police," Josh replied. "But if the captain gets him. Well, the media will murder the rabbi. . . ."

"It sounds like a crazy game to me," Sosie said.

"It's all a game," Ryan replied in a slow, deliberate voice.

"What happens if he is innocent? I mean he could be innocent," Sosie continued, her eyes unmoving from Ryan's face.

"At this stage, that becomes irrelevant. His innocence, I mean. It's the illusion of guilt that matters. You run away from the police, it seems that you're not innocent. You might be. But it doesn't appear that you are if you flee," Ryan declared, his hand reaching for the aqua-mineral bottle; his throat felt sand-dry. She's so beautiful, he thought, as his eyes stared at the sheer cotton blouse that exposed a little cleavage.

"We don't have time for your American form of justice in Israel," Yehuda remarked, as he quickly turned to face the table.

"Sosie's fiancé died in the last bombing," Yehuda added.

"We got even, Papa," Sosie said in a soft voice.

"You never get even, Sosie," Yehuda replied, "It doesn't bring your loved ones back from the dead."

"Enough already, you two," Zeppi chided, as she rose to refill the coffee pot.

"Why don't you take Josh to the new shopping center down by the square, Sosie," Zeppi directed as she walked to the kitchen.

"I'm on call tonight, Mama," Sosie replied.

"Carry your beeper. If anybody calls . . ."

"Be careful, Sosie," Yehuda warned, "Hamas are ready for the next strike, and I don't want you to be in it."

Sosie laughed.

"You still treat me like a child, Papa," Sosie replied, as she rose from the table, adjusted her form-fitting slacks that showed off her curvaceous body, and strolled toward the entranceway to the dining room.

"Mr. Ryan . . . Joshua . . ." she smiled brightly as she held her hand out for Ryan, who was still seated at the table wondering what to do next.

"Let me show you how America can transform the desert beauty of Israel into one massive shopping mall."

Ryan clumsily rose from the table, a bright red flush appearing on his face as he nearly stumbled toward the waiting young Sosie.

"I really think we should spend the night with the rabbi," he said in a reluctant undertone.

"Don't worry Mr. Ryan," Yehuda said, his arms raised toward the ceiling. "We have God on our side. And also my three friends from the Shin Bet, the ones that hid the rabbi from me. They feel so guilty they would give their lives to protect him from those *gulayim*."

"I'll look in on him, Josh," Olsham volunteered, as he drained the last remnants of the red wine from his glass.

"Besides," he continued, "nobody can get into that floor of the King David without triggering an alarm set up by the hotel and Yehuda's three compatriots."

"I'd still feel safer, if you were there." Ryan's concern was clearly evident on his face.

"Okay . . . okay," Olsham muttered. "Yehuda will drive me. Soon as I finish this great wine."

"Now . . . John . . . now," Ryan ordered, as he followed Sosie's quick pace out the front door of the house into the silence of the moonlit street.

Sosie had already jumped into the front seat of the BMW 350i convertible parked at the curb up the street from the house.

"You don't trust anybody . . . do you, Joshua?" she said, as she focused her gaze down the sloping hill in front of the car.

"Too many things can go wrong. There is a lot riding on the rabbi getting back to the States . . . without leg irons on," he replied as he sidled into the black-leather bucket seat of the compact sports car.

"My father's friends are professionally trained like he was. I'm sure they will deliver the rabbi in one piece," she said as she gunned the accelerator. Joshua barely noticed the shift into first gear. They hurtled past the line of parked cars at the curb of the residential street. Any minute now, Josh expected the silent driver to press a button on the dash and soar the black German steel machine into orbit.

"Are we in a hurry?" Ryan shouted above the noise of the windy maelstrom created by the speed of the convertible lurching headlong down the hilly streets of east Jerusalem.

"I'm always in a hurry, Joshua," she replied with a sardonic laugh.

Silently, Ryan sat impelled into the wraparound leather bucket seat, holding onto the handle above the seat. He attempted to appear unconcerned but the deep worry lines around his mouth showed otherwise.

Suddenly, Ryan's eyes were caught by a panoply of bright lights in the near distance.

Sosie reduced the speed of the vehicle as the lights grew brighter and nearer.

"Hollywood USA," she said in a cynical undertone, as she expertly downshifted the vehicle into the lower gears.

"An American's answer to the Mideast crisis," she continued as Ryan viewed the massive lights encircling the power shopping center directly in front of the vehicle.

Sosie drove the vehicle towards an empty parking spot near the entrance to the Super Value Supermarket. As she readied the vehicle to fill the empty parking space, another vehicle, a Mercedes sedan, shot across the front of Sosie's BMW from the opposite direction into the parking spot. A tall, portly man in his mid-forties, dressed in expensive jeans and a Versace shirt, bounced pompously out of the front seat of the Mercedes SE 600 Sedan. Sosie pulled her BMW behind the ponderous Mercedes, as she simultaneously jumped out of the front seat onto the asphalt pavement of the parking lot. She blocked the path of the much larger man, who attempted to go around her without striking out at the seemingly insignificant obstacle in front of him. Ryan slowly extricated himself from the front seat, his knees aching from the contortions of the rollercoaster ride through Jerusalem.

"That was my parking place," Sosie said in a soft voice, a friendly smile crossing her face.

The large man stared down at the little-girl image in front of him, and then uttered in a sneering laugh, "Your space?" he shouted in a voice dripping with sarcasm. "Listen . . . you don't own this parking lot, lady . . . and besides, what the hell are you going to do about it?"

He looked over at Ryan, who was slowly walking toward the two combatants.

"You have my parking space," Sosie repeated in a dramatic, threatening voice. Her arms were braced against the sides of her tiny body, her legs were apart in a pyramidical stance.

"Wait a second . . ." Ryan declared as he lunged forward with his right arm to separate the two unequally sized bodies.

"The marines are here," the man laughed as he struck Ryan

across the chest with the back of his fist, forcing the unsuspecting Ryan to fall backwards before he finally regained his balance.

"Get out of my way . . . you little fuckin' cunt!" the man said as he pushed out towards Sosie's chest with his beefy right arm.

Sosie stepped to the side of the attacker and completed an inside-outside block with her left arm. Almost instantaneously, her left foot side kicked him just above his right knee, crushing the kneecap. As his head dropped to his chest, Sosie then performed a long, back-spinning kick to the right side of his face with her right leg.

As his body fell to the ground, his voice became a curdling shriek. Sosie adeptly turned to face the caved-in man, grabbed his well-coiffed head of hair with both her hands and pulled the entire groaning mass of human pain through the rear window of the giant Mercedes Sedan. Finally releasing the man's head, Sosie stepped back to allow the semi-unconscious body to fall to the ground. The man dropped to his knees, his face a mass of blood-ied pulp from the glass residue imbedded in his distorted features, his voice a series of low drowning groans and cries for help.

With extraordinary strength, Sosie lifted the giant of a man from his knees, tore the front of the expensive silk shirt he was wearing, threw his body against the trunk of the Mercedes and said in a tranquil, even voice, "Mister, I want you to pull your car out of this slot. Here are my keys. Park my car and wait for me until I'm finished shopping. Do you understand me, sir?" her smiling voice containing the same jocular throatiness Ryan had heard over dinner.

With newly gained respect and reverence, the man's hand grabbed Sosie's car keys in his right hand, his eyes still incredulous.

Ryan stood back, leaning against the passenger side of Sosie's BMW, not in pain like the boorish victim, but equally surprised by the recent turn of events. For a swift moment Ryan thought he was watching a Bruce Lee video except for the fact that he was stand-ing next to this superwoman as she demolished an attacking army of evil Huns.

As they walked into the supermarket entrance, Sosie turned her head toward Ryan, pushed her arm through his arm, and said, with a smile, "Parking is a problem in Jerusalem, Joshua."

CHAPTER TWENTY-FIVE

Sosie parked the BMW at the edge of a promontory overlooking the old city. The glimmering lights of Ben Yehuda Street blinked on and off like dying stars. The silence was ominous. Ryan didn't know what to expect from this beautiful young woman who could leap tall buildings and demolish vast armies of threatening hordes with her bare hands.

After an hour browsing through the marketplace and buying nothing, with few words passing between them, Ryan and Sosie left the gaudily lit mall to return to her car and its caretaker. The repentant attacker scraped and bowed as he gladly handed the BMW keys to Sosie.

"You treat all your men friends like that?" Ryan asked, a broad smile crossing his face as he rubbed the caps of his aching knees.

"I try to avoid violence," Sosie replied, as she lit a long Pall Mall cigarette, and puffed luxuriously up toward the sky. She turned toward Ryan.

"I'm sure he would have been persuaded to move his car without surgically removing his," Ryan stated, his voice trailing off as his eyes stared at Sosie's lips puffing away at the massive stogie.

"Balls," Sosie finished his sentence with a chuckle. "You mean his balls, Joshua."

She paused, smiled and reached over to touch Ryan's face.

"You have a classical Roman face, Joshua. A nose too big for the face . . . but promising. A sensuous face. When you have the capacity to kill . . ." she continued, "Well . . . you use . . . or you try to use . . . violence carefully. Talking to that . . . that . . .boor would have not solved anything. Jerusalem is full of them. The nouveau riche. They treat everybody like dirt."

"I think you need more parking lot attendants in Jerusalem," Ryan replied. He couldn't help imagining Sosie out of her white slacks. He felt a surge of erotic tingling.

Touching his face with her hand, Sosie reached over and kissed

Ryan on the mouth. Although initially taken unaware, Ryan quickly recovered as he held her shoulders with his hands and passionately returned the searching kiss. His hand dropped from her shoulder and reached under the cotton shirt. He half expected Sosie to stop his hand, but feeling no resistance, he reached across her flat smooth belly and up toward her breasts. The initial sensation of touching the silky skin sent waves of electric shocks through Ryan's legs and groin. He had been celibate so long, the passion of sex had left him. Now so suddenly revived, it was like an onrushing hurricane drowning whatever restraints remained.

Sosie's hand moved slowly down Ryan's leg, never touching his genitals, and then up across his stomach and up to his chest.

"Do we want to do this?" Ryan suddenly said as he removed his hand from Sosie's breasts.

"I'm surprised," Sosie replied, "Do you find me so unattractive?"

"That's not the point, Sosie."

"What is it?"

"I'm doing business with Yehuda. I need him . . . he might be offended if I seduce his daughter." He paused, smiled, and then continued, his hand tenderly caressing her face.

"Papa lets me lead my own life. I'm a big girl who doesn't need fatherly guidance in my sex life."

She angrily turned the ignition key on and before she could ram the stick shift to the reverse position, Ryan reached over and switched the key to the off position.

"Please," he said in a soft pleading voice. "I'm not rejecting you, God . . ." His eyes devoured her as he continued in a stammer, "I love everything about you, Sosie. I would give up almost anything for the chance to make love to you."

"What's the point?" she demanded in a harsh voice.

"Listen," he said, his hands cupping her tiny face, "I've been down so long, Sosie. This is my chance to redeem myself. To show the world that I'm not a washed-up rummy. Once I was a somebody. A good trial lawyer. Something I've always wanted . . . since I was a kid being kicked around by my father. When the world caved in on me I wanted to jump out of a window. I never thought the pain, the public humiliation, would ever go away. But it did. And I'm here. With a chance to show everybody I'm a good lawyer. That's what I want to do. Be where I was. At the top. And rising again. And now I have a chance to do just that."

"Life is more important. I can't believe that you would put your life on hold . . . a lawyer?" she declared with a disbelieving tone in her voice.

"I know. They probably think of lawyers in Israel the way people do in the States. But to me . . . a lawyer was always someone to look up to. That's what we did when I was a kid. A lawyer wasn't a shyster . . . somebody to watch out for. I want to be the best. Not just for the money . . . but, . . .but . . ." he stammered again, "nothing really changes in this world. We go on. And nothing really changes. But sometimes . . . in a case . . . defending somebody who you think got a raw deal . . . you can make the world change. Just for that case. That person. And that's the way I feel here. The rabbi's case . . ."

"But," she replied quickly, "he might be guilty. You don't know yourself whether he is or not."

"That's not the point. I don't decide either way. But he should have a chance. It's not just him. It's everybody out there. It's the system. If it doesn't work for the rabbi, it won't work for anybody."

Her face pointed up to the star-filled sky, tears welling up in her eyes and then she spoke in almost a whisper, "We believed in the system. Once. And then he died. They all died. Without a system to declare them innocent or guilty."

"Yehuda said it was your fiancé?" Ryan replied.

"Not only him," Sosie almost shouted as she wheeled around in her seat to face Ryan. "He was the last one. There were others before him. There was Benny." Her voice trailed off.

"Benny?" Ryan replied, not knowing how to confront this suddenly fragile child seated next to him.

My brother. My older brother. My only brother."

"Yehuda never mentioned he had a son."

"He'll never talk about it. Ben was the best. He went through the brigade training like he was born to it. And then they . . ." She pointed her face to the north, "The Arabs. They shot him to pieces while he was on patrol . . . in Ramallah. The West Bank. He wasn't even nineteen yet."

"I'm sorry . . . I didn't know."

She smiled as the tears fell down her cheeks. "Don't be. Papa got even. With his . . . his associates . . . the ones watching over the rabbi now. They went to the village and caught every last one of them. They knew, because the murderers boasted publically. Killing an elite Israeli paratrooper was an honor for those thugs. They never lived to boast about it."

"Were they tried?" Ryan innocently asked.

An enigmatic smile crossed her face, yet her eyes burned with fiery hatred as she spoke in a soft, articulate voice. "Tried? Not tried by a court of law. Tried by my father and his men. Strangled by their hands. Every last one. And then they bombed their families' houses. Blew them to little bits. That's our justice."

"But it will go on. . .you kill and they get back," Ryan argued and then continued, "Where does it all end, Sosie?"

"Maybe never. It took us five thousand years to get this little piece called Eretz Yisrael. Maybe never. Until we all become part of the soil. Maybe then," she paused. "And then maybe never."

The shrill sounds of the car phone pierced the stillness of the car and surrounding mountaintop.

"It's Papa. He worries for me. He thinks I take too many chances," she said in a laughing voice as she picked the telephone out of the console.

"Hello, Papa," she said into the cradle of the phone. For what seemed an eternity, she said nothing as she listened to the voice in the phone.

"Yes," she finally said in a depressed voice, "I'll tell him. We'll be there in a few minutes."

She paused and then said, "I'm sure he'll want to go immediately. Shalom."

She placed the phone into the console, turned the engine on, and then rammed the gearshift into reverse, jolting Ryan's neck.

"They got the rabbi!" she yelled above the whine of the engine's noise.

"They got who?" Ryan replied in a shocked voice. "They got the rabbi? Who . . . who did? I thought he was safe?"

"He was . . . they dressed up as Israeli policemen . . . and shot the guards. One was severely wounded."

"Who? Do they know who?" Ryan's voice was rising to the level of hysteria.

"My father thinks it's some captain . . . American team."

"Hurry!" Ryan ordered. "Maybe it's not too late."

"They've already left the country." Sosie said. "They left by private jet. I'm sorry, Joshua."

Ryan noted the cigarette had burnt itself out and fallen to the floor as he held onto the door grip.

CHAPTER TWENTY-SIX

"We have him," Leary declared too loudly, his uneven teeth breaking over his thin lips in a victorious chuckle.

The restaurant was called the Franklin Inn, located just outside Bristol in the rolling hills of eastern Summit County.

The Inn had several rooms on top of the sprawling restaurant so it could qualify as a country bed-and-breakfast facility. The cost of a liquor license was cheaper that way.

It was a Thursday night and the restaurant was filled to capacity. The waiting line streamed out the front entranceway and each waiting customer was given a belt vibrator to wear so the customer would know when to come in from the outside waiting area. The restaurant building was two stories high and looked like a great working barn, except for the massive roadside neon sign shouting the name and face of Ben Franklin.

The Inn was a steakhouse. Massive alcoholic drinks went with the Gulliver-size platters of ribeye, filets, or just plain king-sized slabs of prime rib. Although listed as a bed-and-breakfast inn, the Franklin Inn was only open for dinner and took no reservations.

Leary stared at Judge Albert Sturmer's sharp-nosed face as he spoke in stuttering, frenetic sentences.

"Are you listening to me, Albert?" Leary barked suddenly at the silver-haired judge who was wrapped up in devouring the two-pound porterhouse steak in front of him.

"Yes, Roger . . . I'm listening. I haven't eaten all day. I'm listening. What the hell do you want me to do?" Sturmer replied, his voice flecked with irritation at the young insistent prosecutor seated across the table from him.

"You have to update the warrant for Rubin's arrest," Roger paused as he downed the last of his margarita.

"Besides, I told you I was going to present an indictment to the grand jury for obstruction of justice against that son of a bitch Ryan. I warned him. But no . . . he wouldn't listen to me. Well,

I'm telling you . . . you screw with me and your ass is up a tree." Leary's voice rose as several diners at the nearby tables turned towards him as he spoke.

"Keep your voice down, Roger," Sturmer warned as he continued to cut into his steak and push the large pieces of meat into his mouth. Alternating between the pink slices of beef, the judge gulped down beer from a pewter tankard.

"We shouldn't even be talking together, Roger," the judge warned, his eyes shifting from the half-eaten steak to the completely filled room of noisy diners.

"Why not? Do you think anybody cares if we have dinner together?" Roger replied with a half grin on his face.

"The assignment judge would care, Roger," Sturmer declared.

"Sure," Roger quickly shot back, "and the judicial ethics board would not look kindly at a Superior Court judge owning a piece of the Franklin Inn."

"I don't own a piece of anything, Roger. Estelle does."

"Sure." Leary grinned and then said, "Bullshit, my good judge. Just don't hand me any shit. Okay. We both know I can hang you by your balls."

"Roger, you're spoiling my dinner," the judge replied angrily. Then switching to a deep solemn voice, he continued, "You know, you're nothing like the senator, Roger. You go through life pushing and shoving people. Why don't you have some of the finesse of your father?"

"Because he was him and I'm me," Roger Leary replied in a passionate voice. "Listen, this is no big deal. The son of a bitch, motherfucker killed that woman. I know it. You know it. If we're going to let Ryan bullshit these fuckin' farmers out here . . . well, then, this world is going to go to the dogs. And I ain't going to let it happen. I have a responsibility to the little people of Summit County."

"Sure," the Judge replied, a broad grin on his face, "you don't give a damn about anybody but yourself, Roger. I've known you since you were a spoiled kid throwing a tantrum on the senator's office floor."

"We got him!" Roger Leary's voice blurted out. He started to laugh uncontrollably.

"Roger, stop it!" The judge's face was grim with worry, his eyes clicking side to side to see who could hear Leary's boasts.

"I don't care who hears me, Judge, I don't think I've been this happy since Ryan was disbarred." Leary paused and then called to the waitress to bring him another margarita.

"Roger, I think you've had enough," the judge warned.

"Listen, you old coot," Leary chided as he pointed his forefinger into the face of the judge, "you know what that means? To bring the son of a bitch back in fucking irons. I'll have every national television station waiting at the airport."

"You can't do that, Roger," the Judge warned, gulping the last of his beer. "The trial judge would have to change venue or maybe even call a mistrial, Roger."

"Not if you're the judge, Albert."

"And who says I'm going to be the trial judge? The AJ might pick someone else. . . ."

"Not if I talk to his secretary. She runs the list anyway . . . and she's sort of sweet on me."

Judge Sturmer stared into Leary's face, his thin lips tight against his teeth. "You know you're flirting with obstruction of justice charges yourself, Roger. Besides, if your case against the rabbi is so strong why mess it up with this kind of chicanery."

"Because without a sure conviction I'm out on the street. The governor hates my guts and is looking for any reason to dump me . . . and I ain't gonna give her any. If I convict the mother . . . she has to reappoint me. Do you know what I'm saying, Albert?"

"How did you obtain the extradition order so quickly?" the judge queried in a brusque voice.

"I didn't. The rabbi's political buddies squelched any chance to legitimately extradite him from Israel. So, I had the good captain 'borrow' the rabbi from his hotel room." Leary's feral face was illuminated with a mischievous grin, his hands shooting outward to emphasize his point.

"Don't talk like that, Roger. Not to me. I don't want to know. You hear me? Don't ever tell me about such . . . such . . ." The judge stammered as his mind searched for words.

"What? Now you're playing the vestal virgin, Albert. You remember you signed the warrants to bug Ryan's office."

"But . . . but . . . what do you mean I signed the warrants? You gave me your certifications that it was necessary. You supported those warrants, Roger."

"Sure, I did. But if it blows up in my face, Albert, you're going to make Nixon look like Mother Teresa. We're in this together, Judge. My good judge. Besides," Leary's voice lowered into a goodnatured whisper, "nobody's going to find out. I didn't think we'd ever use those tapes. Got them where I want them, Albert."

"It's kidnapping, Roger. If you didn't get an extradition order signed . . . you know that, Roger."

"Once he's back in Summit County, who's gonna care, Judge. Tell me that. Who's gonna care?"

"Ryan could cause trouble. You know Ryan, Roger."

"That's why I'm getting the indictment against him. When he lands in the US, he'll have enough to worry about keeping his own ass out of jail."

"It's not right, Roger"

"Who cares about right, Judge?"

"Your father would not approve. The senator would not approve, Roger."

Leary's face turned red as the Judge brought forth his father's name. Biting his lip, his eyes closing into a malevolent squint, Roger Leary spoke in muted tones, his voice barely audible.

"Judge, let me tell you something. My father was the biggest crook of all. Things that he did. Well . . . y'know better than anyone, Judge. You were out there in the Pine Barrens. You wore the same white sheets he did. . . . Along with all your cronies. I was a little kid . . . just watching. He brought me out there . . . to learn to hate. Just like you all did. And I saw them . . . you too, Judge. They lynched and burnt that nigger . . . the one from New York that was causing trouble. What was his name? Elias. . . Elias Rubin. . . or something. Just like the good rabbi. I saw them bring the body down from that burning cross. So, Judge . . . don't hand me any shit about right and wrong. There ain't no right and wrong in Summit County. Just whoever holds the rope and the torch. And I'm not going to give up the rope, Judge. Never, do you understand me, old man . . . never!"

Mathias and his wife walked passed Leary's table just as Leary finished his whispered diatribe. They had finished dinner and were heading toward the front-door exit. Leary peered up at Mathias standing by his table.

"You lost, Lieutenant?" Leary asked in a taunting voice.

"Just leaving, Mr. Prosecutor. Anything new in the Rubin case?" Mathias asked, knowing that the prosecutor's office had drawn no real scientific data linking the rabbi to the murder.

"You'll hear soon enough, Mathias," Leary replied.

"A little bird told me the rabbi's on his way back," Mathias said with an innocent grin on his face.

"Yeah. And we're going to buy him a ticket to Trenton State . . . the little room up there. How does that fit in your craw, Mathias?" Leary's voice was loud and biting. Not one to forgive and forget, Leary remembered Mathias's breach of faith in the black soldier's murder case at Fort Dix.

Reporting the prosecutor's overzealous support of the state trooper's beating of the black soldier suspected of killing his white girlfriend at the army base was enough to place Mathias at the head of Leary's shitlist. Nothing Mathias did or didn't do would ever remove the taint of his infidelity to the "cause" . . . to the "brotherhood of law and order" as Leary called his state trooper legions.

"I'm on your side, Pros. I want to see the guilty man convicted. Just like you do," Mathias responded in an even tone belying his repugnant feelings toward Leary.

"Well, call me if you need any help in the case, Pros." Mathias smiled warmly.

"Oh . . . hello . . . Judge," Mathias said as he led his wife past Leary's table. "I didn't recognize you for a second with that beer stein in front of your face." Sturmer had feigned a drinking pose hoping that Mathias would not recognize him in the dark shadows of the restaurant.

"Hello, Lieutenant," Sturmer replied softly. "Nice to see you again."

"Yes, sir, it was," Mathias said as he followed his wife toward the door of the Inn.

Sturmer said nothing for a few seconds. His face was flushed with a pinkish glow. He motioned to the waitress to bring him another beer and then he said, his voice biting and reproachful, "Roger, this public meeting was the wrong thing to do. Mathias could be trouble. You realize that. Roger, listen to me . . . I'm worried."

"Don't be. Mathias won't get out of line. If he does . . . don't worry. I'll make sure he won't cause any trouble . . . not any more," his voice trailed off as he chugged the entire margarita in front of him.

CHAPTER TWENTY-SEVEN

The assignment judge is the lord of the manor in Summit County. Alexander King has been assignment judge for thirty years, ever since Senator Leary pushed his nomination through the state senate. He had been the youngest assignment judge in the history of the state.

Now, he was the oldest. One year left to his retirement. King was not ready for retirement. Only with special dispensation from the legislature would they extend his judicial term. Another year . . . maybe two. It was all politics. And he didn't have his political guru alive. Senator Leary could have done it, King reflected sardonically. Now all I have is his son. And he might be the death of me yet.

Roger Leary sat slouched in the wing chair in front of the Judge's antique desk he was so proud of. It had belonged to his father before him. And his father before him. The Kings had been judges in the state for almost one hundred and fifty years. Serving the public was a family tradition. That's after they made their money in cranberries. The Kings were the oldest cranberry farmers in the state. Still owned 1000 acres of bogs surrounding the Pinelands and they were the largest growers supplying Ocean Spray, the largest national purveyors of cranberry products.

"I had no choice, your honor," Leary said in a muffled voice. His eyes stared out past the judge through the large window in the corner office of the assignment judge.

"You always have a choice, Roger," Judge King replied, his hands clasped in front of him.

"Y'know we'd never have gotten him back here, Judge, if I had to go through channels."

"That is what the law is for, Roger. You're the key law enforcement officer of this county. The law is your bread and butter, Roger." Suddenly the judge leaped from his chair and briskly walked over to the unimposing figure of Leary.

"Why the hell do you do these things, Roger?" he shouted at Leary who continued to focus his eyes out the window of the office.

"Who told you?"

"Goddamnit, Roger. It doesn't matter who told me. What's important is that the AG knows about it . . . so you damn well know that the governor knows about it. And you know I need a favor from the governor . . . like I'm sure you do."

"I know, I know," Roger repeated in a bleating voice. "But, y'know . . . if the Israeli government doesn't make a stink about it . . . who's to know?"

"Roger, you're an ass. The AG knows. And before long the whole world will know," the judge said, his eyes staring at the top of Leary's head.

"Maybe you should look for another job, Roger." the judge's voice was patronizing.

Roger lifted himself from the chair and stared into the aged jurist's weather-beaten face.

"You look for another job, your honor," Leary said in a threatening voice. "I don't have ten million dollars sitting in cranberries on wetlands that should be condemned by the state. This is all I have . . . and I'm not leaving it just because you're too old to contain the enemy."

Judge King walked toward the window in back of his desk. His hand played with the long strands of hair on the side of his head.

"Who told the AG?" Roger asked.

"I don't know. He wouldn't say."

"I bet it was Mathias . . . that son of a bitch is a rogue cop, Judge."

"You ever talk to him?"

"Plenty of times. He thinks he's some kind of crusader."

"Why are you so dead-set against the rabbi?" The judge asked, as he turned to face Leary.

"Because he killed his wife, Judge. And because he thinks he can manipulate the system with his pompous bullshit."

"What evidence do you have? Do you have anything, Roger, to convict him?" the judge asked.

"We're waiting for the DNA results to come back. But even if it doesn't prove he's the killer, circumstantially I've got him by the balls, Judge."

"I wouldn't bet my job on circumstantial evidence, Roger. You've already indicted him so he's going to trial in ninety days. And I hear your best buddy Ryan is defending him. I hope you haven't bitten off more than you can chew, Roger."

"Ryan's an alkie. I might even try the case myself."

"You haven't tried a capital case in ten years, Roger. And I hear you didn't do so good on that one."

"A fluke. I'm ready now. Besides I'll have Ambrosio sitting second chair. She's the best technician in the office."

"Then why the hell don't you let her try it?"

"Because I'm the prosecutor and it's my case, Judge," Leary said in a childish whine. He bolted up from the chair and walked toward the bookshelves against the far wall of the office. His eyes ran up and down the lines of legal books while his fingers touched the leather binders of the law books.

"You're going to need an Ambrosio next to you, Roger. Your former first assistant knows the rules of the game . . . if I remember correctly," the judge paused. "I remember when Ryan was an assistant prosecutor. Always did a good job, from what I remember."

"He was lucky," Leary half-shouted, as he quickly turned and stood behind the wing chair, waiting to leave the chambers.

"Luck has nothing to do with being a good trial lawyer, Roger. You should know that. Ryan felt something like all good trial lawyers. They know what's important to the little guy . . . the guy that sits in a jury," the Judge added cynically. "And he never went overboard, Roger."

"Pulling that 9mm on the jury was a good touch," Roger moaned as he drew his hand from his pants, pointing it at the judge.

"I don't think so, Roger. If you weren't the prosecutor I think Judge Kilmer would have had to put you in the lockup. Anyway he called a mistrial and Ryan convicted the pervert."

"I did all the groundwork and Ryan gets all the credit," Leary continued, the palm of his right hand subconsciously beating against the top of the wing chair. Suddenly, Leary's demeanor changed. His eyes glared at the judge.

"Sturmer has to be assigned to the trial, Judge," Leary said.

"It's up to the draw. Roger . . . you know that."

"No it isn't, Judge and *you know that*. . . ." Leary pronounced each word bitingly. "You call the shots in this county, and you know that."

"Well," the judge said as he resumed sitting in his chair, his hands folded in front of his nose in a tent-like fashion, "I'll see what I can do, Roger. I don't like tampering with the draw system. It leads to hard feelings among the bar."

As he strode to the judge's desk, Leary's body arched straight. He leaned over the edge of the desk and pointed his forefinger straight at the judge's face.

"Alexander," Leary spat the name out along with a spray of foaming spittle, "my father put you in that fucking chair and. . .I can get you out of it. You know what I know about this county. About you. About everybody. And I'm going to use everything I know to keep my job. So if I were you, I'd forget about any draw. *Sturmer is your fucking draw, Alexander!* Remember that."

Leary turned around and marched defiantly out of the chambers, the judge's face a mask of fear and utter surprise.

CHAPTER TWENTY-EIGHT

"Why the hell are we sitting in your car overlooking this dump, Lew?" the chief said in a gruff, cigarette smoker's voice, his eyes peering through the unmarked police car's windshield onto the cavernous pit used as a waste dump by the county.

"Because I think your office is bugged, Chief," Mathias replied without any emotion in his voice.

"Who in God's name would dare bug the chief of police's office. I think you're smoking something funny, Lew."

"Maybe. But I found out that Leary bugged the rabbi's office, his lawyer's office, and anybody remotely connected with the Rubin case. And all the wiretap orders were signed by Sturmer. And guess who I saw eating dinner together . . . nobody but Sturmer and Leary. It just doesn't smell kosher, Chief."

"You didn't go to the AG, I hope, Lew. Leary and his cronies still haven't forgiven you for that other time."

"I called him but he was out. Anyway, it's not just the tapes." Mathias paused, pulled his meerschaum pipe from his jacket pocket, bit at the end and then started puffing on the pipe although there was no tobacco in the cradle. "The DNA results came back, Chief."

"So . . . did he do it? The rabbi?"

"It's not him. Maybe they got the wrong samples. He lived in the house . . . so they could have picked up samples of skin, blood, anything that had nothing to do with the murder. But the sample of skin under her fingernails weren't his." He paused and then continued in almost a whisper, "I think Leary is going to screw around with the DNA results."

The Chief turned anxiously in his seat, grabbed a cigarette and lit up. The smoke filled the car as he exhaled.

"Nobody said he killed her, Lew. Not by himself."

"Leary does. And he's pulling it out of his asshole. He indicted the son of a bitch without any tangible direct evidence, Chief."

"So what," the chief replied. "It ain't the first time somebody's been indicted on smoke and mirrors, Lew. You know that. We used to do that all the time in LA. Just to get the press off our backs."

"Not in this case, Chief. Leary has more to gain by railroading the rabbi into an early trial. Especially after Captain Crunch and his evil bunch are bringing him back in cuffs from Israel. The escape alone could hang him."

"Maybe it won't be admissible," the chief stated.

"If Sturmer's the trial judge, everything the prosecutor puts into evidence will be admissible, Chief. . .and I bet you ten to one that Sturmer's the assigned trial judge."

"Look," the chief said, "I don't care if Adolf Hitler is the judge. If the state has nothing against the rabbi . . . so what's the problem, Lew? Sturmer and Leary still have to answer to the media. And that's gonna be one hell of a TV trial."

"As I told you, I think Leary could play around with the DNA results. Switch samples or something."

"What'd ya mean, switch? The state still has to show chain of evidence to even get the samples into evidence. What's he going to do? Have all the cops and lab techs lie? Some massive conspiracy? Lew, I think you have been reading too many novels. Hey," the chief shouted as he looked at his watch, "I gotta go, Lew. Meeting with the mayor. It's all about money . . . and letting cops go. And still keeping those yombos out of Philly from stealing everything not tied to the ground."

The chief moved his heavy, pot-bellied body from the passenger seat out of the car.

"Look, Lew . . . you're a good cop. Leary's a fucking scumbag. So you watch your ass. He's not the last bad apple posing as a good law and order man."

"But he's a Leary, Chief. And you don't know what that means in this county unless you knew the senator."

"I missed that, thank God. They got them all over, Lew. LA. New York. There are guys who run the town. So what? Justice still comes out."

"I hope you're right, Chief."

Mathias's eyes stared out the window as his mind raced back to his Brooklyn narcotics days so many years ago. It seemed like yesterday. The lice, the grime, the corruption. And the indifference of everybody about it all. It was the way things were done, he was told. Don't upset the apple cart, Mathias. And he did and he left. Now he was here. The same bullshit. . .nothing ever changes. Except the scenery. Only the air is better in Summit County. Nothing changes, his mind repeated over and over again.

"Yeah. . .Chief. That's what I'll do. Forget it all." He paused, "Have a good meeting. Give my best to her honor."

"You got five years to retirement, Lew. Ride it out. Nobody gives a shit whether the system works. They just want to have a system."

"Yeah, I guess. . ." Lew mumbled as the chief limped over to his car located behind Mathias's vehicle.

Lew sat in the front seat staring out onto the dump, the seagulls hovering above as the bulldozers removed the waste from the 50 ton tractor trailers lined up to dispose of their cargo.

That's what it's all about, Lew thought. Waste and shit. Garbage. The seagulls got it right. Shit on the shit.

As he pulled his car out of the parking area, he expected to hear the staccato coughing sound of a Volkswagen Beetle laboring up the highway approaching his parking spot. He could see or hear nothing behind him. Just silence. 'Where the hell was the Beetle? It suddenly disappeared. Thank God for little favors,' he thought. He took a deep breath of air, filling his lungs, as he drove onto the empty highway.

CHAPTER TWENTY-NINE

Paris was beautiful this time of year. The residents left the City of Light in August to the American, German, and British tourists.

Fortunately for the rabbi, the private jet plane carrying him to the States had to refuel before the trip across the Atlantic. Captain Crutchfield secured him in the small kitchen in the rear of the Canadair jet. He was handcuffed to a steel rail. The rabbi recited the *Shema* over and over again to avoid bashing his head against the wall out of boredom and fear.

He had been foolish. Ryan warned him to be cautious. But he was in Israel and he felt invulnerable. Who would ever expect the sixth floor of the King David Hotel to be invaded by American policemen? Illegal. It was unheard of. Yet it happened. To him.

He had never been afraid. Until now. His life had been sheltered. Yet his faith in God had been transitory. Even leaning toward atheism. At times. Even with the Rebbe. The great and only Rebbe. He must have been drunk to voice his concerns about the existence of God to the great Rebbe. But he had and the Rebbe, the intellectual messiah of the Ashkenazi Hassidim had received the mental games in better humor then Rubin had expected.

The Rebbe liked Carl Rubin, who was young, not unattractive and had a deep mellifluous voice that articulated well his troubling thoughts. No one had ever approached the Rebbe with the suggestion that God was not favorable to the Hebrews. Or that, He even existed. Of course He existed, the Rebbe exclaimed as they sat in the old man's study in Crown Heights, Brooklyn.

"God does not live man's life, my son," the great Rebbe would say. "He puts the world in motion and then He says to His children, 'go and experience the world I have given you!' Man does his own evil. God has nothing to do with man's misfortunes."

"But then," Rubin replied, "why does man attribute the good things that happen in our world to the beneficence of God?"

"He still watches over us," the Rebbe would reply. "He still controls the world . . . man's life . . . to an extent."

"I still don't understand," Rubin would reply with great respect. "If He can control the good things of life . . . make them happen . . . why not stop the evil that has happened to His children. Especially to His children."

The Rebbe's snowy bearded face remained gentle—yet concentrated.

"We don't question God, my son. He has His reasons for doing what He does. You need not question His actions, Rabbi," the Rebbe murmured.

But Carl Rubin did. Too much. And the Rebbe told him to leave the fold. Which Rubin did. Not far. But far enough. He cast aside his ultraorthodox observances and sought less structure in the more liberal Reform movement.

No trappings of orthodoxy. Just the plain worship of God. He accepted God on his terms. A human God. With frailties and vices and beneficence. No one knew that the great Rabbi Rubin was an heretic but he was. He formed a body of religion that was his own.

From the beginning of his entrance into the evolving Jewish community of Larchmont Hills, Rabbi Carl Rubin established his philosophy, his voice, and most importantly his charisma. Nowhere had this religious community heard or seen an electrifying persona such as Rabbi Carl Rubin. They flocked to him. Conservative and Reform alike. The words that he preached were repeated to others. From the ashes of an old forgotten Orthodox shul in Larchmont Hills, Rubin helped to build a modern magnificent temple. It was a temple memorializing himself. He had arrived. Evangelistically he was worshipped. As much as the ethereal God whose existence he sometimes disbelieved.

And with the worship of the rabbi came the adulation of beautiful, rich women who had tired of their moribund, money-driven husbands. They needed romantic love. He gave it to them. First, it was a spiritual giving. Then it became more so. He had been tempted and he had succumbed. Religion was merely a backdrop to the physical sharing. His women, his flock, his love, like some rock star, they waited for him, not at the stage door of some seedy theater, but rather at expensive hotels buried deep in the corners of Philadelphia and New York. He forgot his vows, to God, to the temple, and most of all to his wife. She knew nothing for most of their married life. Wrapped up in her charity work and bakery, in her creation of beautiful pastries, in the adulation heaped upon her by food critics and patrons of her heralded pastry establishment, she attributed her husband's diminished sex drive to age, to the stress of his business, his Temple and his God.

The plane landed on a secluded area of Charles DeGaulle Airport. He was left in the kitchen, while his fellow travelers disembarked. No one even came back to inspect the human cargo handcuffed to the rail. He felt alone, more alone then he had ever felt before. In Paris. What a shame, he thought. In the most beautiful city in the world, he was alone. God must be laughing, he thought. A vengeful God.

Paris! Eleanore and he had landed there two days after their wedding. The wedding had been sumptuous. Eleanore's parents spared no expense. The finest in New York, society orchestra, caviar, and the beautiful people, all were present at the wedding. Eleanore's mother was a Bernard, an heir to the greatest department store fortune in America. Eleanore was her only daughter and she wasn't going to be cheated out of a grand wedding. She didn't like Carl.

"Why marry a rabbi," she would tell Eleanore. "A small man, Eleanore. There are tall, handsome doctors and lawyers who would love to spend the rest of their lives with you."

But Eleanore abstained. She had found her man. They shared the same goals, the same dreams, and they were in love, spiritual love, physical love. She was the centrum of his world. For that moment anyway.

And then came Paris. It was the Mount Everest of their relationship. Nothing would ever rival those seven days in Paris.

Arriving in the early morning hours at Orly, they rushed to the hotel her mother had reserved for them. Le Residence du Bois, in the 16th arrondissement with the most exquisite garden she had ever seen. Their first night in Paris they dined at a small restaurant. The wine flowed. They ate and drank and held each other. They laughed at the silliest things. Life was a cabaret.

Time seemed to fade away. As if it didn't even exist. Blurred. Everything tasted of spice, of wine, and of rare ingredients.

And they danced. Waltzes and tangos and rhumbas, the trio of musicians suddenly appeared around midnight to play their violins. As they danced they kissed, young and vibrant and so much in love. They felt the grandeur of Paris. It was over much too soon. As if it had never happened.

And it never happened again. They had had Paris and as the years sped away, they lost Paris. Because the first time in Paris is the best time in Paris. They came back but it was not the same. It never is, the rabbi thought as he realized his right wrist was bleeding from the tight lock of the handcuffs covering his wrist.

His mind raced back to the first time when he had met Eleanore. It was a ball. Eleanore refused to dance with others. She was like a Lautrec portrait of a haughty but giving dancer at La Mistral.

They danced, not talking. He thought she didn't like him. She thought he was pompous. They were both afraid of each other. Until she laughed, her teeth opening to a throaty laugh that was unrestrained and genuinely happy.

"Where have all the years gone, Eleanore? Now you're dead. I can't even remember your face. Why? Why?" he whispered to himself.

He thought about Jeanette. His lovely sister Jeanette. They had been so close as children. The only children of the great Rabbi from Boro Park, their father. The revered orthodox rabbi. Every high holiday his picture would appear in the centerfold of the Daily News, *the* Daily Mirror, *the* Post . . . *all the New York newspapers . . . they would show him* davaning, *his shoulders wrapped with a gold-edged* tallis, *his head covered with the embroidered yarmulke, as it bobbed up and down as he led the other rabbis, all bent over the opened Torah scrolls. Rabbis have been in our family for hundreds of years he thought. What else would the male offspring be? Not Jeanette. She was expected to be a good Jewish housewife and mother of many children, to carry on the ancient rabbinical traditions of the Rubin dynasties. And so I did. Even though I had doubts. Always doubts. About God . . . about our dictated way of life. The*

Orthodox way of life . . . there was no room for deviation. Well, he thought, I had to leave. No one could understand why I had to leave. The Rebbe called me, after he had disowned me. The great living messiah, the Rebbe, called me. To represent him. He rarely left his home base in Brooklyn and now he was much too old to go to Israel. He said I was the only one he wanted to represent him and his flock and his beliefs. That Israel must never give up the sacred lands of Abraham, of Joseph, of Moses. Never! I became his emissary. Disfavored albeit in other things of the Hassidim, but he wanted my ability to articulate his demands to the irreverent rulers of Israel. Diplomatic chazerai *he called it. A practical ruler he was, the Rebbe knew the banal ways of man in this world. I was his voice, O'Israel, deliver to the Rebbe or he would absent his influence and his money from the ruling party's side. His beliefs, his influence, and his power could decide who ruled Israel . . . Especially now . . . because the Prime Minister would be decided by the Rebbe's people. The Rebbe could tip the scales.*

The rabbi turned onto his other side because of the excruciating pain coursing through his shoulders. What a position to be in, he thought. It wasn't just the physical pain. He could live with that. it was the ridicule . . . the loss of favor of his devoted followers. They had thought he was some kind of God . . . and now this. Murder. And he was so careful. Everything he ever did, he planned it carefully. Murder . . . a common criminal . . . chased after. How could it all happen? I was as high as the heavens. My own synagogue, a revered apostle . . . by all who came to hear me. Packed audiences. My sermons even transmitted on the radio. A greater audience than even my father had. Where did it all go, Eleanore? Where?

And Jeanette. My lovely Yetteruchel *(yiddish nickname) My sister. She was the fighter. How many times had she shielded me from the fists of the bigger boys on the block. She was my protector. I loved her for it. But she too wanted her own space, her own world, away from the traditions . . . the unbending traditions of our father, our religion, our family. But how could she fight against such ancient traditions? Five thousand years of it. There was no way that she could prevail . . . unless she left . . . gave it all up for her own world. She did. Migrated to Philadelphia. To the liberality of the University of Pennsylvania. They all went there. The young liberal Jews of the forties. And she was gone. Then she committed the ultimate crime. A Nigerian student became her lover. She had been*

*a virgin as all orthodox Jewish maidens of Brooklyn were in the forties.
She bore his child. A brown-skinned baby. The ultimate crime. And she
named the baby Elias. Elias Rubin. Forever severing her relations with
her orthodox past. Excommunicated by her father, her people. A brown
baby . . . half Jewish and half pagan. I saw her only one more time, he
thought. And the baby became the greatest rebel . . . a leader of the black
revolutionaries of the sixties and seventies. Where are you now, Elias
Rubin? You who forsook your own mother. She died in shame, unloved by
her own son. By her own family. She died so alone. Just like me, the
rabbi cried in a soft voice. Just like me. He felt so sorry for himself. So
sorry for what he had lost.*

His reverie was suddenly shattered by the noise of the folding door
of the kitchen being thrown open.

Two burly attendants walked through the plane to the kitchen.
Without any words, they unlocked the handcuffs and led the rabbi
to the front of the plane. Emerging from the cockpit, Captain
Crutchfield smiled innocently and said, "Good morning, Rabbi.
Hope you had a pleasant evening. Sorry the accommodations
weren't equal to the King David."

His eyes shifted to the two men bringing a metal trunk into the
plane.

"We're going to be in Paris a few hours only. Just time to refuel and clear customs. Unfortunately, the plane has to be inspected
by the French custom authorities, so we must place you in that
trunk. There are holes in the top. Enough to allow you to breathe.
But let me warn you: if I hear any attempt to warn the police of
your presence. Well . . . it won't happen, will it, Rabbi?"

"Y'know, Captain. . . this is kidnapping. I'm just surprised that
a policemen like yourself would break the law."

"Here it is breaking the law, Rabbi. Once we're back in Summit
County, it's just returning a fugitive from justice."

"Call it what you like, sir. But I can't see how any judge will
uphold your actions."

"We'll see, Rabbi," Crutchfield replied, a thin veil of concern
shadowing his eyes. "I have a warrant for your arrest."

"My little knowledge of international law, Captain. Well, my attorney told me . . . your warrant wasn't any good in Israel . . . unless affirmed by an Israeli judge."

"No harm will come to you, Rabbi. Just play ball with us, and we will let the courts in the States work it out."

One of the men opened the metal trunk and the other one grabbed the rabbi by the elbow and forced him inside.

"Easy there," the captain warned the men as the captain walked over to help the rabbi into the trunk.

"I think this is a mistake, Captain."

"Maybe Rabbi . . . but I'm only following orders."

"That's no excuse."

"You'll be all right, Rabbi. It'll only be a few hours and I will check on you every once in a while. You'll be all right." The captain repeated the conciliatory remarks as if he didn't believe it to be so.

After the rabbi entered the trunk, the two men closed the lid and locked it.

"Be careful how you handle that cargo," the captain warned the two men who lifted the trunk between them and started out the plane door to the tarmac below.

Dickson came out of the cockpit as the trunk was placed into a small panel truck.

"He might be right, Captain," Dickson remarked with a note of worry in his voice.

"I only do what I am told, Trooper," Crutchfield replied. "Just like you."

"Did you tell the pros?"

"Tell him what? That I kidnapped the rabbi out of Israel? Sure. I don't take kidnapping lightly, Sergeant. Leary knows everything."

"I got it up the ass when I dumped that nigger in the trunk of my car on the Turnpike."

"That was different, Sergeant."

"How so?"

"You did it on your own. I have direct orders from my superior to do what I'm doing," the captain replied angrily.

"Leary's a little nuts, Captain."

"Coming from you Dickson, that's a compliment," Crutchfield

said, a smile faintly discernable on his broad pockmarked face.

"Once was enough for me. I almost got booted out of the corps. For doing what I was supposed to do. Fucking niggers. You get more then one together and they start a riot."

"Just watch over the rabbi, Dickson."

The panel truck swerved off the airport road leading to the warehouse on the far side of the private section of DeGaulle and disappeared as it bounced over the grassy ruts of the path leading to the airport exit. Dickson jumped down the steps of the plane onto the ground and pulled his cell phone out of his jacket.

Frantically he punched the numbers into the phone block and pushed the phone to his ear as he spoke hurriedly into the mouthpiece. After he finished speaking, he waited a few moments before he shoved the phone back into his jacket and whirled around to face the exit door of the plane.

Captain Crutchfield watched the trooper's nervous movements and then shouted down to Dickson who faced him with a glazed look in his face.

"What the hell are you standing there for, Dickson?"

"Those two guys, Captain."

"They're airport people."

"I don't think so, Captain. If they are, they were supposed to store the trunk in the warehouse up yonder. They left the airport. I called our people at the warehouse. They never got there, Captain."

"You fucking idiot, Dickson! I told you to watch them. Goddamnit!" Crutchfield shouted as he spat the words out of his mouth.

"I thought they were our people, Captain . . . I swear."

"Find them, you asshole. Go get your asshole buddies and find them. Goddamnit! We leave in five hours, Dickson. If he's not back by then, you better take up residency here. You got me!" The captain's face was beet-red as he almost fell coming down the ladder of the plane. He knew the rabbi would be impossible to find in the maze that was Paris. Especially if the two men were Israeli agents . . . which he figured they probably were.

CHAPTER THIRTY

He wanted to see her one more time. All he could think about . . . dream about . . . was Sosie. Ryan knew, from the first kiss . . . from his first touch of her body . . . he would be obsessed by her. She was everything in a woman he wanted.

But he was leaving. Yehuda was hustling him onto an El Al plane to Paris . . . to follow the kidnapped rabbi. 'It always happens like that,' he thought. 'You can never space events far enough apart . . . everything happens at once. '

Ryan sat impatiently at the small coffee table in the Tel Aviv Airport café . . . waiting. 'Always waiting,' he thought. 'Where was she?' his mind shouted.

He looked at his watch anxiously. Twelve noon. And the plane leaves at twelve-forty-five. Can't even depend on El Al's reputation for late departures. 'With my luck,' he thought, 'the plane will take off early.'

Suddenly, Sosie appeared at the entrance of the café, asked something of the hostess who pointed to Ryan at the table near the window. She smiled that delicious smile which caused her eyes to crinkle into oval slits. Ryan followed her body as she glided sensually across the café floor, her back straight, her ample bosom lustfully raised. Her face ignited with unrequited joy as her ocean green eyes stared directly at him. Never wavered. He rose clumsily, almost knocking over his chair, as she melted into his arms. They kissed, slowly at first, then hungrily, with passion. That distinct monment, he felt that the world was good. That his life was good.

"I almost missed you . . . ," she said in a soft, husky voice.

"Traffic is getting as bad as parking in Jerusalem," she laughed as she spoke.

"Hope you didn't meet your friend in the Mercedes en route," he replied. She laughed heartily, without restraint. With her whole body, she enveloped him with her joy.

"My father is ruining my love life, Joshua."

"We have to go . . . the rabbi . . . "

"I know . . . but I still don't like it."

"I don't want to leave," he replied.

"Come back then . . . "

"Maybe when it's all over."

"Will it ever be? Over, I mean."

They both sat down alongside each other. He ordered coffee for both of them and then reached over to touch her hands that were resting on the table. For several endless moments, they sat there, hypnotically staring into each other's face. He could feel the electricity of her hands and body shooting up through his arms, finally lodging in his brain, compounded by the lavender scent of her body, overwhelming him.

"We don't even know each other," the words fluttered out of his mouth.

"I know you, Joshua Ryan. I don't need any more time to know how I feel about you."

"You're not afraid? I mean . . . you could be making a mistake . . . "

"Maybe," she answered, her hand climbing lazily up his forearm sending shudders up to his shoulder. "I don't think so," she added.

"I'm not innocent, Joshua. You're not the first boy I've . . . well . . . liked very much . . . "

I think it's more than liking," he replied. "But," he stammered as he tried to collect his thoughts, "I can't explain it . . . except the physical . . . there's no doubt there is . . . an attraction."

She laughed. "Maybe that's all there is . . . a passing attraction."

"Do you think that's it?"

"You Americans are strange people. You need answers for everything. Why not just enjoy it . . . for how long it lasts . . . enjoy the moments."

"I thought that's how the boy is supposed to feel . . . grab it while it's hot."

"Not in Israel . . . we don't have the time to play games . . . "

He sipped on the already cold coffee hoping the caffeine would supply his mind with memorable words of love. He had never wanted somebody so much . . . not just for the physcial . . . that surely was there . . . but also to have someone who wasn't afraid to bite off a slice of life no matter what the consequences were.

"Do you like music?" she suddenly asked.

"What kind?"

"Classical . . . you know . . . Beethoven . . Mozart . . . Ravel . . .", then she added, "Tim McGraw?" She laughed again.

"Country . . . I like country . . . and yes . . . classical also . . . my father . . . probably the only good thing I got out of him . . . he loved the old masters. He would make me listen to the symphony hour on our old Bendix radio. It must have rubbed off."

"In Israel . . . to weather the killings every day . . . we must have the music of Mozart and all of them . . . without the music we might as well give the land back to the Hamas."

"Don't you fear . . . you know . . . that one of those bombs is going to explode right in front of you . . . kill you?"

She smiled, just parting her lips. She sipped the coffee as her eyes scanned out the window toward the skyscrapers of Tel Aviv in the near distance.

She pointed her finger out toward the city outline as she said, "You see out there, Joshua. Tel Aviv. Almost as many people live there as in New York City. Anyone of those millions of people could die . . . torn to shreds by those horrible suicide bombs. If we worry about it everyday . . . we can't go on living. Dying is all around us. If we fear it . . . well . . . we can't do anything else except walk around with our head between our legs."

She paused and then stared at him for an everlasting moment. Something about her face, every part of it, captivated him. Her body movements, so fluid, so unafraid. 'Goddamnit,' he cursed silently to himself, 'where is the fear . . . he was afraid of almost everything . . . where was the fear in Sosie?'

"Did I ever tell you about my football career?" he said with a feigned air of bravado.

"Is that like soccer?" she asked in a mocking voice.

"Sort of . . . I was pretty good . . . for a while they thought I could make it to the pros. But then . . . well . . . I got banged on a few times too much . . . my knees . . . "

"And then? Did your life end?"

He laughed for the first time. A belly laugh. A joyous laugh.

"You should laugh more often," Sosie exclaimed. "You have a nice laugh, Joshua."

"You are very good at analyzing the life and times of Joshua Ryan."

"How so?"

"I thought my life was ended when I couldn't play football anymore. That's all I ever did well. Maybe my life did end then," he paused and grinned foolishly, "Until now . . . "

They held hands tightly. She reached over the table and kissed him on the lips. His hand tenderly brushed her golden, sun-streaked hair.

"Too bad you have to leave," her voice taunted him.

"I know . . . you cannot even imagine how much I want you."

She laughed again as she rose from the table.

"Enough torturing each other, Joshua Ryan. My father wants you to accompany him to Paris. Next time . . . "

"Will there be a next time?"

"If you want it, it will be."

They embraced in the corridor outside the café. A tender embrace that lingered for several minutes. Their bodies and lips touching, taunting, and yet unfullfiling their obvious yearnings for each other.

"Go with God," she said as they released each other.

"I love you," he whispered without thinking.

"Maybe you do . . . and maybe I do, Joshua . . . Hopefully we'll find out when we next meet."

He watched her walk away. Her body barely touching the ground. She turned and smiled at him. For a moment he thought he saw a glint in her eyes. 'Can you see love in a woman's eyes?' he thought. 'Maybe,' he answered to himself. 'Maybe,' as he walked to the gate where his plane to Paris awaited him.

CHAPTER THIRTY-ONE

Racing to Paris, they ran through Ben-Gurion Airport like the old O.J. commercial for Hertz. Yehuda led the way, a small leather shoulder bag bouncing off his back as he pushed pedestrians out of the way. Ryan brought up the rear, his knees aching miserably. Olsham ran breathlessly, proudly showing off his daily ten-mile training runs through the hills of Summit County. Ryan had vehemently objected to Yehuda tagging along after the debacle at the King David.

But he relented after Yehuda convinced him that he knew Paris better then he knew Jerusalem.

Yehuda had spent almost two years at the University of Paris receiving a master's degree in archeology from the Sorbonne. Besides, Yehuda was assured that his woebegotten buddies on the Shin Bet wanted to make amends for their faux pas allowing the rabbi to be snatched right from under their noses. Paris was a second home for the counterintelligence work of the Shin Bet. And probably every other national intelligence agency in the world.

Arriving just before the gate closed, the trio trudged down the air corridor to the plane, Yehuda smiling his way to the first-class section of the El Al 747. Everybody seemed to know him. Ryan's doubts slowly dissipated as he observed Yehuda work the El Al attendants. Never have so many melted through El Al security so effortlessly. Yehuda had badges for every occasion. He must specialize in security clearances, Ryan mused, as he sat comfortably in the oversized first-class leather seat alongside Olsham who had already engaged the petite stewardess in verbal foreplay.

Yehuda disappeared into the cockpit of the massive plane and reappeared as the plane made its way down the runway. His face was aglow with a knowing smile. Exhaustedly, he threw himself down into the seat in the center of the plane, ordered a yogurt drink from the steward and bent over to whisper to Ryan and Olsham.

"They don't have much of a head start, Joshua," he said in a small but confident voice.

"The pilot checked with the control tower and their flight plan shows that they left for Paris no more than twelve hours ago. They had to land in Paris for refueling. My people are already at DeGaulle. I don't think we will be far behind."

"What happens if they get on and off in enough time?" Ryan declared.

"They won't," Yehuda answered.

"How can you be so sure?"

"Because our people are at the airport. And the private planes can only land at one section of DeGaulle."

"We thought the King David was a safe haven," Ryan replied.

"King David was my fault," Yehuda admitted.

"We underestimated the good captain," Olsham interjected as he downed a tequila sunrise.

"Who'd ever think he'd go so far?" Ryan said as his eyes peered out the window onto the disappearing skyline of Tel Aviv.

"Pensions do that to you," Olsham said.

"Breaking the law is not what I expected of the captain," Ryan insisted.

"He's had enough, Joshua," Olsham added. "I've known him for over twenty years. I've seen him go from a downright coura- geous chief of detectives to a cop who just wants out. His wife died of Lou Gehrig's disease a year ago and he doesn't want to die with Leary pissing on his grave. That fishing boat in Tampa looks awfully good, I guess."

The steward strode briskly down the aisle and handed Yehuda a fax. Yehuda put on his glasses and quickly read the one-line mes- sage. Turning to Ryan he smiled.

"They got him. Our compatriots stole him away from your friend. He's safe in the Jewish section of Paris. One of our friendly houses."

Ryan tried to stop the smile from crossing his face. He had been disappointed too many times in this Keystone Kop search; he was afraid to feel any sense of relief.

"You sure, Yehuda?" Ryan questioned in a disbelieving voice.

"That's what the paper says, Joshua. I knew they weren't happy with letting him go."

"Now we have to reach him before they have a chance to find him," Ryan muttered in almost a whisper.

"They have to find him first. And the Left Bank of Paris has more winding streets than Mea Shearim. Besides, they have to clear customs and the French do not want to be in the middle of an international kidnapping incident with an American rabbi as the victim."

"So we thought in Jerusalem, Yehuda," Ryan said.

"We all make mistakes, Mr. Ryan," Yehuda replied in a sullen voice.

"What time do we arrive?" Ryan added.

"In about five hours. It'll still be light. Maybe we'll see your client before the day is out." Yehuda replied as he closed his eyes and fell fast asleep before Ryan could offer any reply.

As promised they arrived in Paris before 6:00 p.m., the sun still bright over the Paris city line. One of the Shin Bet agents met them at the gate and hurried them through passport control and customs.

"How is he?" Ryan asked to the burly, large man known as Pinny who was leading the way to the ancient Citroen at the curb, outside the main exit.

"He's fine. He didn't like his accommodations. In the trunk, I mean. But he's fine now. Davening in the little shul up from Goldy's Delicatessen."

"You did a nice job," Ryan admitted casually.

"We don't usually make such large mistakes," Pinny replied. "It was the only thing left to do."

"How's Abie?" Yehuda asked.

"Chest wound. But he'll live. He wanted to jump out of his IV and come but we insisted he would only be a burden." Pinny laughed.

The old Citroen wound its way through the departing airport traffic, Pinny honking the horn angrily as he frantically darted from lane to lane on the two-lane highway to Paris.

She had talked about Paris so lovingly, Ryan thought of his ex-wife's repetitive incantations about her unfettered student days at the Alliance. Pronounced *All . . . i . . . ance*, she said so precisely, treating him like a child who just couldn't imagine what true Francophiles understood about the City of Love.

Why can't we travel more? When I was single I traveled all

over. Why are we tied to this shithole? she whined. Then he retreated. Silence. He stopped fighting back. It wasn't worth it. There was no avoiding her unpredictable rages about how she suffered by marrying Joshua, her cultural inferior.

Looks like any large city in the States, Ryan mused to himself as his eyes darted from the bucolic greenery of the Paris suburbs to the growing mountains of office buildings. He wondered what she was going on so much about. Then the car sped from the Peripherique Highway past Porte de Clignancourt, through Porte Dauphine, leading to the Avenue Foch. Massive trees lined the great boulevard as the car traveled up the six-lane avenue, the illuminated Arc de Triomphe in the near distance. It was well after 7 p.m. and the sun was still prominent in the cloudless blue sky, with shades of darkness approaching from the west. Ryan could almost see the upper rim of the full moon fighting its way towards center stage of the Parisian skyline.

Pinny entered the chaos of the Arc's multi-channeled traffic circle, a smile crossing his heavy jowled face, a long Gauloise cigarette dangling from the corner of his unshaven mouth. His hand pounded constantly on the horn as he negotiated his auto through the frenetic merging lanes.

Ryan covered his eyes as the Citroen just missed the ungiving lines of taxicabs, trucks, and passenger cars all rushing toward the other end of the Arc. Suddenly the Citroen emerged from the unending circle enveloping the Arc de Triomphe onto the multi-lane boulevard of the Champs Elysees. The wide boulevard sidewalks were bordered by retail shops, sidewalk cafes and restaurants, their bright lights dancing through Ryan's mind. He finally realized what Helen had been ranting about.

People filled the sidewalks; all meandering at their respective paces. Laughter could be heard above the raucous din of the automobiles crawling down the avenue. It was a scene out of a Pisarro painting, he thought. Everything in its place, yet no discernable force controlling this theatrical production.

A tiny Fiat suddenly appeared as it plowed through the Champs traffic from a side street, heading toward the passenger side of the Citroen. Ryan saw it first since the boxy Fiat appeared to be heading straight toward him. Pinny, nor any of the other passengers, took any notice of the hurtling car, until Ryan shouted in a shrill voice, "Watch out!"

Pinny's head turned toward his left and swerved the Citroen toward the right, almost striking a Mercedes in the middle lane. Pinny continued into the middle lane and finally stopped on the sidewalk, the car's bumper leaning into a lightpole. The Fiat struck the Mercedes broadside. The driver then backed the tiny car out of the cavernous hole in the side of the Mercedes, shot the gear shift into reverse with a squeal, backed the vehicle into another car heading up the Champs, and then careened down the Champs into the outside oncoming traffic lane.

Yehuda jumped out of the Citroen, crawled alongside the gravel of the tree-lined sidewalk, pulled the .32 caliber Beretta pistol from his leg holster and crouched over the front fender of the Citroen, the pistol lodged in his two hands aimed at the fleeing Fiat. Realizing that the offending vehicle was out of range, Yehuda returned the pistol into the leg holster. He stood up, and with an enigmatic smile on his face, opened the back door to allow Ryan and Olsham to exit from the vehicle.

"Welcome to Paris, gentlemen," Yehuda announced as if he were leading a tourist group through Jerusalem.

"I was starting to like the city," Ryan said in a voice filled with relief.

"Fortunately, Pinny was at the wheel," Yehuda remarked as he pounded Pinny on his round-shouldered back. "Nobody can kill a Tel Aviv taxicab driver."

"Not even in Paris." Pinny smiled a gap-toothed smile.

"Who were they?"

"Who knows?" Yehuda replied. "Anywhere we go, we expect unfriendly people. That's the burden of being an Israeli."

The blue uniformed gendarmes pushed through the gathering onlookers surrounding the beached Citroen. Yehuda pulled out his wallet, flashed an indiscernible piece of identification and spoke in whispered French to the inquiring policemen. Smiling brightly as Yehuda patted the taller gendarme on the back, the policeman pushed the crowd back while his companion halted traffic along the Champs to allow Pinny to back the Citroen off the sidewalk onto the street.

Ryan, Olsham, and Yehuda entered the car, Yehuda waving farewell to his new police friends and the Citroen sped off toward the Place de la Concorde circle.

"New friends, Yehuda?" Ryan asked.

"We all belong to a worldwide fraternity of policemen, Joshua," Yehuda replied without any bravado in his voice.

"It's their guilt complex," Pinny added as he entered the Place de la Concorde circle as offensively as he had traveled around the Arc de Triomphe.

"Guilty about what?" Olsham asked.

"About their Jews," Yehuda said. "They could have done more during the war."

"What about the great French resistance?" Ryan asked as he anxiously noted how Pinny drove around the traffic circle.

"That's the myth created by Truffaut and Malle," Yehuda remarked as he opened the window of the vehicle to allow the cigarette smoke from Pinny's Gauloise to drift out into the nighttime Parisian air.

"A thousand resistance fighters don't make an army of revolutionaries," Pinny interjected. "They all sat around while the Boche sent the French Jews to Auschwitz or wherever there was a vacancy. Now being Jewish is popular in France. Who knows when we will come into disfavor again."

"Can we expect any help from the French?" Ryan asked.

"The French won't help either side," Pinny said as he sidled the Citroen into the entranceway of the Hotel Le Bristol.

"Unless there is a formal request from your government," Yehuda said, adding quickly, "Anyway, we'll have the rabbi on his way to the States well before anyone can file a formal request through channels."

"If we can get my client on a plane back to Philadelphia . . . without incident," Ryan's voice trailed off as he stepped out of the car onto the sidewalk alongside of the elegant ten-story hotel.

Pinny stayed in the driver's seat as he remarked to Yehuda, "I'll stay with the car, Yehuda."

"Meet us here in an hour. We'll go for a light snack . . . with the rabbi."

"Be careful," Pinny warned.

"Pick the rabbi up when you come. And Pinny . . . do you have your sidearm?"

"Never leave home without it," Pinny said with a crooked smile on his face.

"We'll need a safe 24 hours, Pinny," Yehuda warned, as he stood by the front passenger window.

"Nothing will go wrong, Yehuda."

"If it does . . . well, Mr. Ryan will not be happy."

"I will call Barak to make sure the restaurant is empty."

"Go with God, my friend," Yehuda said as he grasped the extended massive hand of Pinny.

"Go with God," Pinny replied.

He pulled the car away from the curb into the crowded narrow Rue St. Honoré and disappeared before Yehuda had stepped onto the curb alongside the hotel.

The two-bedroom suite was much more then Ryan had expected. Yehuda had mysterious connections with hotels and police around the western world.

Cradled at the far end of the suite was the marble bathroom with a roman bathtub. The large bedrooms were divided by a well-appointed living room containing a massive entertainment wall unit. Computerized hell, Ryan thought.

"Drink?" Olsham shouted from the living room as Ryan stepped out of the marble-walled enclosed shower, wrapping himself in a soft body towel.

"You'll need a liver transplant after this trip, John," Ryan said in a lighthearted voice as he walked into the living room with the towel loosely wrapped around his body.

"It relieves the tension."

"Yeah . . . I know," Ryan replied.

"I got it under control, Joshua," Olsham declared confidently.

"So did I. Then it's suddenly not, John. Then it's on its own. You need it all the time."

"I don't need it, Josh," Olsham defended his position.

"When was the last time you went without it, John?"

"Whenever I want. Look," his voice was pliant and conciliatory, "I know what you went through, Josh. But that's different. You had your baggage. I don't have it. To me . . . well, to me, booze is like . . . well, like sex. I can go without both. It's not like I can't. You understand?"

"Yeah," Ryan laughed. "Now I know you're BSing me, John. I can't see you going without sex for a day."

"I have been celibate this trip," Olsham replied with a smile, then added, "Almost anyway."

"When?" Ryan declared in surprise. "I was with you almost all the time."

"Triana. The stewardess. On the plane."

Ryan laughed as if all the tension of the last few days had been unleashed.

"You son of a bitch!" Ryan said as he laid down on the massive pillowed couch.

"No wonder you had to go to the bathroom so often. The rabbi should get a rebate on your fee."

"They have to make those bathrooms bigger," Olsham replied as he handed Ryan an iced glass of tomato juice.

"This city sure beats Summit County," Ryan said.

"Anything beats Summit County."

He wondered why John stayed in the county. We all have a story, he thought painfully to himself. Then he smiled and his eyes focused again on the luxurious room and he knew that the past is the past and you have to forget it, or remember it and digest it, and then go on. There is no other way, Joshua Ryan, he thought ruefully.

"She's nice," Olsham's voice broke through Ryan's reverie.

"Who?" he replied.

"Who? You know who I mean, Joshua. Sosie. Yehuda's girl. Who? Who the fuck are you kidding, Joshua Ryan. I see those eyes you had for her. Even Yehuda noticed it."

"You never date a girl in another borough, Olsham," Ryan said as he rose to get dressed in the bedroom.

"For Sosie you do."

"Maybe. But the Bronx is the Bronx. And I'm a Brooklyn boy. The subway doesn't extend to Jerusalem, John."

"You better talk to Yehuda. That's if you ever catch a ride back to the old country."

"Nothing to talk about. I got a client to defend. And she's not coming to Bristol."

"You never know, Joshua. You just never know," Olsham drained the last half of his tequila, walked into the bathroom and proceeded to shower. Ryan stood naked in front of the living room window wondering if he would ever see Sosie again.

Pinny was on time. Waiting in the old Citroen at the curb of the elegant street filled with the fashion houses of Versace, Ungaro, and Hermes; the dusty automobile seemed out of place.

When they were seated in the car, Pinny recklessly backed up to Avenue la Montaigne against a backlash of Gallic obscenities hurled at him by the waiting taxicab drivers. Pinny smiled and drove past the Grand Palais, across the Pont Royal onto the Quai Voltaire. Ryan's eyes feasted on the limestone empire buildings of all sizes and elegance, expecting Napoleon to emerge leading his troops to war.

Pinny drove with reckless abandon down one-way streets, across the St. Germain de Pres, around the Luxembourg Gardens, then back to the St. Germain with its snarling taxicabs and anxious Saturday night residents scouring the boulevard for a good place to park. With a jolting lurch, the Citroen came to a stop in front of a small storefront restaurant just off the Place Von Furstenburg behind l'Abbaye St. Germain. Simple lace curtains covered the small windows of the bistro. Toward the back of the restaurant, near the kitchen, barely visible, sat Rabbi Carl Rubin alongside Moishe, also known as Boris of the Shin Bet. Not speaking, they were each smoking, Moishe a Gauloise, the rabbi, his pipe, staring at the empty walls.

Observing Ryan, the rabbi rose to shake hands. Pinny pulled four chairs over to the table where the rabbi was seated.

"Good to see you're okay, Rabbi," Ryan said with obvious concern.

"I'm sorry to cause you so much trouble, Mr. Ryan," the rabbi replied with a wide perfect smile etched across his now shaved face.

"Your beard is gone," Olsham remarked.

"On advice of my Israeli friend here," the rabbi replied.

"We thought it would be easier to hide the rabbi without the beard," Yehuda said.

"Where are you staying, Rabbi?" Ryan asked more of Yehuda.

"We have a safe house on the Rue de Tempe. Just up the street from the Hotel de Ville," Yehuda answered.

"Who is *we?*" Ryan asked.

"We is the Shin Bet," Pinny's gruff voice barked out.

"I thought the government would not get involved?" Ryan asked as a short, stocky waiter approached the table, rubbing his hands as if he were a maître d' in a French film.

"Gentlemen," the waiter said in a garrulous voice, "it's good to see you back again. Yehuda, how is your daughter, Shoshana? Lovely young lady. She stayed with our family when she attended the Sorbonne."

"Sosie's fine. She sends her love . . . to all of you," Yehuda answered as he grasped the extended rough-hewn hand of the waiter.

"Schmiel here," Yehuda added, "is the real resistance. Schmiel, they want to know about the great French resistance during the big war to end all wars."

"Not many of us are still alive."

"There weren't many to start with," Pinny interjected cynically.

"Pinny, stop with the debate already," Moishe said as he stuffed a thick slice of bread into his mouth. Schmiel left to retrieve menus.

"It's not a debate, my brother of all brothers," Pinny replied with a wave of indignation, "it's the truth."

"Moishe and Pinny are French," Yehuda said.

"We are Israeli," Pinny shouted.

"Nobody's Israeli," Yehuda added. "Except Sosie and me. Everybody is from someplace else. A nation of immigrants."

"We were children. Pinny remembers nothing. Just what Papa told us," Moishe said, as his mouth continued to chew into the bread he stuffed into his mouth.

"They killed all of our cousins. Our aunts and uncles. Papa's brothers. Why do you take it so lightly, Moishe?" Pinny asked in a demanding voice.

"Because it's over. Everybody in Israel lives in the past. Never forget. Vengeance is mine, said the Lord. Well, I'm getting too old to wreak vengeance on enemies that are older then me. Let the dead lie in their graves. What good does it do to damn the French for what they should have done fifty years ago?" Moishe's voice was dry as he spoke. He had finished all the bread in the basket before him.

"It's the hypocrisies of the French, I guess," Yehuda offered without passion in his voice.

"They could have saved the Jews but they didn't. It would have taken such little effort," Yehuda added.

"There was no resistance," Pinny bellowed, "it's all make-believe. Like everything else. All make-believe."

"Maybe that's the reason we Jews feel something toward each other," Ryan said in a pensive, quiet voice.

All at the table stared at him in apparent surprise. The silence that followed was interrupted by Schmiel arriving with large menus and an even larger wine list.

"Here are the menus," he said, "but I'd rather order for you. It's my chef . . . and I know what my friends should have. Is that all right?"

"I'd let you order for me at Lasserre, Schmiel. You've always been right," Yehuda said as he rose to grasp the short man around the shoulders in a loving embrace. He then spun the short stocky body around and kissed him on both cheeks.

"That's for being so wonderful to my Sosie," Yehuda said proudly.

Schmiel brought platters of escargots smothered in garlic and melted butter sauce, salads garnished with truffle shavings. And then servings of coq au vin and duck a l'orange, albeit in separate platters. Dipping into the sauces with the freshly baked chunks of hard-crusted baguettes, drinking glasses of Rothschild Pouilly Fuisse from chilled bottles, the diners' conversation was immersed in the sounds of joyous feasting among friends. Schmiel pulled up a chair and poured himself a glass of wine, offering toasts of health and happiness to the group.

"Thank God I don't live in Paris," Pinny remarked between glasses of wine and coq au vin. "I'd be three hundred pounds."

"You *are* three hundred pounds," Moishe replied quickly.

"On your mother's head." Pinny belched.

"Mama even knows you're three hundred pounds, Pinny," Moishe replied.

"More to love," Pinny said, his eyes darting to the five-layer dessert cart tucked in the front corner of the restaurant.

"Schmiel, what are you doing sitting with the customers," Pinny clucked.

"Up . . . up . . . bring over that dessert cart. *Schnell, schnell . . .* you *schweinhundt.*"

"My little brother knows a few obscene words in twenty languages," Moishe said.

"All related to food," he added.

After several portions of tarte aux pommes, Napoleons, and chocolate profiteroles, the men sat silently around the table sipping tiny cups of espresso.

"When are we leaving?" Ryan asked, turning down a brandy from Schmiel.

"We can't use a commercial airline, Joshua," Yehuda replied. "If the French are forced to restrain the rabbi here pending formal extradition proceedings, he could be here a month."

"There's an old friend of mine from the early flying days operating a charter air jet company out of Orly," Pinny remarked between mouthfuls of profiterole.

"Does he have a plane that can make the distance?" Ryan queried.

"One stop in Newfoundland."

"I must get the rabbi back to Summit County for an arraignment hearing by Tuesday 9 a.m. That gives us two days to get out of France and land in Philadelphia."

"And if he doesn't make it?" Yehuda asked

"They'll fix bail at a million dollars and we'll never get it reduced once we surrender to the police."

"Then it's Tuesday," Yehuda declared.

"Just a little side question, gentlemen," Olsham said, accepting Schmiel's offer of a brandy glass full of Grand Marnier.

"How do we get the rabbi out of France without the French . . . and the good captain . . . knowing about it? I presume we still have to go through customs. Passport control. . ."

Each of the men looked askance at each other until Pinny smiled and said in a rush of words, "The trunk. The same trunk your friend put him in when he arrived in Paris."

"Gentlemen," the rabbi raised the palm of his hand in defiance to the suggestion, "I've had enough trunks for one trip."

"No. I think Pinny is right," Yehuda exclaimed. "In fact, I have a better idea. Why don't we put the rabbi in a coffin. We can convince the French customs that the dead man is being flown back to the States for burial. No one will look at the body. They never do when the body is leaving the country."

"What about US Customs?" Ryan replied quickly.

Olsham finished his brandy and stood up, peering out the small front window of the restaurant.

"Don't you think we should have posted a guard, gentlemen . . . outside the restaurant," he declared brusquely.

"We have people out there, Mr. Olsham," Pinny replied.

"I don't see anyone."

"That's why they are so good," Moishe interjected.

Olsham returned to the table, sat down and then said in a slow monotone, "The military. They never check a military coffin. I should know. I brought many a buddy home from Vietnam, on commercial jets. They never check. Out of respect."

"How do I breathe?" the rabbi asked in a less than agreeable voice.

"The same way you breathe in a trunk," Yehuda said.

"We can also fix you up with an oxygen portable tank if you get claustrophobic in there. You whiff in the pure oxygen," Olsham said, then added with a grin, "It's the greatest high in the world, Rabbi."

"Better than first class on El Al, Rabbi," Pinny said.

"How do you know, little brother. You never flew first class on El Al," Moishe quickly remarked.

"How do you know everything about me, Moishe? What do you do, follow me around. There's plenty you don't know about me. Plenty."

"And these are the two soldiers who fought side-by-side with me over the Jordanian lines to the Old City in 1967?" Yehuda declared with a smile.

The air of good humor was suddenly shattered by the wail of discordant sirens filling the inside and outside of the restaurant. Without hesitation, Yehuda directed that Pinny lead the rabbi,

Ryan, and Olsham out the back door of the restaurant into an alley leading to the tiny square of Place Von Furstenburg.

"Moishe and I will walk out the front and see what the French police are all excited about. I'm sure your friend the captain had something to do with it," Yehuda added. And then instructed quickly to Pinny, "Take them through Lavoisie. The silk shop. He's one of us. And you'll find you're on the Rue de l'Abbaye. Follow that up to the Quai Voltaire, and then taxi back to le Bristol. Understand, Pinny, my friend?"

Yehuda's demeanor was even, his face wreathed in a smile, as if he were merely taking a leisurely Saturday night stroll. Pinny lifted his great bulk out of the chair with surprising agility, grabbed the arm of the rabbi and started for the kitchen in the back of the restaurant. Ryan and Olsham followed.

As Pinny entered the swinging doors of the kitchen, Yehuda shouted, "Pinny, remember to call your friend with the plane. We'll need it sooner then we thought."

Yehuda and Moishe walked slowly to the front of the restaurant as the boxlike French prison wagon pulled over to the curb. Frenetic gendarmes armed with nightsticks rushed out of the back of the wagon. Yehuda tried to engage the sergeant in conversation as the policeman directed his men to surround the restaurant. A Renault 21 sedan pulled up behind the wagon and a young lieutenant of the French Sureté approached Yehuda and Moishe who were leaning against the adjacent building. From the rear of the Renault, Captain Crutchfield appeared, followed by Dickson.

"That's him, Lieutenant!" Crutchfield shouted to the young officer who had just instructed his men to surround the restaurant.

Yehuda smiled. Moishe pulled a Gauloise from a crumbled pack and lit up.

"Good afternoon, Captain," Yehuda said in a pleasant voice in French.

"Where is he?" Dickson barked as he fronted the captain and stood, legs apart in a threatening stance, glaring at Yehuda.

"Who?" Yehuda replied.

"You know who . . . whatever your name is," Dickson said as he moved closer to Yehuda, their noses almost touching.

Yehuda spoke in almost a breathless whisper, again in French, to the young French lieutenant who said nothing, his right hand on his leather holster at his side. The lieutenant replied, in French, to Yehuda, his face hiding a growing smile.

"Fucking frogs," Dickson bellowed, not caring who heard him.

"Shut up, Dickson," the captain instructed, as he pushed Dickson's well-muscled body to the side and directed his attention to Yehuda.

"I have filed a formal extradition petition with the French department of justice. So let's stop crapping around and turn the rabbi over before somebody really gets hurt," the captain announced.

"Putting him in a trunk would be considered harmful to his health, Captain," Yehuda replied.

The sergeant walked over to the group gathered on the sidewalk, saluted and then spoke hurriedly to the lieutenant.

The lieutenant turned to Captain Crunch and said in perfect English, "Sir. . .my sergeant tells me the restaurant is empty and there is no one outside the restaurant that fits your man's description. I'm sorry. But I think that we have been too late."

The young man smartly saluted, faintly winked to Yehuda, and called to the gendarmes to withdraw.

A small Fiat pulled up to the back of the departing prison wagon and Yehuda could see the man who had been present at the Jewish Quarter in Jerusalem with Captain Crutchfield, driving the sedan.

"This car looks familiar, Moishe," Yehuda remarked in a loud clear voice.

"Fiats are common in Paris, Yehuda," Moishe replied.

"Not one with two bent fenders and smashed headlights, Moishe."

"Lousy French drivers. They're always getting into accidents," Moishe replied, his mouth puffing dramatically on the almost burnt-out Gauloise, the smoke assaulting the captain's face with a fury.

"You fucking wiseass Jews," Dickson spewed out the words with hatred. "You think you can run this world. Well, wait till we get back to our home ground. You'll see good ol' American justice at its very best."

He jumped into the passenger seat of the Fiat before any reply could be uttered.

"You should control your men, Captain," Yehuda warned.

"I don't want the rabbi to be killed, Mr. Ben-Zvi," the captain said as he opened the rear door of the sedan.

"I'll tell him, Captain. I'm sure it will comfort him."

"You'll never get him out of the country alive, sir," the captain replied.

"Don't bet on it, Captain. We'll see you in your country on our terms. The rabbi will be delivered whole. As his lawyer wants . . . as the rabbi wants. *Bon voyage, mon capitain*." Yehuda saluted as the Fiat screeched away from the curb heading toward the Rue de l'Abbaye.

Yehuda's stone face turned to concern. Quickly, he walked to the corner of the small street, turned left into the Place Von Furstenberg. The street was dark.

"We better make sure, Moishe. Call for backup. They're on foot and I don't know how fast your brother can move with all the luggage he's carrying."

Moishe withdrew a cell phone from his leather jacket's inside pocket. He punched in some numbers, spoke quietly in Hebrew and then placed the phone back into his jacket.

"They are at Odeon. Maybe five minutes, Yehuda."

"Maybe five minutes too late, Moishe," Yehuda replied.

Yehuda's eyes peered up the tiny street to the Rue de Bonaparte and into the square surrounding the Abbaye. To the left was the St. Germain de Pres. Has Paris changed so much, he wondered, or is it me that changes every time I visit it? From generation to generation, the young from all over flock to Paris. Liszt, Prokofiev, Mozart, and Chopin, they all came, studied, created beautiful music, and died longing for the youth so rapturously spent in a city that never changes. It only changes people. And it was so when I was young, Yehuda mused. It tied you to her bosom with happiness and then left you with eternal sadness to be there when you went home.

1959, 1960—was it that long ago, Yehuda thought as his eyes followed a young couple embracing. His ruminations continued. What did I know? I was wrapped up in my love for things that happened in the long past. I cared not for today. The past was mythical. We forget the hurts of today when we delve into the past. My thirst for knowledge of the ancient world was unquenchable. And where better to learn of the civilized magnificence of archeology but in Paris, he thought.

Yehuda had graduated from the University of Tel Aviv with honors in ancient Middle East civilizations. When he craved a far-wider knowledge, he gravitated to Paris. His basic service in the Israeli army completed, he kissed his parents good-bye and booked an Israeli freighter heading for Marseilles. Then he hitchhiked along the country roads of France, through Provence. He finally arrived in Paris six months after he had left Haifa's harbor. Affable and handsome, Yehuda made friends wherever he traveled, learning the language from the people he met and loved.

Both men, as well as women, loved his exuberance for life.

Arriving in Paris at the end of 1959, Yehuda registered for the spring term at the university in the graduate archeology curriculum. His knowledge of the ancient world bedazzled most of his scholarly professors at the university. Within months he had won a graduate instructor position teaching undergraduates various courses in ancient civilizations.

In one of those courses, she was there. Zepporah Wilkenfield, Zeppi to her friends, sat in the front row of Yehuda's class, taking copious notes. She smiled affectionately at him. Yehuda was used to such flirtatious advances by young female students. He had bedded many in the short time he had started teaching. The only rule he demanded was that they realize the relationship was not permanent and that he was offering no commitment at all. Marriage was not in his plans. Not for years. His love was with the past.

They went to Deux Magots after class one afternoon. They sat at an outside table observing the springtime lovers walking by the bar. They drank Pernod and espressos as they spoke about Herod, Caesar, and Abraham. Yehuda had recently turned agnostic. It was a trend in Israel among the young to question the existence of the Almighty. He listened to rebuttal but accepted little in response.

Zeppi, at first, was taken aback by his questioning and his violent perspective of the future of the Jewish people. Yet, he learned to listen to her husky, slow-speaking voice. She articulated her beliefs so well. They only spoke in French. She was classical in her language, he was a peasant in his understanding of the French of the countryside. Her accent was Parisian. His was of Provence. Phonetics. Sounds. His ear was trained for language. He spoke Hebrew, English, and German as well.

Yehuda was not to be thwarted in any way when it came to discovering the past. And language was the highway to the past.

He met her mother. Her natural father had been killed at Auschwitz in 1944, three years after she was born. Marched into death by the Vichy underlings of the German occupiers. Zeppi remembered the day he was taken from the apartment. She and her mother were hiding in a Catholic neighbor's apartment across the street when the SS came. Her father had to stay or else the Germans would continue searching for the entire family.

"Go, little *tsatskala* (little toy, little loved one)," he instructed with a loving flourish of his head. He left that day and died within a year. An innocent, a professor of nineteenth-century history at the Sorbonne, the French gave him up without a fight.

Yehuda had gone into his atheist diatribe. He was angry. He was always angry when he heard stories of the Jews and the massacres and the acceptance of it all by the Christian world. Even the Jews accepted it.

Yehuda remembered that fall afternoon well. They had been dating, off and on for six months or so. Yehuda had barely kissed her. Zeppi wondered if he considered her unattractive. She knew of his reputation as a lover. Even in Paris, Yehuda was envied for his romantic encounters.

The leaves were falling. It was the Bois de Boulogne, lunch at Le Pre Catalan. It was her birthday. She had just turned twenty.

Sitting at lunch on that glorious Parisian fall Saturday afternoon, they ate hungrily. The sumptuous foods engulfed their stomachs but the red wines of Provence filled their heads. They laughed and cried and argued and held hands and silently fell in love. She had been his friend. He had very few friends who were also his lovers. Confused, Yehuda wanted to leave. But he didn't. He sat with the luxury of the Bois at his feet, not knowing what to say or do next.

He recognized the danger that lurked behind that china-doll

smile of this innocent temptress who sat across the table from him. He knew she wanted to make love. Her fiery blue eyes evoked passion, her fingertips on his hand caused him grave concern. They were lightening rods stirring him. He knew this encounter would not be his usual slam-bang affair. Zeppi was more. He would rather not, he thought. There were easier ways.

They walked. Through the leaf-strewn paths of the Bois, ostensibly going to the Metro stop. It's the long way to the Metro, he thought. So what? he consoled his mind. What could happen in a forest filled with horse riders, walkers, and bicycles?

Hand in hand, they strolled through the trails. It started to rain. They hurried deeper into the woods, away from the trail, seeking shelter from the lightning and the wetness. They found each other. Lovers. He forgot she was a friend. She was now a lover. The cable had snapped. For each of them.

The rain stopped. They had mixed feelings of guilt, love, satisfaction. Mostly both were wondering what the hell was next.

"Can we still be friends?" she asked.

"I never had a friend who was a lover," he replied.

"I want to be your friend more than your lover, Yehuda."

"We'll try."

"Am I like all the other ones?" she asked petulantly.

He remained silent.

"This is not my first time," she admitted.

"Neither mine," he said.

"He was a lieutenant in the army," she continued in a whispering voice.

"You don't have to tell me anything, Zeppi."

"We were going to get married."

"And."

"He was killed in a motorcycle accident. Last year," she said in a dry voice.

"Such things happen," he said to console her.

"I don't have much luck with men in my life," she said soulfully.

"Before him, it was Papa," she added.

"You don't blame yourself for your father's death?" he said.

"I was three years old. Looking out the window. Behind the

curtains. And I saw them beat him. He was a passive man. I couldn't do anything. I just stared as they threw him into the truck. I knew he was looking up to me in the window."

"We were already in Palestine when the war broke out," Yehuda said as his hand stroked her long, brown hair, wet from the rain.

"You were lucky."

"Maybe," he admitted.

She continued, "When I was just a baby, my family traveled across the German border . . . the family had lived in Berlin for over a century . . . into France, with a caravan of circus people. Under the floorboards of their wagon. We thought once we got to France we would be all right. The French would protect their Jews. We all thought that. But we were wrong. First Papa. Then Samuel, my older brother. He was about twelve. We never saw them both again."

"That's why we fight so hard for every inch of land," Yehuda said with a trace of anger in his voice.

"God didn't protect us. Papa said God would protect us," she continued.

"We depend on ourselves," Yehuda said, a note of defiance in his voice.

"I can't even remember his face now." She paused and stared at Yehuda's eyes. "He had such a beautiful face. Just like yours, Yehuda."

She then smiled and the world seemed to open up. The rain clouds disappeared and Yehuda saw sunlight in her face. He knew then that he wouldn't escape. Goddamnit, he cursed to himself.

"I adore you, Yehuda," she said matter-of-factly.

"Please," he defended futilely.

"You don't have to say anything. I don't expect any long-term commitments from you. I just want you to know how I feel." She paused and then sat up and stretched like some jungle cat waking up from a long sleep.

"I don't want to be loved, Zeppi. I'm not ready. . . ."

She laughed in a deep throaty voice.

"Why?" she said, "Is the great Yehuda Ben-Zvi afraid?"

She leaned over to kiss him square on the mouth.

"We should continue being friends," he lamely muttered.

"We will be. Always, Yehuda. I need you as a friend more than I need you as a lover," she replied.

"But," he interjected quickly, "we can still . . . y'know . . . make love. Friends can make love," he added.

"Not anymore, Yehuda," she stated with authority as she rose from the wet, leaf-strewn ground.

"The only way we'll do it again is after you crush the glass under the huppa." Her voice was taunting yet so innocent.

They were married three years later in Jerusalem.

CHAPTER THIRTY-TWO

The Left Bank of Paris was easier to escape on foot than in a car. Winding narrow streets sometimes ended abruptly in a small alley. Most streets eventually terminated at the banks of the Seine.

Pinny half dragged the rabbi up the Rue de Seine onto the Rue Bonaparte and finally onto the Quai Voltaire. The smell of the ancient Seine caught the rabbi flush in the face. Ryan and Olsham carried up the rear, always peering over their shoulders for the oncoming enemy.

At the Quai, they made a quick left turn toward the Musée D'Orsay, the old railroad station converted to a museum. Within a short distance of the Musée, they all could hear the misfiring of a vehicle directly behind them.

"In here," Pinny instructed briskly, "I think they might be right back there."

He pushed the rabbi into a side entrance of the Musée that led to a long, narrow corridor. A single fluorescent light illuminated the passageway. Ryan and Olsham followed.

Pinny stopped suddenly. He motioned for them to stop as he backtracked down the corridor to the swinging doors of the entrance. Peering through the doors, he saw the Fiat draw up to the curb. Turning quickly, he adeptly double-timed toward the trio and with the wave of his hand, he ordered them to follow him through the single door leading to the rear of the museum's lobby.

"They know where we are," he breathlessly uttered in anger. "We have to get lost in the museum. Follow quickly. I know the museum well from when it was a railroad station. Just follow me and don't say a word."

"How the hell do they know where we are?" Olsham complained.

In the side hall of the foyer of the almost empty museum, Pinny abruptly stopped and pulled the rabbi into a corner pocket where the Daumiers were hung. Pushing the rabbi roughly against the wall, Pinny pulled the rabbi's arms toward the ceiling.

"Straddle your legs, Rabbi," Pinny commanded. The rabbi peered over at Ryan for advice, but Ryan only shrugged his shoulders, and the rabbi complied.

Patting the rabbi down from his head to his groin, his legs and then his ankles, Pinny's hands moved like voracious octopus tentacles. Finding nothing, Pinny turned toward Ryan and Olsham then quickly turned around and faced the rabbi. Without warning, he grabbed the rabbi's thick mane of hair and crudely ran his stubby fingers through the hair. The rabbi's face grimaced with pain as he struggled to push Pinny away. A victorious smile found its way over Pinny's large face as his right hand pulled a microscopic piece of metal out of the rabbi's hair and scalp.

"Here's the little bugger," Pinny almost shouted. "I knew they couldn't find us without some electronic trailing device on one of us."

Showing the tiny metal square to Olsham and Ryan, Pinny moved quickly up the side display room toward the back of the serpentine hall of the museum. The loudspeaker announced that the museum was closing in twenty minutes and the voice instructed all persons to head for the entranceway. Ryan and Olsham looked toward Pinny who appeared to field a deaf ear to the closing instructions. He hurled the electronic bug down a side hallway.

"They'll be checking the front entrance," Pinny said. "We have to get to the fourth floor. There's a fire escape leading down the back of the building. Hurry, don't look back."

Up the series of short flights of steps separating the display rooms, Pinny ran as if he were an overweight Olympic track star. Even Olsham, his well-trained body used to a vigorous pace, had difficulty keeping up with the disappearing rotund form of the gigantic leader of the pack.

The footfalls of hurried chasers echoed through the marble-covered alcoves, their plain walls filled with striking nineteenth-century paintings. Then the muffled sounds of voices trailed after the fleeing quartet.

Ryan stopped near the last display room, his knees too painful to continue.

"You must not stop!" Pinny whispered in a frustrated voice.

"My knees," Ryan complained.

"Mr. Olsham," Pinny demanded, "Carry your friend if he can't make it. We just have to get to the end of the hall, and then we will be safe. Hurry, please . . ." Pinny implored.

Ryan rubbed his swollen aching knees vigorously, crouched down onto the floor and then rose, pain etched on his face, and then started up the last flight of steps.

They rounded the corner. Pinny stopped at the miniature replica of Paris of the nineteenth century. Suddenly he disappeared into the shadows of the darkened hallway, the mammoth Paris model obscuring his disappearing hulk.

"Pinny," Ryan half shouted, his feet almost stumbling.

Nothing was heard except for the patter of running feet over the marble walkways behind them.

As quickly as he had disappeared, Pinny reappeared from behind the Paris model, his face covered with a mischievous grin.

"Follow me, gentlemen. I knew it was still here."

The trio followed Pinny around the model city. Magically he uncovered part of the heavy plastic top of the Paris model, opened the miniature building designated as Napoleon's Tomb, and started to descend into the marble floor. Pinny flicked on his cigarette lighter as they followed him, each man holding onto the man in front of him in the pitch-black underground tunnel located at the bottom of the stairs.

"I hope your knees will hold out, Mr. Ryan," Pinny said, "We'll have to climb four flights of stairs to get to the exit."

"I'll make it," Ryan said meekly.

Within seconds after they had closed the miniature Napoleon's Tomb, they could hear the voices and hurried steps above the tunnel.

"They left this tunnel when they changed it from the railroad station," Pinny said as he pushed open a small wooden door that led into the stairwell leading to the upper floors of the museum.

"How much time do we have?" Olsham asked as he strode abreast of Pinny.

"Five minutes. They'll know we're not on the main level. Unfortunately, the escalators are shut down," Pinny said as he stared at the struggling Ryan.

"Will you make it, Mr. Ryan?" he added.

"It's these goddamn knees," Ryan complained as his limp increased noticeably.

"Four flights, you say," the rabbi said, his chest heaving from the frantic running efforts.

"We have to get to the back of the rooms holding the Impressionists. There is a fire exit that leads to the outside street. We must get there before the museum closes. They put the alarm on when they close. So I am asking all of you to hurry."

As they climbed the steps, Ryan could see through the glass enclosure into the main hallway of the museum. Captain Crutchfield and four other men were scurrying around the bronze and marble statues located in the rising center of the hall, all appearing to head for the side of the hall where the staircase was located.

After two knee operations, I have to go through this shit, Ryan thought, as he attempted to place his legs on the stairs in such a way as to limit the agonizing shooting pains filling both kneecaps. His mother told him Jewish boys don't play football. Ryan wanted to please his father. The only appreciation his father ever displayed. My son the hero, he would always say sarcastically.

What a way to see Paris, Ryan thought as he trudged painfully up the wide staircase trying to keep up with the others.

As he grasped the thick marble rail of the staircase, Ryan's eyes marveled at the soaring old glass ceilings preserved when the museum was converted from the Gare D'Orsay train station. The sheer cubic volume of the free spanning space was a marvel of human creativity. It brought the wondrous sky of Paris into the building and provided background for mankind's greatest works of art. In Paris, nothing took center stage. Every work of art or piece of architecture was just another piece of the great puzzle that was Paris.

At the third level, Pinny stopped at the landing and waited for Ryan to bring up the rear. The rabbi sat down on the first step of the staircase, his head in his hands, his heavy breathing noticeably loud.

"Too much good food," Pinny said with a grin on his sweating face.

"How far?" Ryan asked in a husky whisper.

"One more flight, Mr. Ryan. One more flight. We don't have much time. The museum closes in five minutes. It's probably the only public building in Paris that closes on time," Pinny said.

"I don't hear them," Ryan observed as he sat down by the side of the rabbi.

"They probably found the elevator."

"How can we beat them to the fourth floor?" Olsham asked.

"They'll stop at each floor to look for us. Anyway, whoever reaches the fourth floor first. Well, anyway . . . let's get going. It's only one more flight," Pinny advised as he agilely started to climb the steps.

"I'm sorry, Mr. Ryan," the rabbi said as he helped Ryan up from the step.

"Don't be, Rabbi," Ryan replied, a slight smile on his face. "Ten years ago I would have made it to the top without a sweat. But that was ten years ago."

The gear sounds of the running elevator could be heard outside the staircase, seemingly a few feet away on the wide landing surrounding the great hall.

"Come on!" Pinny half yelled from the top of the middle landing of the staircase. "They'll be searching the third floor in a few seconds. We must hurry, gentlemen."

Forgetting his shooting pains, Ryan bolted quickly up the steps just behind the disappearing body of the rabbi who was rounding the corner of the winding staircase.

At the fourth level, Pinny held the door open to the exhibition floor. Inside on the platform, Ryan's eyes took in the panorama of the soaring main hall. The glass ceilings were crisscrossed with ribbons of bronze that bound the never-ending curved roof together. Through the vastness of the glass roof, Ryan saw the sky of Paris.

"We are now closing the museum," the voice bellowed through the loud speaker. "Please exit immediately."

Pinny corralled his charges down the landing into the small display rooms filled with nineteenth-century Impressionist paintings located toward the front side of the museum building. The faces of the subjects in the paintings were alive in the darkness of the building. Like having a thousand eyes staring at you as you passed, Ryan thought, hurrying to keep up with the fleeting body of Pinny.

Pinny stopped alongside a metal unmarked door. It seemed to lead to another hallway off the landing.

"Why are we stopping here?" Ryan asked of Pinny.

"Because this is the fire exit," Pinny replied.

"It's unmarked," Olsham said.

"It's not the official exit," Pinny replied. "But it leads down a small hallway to the outside staircase of the building."

"The elevator is stopping on the floor!" Olsham exclaimed.

"We must get to the staircase before the museum is closed. Or else the door will not open. Let's go, gentlemen," Pinny ordered.

Without hesitation the quartet ran down the narrow hallway outside the fourth floor hallway. Pinny stopped at a metal door at the end of the hall. He looked at his charges momentarily before he pushed at the door. It did not open. He pushed again. It still did not open. The noise of heavy footsteps and voices could be heard in the landing several feet away from where the quartet were standing.

"It won't open!" Pinny said with an anxious voice. Beads of sweat could be seen gathering on his jowly face.

"Let me try," Olsham said, as he drove his broad shoulder into the center of the ungiving door. The voices and footsteps grew closer.

"Son of a bitch," Olsham shouted. "It's stuck."

"Try again, John," Ryan instructed.

The second attempt by Olsham drove the door outward with a noticeable clang as it opened against the steel outside staircase. Suddenly the voices stopped and an eerie silence prevailed.

Pinny seized the moment and pushed the rabbi through the open door. Ryan and Olsham followed. Down the steel fire escape staircase the quartet descended. When they reached the second landing, they could hear Captain Crutchfield's heavy voice ordering them to halt or he would shoot.

Ryan looked quickly over his shoulder as he rounded the last leg of the staircase and saw Dickson kneeling on his knees, his 9mm automatic held in two hands, aiming the weapon at the rabbi's descending body. Then he fired.

At least three bullets ricocheted off the metal superstructure of the stairwell, but the quartet continued on until they established a firm footing on the concrete patio at the side of the museum building.

"Stay against the wall!" Pinny's voice was loud and demanding. The bullets were hitting the wall outside of the museum, but Pinny crouched and nearly crawled toward the edge of the gigantic terrace leading to the side street alongside the museum. His flock followed.

Out of nowhere, the omnipresent Citroen emerged with Moishe and Yehuda in the front seat.

Pinny shepherded his three charges into the backseat and he jumped alongside of Yehuda in the front seat. A stray bullet struck the roof of the car but bounced off randomly, striking at the curb of the street.

The Citroen disappeared down the Rue de Lilles.

CHAPTER THIRTY-THREE

The funeral procession to DeGaulle Airport was short and resplendent with three black Mercedes limousines following one another like sheep to the barn. It was nearly sunrise, a strange time to bury someone. Especially at DeGaulle.

Yehuda drove the lead vehicle, the gilded casket enclosure in the back of the vehicle. Ryan sat beside him all dressed in black. The other two Mercedes limousines were driven by Moishe and Pinny with Olsham riding shotgun in Moishe's limo.

Yehuda flashed his security badge at the gate to the private sector of DeGaulle Airport and the guard summarily passed the funeral cortege through the gate.

A Lear ten-seater private jet sat waiting just inside the gate at a special hangar used often by foreign diplomats flying quietly out of France. Pulling up to the jet, the funeral line stopped at the tarmac leading up to the open door of the plane. Quickly, the four men exited their vehicles and unloaded the casket from the first limousine and carried it up the steps of the waiting jet. The bronzed, white-haired pilot emerged from the cockpit and led the procession to the back of the jet. The casket was placed behind a curtain in a room that served as the master bedroom for the plane.

Triana also emerged from the cockpit, her long legs following the procession to the back of the plane. She was wearing her El Al stewardess uniform.

Ryan smiled as he saw Triana. Olsham kissed her on the cheek as he passed her in the aisle leading to the front of the plane.

"Pinny must be your best buddy to arrange your favorite stewardess on the flight back," Ryan said in a plain, even tone.

Olsham just grinned as the four men walked down the steps to the tarmac.

"What now?" Ryan asked.

"We wait," Yehuda replied.

"For what?" Ryan persisted.

"Our friends in the French customs bureau," Pinny interjected.

"We can't leave until they endorse the exit paperwork," he added.

"What happens if they want to look into the casket?" Ryan asked doubtfully.

"They won't," Yehuda answered.

"They never do," Pinny added.

"Hopefully we don't start a precedent," Ryan said, his eyes spotting the two French uniformed custom agents walking slowly from the gate area.

Pinny nudged Yehuda and then whispered.

"It's not Langois," he said with a note of fear.

"I thought you said he was on duty this morning," Yehuda replied, obviously angry at Pinny.

"He always is."

"He's on Sunday?" Yehuda asked.

Moishe's face contorted with wonder as if he suddenly realized it was Sunday.

"I forgot, Yehuda," Moishe admitted contritely.

"I hope he's a friend," Pinny joined in.

"We'll know in a second," Ryan said, as the French uniformed duo marched grimly toward them.

"Bonjour," Yehuda greeted them happily.

"Bonjour, monsieur," the lead French customs agent replied in a chilly voice. He was not smiling as he spoke.

Yehuda handed over the medical certificate of death and the exit papers that had been so carefully forged by the French handwriting experts usually employed by the Shin Bet.

The custom agent carefully read the documents and then handed them over to his associate. They both stared suspiciously at the quartet of black dressed men surrounding the steps to the plane.

"Why are you leaving so early?" the lead agent said in slurred French.

"There is a ceremony in Philadelphia this afternoon for the dearly departed," Yehuda answered in a provincial French accent.

"Has the casket been inspected by customs?" The agent asked. His face was scarred with a line that ran from his temple to his jaw. It appeared red from the morning sun.

"We have the medical certificate, monsieur," Yehuda answered instantly.

"It still has to be inspected," the lead agent insisted.

"You may if you want. . .but. . ." Yehuda replied and then asked the agents to follow him to the rear of the plane. After several minutes of hand-filled conversations between Yehuda and the French agents, Yehuda returned alone. The scarred agent had endorsed the exit visa with his stamp and signature.

"A friend?" Moishe asked, an insane grin across his small face.

"Probably hates Jews," Yehuda answered. "Also probably hates homosexuals too,"

He paused to exhale the morning's frosty air.

"So?" Pinny asked anxiously.

"So . . . I told him our dearly departed friend died of AIDS. And that to look on his face and body is to throw up your breakfast. You know a Frenchmen hates to lose his meal over a job. *Le toute est là.* (It all boils down to that)"

Ryan laughed for the first time in days. He actually realized he was going home.

The crossing was uneventful except for the disappearance of Olsham and Triana. The rabbi rose from the dead and joined Yehuda and Ryan in a game of pinochle. Fortunately there was a second stewardess serving the trio's food and drink requests.

"How do we get past your customs people?" Yehuda queried as he pensively arranged his cards in his hand.

"I haven't figured that out yet," Ryan admitted.

"We land in less than two hours," Yehuda replied.

"They won't be expecting the rabbi," Ryan declared.

"Maybe he should just walk through the gates," Ryan added.

"I'm sure the captain has notified the police," the rabbi declared.

"Maybe not," Ryan said, his eyes fixed on his cards. Between playing the cards, he sipped a cranberry juice and club soda with half a lime squeezed in it.

"A coffin might be difficult. Customs are looking for narcotics. Hidden containers that appear innocent, such as a coffin. Walking right through the gates might be the best way," Ryan added.

"What about his passport? He has to go through passport control?" Yehuda asked, staring directly at the rabbi.

"I don't know," Ryan replied. He pensively sucked on the squeezed-out half lime.

"Maybe Olsham has some suggestions," Ryan added as he peered back to the curtained bedroom area.

"That's if he is still alive after Triana," he added with a smile.

"He has an appetite," the rabbi said.

"Youth . . . I guess," Ryan replied.

They played silently for another twenty minutes before Olsham and Triana reappeared from the rear of the plane. Olsham was adjusting his Calvin Klein jeans while Triana nonchalantly walked to the front of the plane into the cockpit.

"Poker's a man's game," Olsham said as he pulled a chair up to the table where the trio were playing cards.

"The rabbi doesn't gamble," Ryan offered. "Besides, I didn't think you had time to play cards with us."

"Joshua . . . I think you're jealous," Olsham replied with a lusty smirk.

"We're trying to figure out how to get the rabbi through customs," Yehuda said.

"What about the coffin?" Olsham replied.

"I don't know if I can get back in there," the rabbi said, his head nodding toward the back of the plane where the coffin was situated.

"Besides," Ryan added, "we might have it searched. And the customs boys would be surprised to find a live corpse in there smelling pure oxygen."

Olsham picked at the club sandwich sitting in the middle of the table separating the chicken from the toast. His eyes narrowed to almost closed slits as he stared out the sun-drenched window, his mouth chewing on the slivers of chicken.

"Aren't we stopping in Newfoundland?" he asked.

"The pilot thinks we can make it to Philadelphia. Stopping could mean further inquiry about the coffin," Ryan replied.

Ryan rose from his chair and walked over to the bar standing against the side of the plane. He poured another cranberry-juice cocktail, and then drank half the drink in one gulp.

"Gentlemen, we're getting close to touchdown time," Ryan declared.

Olsham leaned back in the plush leather chair, his hands clasped behind his head, and he said with a deliberate voice. "Maybe he doesn't have to go back into the coffin. Maybe there is another way."

"Speak, brother," Ryan demanded.

"The pilot. They're about the same size. The rabbi and the pilot. Dress the rabbi in the pilot's uniform and use the pilot's passport."

"What does the pilot do in the meantime?" Ryan asked.

"Stay with the plane. After we get the rabbi into the lounge area, I send the passport back with someone at El Al. Right, Yehuda?" Olsham asked.

"The pictures are different," Yehuda remarked.

"So what?" Olsham defended.

"They rarely look at the picture in the passport. They depend on the computer. Besides, we go right through the airline employees control station. They never bother the pilots," he added.

"Maybe, Mr. Olsham is right," the rabbi said in a voice filled with relief.

"Do we have a choice?" Yehuda asked.

"Not if the rabbi won't get back into the coffin, we don't," Olsham observed.

"I hope Crutchfield isn't waiting for us," Ryan said.

"Let's hope he's still in gay Paree," Olsham replied.

"I'll talk to the pilot," Yehuda said as he rose from his chair.

"If he's a friend of Pinny's we should have no trouble," he added as he walked toward the cockpit.

"Send Triana back," Olsham yelled to the departing Yehuda, "There's still another hour."

"Just keep your mind on business, John," Ryan said half seriously.

"I think better when I'm with a beautiful woman, Josh. You should try it sometime."

"Yeah, I should," Ryan muttered.

The plane landed without incident at the Philadelphia Airport. Executing Olsham's plan, the quartet walked through the airline-employee passport control gate as if they had been doing it for years. Fortunately the pilot's uniform adequately fit the rabbi's slightly more rotund body. With professional aplomb the rabbi led his civilian employees through the gate as if he were a real pilot. The only problem arose when a custom agent stopped the four men just before they left the secured area of the airport. He insisted on searching the rabbi's hand luggage, which contained various religious items such a his tzitzis, bible, and tallis. Yehuda interceded in the agent's interrogation of the rabbi by declaring that they were gifts for the rabbi's ancient grandfather. The agent stared into the rabbi's face as if he had recognized who he was. After Yehuda flashed his El Al security ID card, the agent released them to exit the area. He kept looking after the rabbi as they hurriedly left the area into the airport ticket hall. Yehuda saw the agent walking toward the passport-control officer who had examined their passports moments ago.

The four of them rushed outside the airport exit doors and Olsham waved for a cab at the curb.

After they pulled out, Ryan could see the customs officer rushing to the exit with two Philadelphia policemen right behind him. It was obvious that the rabbi was a wanted man.

CHAPTER THIRTY-FOUR

"Roger," Ryan spoke in a low, even voice into the receiver.

"Ryan? Where are you?" Leary replied, while he waved to his aide to try and trace the call.

"Around. Did you miss me, Roger?" Ryan continued tauntingly.

"We're friends, Joshua. Why wouldn't I miss you?"

"Cut the bullshit, Roger," Ryan answered in a flash of anger. "You know why I'm calling. You've had your gestapo after me for the last week."

Ryan paused and let out a deep sigh and then continued, "I'm ready to bring the rabbi in if we can make a deal on the bail."

"Sure, Joshua. I'm always reasonable. You know that." Leary was quiet for a breathless second then continued, "Let me see. He's a fugitive from justice. He left our little state after he was indicted."

"That's bullshit, Roger!" Ryan shouted. "You know he hadn't been indicted. You indicted him after he left. You know that!"

"Prove it. You can't, Ryan . . . *you know that!*" Leary's voice trailed off into short breaths of sucked-in air as if he were undergoing an asthma attack.

"If you don't bring him in voluntarily and we catch him . . . well, I don't think it's going to look so good. Anyway, that's the reason you brought him back yourself, Ryan."

"I'm not bringing him in until we agree on bail, Roger."

"Do what you want to do, Ryan. No deal. He ain't leaving the County jail until he goes to the death house in Trenton. You hear me, you scummy motherfucker!" Leary screamed hysterically into the phone.

"Then I get a court order from the AJ . . . before he comes in."

"Try it," Leary yelled, "Just try it. You'll see what good it will do you."

"We're not getting anywhere, Roger," Ryan replied in an almost whisper. "I'll see you in court."

Ryan hung the receiver back on the pay phone cradle. He looked around the strip center. Finding nothing unusual, he walked back to the Corvette sitting in front of the WaWa convenience food store. Olsham was behind the wheel.

"Any good?" Olsham asked as Ryan swung into the dark brown leather bucket seat.

"He's being a prick as usual," Ryan replied. "I'm going out to see Judge King. It's too much of a chance to bring the rabbi in without a deal worked out before."

"Will King deal? He's the senator's boy. Y'know that, don't you?" Olsham asked rhetorically.

"The senator's dead, John. I can't believe the assignment judge won't treat the rabbi fairly."

"Don't you believe it. They're all cut from the same cloth, Joshua. You should know that by now."

"Well, anyway, I'll go see him. Maybe Roger will show some sense." Ryan paused as his eyes rested on the countryside filled with sheep and wondered how trouble like this could invade such a bucolic peaceful place.

"I think you should apply for a writ of habeas corpus in the federal court in Trenton, Joshua," Olsham suggested.

"Premature, John. The rabbi would already have to be in custody. Anyway, what are the grounds?"

"Police brutality. Y'know the rabbi won't be safe in the county jail, Josh. Leary will make sure his stay will be . . . what is it . . . uncomfortable."

"Unfortunately I can't prove that, until the rabbi is actually incarcerated. And I'm not taking that chance until I work out a bail agreement. King will listen."

They sat in the 'Vette silently peering through the windshield into the empty convenience food store. Olsham flicked on the CD player and the Frank Sinatra recording of duets with all of Olsham's favorite singers wafted through the speakers.

"I betcha Crutchfield's back . . . with his gorilla, Dickson. That sucker can't wait to get his hands on the rabbi, Joshua."

"Drive me to the courthouse, John. Everyday we wait . . . the rabbi could be picked up. And all the trouble we went through will be for naught."

Olsham shifted the floor gear into reverse and then accelerated the bullet-nosed car forward into the two-lane highway leading out of Fayetteville toward Bristol.

"How long will he be safe at your uncle's cabin?" Ryan asked.

"Who knows? The place is stuck in the middle of the Pine Barrens. I don't think anyone at the pros's office knows he's even my uncle. But who can tell?"

Ryan knew full well that the assignment judge owed his very job to Roger Leary's father, the late state senator.

The question was whether Judge King still clung to the umbilical cord that tied him to the late senator's political influence even though the senator had been dead for over two years. Ryan thought that it was worth a chance. What the hell could happen if he says no, Ryan thought.

Olsham stopped the car in front of the white-pillared entrance to the antebellum courthouse.

Ryan got out and said in parting, "Stay around, John, we may need to execute plain B if all else fails."

Olsham's face contorted in a quizzical mask.

"What the hell is plan B, Joshua? I don't even know plan A."

"Now is plan A. Plan B, we'll have to decide if all else fails."

"You said that . . ."

"Stay loose. I should be out within the hour. If not, call the Texas Rangers to rescue me," Ryan said with a hearty laugh.

"Just be careful, Joshua."

Ryan smiled as he walked briskly through the front doors of the courthouse. Olsham pulled the car away from the curb and drove it up the road to Buzzies Bar. He needed a drink while he waited.

On the top floor of the six-floor courthouse, Ryan exited the elevator. He looked to the right where Judge King's chambers were located but then turned left to the section of the building marked SUMMIT COUNTY PROSECUTOR'S OFFICE. At the reception window he told the young girl that he wanted to speak with Roger Leary. The girl buzzed Leary's office, waited a few seconds for a reply and then ushered Ryan into the waiting room.

"Shirley will be out to get you, Mr. Ryan," she said sweetly as she motioned for him to take a seat.

The anteroom was empty except for another receptionist situated in front of the waiting area. She smiled flirtatiously at Ryan, then turned to answer the small central bank of phones.

Ryan pulled *Sports Illustrated* off the coffee table situated in front of his chair. Leafing through it absentmindedly, he thought of the score of years he spent in these very offices. New faces, new people, he thought, nothing remains the same. Shirley was still here. She covers Leary's ass all the time, always did! She used to be the senator's secretary at the tail-end of the senator's career. When he died, she became Roger's part-time mother confessor and full-time administrator.

"How are you?" Shirley asked in a patronizing tone. She had somehow appeared out of nowhere.

"Fine, Shirley. And how is Morty?"

"Dead. Last year . . . I thought you knew."

"I'm the last to know. He was a great guy."

"We had thirty years together. God needed him more then I did, I guess. Anyway, it's good to see you again. You are certainly looking better then the last time I saw you."

"Thanks. I would have liked to have come to Morty's funeral . . . if I had only known," Ryan said in a soft, honest voice.

Her face suddenly changed from friendly to an officious facade as she said, "Please follow me, Joshua. Mr. Leary will see you now."

Ryan followed the tiny, robust woman as they wended their way through the maze of offices. At the end, in the far corner of the building, she stopped, opened the door for Ryan, and closed it behind him after he had entered.

Leary's back was to Ryan. His chair was facing out the window overlooking the tall pines in the rear of the courthouse. Ryan stood there for several seconds before he spoke.

"How are you, Roger?"

"Sit down, Ryan," Leary whispered in a tight-clenched voice.

Ryan sat in the armchair in front of Leary's desk. Nothing was said for about two full minutes, both lawyers staring out the window.

"So you're back, Ryan?" Leary finally said as he whirled his chair around to face Ryan.

"Body and soul, Roger."

"I guess you haven't heard?" Leary smiled as he spat out the question.

"Heard what?"

"You've been indicted, Joshua my boy," Leary smiled broadly as he spoke.

"For what?" Ryan's voice was filled with a mixture of anger and fear. His eyes were narrow slits as he stared at the slumped narrow body of Leary overwhelmed by the great leather judge's chair he sat in.

"Obstruction of justice. Just as I promised you two weeks ago."

"Bullshit, Leary. You know you can't indict a lawyer for helping his client."

"Yes I can. A sealed indictment that Judge Sturmer is holding in his safe. I didn't want the publication of the indictment to scare you away," Leary rose from the chair and stood on his toes over the desk, his eyes burning into Ryan.

"I'm leaving, Roger. There's no talking to you." Ryan raised up from the chair just using his arms. Leary pushed the intercom button down on his phone and told Shirley to get Dickson from the next office. Ryan walked toward the exit door of the office. Before he could open the door, Dickson marched through the side door of the office, grabbed Ryan around the neck with his mammoth right bicep and pulled Ryan to the floor facedown. Dickson then roughly handcuffed Ryan's wrists behind his back while he placed his knee into the small of Ryan's back. Ryan winced from the sharp pains that coursed through his lower back.

"You're making a big mistake, Leary," Ryan mumbled the words out of the side of his mouth in garbled syllables.

"Maybe. Maybe not, Ryan. Tell me where the rabbi is and I'll let you go. If you don't, Dickson here . . . your old buddy . . . will lodge you in the old county prison. All alone except for Dickson," Leary paused as he wiped the saliva from his mouth with a crushed handkerchief he pulled from the back pocket of his pants.

"I can't do that. You know I can't do that, Leary" Ryan replied in a voice filled with pain.

"Then off you go, my dear departed friend. I will leave you in the good hands of your warden Dickson. When you're ready to talk, he'll bring you back here. If not, I'm afraid you're not going to like the accommodations. Will he, Sergeant Dickson?" Leary asked of the smirking Dickson.

Dickson pulled Ryan up, the handcuffs cutting deep grooves into Ryan's wrists.

Unsteady on his feet, Ryan asked, "I can make a phone call?"

"No you can't. This is not an official arrest. Call it a pre-arrest. Questioning of a suspect."

"If I'm indicted it's an arrest, Leary. Y'know the goddamn rules!" Ryan shouted.

"There are no rules in my county, Ryan. I make the fucking rules here. When I want you to call somebody I'll tell you when."

With a nod of Leary's head, Dickson pushed Ryan through the side door of the office down a long narrow hallway that led to the Judges' private elevator. At the basement level, Dickson shoved Ryan's stumbling body out of the elevator into a tunnel of walkways. Wrapping around the utility mechanical room of the courthouse, they walked from the courthouse to the door leading to the annex containing the oldest courthouse building and jail in the country. Dickson pulled Ryan up the crumbling staircase onto the first level of the jailhouse.

The grey masonry walls were scarred with long forgotten graffiti, slabs of white detritus hanging off the walls as if some giant malcontent had ripped the walls into shreds with his massive hands. The block of cells were dark except for sprigs of sunlight beaming through tiny barred windows located in each cell. No toilets were evident in the cells, just a large pail in the corner of the cell, located at the end of the rusting cots thrown against the wall. The noise of scurrying vermin could be heard but the source could not be readily seen because of the shadowy darkness of the block.

Dickson kicked Ryan into the first cell, the heel of his snakeskin boot striking Ryan just above the buttocks. He fell forward, landing on his chest and stomach, his face striking the end of the cot. Blood trickled down the side of his face from the gash forming at the far right temple of his head. His hands were still handcuffed behind his body. For the first time in years, he felt greater excruciating pain in the rest of his body than in his ailing kneecaps.

Dickson walked into the cell and unlocked the handcuffs. He

grinned sadistically when he saw the blood from Ryan's face trickling onto the debris-filled asphalt floor.

"Just like being in court, counselor," Dickson said in a gruff, deprecating voice. "I betcha you'd like to call the AG to tell him how the police beat the shit out of you, eh, counselor?"

Ryan raised himself from the floor and sat at the edge of the rusting cot. He rubbed his wrists with his hands. Observing the blood on the floor, he felt the gash at the side of his forehead.

"You're not too bright, Sergeant. You usually don't leave any scars on your victims," Ryan said, his eyes peering at the blood on the floor.

"Nobody's going to believe a washed-up rummy like you, Ryan. You drunks are always falling and hitting your heads on the gutters."

"You know I'm not going to tell you anything about my client, Dickson," Ryan said.

"We'll see. You ain't so tough outside of a courtroom, counselor. *You're in my courtroom now!*" Dickson shouted, as he drove his highheeled boot into the side of Ryan's sitting body, causing Ryan to fall onto the broken springs of the cot, his hands grabbing onto the rails in order to prevent falling onto the floor. From the sound Ryan heard, he knew Dickson had cracked one or more of his ribs. The ensuing stabbing pains in his side and abdomen proved he was right.

Dickson removed a rubber truncheon from the back of his oversized camouflage fatigues and repeatedly punched the 6 inch round object into the palm of his hand.

"Get up, you motherfucker!" Dickson yelled at Ryan, who managed to regain his sitting position on the rail of the cot.

"You should think about what you're doing, Dickson," Ryan warned, his hand rubbing his side.

"I know what the fuck I'm doing, Jew boy," Dickson replied, beads of sweat glistening on his baggy, vein-filled face. Suddenly he whacked Ryan across the back of the neck with the rubber truncheon. Ryan fell forward onto the floor, his hands barely able to prevent his face from striking the floor.

Again and again, Dickson pummeled the back of the head and neck of Ryan until Ryan's eyes closed and the only sign of life in his body was a sporadic twitching movement. Dickson suddenly stopped the barrage of blows. He closed the cell door, and peered through the bars to see if Ryan was moving. Noting the slight breathing motion of Ryan's body, he then proceeded to lock the cell door with a ring of keys dangling from his wide, turquoise-studded cowboy belt. He laughed to himself as he trudged out of the cell block to a small office located at the end of the hall. He called Leary.

Ryan was unconscious for almost an hour. He awoke to a hot streaming beam of sunlight that caught the corner of his eye. With a shivering start, his eyes opened to a blinding headache that seemed to permeate every brain cell in his head. His eyes teared from the pain. The red blood from his temple poured into the corner of his eye.

CHAPTER THIRTY-FIVE

Shirley walked to the far corner of the office and went into a small conference room. She closed the door behind her. Picking up the phone book, her eyes searched for John Olsham's home phone number. She hoped he was listed.

After a moment, she noted the business phone number of Olsham's private investigation office. She dialed the number after searching for anyone coming down the hall.

"Is John Olsham there?" She whispered into the phone.

"I'm sorry," the voice replied, "this is the answering service. Can you please give me your phone number and Mr. Olsham will call you back."

"Just tell John that Ryan's in trouble. He'll know what I mean."

She abruptly hung up the phone. Her eyes darted out the small window of the office and she noted Leary walking briskly down the hallway. She hoped no one had been listening on the line.

Olsham finished his beer draft with a gulp, as he swung his body around from the bar. It was over an hour since he had left Ryan at the courthouse entrance. He started to worry. An hour should have been enough time to sort things out with the assignment judge. Olsham knew things could happen once you entered those courthouse doors. You could lose control of your future.

He walked slowly to the pay phone located in back of the dark wood paneled bar. Why do all these raunchy country bars look alike, he thought to himself as he dialed his answering service. He was hoping that Ryan had called to explain his delay.

"Yeah . . . it's me. Who? Did you get the name?" he spoke in a rush of words into the phone speaker.

"Goddamnit, Sophie. You're supposed to get the caller's name. Now who the hell was that? She said what? Ryan was in trouble?. What the hell does that mean? In trouble with whom? Where the hell is he?" He expected answers and was frustrated when none were forthcoming.

"Okay. Next time get a number I can call back." He paused with a deep breath and spoke with the air rushing out of his mouth along with the words. "Do you have Sam Levine's phone number? Should be in the Rolodex of numbers I gave you. Yeah. L-E-V-I-N-E."

He spelled the name with an exaggerated effort.

"Look . . . he's in Florida somewhere. If you don't have it, call down to Florida. You must have a number there. Call me back here. Here's the number."

He gave the answering service the number at the bar. After he hung up the receiver, he stood against the wall for several seconds wondering what the hell to do next. He knew he should have accompanied Ryan into the courthouse. At least they would have had to dump on two people instead of one. He cursed to himself as he walked back to the long wooden bar.

"Give me another beer, Frankie," Olsham ordered to the bar-keep.

After about three beers, the pay phone rang. Olsham, slightly unbalanced from the beer, slowly walked over to the pay phone.

"Yeah . . . it's me," he said into the receiver, "That's him. Where? Turnberry? Sounds right. Yeah. North Miami. I think that's where he's at. What's the number? Wait a second, I need to get a pencil. Frankie," Olsham yelled across the bar, "Can you throw me a pencil?"

Frankie threw a pen over to Olsham, who withdrew a match-book cover from his pocket and wrote the phone number down on the inside of the cover.

"Thanks, Sophie. Good job. Yeah . . . I'll call . . . within the hour."

Olsham hung up the phone, retrieved his phone credit card from his wallet (he always forgot the number) and dialed the Florida phone number. The phone rang for about a minute. Just before Olsham was about to hang up a deep male voice muttered something into the receiver.

"This is John Olsham. Calling from Bristol. Are you Sam Levine?" Olsham asked in a hopeful voice.

"Who wants to know?"

Olsham shouted in an exasperated voice. "Look, I'm Ryan's

friend. You know Joshua Ryan? Well, if you're Sam Levine, you better stop fucking around and start to talk. Okay, I'm sorry. Things are happening so fast up here my mind is off track. Sure . . . I'll hold on." Olsham kept the receiver taut against his ear as if to loosen the grip would disconnect the voice at the other end.

"Okay . . . yeah," Olsham spoke excitedly into the phone. "Look Mr. Levine. Okay, I'll call you Sam. Y'know about the case that Ryan is handling . . . the rabbi. Yeah. That's the one. Well, we just got back with him. That's right. We brought him back to the States in one piece. Yeah, he's safe. But I'm not so sure about Joshua. What? Yeah, Joshua. Well, I left him at the courthouse about an hour ago . . . he hasn't come out. Worried? Sure I'm worried. Because my answering service got some anonymous call from a woman that said he was in trouble. I wish I knew, Sam. All I know is that he went into the courthouse over an hour ago to see the assignment judge. Yeah . . . it's still Judge King. He wanted to make a deal about bail . . . for the rabbi. Before we handed him over. Ryan was afraid what the hell they would do to him once he was in their custody."

Olsham paused in a breathless manner, put the end of the pen in his mouth and sucked on it. He listened for about a full minute before he said in a low, unsure voice, "Okay. I'll call Judge King's chamber. I don't know if he'll talk to me. If I can't get any information I'll call you back. Well," Olsham paused to think and then continued, "Maybe you should, Sam. I got a rotten gut feeling that Leary's up to something. He must have been really pissed that the captain couldn't bring the rabbi back in a cage. You know Leary . . . Yeah, fly up. Call my answering service. Here's the number."

Olsham recited the number and continued, "Just tell my girls the airline and the time you arrive. I'll pick you up. I got a 'Vette, a black 'Vette. You can't miss it. Philly Airport. Make sure you tell her which terminal. Okay, see you in a little bit. Yeah . . . I'm gonna get to the judge. Somehow. Thanks again."

Olsham placed the phone onto the cradle and quickly walked out of the bar into the rain.

CHAPTER THIRTY-SIX

Ryan tried to urinate into the rusted waste pail. As if the dam gates had been lowered, nothing came out. His ribs ached, his lower back seemed on fire with tremulous sparks running chaotically down his legs. He held onto the rail of the bed as he stood there.

Suddenly, with excruciating pain coursing through his groin and penis, chunks of blood flowed out of his penis. The blood sprayed beyond the opening of the pail, onto the blackened walls. He let out a groan as the blood continued to run out of his body. After almost a minute, the flow of liquid stopped and a horrible burning enveloped his groin area running up to his abdomen. He turned away from the pail and vomited dry phlegm over the cot. For an eternity the vomiting continued without abatement. Very little came up, just the gray sputum of bile that lodged in his throat. He gagged, his hands grabbing his throat. He couldn't breathe.

He fell to the floor, his throat in violent convulsions attempting to suck in the stagnant air of the ancient cell.

The next thing he felt was Dickson prodding him in the broken ribs with the rubber truncheon. Softly at first, but when Dickson saw Ryan's eyes open, he increased the velocity of the truncheon, right in the area of Ryan's bruised ribs.

Without mercy, Dickson pulled Ryan by his belt up from the floor and lodged him in a chair Dickson had brought into the cell.

"You're not falling asleep on me, are you, Counselor?" Dickson said, his face etched with a sadistic grin.

"Fuck you, dickhead," Ryan spat the words into Dickson's face.

Dickson lurched back in surprise, wiped the spittle from his face with the back of his cowboy shirtsleeve, then proceeded to beat Ryan across the head and back with the rubber truncheon. Ryan threw his hands up to ward off the violent blows but after a few seconds his body slumped out of the chair onto the floor.

"Get the fuck up, you motherfucker!" Dickson yelled hysterically at the inert body, his narrow-tipped snake boots kicking into Ryan's ribs.

Ryan's breathing could barely be heard. A look of sudden concern crossed Dickson's face. He knelt down to place his forefinger on Ryan's throat, when suddenly Ryan came alive and jerked his head into Dickson's face. Ryan heard Dickson's nose break, the blood rushing out of the inflamed nostrils. Dickson fell backwards. Ryan tried to raise his aching body from the ground but it wouldn't move. Dickson grabbed his bloody face, stared at Ryan attempting to rise, and then Dickson lunged forward onto the back of Ryan.

Repetitively he banged Ryan's head onto the solid asphalt floor, his right hand tearing at Ryan's hair. Up and down, Ryan's face struck the floor.

"You motherfucker . . . you fucking motherfucker!" Dickson hysterically screamed as the blood from his own face spread over the back of Ryan's head.

Dickson finally realized that Ryan was indeed unconscious. As if he had been suddenly instructed to stop, Dickson dropped Ryan's face against the bloodied ground. The corner of the cell was reddened with splotches of human blood all over the walls and floor. Surprisingly, Dickson felt his penis getting hard as he lifted himself off the still body of Ryan. He almost achieved orgasm.

Dickson left the cell and returned with a bucket of water that he dumped onto Ryan's head. Ryan still didn't move. Dickson rolled Ryan over and started to pound on Ryan's chest as if he was performing some sort of barbarous CPR. He reached over to Ryan's neck while feeling the pulse, lifted himself off his knee as he spat into Ryan's still face.

"You'll live, you motherfucker!" Dickson said as he closed the cell door with his key. "Next time, I'll kill you. Understand me? Next time, I'll send you to the other side!"

Ryan lay in a pool of blood for almost an hour. His body started to jerk spasmodically as the pelts of rain came in through the unprotected window of the cell. The rainwater slowly washed away the blood of his temple but the matted blood on the back of his head remained. His eyes opened to the crawling of a gray rat near his head. Repulsed by the sight of the rat, he turned sidewards onto his broken ribs, his body releasing a shout of pain as the weight of his body crushed on the already torn rib cage. The rat scurried into a hole in the wall located in the far corner of the cell.

"I hate rats," Ryan thought. "What am I doing lying with rats?"

The image of the rat buried into the forefront of his scarred brain. With great suffering, he managed to lift himself up off the ground onto the side of the scattered cot. Standing up, he righted the cot and sat on the rail, his hands searching his neck and head for the source of the hot shards of pain running through his head and neck.

He turned his head toward the window of the cell and realized the rain was pouring unabated into the cell. Pushing on a rusted rail of the cot with his arms, Ryan lifted himself onto his buckling legs, almost falling to the ground, grabbing onto the wall with the palm of his right hand and then stumbling over to the window. The bottom of the window was about three feet above his head, but the rainwater poured over his head and face in diagonal sheets of pleasure.

Aquarius, that's what my mother used to say I was. Water baby. "God do I miss her," he muttered to himself.

Wanting to peer out the window, Ryan reached out for the fallen chair, placed it against the cell wall under the window, and precariously stepped onto the platform of the chair, his hand placed against the cell wall. His eyes bathed in the greenery of the fields behind the old jail.

Ryan stood on the chair for almost an hour, his mind bouncing back to the disturbing past and traveling light years forward into the future. Sosie came to mind. He saw her face before him. The soft pallor of her skin, her body, and most all her caring voice. He thought she really cared for him. Why, he didn't know. He always felt that he didn't deserve to be loved. His mother would always say she loved him, that he was great and marvelous and bright, but he never believed any of it. She was a Jewish mother and all Jewish mothers tell their sons how wonderful they are.

He looked to his father for praise. It never came. Just cynical jibes that destroyed his feeling of worth. Why, you old bastard? Ryan thought and then uttered the words in a loud voice. Why was it so difficult to tell me that I was good? Even in football. You never would come right out and say I was good. Never. It was too much to expect. That fucking rummy. Why? "Dad . . ." He uttered the name in a hoarse, crying voice. "Dad," he repeated. "Why?"

He lowered himself from the chair and sat in it, the rain pouring onto the back of his bloodied head and neck. He placed his face into his hands and cried. For what, he didn't know. Was he feeling sorry for himself? Probably. Maybe it was the fear of dying in this abandoned cell. Fear . . . that is all that Joshua ever had in the last ten years. He could never seem to conquer the black side of life. "Why couldn't I be like Sosie?" he mused. Never afraid of what the future holds. She just faces the demons when they appear. No quarter given. "Teach me, Sosie," he muttered. "Tell me how . . . I'm so tired of waiting for the next attack . . . from wherever . . . and then trying to meet the challenge. And always doubting whether I can. Only in football . . . I was never afraid . . . until the tearing . . . my knees . . . the pain before and after the surgeries . . . and then . . . laying in bed . . . gathering up my fears . . . one after another . . . they ganged up on me . . . till they overwhelmed me . . . I was always afraid after that. Where are you, Sosie, my fearless one . . . Where are you?"

Ryan mused about how he wanted to grow up so fast. To get away from his father's control and his unpredictable rages. Every day was a battle to avoid him. You never knew what he would throw at you. Verbal or physical. Sometimes the words were much more punishing then his fists. 'He took away any shred of self-esteem I had built up,' he thought. Why? Was I such a hateful kid? Maybe it was my fault. Maybe it was.

Ryan remembered looking up to the fifth floor of Kings County Hospital where Michael Ryan had been placed after he fell apart, almost killing himself by jumping in front of a subway train. Drunk and sotted with the bullshit coming out of his mouth, they placed him in the psychiatric ward of the mental hospital. Joshua was barely sixteen when he saw him, pacing in that ten-by-ten foot cage. The residents following each other as if John Phillip Sousa was playing his marching music. Each tagging along after the other. A world lost to the minds of the deranged. Never me, Ryan said to himself over and over again then. I'll never be stuck in a cage. Not me. Never.

But here he was in a cage no bigger then King's County Hospital's fifth-floor cage. Except he was alone. No other residents to follow him. Perhaps to die alone.

He thought of Helen. And Sosie. They are so different. Helen was so callous, uncaring, almost enjoying my alcoholic depression. Why did she hate me so much? And why does Sosie blindly offer me herself . . . without reservation . . . and we don't even really know each other. Yet I feel I have known her all my life. What a terrible shame . . . stuck in this god-forsaken cell . . . never knowing whether I'm ever going to get out . . . and Sosie out there. Somebody I've been waiting for all my life.

The rain stopped and he could feel the emerging rays of sun start to warm his battered neck and head. He stood up, wobbled briefly, then walked slowly to the cell door. It was floor to ceiling bars. The corridor ran down toward a section of offices where Ryan could hear Dickson speaking on the phone.

Dying. He never actually thought about dying since he contemplated self-destruction when the publicity became unbearable. Except for Sam, the whole world seemed bent on destroying him. Looking out that twentieth floor window of his Philadelphia lawyer's office window, he imagined himself opening the window and diving out into the freedom of pure air, just give it all the fuck up, what else was there to do. He couldn't see the end of his troubles. How do you defend yourself when you don't even know who you are defending against?

He remembered the assistant attorney general assigned to his case. Some pimply-ass kid just out of Harvard Law wanting to make a name for himself. And Ryan was his vehicle to fame and fortune. Sitting in that dank interrogation room, the lieutenant of the state troopers to his left, and the kid Perry Mason grilling Ryan as if he were some punk kid off the street.

"Listen," the assistant AG solicited with a conciliatory voice, his smooth hands reaching out to touch Ryan, "I don't want to send you to prison. Hard time would kill you, Mr. Ryan."

He paused. The smile displaying an even row of white teeth that seemed hidden by the immaculately manicured brown mustache that bobbed up and down as he spoke, "Let me call my boss up and make a deal for you. One year . . . and maybe you're out in six months. We'll get you into the reformatory. No hard time. Y'know if the other prisoners know you're a cop . . . well, it'd be real hard on you. What do ya say?" He pleaded as if Ryan were a young virgin with his legs apart.

Sam Levine killed all that plea-bargain bullshit. With thinly veiled threats, they agreed to plead nolo contendre to the misdemeanor, no felony plea, and he walked free except for the eighteen- month probation. At least he would survive the disbarment proceedings. Suspension for six months. Sam made sure he attended the private counseling session at the Darby Clinic, a state-supported rehab institution. The Supreme Court received all the favorable reports of Ryan's rehabilitation. The Court could empathize with the human frailty of drunkenness but if he had taken a dime from anyone, Ryan would be sleeping on the Bowery; homeless and without a profession.

But you didn't jump, he thought. It worked out . . . like your childhood, it worked out. Maybe it wasn't meant to be, like his mother would always say. Not your time, Ryan.

He learned for the first time what it was to hold the wrong end of the stick. Outside of his father, he had never experienced the brutality of the outside world. The applause, the adulation of being a football hero, and then the star of the all-powerful litigation team of the Summit County prosecutor's office, it didn't prepare him for the overt scorn heaped upon his head when the accident happened.

The kid had almost died.

Aggravated assault downgraded to driving under the influence of alcohol and simple assault. The Harvard lawyer squealed like a pig. He wouldn't accept the plea-bargain. He yelled at Sam. But Sam just smiled his leprechaun's smile, more like a male Mona Lisa, Ryan thought. The AG's office didn't want the wound to fester publically. They had allowed the first assistant prosecutor to continue to try cases even though he had been openly drunk in Court on numerous occasions. The prosecutor's office should have known about Ryan's weakness long before he drove over an innocent child. Cover-up, yelled Sam Levine, the lawyer for the covered-up malfeasant. Strange to hear it from your own lawyer, Ryan thought with a smile crossing his face. That was Big Sam, he pulled rabbits out of his ass.

Yet it was never over. The shame followed him wherever he went. The whispers, the finger-pointing. Ryan knew he was the object of the silent scorn of his fellow members of the bar. They never forgave. Why should they? Ryan would always be vulnerable, roadkill for the carnivorous practitioners of the law. But now, this case, the rabbi's case, could mean resurrection, revival of his vaunted career.

He could show them all that he was still a trial lawyer. A good one.

Fatigued, he sat down on the floor, his back to the wall and fell asleep. He had no more daydreams left to hold off his sleep.

CHAPTER THIRTY-SEVEN

After Olsham picked Sam Levine up at the airport that evening, he drove directly to the Larchmont Hills police station. They were looking for Lieutenant Mathias who had already gone off duty. Reluctantly the desk sergeant phoned Mathias at home and told him that Olsham and Levine wanted to talk to him. Mathias said he would be right down.

"How the fuck do I know where he is?" Mathias shouted defensively as the three men sat around an old desk in the detectives' room on the second floor of the Larchmont Hills Police station.

"Nobody at the courthouse has seen him," Olsham replied, his teeth clenched tight against his lips.

"Maybe he left without telling you," Mathias declared. He lifted his meerschaum pipe out of his jacket pocket and stuck it into his mouth unlit.

"He would have called my answering service," Olsham insisted.

"Did you check the other bars in town?" Mathias said without meaning the words that came out.

"Not fair, Lieutenant," Levine said, his large bulky body uneasily lodged into the tattered chair he was sitting in.

"I'm sorry, Mr. Levine. I'm just angry over the whole situation. You know," Mathias sucked nervously on the stem of his pipe, "I had nothing to do with this. Y'know, indictment and all. We just passed the medical findings and the results of our investigation over to the pros' office, and . . ."

"He indicted the rabbi . . . on what?" Levine queried in a disbelieving low voice.

"Circumstantial, I guess. There's nothing in the evidence I turned over to suspect the rabbi. . . ." Mathias sat silently for a moment.

"I'm not supposed to know. But, I don't think what Leary did was right. Maybe that's why Ryan can't be found," Mathias said in almost a stammer. His mouth was dry and he appeared to be having trouble breathing.

"Are you all right, Lieutenant?" Levine asked, instinctively extending his hand to Mathias.

"Yeah. I'm fine. All this bullshit is getting to me. Listen. I found out a couple of days ago Leary had Ryan indicted on obstruction of justice charges. Nobody's supposed to know. A sealed indictment held somewhere. But Leary went ahead and indicted your boy."

"Obstructing what?" Levine asked with an incredulous look on his face.

"Helping the rabbi leave the country. Aiding and abetting a fugitive. Y'know Leary . . . he would indict his own father," Mathias replied.

"The rabbi left the county, before he was indicted, on his own accord, Lieutenant," Olsham said, his mind craving a drink.

"Maybe. But y'know the grand jury. Leary has them in the palm of his hands." Mathias's voice trailed off into an inaudible whisper. As if he were back in Brooklyn Vice, trying to defend his corrupt fellow cops. Not again, he thought angrily.

"Well, what the hell do we do now?" Olsham demanded.

"I could wake a federal judge up and petition for a writ of habeas corpus," Levine declared absentmindedly. "That's if we can locate him."

"He's up there," Olsham shouted, his face pointing in the direction of the county courthouse.

"The courthouse is closed. Maybe he's in the jail out back," Mathias wondered aloud.

"Leary wouldn't be that stupid," Levine replied. His thick-lipped mouth was vigorously chewing on two sticks of artificial sugar gum, the only taste of sweetness Sam was allowed owing to his resurging diabetes.

"Where's the rabbi?" Mathias asked.

"Safe," Olsham replied.

"I'm on your side, John," Mathias offered.

"He's not at liberty to tell you, Lieutenant" Levine interjected.

"Why not?"

"That's up to his lawyer," Levine replied.

Mathias stared quizzically into the yellow pallor of the lawyer's full-moon face. Mathias had never seen Levine in a courtroom but he heard he could make a red-neck Piney cry in a civil rights trial. He spoke simple truth, Levine did. Nothing complicated about his theories. Sam never considered himself a smart-ass. His humility was the hallmark of his openings and closings to the "simple folk," as he so affectionately called his jurors. They looked at him with an air of superiority, as if he were a simpleton trying to please them. But he always got them in the end. Hypnotically, he weaved his client's story. And that's what trials are all about.

Levine would preach to the young lawyers who had the sense to listen to his earthy wisdom. Tell a story. Like Cinderella. You're Walt Disney, hypnotizing the kids with your colorful animations. Except he did it with words. And actions. Spectators were always amazed at the litheness of his immense body. Jackie Gleason in ballet slippers. Don't move too much, he would tell his acolytes. Just enough to keep 'em awake. They want a show, give it to them. They paid for their tickets. They deserve a show, he would preach.

Sam loved the television evangelists. Jimmy Swaggart was his hero. Even after he got caught with his pants down. He still was the greatest, Sam would preach. A preacher man. That's what the world needed. More preacher men. And then when they fell to the ground you knew they were really human. It made everybody feel good when the cloth of God unraveled. Warts and all. God, I loved Jimmy Boy, Levine would mutter to anyone who would hear him. He even sent contributions into the television ministries with pugnacious barbs attached to his anonymous contributions.

He knew they didn't believe. Like he didn't believe. What's there to believe? They knew the truth and so did Sam Levine. It was money and power. With that you got laid. And he got the same thrill when he won the jury over. He had seduced them. Men and women alike. With his words. He didn't have to touch them. Physically, that is. He always touched them with the words. They never knew what hit 'em. Until they went home. They wondered why. The jurors somehow knew that they voted the right way. Sam's way.

And Ryan listened to the old weaver. Avidly. He knew a good magician when he saw one. With those chubby hands, he pulled the pigeons out of his pockets. Sam was the father Ryan never had. Not that they buddied around. Occasional drink, when Ryan drank. They ate together. Great meals by great chefs. That's the only way to live, Levine would preach.

Levine was married once. For about a year. A Russian immigrant who was waiting on tables on the East Side of New York. Before he knew it, he was her admission to the American gold fields. Citizenship. So what, he would reminisce. What difference does it make if she took him over the coals. Sam Levine never took life that seriously. He laughed at his foibles. Except for the Trial. Senator Leary's doing. They almost got him. It would have been all over. Except for a good lawyer. The one defending him.

At the end of the trial, Levine knew it was time to leave. Next time the senator would surely get him. Déjà vu, I guess, Levine thought as he observed the chaos of the detective's room around them. Now it's Ryan's turn. Again. Sam marveled that Ryan ever made it through the horrendous gauntlet of public scorn the first time. But the kid did. There was something about people like us, Sam mused. Ryan and him. Like father and son they fought off the huns of hell.

What is the threshold of pain when you finally give up? A lawyer never really wins if he's the defendant. Even after acquittal, the cloak of guilt shrouds his future forever. Why do it? Levine thought. There's easier ways to make a living. Why do it? He never knew why.

"We can't do anything tonight," Levine said as his own voice broke him out of his silent reverie.

"If he's in there," Olsham said in a dubious voice, "Y'know Sam, he might be in there with Dickson and his chums."

"Maybe I can do something," Mathias offered. "I know somebody who's got an in with the Pros's office."

Sam gazed at his wristwatch and then said,

"It's after 9."

"I'll call him," Mathias replied.

Mathias lumbered out of his chair and went into a private office in the back of the large room. He closed the door behind him.

"Should we tell him, Sam?" Olsham asked.

"What?" Levine answered in a croaky voice.

Sounds like a frog who talks, Olsham thought. "Where the rabbi is. Y'know, at Uncle Lester's."

"We'll see. Let's hear what he has to say, John."

Mathias returned slowly from the rear office. His face displayed no emotion. Sort of looked like Sergeant Friday in *Dragnet*.

"Well?" Olsham asked impatiently.

"He says he'll call," Mathias answered drily. He had stuffed tobacco in his pipe and was puffing on it in deep drags. The smell of the cherry tobacco permeated the musty room.

"Why are you doing this, Lieutenant?" Levine asked.

"Ryan always played it straight with me, Mr. Levine," Mathias replied, as he sat down in the tattered chair.

"Did you ever see him play football?" Levine asked as if he were trying to make conversation.

"I heard about him,"Mathias replied.

"Good arm but he couldn't get around the linebackers. His knees kept getting busted up," Sam said in an uncritical voice.

"We all get busted up sometimes," Mathias replied wistfully. His eyes stared out the window of the second-floor room as the rain intensified outside the station.

"He needs to get back in there again and win, Lieutenant," Levine said matter-of-factly. A trace of a grin crossed his face almost showing his small front teeth.

"I saw him once in court, y'know," Mathias said. "It was a capital case. Some guy had butchered his wife. No real evidence. Just circumstantial. Like this one. Had Buster Hatfield on the defense side. And McGowen on the bench. Hatfield was his favorite. Judge McGowen . . . they were kissing cousins from way back. No matter what Ryan did . . . McGowen would flavor his voice against the prosecution. I think it was one of Ryan's first capital cases . . . and Hatfield blew Ryan away to the jury. 'Can you believe such an inexperienced prosecutor?' Hatfield would cry to the jury."

"And Ryan just came back in his closing. Admitting he was inexperienced. Even lied to them about just being out of law school and all. He always had the innocent look. Well, Hatfield couldn't believe the jury hung his client . . . balls and all. I heard that Hatfield crawled back to McGowen's chambers crying like a baby. Just couldn't believe a young punk like Ryan could beat him. McGowen wanted to grant a new trial . . . but Ryan was careful.

He made no mistakes that McGowen could sink his teeth into. Anyway, I don't think Hatfield ever took Ryan for granted after that."

The telephone in the rear office rang. Mathias painfully lifted his weathered body out of the chair and slowly walked to the office. He closed the door behind him. Both Levine's and Olsham's eyes followed Mathias to the office.

For about a minute or so Mathias listened. Grunting a few affirmative responses into the phone, Mathias hung up the receiver and walked back to the table where Olsham and Levine were seated. He sat down in his chair, pulled out a bag of tobacco and stuffed a new wad into the bowl of the pipe. Carefully he lit the bowl with a shiny silver lighter. Puffing expansively on the pipe for several seconds, he said in almost a southern drawl, "He's in there all right."

"Ryan?" Olsham shouted.

"Yeah. Ryan. My guy's contact saw Ryan in Leary's office about three or so. Next thing she saw . . . my guy has a girlfriend in Leary's office. The next thing she saw Ryan was gone."

"Where?" Levine asked impatiently.

"Don't know," Mathias replied. "but she also saw Dickson in one of the offices. She thinks Dickson has something to do with Ryan's disappearance."

"Where the hell could they keep him?" Olsham asked.

"If he was put in the county jail . . . I can find out. But I don't think that he's there," Mathias declared.

"The only other place . . . well, it hasn't been used for twenty years," he added.

"The old jail?" Olsham asked.

"Maybe," Mathias offered. "There's a corridor in the basement of the new courthouse that leads to the old courthouse and the jail. Nobody ever uses it anymore."

"Anyway to get into it?" Levine asked.

"Not that I know about, unless you have a key," Mathias said.

"Unless we break in," Olsham declared. He rose from his chair and walked to the window. The heavy rain pelted the closed window like a crazy series of drumbeats.

"That's a first-class felony," Mathias instructed.

"So what? If he's in there with Dickson . . . what's a first-class B&E against murder, Lieutenant?" Olsham asked in a biting voice.

"I don't think Dickson would be that stupid," Mathias replied.

"Tell that to the black hitchhiker he stuffed into the trunk of his trooper car ten years ago, Lieutenant," Olsham's voice rose angrily.

"There's been times Sergeant Dickson has not shown discretion in the past, Lieutenant," Levine said. Rising from his chair, Levine walked over to the automatic candy and gum machine, dropped two quarters into the machine and picked up the Trident package out of the deposit slot. He unwrapped the gum and shoved two pieces into his mouth.

"What do you want to do, Mr. Levine?" Mathias asked.

"Will you help, Lieutenant?" Levine replied.

"Maybe. Wouldn't it be better to get that writ?"

"No grounds, Lieutenant. No federal judge is going to stick his neck out and grant one unless we have something more concrete than an anonymous tip that Ryan is being kept in an old jail against his will."

"My guy is reliable."

"We'll need more," Levine replied.

"We don't have time to fuck around doing it the right way!" Olsham shouted in an unrestrained voice.

"We're all anxious about him, John," Levine declared in a calm, hoarse voice.

"Let's call Yehuda," Olsham announced suddenly.

"What does Yehuda know about the old jail?" Levine asked.

"He knows how to break into it," Olsham replied as if he were critiquing an actor in a play.

"I thought he was a tourist guide," Sam replied innocently.

"He is . . . but he does other things." Olsham walked nervously to the window as the full moon broke through the disappearing rain clouds. "It's stopped raining."

"The only way I can see getting in is through the roof," Mathias volunteered.

"We'll need some cutting tools." Olsham turned and walked to the opening of the staircase.

"Where are you going, John?" Levine's voice was unnerved by the skittish movements of Olsham.

"To get Yehuda."

"They have telephones." Levine rose from the chair and lumbered to the next desk with a phone sitting on top of it. "What's Uncle Lester's number, John?"

"I'll call. Uncle Lester doesn't answer the phone unless he knows you." Olsham picked up the phone and dialed the number.

"Since you are on board, Lieutenant, the rabbi is with Uncle Lester," Levine confessed.

"Now all I have to find out is who Uncle Lester is," Mathias replied.

"Lester," Olsham barely whispered into the phone. "Yes it's me, don't hang up."

Olsham shouted hurriedly into the receiver, "I'm at the station. Larchmont Hills. Yes . . . Little Jerusalem."

Olsham's voice continued in a hurried prattle as if the speed of his words could decide life or death. "Forget about it, Uncle. Yes, the Jews haven't put me in jail. Is Yehuda there?"

Olsham's knuckles rapped loudly on the hard-topped desk as he waited on the phone.

"Yehuda," he said with a sigh of relief, "we can't find him. Mathias thinks he could be in the old jail. Yes . . . next to the courthouse. The problem is we have to get in tonight."

He paused to listen, his knuckles rapping louder in intensity.

"Ask Uncle Lester what tools he has there. We'll need something to cut through a roof. I think it's flat . . . tar and plaster," Mathias said.

"I wonder if Leary knows?" Mathias asked.

"Dickson wouldn't do anything on his own," Levine replied, his bespectacled eyes concentrating on Olsham at the phone.

"Where's the captain?"

"Not far from Leary."

"I can't believe the captain would be part of all this," Mathias said.

"Murder is only one level removed from kidnapping, Lieutenant. The captain is caught in a box. He's old and tired and he wants to just sit out there and fish in the warm sun. I know how he feels. Except I hate to fish."

Olsham hung up the receiver.

"So," Levine asked of Olsham.

"Yehuda is taking Lester's pickup truck. I just hope Uncle Lester has the right tools."

"How's the rabbi?" Levine asked.

"Nervous. He feels responsible for Ryan."

"We better go," Olsham announced as he headed toward the staircase.

"You sure you want to go, Lieutenant?" Sam stared into the immobile square-jawed face of the policeman.

"Someone has to protect you criminals." Mathias's face broke into a wide, affectionate smile. The deep ridges of skin crinkled under his eyes.

Olsham led the trio down the steps of the police station into the warm evening night.

CHAPTER THIRTY-EIGHT

Ryan woke up with a nervous start, hitting his head against the cell wall. A small lightbulb swayed back and forth in the corridor outside his cell. The spray of light from the bulb glared into Ryan's eyes, as his hand rubbed the newly injured top of his head. The only other light in the cell block emerged from the office at the end of the corridor.

Ryan crawled to his knees and tried to pull himself up along the wall. His head was filled with pain and sleeplessness, his mouth oven-dry. Where did all my spit go, he thought as he searched for saliva in his mouth with his tongue.

His eyes absentmindedly glossed over the graffiti scribblings on the wall. Almost fully extended, his arms braced against the wall, the corner of his eye stopped at the frantic scratchings etched into the wall. Ryan brought his face closer, his nose almost touching the slimy wall. He moved his head to the side to allow the fickle shafts of light from the corridor bulb to highlight the several words inscribed in the wall.

Help me . . . Help me, Ryan read. He squinted his eyes in an attempt to read the unclear signature under the pleadings. Just barely he deciphered the name. *Elias Rubin*, and a date under the name. *1972, June.*

The seven had a line through it, similar to how the Europeans wrote their sevens, Ryan thought, his head's confusion slowly clearing.

Ryan pulled his hands from the wall and stared at the writing.

Elias Rubin, he repeated the name to himself. 1972. He muttered. What the hell was happening in 1972? He thought the jail was closed. The Vietnam War came to mind. Protests. Fort Dix. Summit County was a hotbed of antiwar demonstrators that surrounded the bases. Down from New York. "Before my time," he thought. The new jail was overflowing. Probably used this old jail for the overflow.

Elias Rubin, he muttered again. As he held his hands against the cold steely bars, his head ruminated back to his student days. He was in high school in New York but he followed the rebels. Mostly from New York. Jews and blacks together, just like in the old civil rights days in the South in the '60s. It must have been like the south in the '60s in good ol' Summit County, he mused sardonically. Blacks and Jews together. Ryan smiled at the thought of blacks and Jews marching down Main Street in protest.

Senator Leary would never have allowed it. The Klan had their headquarters in Bristol. The rumors about the bonfire meetings in the Pines still persevered twenty-five years later. All the good ol' boys were there. White sheets and all. Didn't Roger mention the burnings when he was drunk out of his mind at Carlisle? The old senator would take the young boy to the meetings. To get him good and ready to lead the good ol' boys in the future.

Ryan sat down against the wall, his hand rubbing his forehead in a spirited effort to recollect the ramblings of Roger Leary. It was hard to decipher what he said when he had too much to drink, Ryan thought. His lips got thick, swollen from the beer but the words flowed unevenly from Roger's mouth. 'The nigger from New York,' Ryan remembered that Roger would repeat the phrase time and time again. Like he was trying to purge some horrible event from his subconscious.

Roger had few misgivings or scruples but the "nigger burning" seemed to have cornered the slim line of morality that nestled in the cracks of Leary's insulated conscience. At times, Roger wanted to tell his ol' buddy, Joshua Ryan, about it, but he never went that far. And Ryan didn't want to know. He realized even then that Leary was his meal ticket to a trial position in Summit County and if Leary told him something that was shady, Ryan might have to reveal it. . .ethics and all.

With the heel of his hand, Ryan smacked his forehead as if the self-abuse would jog his memory.

Elias Rubin! He almost shouted. Sure . . . the black fellow. His mother was a Jew. But he used to boast about his blackness. Columbia University. The student riots in the '60s. Great speaker . . . had a following that would follow him to hell. Anyway to Summit County . . . the military bases . . . The TV stations loved it. "The Black

Jew!" Ryan thought. What a combination to fuck with in Summit County in the '70s. The senator must have had a heart attack. His sense of order destroyed. The senator and his reactionary cronies had held the big-city libertines at the gates for fifteen years . . . but the antiwar demonstrators would not be held forever in restraints by a bunch of Pinies.

They never found Rubin again. Disappeared from the face of the earth. The FBI scoured Summit County for his whereabouts, Nixon trying to divert attention from Watergate to the good deed of fighting his own reactionaries. Kill two birds with one stone. "Nike" they called Rubin. "Nigger-kike," to the unappreciative rednecks.

"He was here!" Ryan shouted. 'Where did they put him?' he asked himself. "That's what Roger has over all these mothers," Ryan exclaimed aloud, not caring if Dickson heard him or not.

The door to the office creaked open as Dickson strode menacingly down the corridor, the rubber truncheon in his right palm swinging alongside his stocky body. He stopped at the cell door. Ryan looked up from his seated position, a wisp of a smile on his blood-clotted face.

"You're up, Counselor?" Dickson's face lit up with a sadistic grin, displaying his gap-toothed mouth.

"Do we need any more persuasion, Counselor?" Dickson added as he opened the cell door.

"The rabbi went to heaven, you motherfucker!" Ryan shouted as he jumped to his feet and brought his hand to Dickson's throat. Dickson was caught off-guard momentarily as the two bodies hurtled out of the cell-door opening into the corridor. Regaining his composure, Dickson brought the truncheon up under the chin of Ryan's face, snapping Ryan's head back against the steel bars of the cell. In slow motion, Ryan's body slumped down the bars of the cell and he crumbled on the gray-painted asphalt floor. Ryan's tongue lay askew out of his mouth as blood seeped onto his lips, his eyes still open but lifeless. Dickson thought Ryan was dead as he knelt by the inert body to confirm. Ryan had stopped breathing. Feeling no pulse, Dickson rose and quickly walked up the corridor to the office.

CHAPTER THIRTY-NINE

Yehuda and Olsham left the pick up truck parked against the curb in front of the old jail. Remaining inside were Levine and Mathias in the passenger seats. Both stayed silent as their eyes followed Yehuda and Olsham as they climbed up the extension ladder placed against the side of the red-brick jailhouse.

After both Olsham and Yehuda reached the flattop roof of the jail, Yehuda pulled the ladder onto the rooftop of the one-story building. The two men half crouched along the roof of the jail until they stood over the air vent in the middle of the rooftop.

Mathias puffed nervously on his pipe, his eyes staring out the windshield of the battered truck. Levine played with the volume nob of the old car radio and stopped at the classical station aired from Philadelphia.

"When I lived up here, I had season's tickets to the concerts," Levine said in a mellow voice.

"We go every once in awhile. . . Joanne likes to go. . .I like country." Mathias paused and then turned his head to look at Levine's smiling face.

"I spent a summer in Colorado listening to country music," Levine replied. "Real country."

"The only kind," Mathias agreed as his eyes observed the Bristol police car slowly winding its way up Main Street toward the truck.

"Friends, I hope," Levine said as he saw the approaching patrol car.

"We'll see. Some of these Bristol cops believe in shooting first and asking questions later."

The patrol car stopped in the street opposite the parked truck. The driver of the car flashed a handheld searchlight into the cab of the truck. Mathias leaned forward from the passenger seat and declared in a voice bordering on loud, "Hi, gentlemen, I'm Lieutenant Mathias from Larchmont Hills. Just waiting for a buddy to come out of the Washington House up the street."

Mathias referred to the corner bar located at the end of Main Street.

The policeman driver focused the light on Mathias's face.

"Hi, Lieutenant," the policeman said, "We've had a rash of burglaries on this street in the past week."

"It's that Philadelphia crowd, officer. If I see anything suspicious I'll call it in."

"Thanks, Lieutenant," the officer replied as his flashlight pointed to the rooftop of the old jail. Observing nothing unusual on the rooftop, the policeman pulled his patrol car up the main street.

"Glad you're here, Lieutenant," Levine remarked with a deep sigh.

"They'll be back. We've got fifteen minutes, Mr. Levine."

Yehuda and Olsham started to cut through the tar paper roof with the battery-operated circular saw, the grating noise reverberating ominously over the quiet street. Levine's forehead broke out into a cold sweat. Mathias increased the puffs on the stem of his pipe.

Suddenly the noise stopped. Levine could no longer see the bodies of Yehuda and Olsham on top of the roof. They had suddenly vanished.

Yehuda dropped the ladder down the opening in the roof until the bottom of the ladder struck the asphalt floor of the old jail. Bracing the ladder against the opening in the roof, he climbed down the ladder to the floor below. Olsham followed. The darkness was pervasive. They both dropped to the floor, not knowing where they were. Sounds could be heard emanating from the other end of the jail.

"Where the hell are we?" Olsham whispered as he crouched against the wall of the corridor.

"It's my first visit here, John," Yehuda replied sardonically. "I think we hit the corridor between the cells. I hope we're not in a goddamn cell."

The light at the end of the corridor suddenly reflected toward them.

"Get down!" Yehuda warned, as he dropped to the floor. Olsham followed automatically.

"The ladder!" Yehuda muttered under his breath.

"Can't do anything about it now," Olsham replied.

The light sprayed the wall passing the ladder, then reversed and focused on the ladder.

"They got the ladder!" Olsham whispered to Yehuda, who was crawling along the corridor against the cell doors.

"Forget the ladder," Yehuda whispered angrily.

The light suddenly blinked off, leaving the corridor in total darkness.

"What happened?" Olsham croaked in a fearful voice as he crawled along the wet floor.

"Whoever it is, he's too far away to see the ladder. Just take it slow, John."

"Its like being back in Vietnam," Olsham replied as he pulled alongside Yehuda. They both rested against the cell bars, breathing heavily.

"We're out of shape," Yehuda said breathlessly.

"So how do you like America?" John asked with a chuckle in his voice.

"Next time, I take another tour."

They both silently laughed.

"Where do you think he is?" Yehuda asked as he raised himself to a standing position.

"Joshua? Probably in one of these cells. I've been here one time before. I think this corridor leads to the end of the cells and into the front office."

"There's a light at the end of the corridor," Yehuda observed.

They both stood momentarily against the wall of bars of the cells.

"We gotta move along, Yehuda," John instructed.

"I'm trying to get used to the darkness." Yehuda paused and then started to inch down the corridor, "Okay, let's move . . . quietly . . ."

Olsham followed behind Yehuda.

After lumbering about 100 feet or so, they observed the swinging lightbulb in the front of the corridor. They saw Ryan's body slumped against the bottom of the bars on the floor outside the cell.

Yehuda rushed to the unmoving body. Quickly, he straddled Ryan's body and applied CPR against the still abdomen.

"Is he alive?" Olsham asked as he dumbly stood at the side of Yehuda's ministrations.

"Barely. He swallowed something. Probably his own blood," Yehuda declared as he continued to feverishly pound against Ryan's chest with the heel of his hand. Frantically Yehuda moved his hands under Ryan's diaphragm in order to jump-start the breathing process. After about thirty seconds, Ryan's eyes blinked sluggishly and he started to cough up chunks of blood onto Yehuda's chest.

"Your friend is alive," Yehuda announced as he lifted himself off Ryan's now breathing body.

Yehuda and Olsham reflexively turned their heads toward the far office door as it slammed open against the wall. Dickson's broad body could be easily seen as he quickstepped down the corridor.

"Hey!" Dickson yelled at the standing men alongside the semi-conscious body of Ryan. He pulled his sidearm out as he menacingly stepped up to the three men, pointing the 9mm at them.

"Put it away, Sergeant," Olsham warned. "You've done enough for one night."

"Fuck you, Olsham. You broke into a government facility."

"Almost killing a defendant's lawyer doesn't hold you up for a Nobel Peace Prize," Olsham replied.

"He's a fugitive. I'm just doing my duty."

"Yeah . . . tell that to the assignment judge, Dickson."

Yehuda walked in front of Ryan's body and spread his legs into an offensive straddle, his hands in front of his thighs. Yehuda warned, "Put the gun away, Detective."

"You're all under arrest," Dickson replied, as the words tumbled out of his mouth.

Ryan's eyes sparkled as he observed Olsham and Yehuda above him. Yehuda's face was a blank mask, offering no emotion. Dickson stepped closer to Yehuda, the 9mm held firmly in his right hand pointed at Yehuda's abdomen.

"Lieutenant Mathias is sitting outside, Dickson," Olsham warned.

"So what?" Dickson replied, with a sneer across his blustering face.

"I'm only doing my duty. Counselor here is my guest. He's here for a friendly interrogation. Voluntarily like."

"Give me the gun," Yehuda asked dispassionately, his left hand reaching for the gun.

"You're all going to be my guests. Breaking and entering into a government facility is a first-class felony in this-here state," Dickson warned as he reached for a set of handcuffs hanging on his belt.

"Just turn around and put your hands against the bars like good little boys." He waved the barrel of the gun at Yehuda and Olsham.

Yehuda's extended left hand jerked upward and across like a bolt of steel striking the right forearm of Dickson's gun hand. Wincing with pain, the gun dropped from Dickson's hand. The heavy metallic sound of the gun hitting the asphalt floor reverberated through the eerie silence of the old jail causing several resident bats to flutter from the eaves of the ceiling.

Yehuda whirled his body away from the frantic Dickson, who attempted to retrieve the gun from the floor. Yehuda's left leg rocketed out from his body catching Dickson in the chest as Dickson bent toward the ground. Dickson fell backwards, his body forced against the corridor's wall. With a gymnast's agility, Dickson recovered his balance and lunged headlong at the turned body of Yehuda striking him in the rib cage. Yehuda fell to the ground, Dickson straddling Yehuda's unprotected side as he viciously pummeled Yehuda's head. Yehuda responded by driving his free elbow into the abdomen of Dickson's flailing body.

While still on the ground, Yehuda's heel of his right foot lashed out and struck Dickson in the testicles, causing Dickson to scream hysterically from the mind-bending pain coursing through his entire body. Yehuda rose, touched the blood pouring out from his nose and then turned momentarily away from Dickson.

Dickson dove for the gray-barrelled 9mm lodged against the outside corner of the nearby cell. Ryan's leg appeared from nowhere, the heel of his foot cracking Dickson's arched kneecap. Dickson grabbed the injured kneecap and cried out in savage pain, his body falling backwards against the unconscious Yehuda. Olsham reached down and picked up the gun and coolly swiped the butt of the 9mm against Dickson's skull. Dickson rolled away from Yehuda, blood pouring out from an open gash in his head, his eyes staring blankly up at the ceiling.

"You didn't have to do that, John," Ryan preached softly.

"He was resisting arrest, Joshua. Plain as day. Just doing what Dickson would do in the same situation."

"Help me up, John," Ryan asked.

"You look like you did after the homecoming game at Penn State when the line mauled the shit out of you, Josh."

Ryan smiled, caked blood dotting his face.

"What do we do with Dickson?" Olsham asked of Ryan, who had rose and stood over the unconscious body of Dickson.

"We leave him here. I'm sure he'll forget tonight's activities."

"What about you? We'd better do something about you."

"It's a trade-off, John. If I bring charges against Dickson, he counters with assault on a police officer, B&E against you and whatever other bullshit charges Leary comes up with. It all washes out anyway at the pretrial conference." Ryan paused and then walked back into his cell. Leaning against the lower portion of the wall, pain shooting through his entire body, he fingered the etched inscription.

"You see that, John." Ryan pointed to the name. *Elias Rubin*. The date inscribed under it, 1972. "Remember 1972, John? You were still a noncom in the army."

"I missed all the hullabaloo. What are you getting at?"

"The riots at the bases . . . spilled out to Bristol. It was led by a brown-skinned Jew named Elias Rubin. He was here one day and gone the next."

"I read about it . . . but nobody ever found the body."

"He was here. Right here in the old jail. The same cell where I spent the night."

"Sam's outside. Wasn't he assistant pros in those day?" Olsham asked.

"Anyway, Yehuda looks like he's ready to leave. Hey, Yehuda, how you feeling?"

"Like an elephant sat on my head," Yehuda replied.

"Is he dead?" Yehuda added, as he stared at the lifeless body of Dickson.

"Should be," Olsham responded, nudging his toe against Dickson's body.

"He's alive," Olsham added as Dickson's chest convulsed for air.

"How do we get out of here?" Ryan queried.

"Either we bust out of the front door or climb the ladder up through the roof," Olsham replied.

Yehuda walked to the office at the end of the corridor. Facing the front door of the jail, he kicked at the decaying, flaked wooden door. After several attempts, the wooden slats of the tall entranceway buckled and the door disintegrated into broken shards of wood.

"Gentlemen," Yehuda bowed and beckoned Ryan and Olsham to follow him through the opening in the fractured door.

Levine and Mathias exited the cab of the truck and met the trio in the middle of the dirt path leading from the jail. Levine wrapped his beefy arms around Ryan and hugged him to his chest. Ryan groaned in pain.

"Sorry, Sam . . . the ribs," Ryan declared in a muffled voice.

"We thought the son of a bitch killed you!" Levine replied, tears welling up in his eyes.

"Almost," Ryan muttered.

Mathias removed his black leather jacket and wrapped it around Ryan's shoulders.

"I'm sorry," Mathias said.

"For what?" Ryan replied.

"For all the good cops out there who get tainted by a degenerate like Dickson."

From the near distance, the lights of the approaching patrol car could be seen.

"Guys . . . help Joshua into the back of the truck . . . Hurry . . . ," Mathias instructed. "Sam and I will get into the cab. No need to raise any flags with these township cops."

Following Mathias's instructions, Ryan, Yehuda, and Olsham crawled into the truck bed facing down on the steel ribs of the platform. Ryan's body pulsated with intense pain. Mathias and Levine entered the cab just as the patrol car pulled alongside of the truck.

"Still here, Lieutenant?" The young policeman asked in a noticeably suspicious voice.

"Still here," Mathias smiled as he lit his pipe with a silver lighter.

"Well, be careful, Lieutenant. The town has changed since I

was a kid," the policeman declared. "Before all these yambos came across the bridge." He smiled a knowing smile.

"Yeah," Mathias replied. "That's progress, I guess."

The policeman laughed and drove slowly down the deserted street. At the direction of Olsham, Mathias drove the rusted pick-up truck out of Bristol along the perimeter road running outside of the sanctified Pine Barrens.

"Nobody lives out there," Mathias yelled back at Ryan, now sitting on the tool chest situated on the edge of the truck-bed.

"My Uncle Lester does," Olsham yelled in retort.

"Since when?" Mathias asked.

"Since he got booted out of the state troopers for drinking on duty. And other things he wouldn't do," Olsham declared, the pine breeze hitting him in the face as he sat next to Ryan on the elevated tool chest. Yehuda had rolled over on his back and stared quietly at the starry sky.

"I thought these were sacred lands," Levine chimed in.

"Not to Uncle Lester. He built a log cabin out here in no-man's land. Nobody bothers him and he doesn't bother anyone either," Olsham replied.

"I guess your client is out here?" Mathias asked of Ryan.

"You guessed right, Lieutenant." Ryan gingerly moved over to the other side to sit on the railing of the truck-bed and then shouted at Levine. "Sam, have you ever heard of a guy named Elias Rubin? Sometime back in 1972. June, I think. Have you?"

"Sure, why do you ask, Josh?"

"His name was etched on the jail's wall. With the words *Help me* over his name. Wasn't he the Columbia University rebel leader during the Chicago Riots in 1968?"

"Great speaker. Heard him speak in New York. At Foley Square. Right in front of the federal courthouse." Sam replied in a thoughtful voice. "Must have been 25 years ago. He disappeared suddenly. Right around here."

"I know," Ryan agreed, his eyes noting the truck entering a little-used dirt path winding its way through clumps of pine trees reaching out across the path.

"You were in the pros's office then, Sam. Did they ever find anything. Didn't they have the feds out here?"

"Sure. They had dogs, helicopters. Even Nixon made a visit to appease the black voters. It happened during the 1972 presidential campaign," Levine said.

"And what happened?" Ryan persisted.

"Nothing," Olsham interjected. "We found nothing."

"Or maybe you were told to find nothing, John," Ryan said.

"The senator was the pros then," Levine declared, as the truck slowed down to a dead end in the path.

"This is it." Olsham jumped over the truck-bed railing onto the white sandy ground.

"This is what?" Mathias questioned as he slowly exited the cab.

"Lester's compound." Olsham laughed.

"I don't see anything." Mathias replied.

"You will. Follow me. It's way back in the woods. Watch out for rattlers." Olsham chuckled innocently.

They could hear the raucous barking of a large dog coming out of a wood fenced compound no more than a hundred feet from the end of the dirt road.

"That's Lyndon Junior," Olsham reported.

"The dog?" Levine questioned.

"Named after our great president. Uncle Lester revered Lyndon Johnson. Another Piney like Lester. Anyway, Lester has had Lyndon Junior for about ten years. Before that, he had the original Lyndon for God knows how long," Olsham stated as he led the men into the compound. From the near distance, they could see the glow of oil lamps issuing from the inside of a one-room log cabin seemingly caught in a time warp.

"Lester!" Olsham yelled.

"It's me, John Boy . . . keep Lyndon inside the house."

"Lyndon don't like strangers," Olsham addressed to the group followers.

Trudging through the pine-covered ground, occasionally tripping over hidden tree stumps, the group approached the log cabin. Except for the full moon, the log cabin could be missed by the unwary pedestrian. Then the barking resumed. Loud and threatening, the barking continued unabated.

"Hope his bark is worse than his bite," Ryan stated, a note of fear in his voice.

"He's a dear," Olsham replied. "Once he gets to know you."

"If we get that far." Ryan said.

"Uncle! Are you there?" Olsham yelled as he stopped the group about ten feet from the front door.

A giant head of a German shepherd appeared in the open window alongside the front door. Foam coming out of its mouth, it had its massive paws on the front sill, its body primed to leap forward.

"He doesn't look friendly, John," Levine declared as he stopped in his tracks.

"Lester!" Olsham shouted. "Goddamnit, Lester. Where the hell are you?"

Suddenly, a half-nude cadaver-like figure threw the log cabin front door open, a 30-30 double barrel shotgun cradled comfortably in his hairy arms.

"Who is there?" Lester croaked, his hand over his eyes as if to ward off the glare of sunlight in the pitch-black night.

"It's John Boy!" Olsham yelled.

"Stay here, fellows," Olsham added as he strode quickly up the barely discernable sandy path to the front door. The figure leveled the shotgun toward Olsham.

"Put that fucking shotgun away, you old fool!" Olsham yelled.

"You gotta be careful, John. Those galoots out there, just waiting for me to let my guard down," Lester's deep baritone voice sounded as if somebody was rubbing two pieces of sandpaper together.

"Come in, gentlemen," John shouted to the four waiting men.

"Who are these fellows?" Lester asked demandingly.

"Lester, you already met Ryan and Yehuda. The other two are friends also."

"You got a lot of friends lately, John."

"Call Lyndon off," Olsham instructed.

"He won't hurt—he's a pussycat," Lester replied and then added, "Lyndon, get your ass off that window sill!" The dog obeyed immediately and loped across the cabin and laid down in front of a giant rock fireplace.

The cabin walls were covered with photos of Lester in a state trooper's uniform performing various feats of police work. The eclectic pieces of furniture that filled the cabin gave off the impression that a deranged interior decorator had deposited all her unwanted furniture in Lester's cabin. Stationed in the middle of the one-room cabin was a shredded couch, the springs of the undercarriage clearly showing. Several wooden chairs dotted the remainder of the cabin. The only light came from two oil lamps situated at either end of the cabin. Covering the wooden floor was a polar-bear skin, its whiteness dulled by stains and muddy debris. The smell of unwashed bodies and dog urine permeated the dark cabin air.

Lester smiled a craggy-toothed smile showing the four remaining teeth in his mouth as he greeted the assemblage.

"Never had so many people in my cabin at one time," he coughed as he spoke, a smoker's hack.

"How long you been out here, Lester?" Levine asked as he walked over to the fireplace.

"Thirty years come November," he answered quite proudly.

"Lester is half Indian," Olsham declared. "The Powhatens. The same tribe that Pocahontas came from. The other half is drunken Irish, eh, Lester?"

Lester cackled as he showed the quart of whiskey he had hidden behind him.

"Drink anyone?" He offered the bottle magnanimously to the circle of men surrounding him.

"Lester makes his own stuff here," Olsham informed. "Right behind the outside door there. He has a still that rivals Jim Beam."

"Got my grandaddy's recipes," Lester said. "Straight from Virginia."

"How long was he a state trooper?" Mathias asked of Olsham, who had retrieved a warm bottle of beer from a wooden box in the corner of the room.

"About six years. He was disabled out." Olsham pointed his forefinger to his head.

"I ain't crazy, John," Lester replied, somewhat offended.

"I didn't say you were, Lester."

"They got to me," Lester rambled in a hoarse voice. "They wanted me to do things I didn't think were right."

"Lester knew Elias Rubin," Olsham announced.

"That guy from New York," Lester added. "Talked too much. The senator didn't like people who talked too much."

"Lester drove the senator around in the senator's Mercedes," Olsham declared.

"The senator didn't like anyone who told him what to do," Lester said, as he lifted the quart bottle of liquor to his mouth and chugged. Wiping his mouth with his scrawny bare arm, shaking his head like a wet dog trying to get dry, he smiled happily, his eyes glazed over with a dull film.

"He talked too much," Lester repeated. "They weren't going to do him. Y'know . . . but he kept on talking. Liberal bullshit. They had the fire going. The cross and everything. Didn't seem to scare this fellow. He smiled a lot. Like someone was protecting him." Lester laughed an evil laugh and then continued, "Well, nobody was there to protect him. Nobody at all. Should have kept his mouth shut."

"What happened, Lester?" Mathias asked.

Lester had moved himself in front of the fireplace to a slat-backed wooden chair. He glanced over at Olsham, who nodded his head.

"John doesn't like me to tell the story . . . right, John?" Lester said as he stared at Olsham.

"If you want, Lester," Olsham replied.

"Tell us what?" Ryan demanded in a strong voice.

"He was there. Lester was there," Olsham reported. "He drove the senator to the meetings. Out at the Piney campground," Olsham reported.

"By the way, where's the rabbi, Lester?" John added suddenly.

"Oh, that fellow you left here. He wanted to get some fresh air. He'll be back, he said," Lester replied.

"I told you to keep him here, Lester," Olsham answered in an aggravated voice.

"He wanted to look at the lake."

"What lake?" Ryan asked, equally fearful about the rabbi's disappearance.

"They got a spring back there." Olsham pointed toward the rear of the cabin.

"He wanted to see where they did in that New York fellow. He said he had heard some rumor about what happened at the campsite. But I didn't tell him, John," Lester said.

"Rubin?" Ryan asked.

- 217 -

"That's the guy. Didn't look like a Jewish fellow . . . black . . . not dark but still black."

"We better start looking for the rabbi," Ryan instructed as he limped toward the front door.

"Stay put, Josh. You're in no condition to go hiking out there," Olsham said.

"Anyway, you'd get lost out there. We'd have to search for both of you. The back only goes to the lake . . . and then it drops off to nothing. There's a small mountain out there. Dead ends. He can't climb it. Anyway, at the base of the mountain there is a campground. I think the cross is down. It's just a bunch of dirt and old ashes."

"So what happened to this black kid?" Mathias asked insistently.

"Lester was told to leave," Olsham declared.

"But I didn't," Lester replied. "I knew something was up. That guy was shooting his mouth off about something or other. I seen Dickson . . . my old buddy . . . punch him in the mouth. Well, let me tell you, that nigger got right up laughing. Dickson couldn't believe that anyone would laugh at him. So he hit him again. Then he kicked him in the stomach . . . when he was down. That sucker didn't laugh anymore. Just laid there . . . like a sack of shit."

"They kill him?" Mathias asked.

"Not then. After a spell he got up again. I was hiding behind the trees. Scared shit they were going to find me. Dickson pulled out his gun. That big piece he always carried. Told the black fellow to jump into the fire."

"Did he?" Levine chimed in incredulously.

"You crazy?" Lester shrieked. "That nigger was no dumb nigger from Philly. He told Dickson to jump into the fire himself. He shouldn't have laughed again. Right into Dickson's face. Right in front of all them people. Dickson didn't like that."

"Lester . . . stop creeping around," Olsham declared, "Tell them what happened already."

"Two troopers . . . including Dickson . . . grabbed the guy around the neck . . . and tossed him into the fire. A real bonfire it was. Well," Lester swigged down a good part of the quart bottle of liquor again, the brown clear liquor dripping down his hairless chin. "He crawled out. His shirt's on fire. But he crawled around on the ground yelping and screaming. Everybody just looking at him. You couldn't see who was there because they all had them white hoods on. Dickson kicked him again. He tried to run away . . . crawling around on all fours. But Dickson kicked him in the ribs . . . with those steel-jacketed boots. That sorta let the air out of the nigger's chest. He just dropped on the ground like a sack of potatoes. Then the senator got tired of all that bullshit, and he told Dickson to get on with it."

"Who was there?" Ryan asked impatiently.

"Couldn't tell. Except for that kid. He weren't wearing a hood."

"What kid?" Ryan asked.

"The Leary kid. The senator's son. He was always there. The senator was sort of breaking him in. To keep up the ol' family tradition, I guess."

"And then what happened?" Ryan persisted.

"I guess the senator was tired. It was getting late, y'know. So he told Dickson and his buddy to grab the nigger and tie him to the stake."

"Where was the stake?" Ryan asked.

"Right behind the fire. The fire was just starting to grow back towards the stake."

Suddenly the booming voice of the rabbi blasted from the front door. He walked confidently into the room and walked to the fireplace hearth.

"We thought you were lost, Rabbi," Ryan said.

"I was . . . but I traced my footsteps back. Not much out there," he paused and then added cryptically, "except for that campsite."

"Nothing there," Olsham reported.

"The ashes," the rabbi replied. "The ashes are still there."

"Just pine boughs and white sand, Rabbi."

"Elias Rubin . . ." Ryan absentmindedly muttered the name.

"Rabbi . . . Elias Rubin. Have you ever heard?" Ryan's sentence dropped off as the rabbi's face contorted in obvious pain.

"He was my sister's boy," the rabbi finally said in a low voice, barely audible. The diminutive rabbi walked toward the window and looked outside.

Each member of the group, except for Lester who was still swigging on the almost disappearing whiskey in the quart bottle, looked at each other. Ryan walked over to the rabbi, who was noticeably shaking as he continued to stare out the window into the pitch black night.

"Elias Rubin was black, Rabbi," Ryan declared.

The rabbi turned suddenly around almost hitting Ryan with his elbow, his face twisted with pain.

"Yes . . . I know, Mr. Ryan. My sister . . . her name was Jeanette. Named after my grandmother. She had an affair with . . ." His voice trailed off as if his throat could not utter the remaining words.

"Anyway," the rabbi continued, "She was a student at the University of Pennsylvania in the late '40s. A time when America was very color conscious . . . skin color. You know what I mean, Mr. Ryan."

"Yes . . . I think I do, Rabbi. But your sister . . ."

"She was young. You know how liberal the generation of young Jews after the war were. She was for equality. For everybody. She marched for the Communists. Everyone was equal. And she practiced what she preached. Anyway, she fell in love with a Nigerian student at the university. Nobody knew. She would never tell my parents. My father was an old Orthodox rabbi in Boro Park. Our family has always had strong religious traditions. "

Y'know what a Kohen is, Mr. Ryan?" The rabbi's question threw Ryan's mind off-guard momentarily.

"Yes, Rabbi, I think so," he replied innocently.

"Well, we . . . my ancestors were the high priests of the tribes of Israel. Nothing was done without a Kohen witnessing the ceremony. Even today, the Jews revere their priesthood. Well, she had a baby. Elias they named him. We didn't know, not for years that she had had a baby. The father . . . the black fellow went home. Leaving her with a half black, half Jewish baby in a strange city, without help. So she quit school and became a domestic. That's all she could do. Cut off all ties with the family . . . until . . ." He again stalled in his recitation as his hand brushed against his face. Ryan could see that the rabbi was silently weeping.

"My father found out," he continued softly. "The grapevine for such a thing is pervasive. And then he cut her off. Refused to even hear her name . . . to see her. Kaddish was said. The ceremony for the dead. He couldn't believe his own daughter would forsake our sacred traditions."

"You must understand." The rabbi lifted his burning eyes and gazed directly into the eyes of the listeners, all standing transfixed in their respective places, "My father's generation didn't march with the blacks at Selma. They were as narrow-minded as any redneck from the south. They believed in separation of the races. *Schvartza* was a denigrating word. Like *nigger*."

The rabbi's tongue almost caught in his mouth before the slang name came out.

"Elias was her son. They lived in a black section of Philadelphia. She wanted him to feel secure. She knew her people . . . the Orthodox Jews . . . would never tolerate a black child. Not for the daughter of a Kohen." He paused again and walked to the large fireplace at the back of the room.

Then he turned around and continued,

"She missed being a Jew. The tradition was her whole life. She would sneak into the Orthodox synagogue in northeast Philadelphia every chance she got. Elias went with her. She had to cover his head with a babushka so no one could see his black face. Well, it was enough for me. I was the advisor to the most revered Orthodox Jew in America . . . the Rebbe . . . and I told him. And he told me that I would have to cut her off from me. Surgically remove the memory of her from my mind."

Tears rolled down the smooth skin of the rabbi's face. His deep, mellifluous voice cracked with emotion.

"Well anyway, when the husband left . . . I shouldn't say 'husband' because they never married . . . she wouldn't go through a civil ceremony. She lived alone. And I came down here to see her. She had aged a hundred years. Her delicate white skin was wrinkled and gray. Her eyes bloodshot and ringed with dark circles because she could never sleep through the night."

"And Elias?" Levine asked.

"Yes . . . Elias. Elias became the ultimate rebel. He hated his mother because she was white and Jewish. He was proud to be black. His people, he called them. *She was the enemy*! He followed the teachings of Malcolm X. He became a black Muslim. He had forsaken his mother. She couldn't take the estrangement from her only reason to live. Her son. Well—" the rabbi's voice had regained its composure and he spoke each word clearly—"She died of a broken heart. She had no will to live. And when Elias disappeared she gave up. She died crying his name on her lips. She had loved him so much she had forsaken her religion. But she finally found peace."

Sounds of owls breached the stillness of the cabin. Each figure stayed in its place as if to move would shatter the world itself. The night air blowing through the cabin had almost cleansed the horrid smells.

"Do you know what happened to Elias?" Ryan asked as he moved alongside the rabbi.

"Just rumors. This was an awful place when I first moved here, Mr. Ryan," the rabbi replied. And then added, "He was a difficult young man."

"They were difficult times, Rabbi," Sam Levine's voice echoed through the cabin.

"We think Elias Rubin was killed out at the campsite," Ryan said.

"I had a feeling," the rabbi replied. "That's why I went out there."

"It was over twenty-five years ago, Rabbi," Olsham declared. "There's nothing left out there.

"Yes there is . . . here." The rabbi handed Ryan, who was close to him, a slim gold ring. "I dug under the ashes and leaves by the stake . . . about two feet under . . . I found it."

"Read the back," the rabbi instructed.

"Just some Hebrew letters," Ryan reported.

"That's the ring my sister received from my grandmother before she died. She gave it to Elias."

"All these years. . .," Ryan mused aloud. "How could the campsite be so . . . " Olsham interjected. "How? I'll tell you how. Lester had Lyndon, the original German shepherd and then Lyndon Junior. That ugly sonofabith . . . with his head sticking out the window, guarding it. Why?"

"Who the hell knows why, but Lester . . . for whatever reason and only God and Lester know . . . wanted the campsite like it was twenty-five years ago . . . as if he was preserving the evidence." Olsham smiled and then continued, "Lester never forgets . . . Never . . . ."

"I spoke to Elias one time," the rabbi volunteered. "One time. We had to meet on neutral ground, he insisted. Some black bar in north Philadelphia. He was surrounded by his followers. He called me a dirty Jew. A coward. For not standing up for the poor. Well, you know the speech. He hated the Jew as much as the rednecks of Summit County did."

"And he probably died because he was a Jew," Levine offered.

"These good ol' boys had a lot of reasons to hate him," Olsham said.

Yehuda stood silently through the entire dialogue. His mind racing through the events following the death of his own son at the hands of the Arab terrorists of the West Bank. *Gulayim* he thought. The same everywhere. He remembered Ben's dark-tanned face and the whiteness of his teeth when he laughed. How quickly a family can degenerate with one event. Murder is universal. The differences of men make us murderers, he thought. The anger he felt when Ben died. Insanely, he led his own legion through the Arab village slaughtering the family of the terrorists, indiscriminately butchering anyone remotely thought to be related to his son's murder. How different were we than the killers of Elias Rubin, he thought. I am not cut from the same cloth as these hyenas, he rationalized. "Aren't you?" the other voice replied. He killed no one, he should not have died, Yehuda's thoughts referring to Elias Rubin.

"Captain Crutchfield was there," Lester suddenly blurted out.

"Where?" Ryan asked sharply.

"At the burning. He was there," Lester repeated.

"How do you know it was him, Lester?" Levine asked, his forehead wrinkling.

Mathias rose from the wooden chair. He waited alongside Lester for his reply.

"Because I know it was him. He wasn't wearing any sheet or anything. He refused to do so. But the senator made him go. Y'know, the captain tried to cut the boy down. Even when the flames started to grow. But Dickson wouldn't let him in. And the senator told him that if he went near the stake the captain might as well move on. So he stood there, like the rest of them. Just watching the flames grow . . . and," Lester paused to swallow and his breathing became heavy but he finally continued, more slowly than before, "some of them couldn't watch the boy go up in flames. The screaming was just so . . . Anyway, some of them took off their hoods and vomited. God, it was terrible. I still hear that boy's screams and you could see his face just before the flames reached up and tore him apart."

"Tell'em who they were, Lester," Olsham instructed.

"The guys without the hoods?" Lester asked.

"Yeah . . . tell'em."

"It was the two judges. They left after they barfed. Even the senator couldn't stop them. They just pulled off their sheets and walked away."

"Sturmer?" Ryan asked.

"And guess who else?" Olsham added.

"Who?" Ryan asked.

"King. The great exalted assignment judge. He wasn't that then. But he was there. Just another one of the good ol' boys, Joshua."

"So Roger has them all?" Ryan said. The German shepherd stirred from his resting position in front of the fireplace. His head bobbed up as if his ears had caught a strange noise from outside the cabin.

"Lyndon is restless," Lester observed.

"Nobody followed us," Mathias replied.

"Does anybody know what Lester witnessed that night?" Levine interjected.

" Not unless Lester opened his big mouth," Olsham said.

"Maybe they think he's harmless," Mathias added.

"He never drove the senator after that night," Olsham says. "The senator let him go . . . so he left the troopers."

"And now the rabbi," Ryan observed. "The circle is complete. No wonder Leary wanted the rabbi. He probably thought he's following in the senator's footsteps. Just what Pop would want."

"But why the judges?" Mathias queried. "What do they have to gain?"

Levine smiled an enigmatic smile. He placed two sticks of gum into his mouth, savoring the sweet artificial flavor for a few moments, then spoke,

"Judges are not elected in this state. You need political clout to get appointed to the bench. And more importantly . . . to stay on it. The senator ran the county and without his approval nobody, Republican or Democrat was approved. And King always wanted to be assignment judge. That takes real political clout which only the senator could provide."

He paused momentarily to concentrate on chewing the gum and then continued, "I guess that's why they were there. The senator wanted their commitment. Sort of like the Mafia demanding their soldiers make their bones. Kill somebody for the boss. Same thing here. The judges just made their bones by witnessing Elias Rubin's execution."

"Why kill Rubin?" Mathias asked innocently.

"I guess because he was the frontal attack against everything the senator and his cronies had built up over the years," Levine replied in a pedantic tone, as if he were lecturing a group of young law students. "Rubin was the opening of the festering wound that this county suffered from. No one had ever bothered to search under the skin . . . not until Elias Rubin brought the big-city media down to little ol' Summit County. The glare of the public microscope was too much for the senator. He had his way for over a quarter of a century . . . and Rubin was going to destroy it all."

Mathias puffed nervously on his pipe. Realizing the tobacco was unlit, he went to the front door, opened it and banged the pipe bowl against the wood railing of the porch.

"I think the rabbi here has the same problem with the senator's son," Mathias said in a low, officious voice. "Roger Leary will do anything in the rabbi's case to get a conviction. No matter what. Also, I know you know this already, Mr. Ryan, but it would be impossible for the rabbi to get a fair trial in Bristol. Leary will stack the jury with the farmers out north of Larchmont Hills."

"If Sturmer's the trial judge, he'll never cross Leary by sending it out of the county," Ryan answered.

"Change of venue goes to the assignment judge, Joshua," Levine commented drily.

"Still, King won't cross Leary either. Not if little Roger can pull the plug on the AJ by what he saw twenty-five years ago."

"Then what do we do?" the rabbi's voice chimed in with an apparent note of concern.

"The appellate division is the only answer. An emergent appeal to the higher court," Ryan said.

"Never win," Levine declared. "It's interlocutory in nature. They rarely grant interlocutory appeals. They tell you to try the case and then bring the whole mess up at one time. They think that's efficient justice." Levine added.

"We have a bigger problem now," Ryan stated, his eyes piercing the black night outside, "How do we keep the rabbi out of jail . . . now . . . up to trial."

"I may have the solution, Counselor," Mathias said. "I take the rabbi with me into Larchmont Hills police station. We call the municipal court magistrate. Y'know him, Mr. Ryan. Anyway, he's a fair guy. He'll set bail at a reasonable sum. We post it and the rabbi goes free."

"What happens at the county arraignment hearing? Or even before that, when Leary petitions the trial court for more bail?" Levine asked.

"There's no reason to overturn the municipal court's bail number," Ryan stated, "as long as we can show the bail number was based on realistic facts such as the rabbi's long-term ties to the community and that he ain't going anywhere."

"May not work, Joshua," Levine opined. "Leary is going to argue that the rabbi escaped this jurisdiction already."

"But he didn't escape, Sam," Joshua interjected. "I could show that he left the county before the indictment was returned. If so, he was never a fugitive because he never was charged before he left the county."

"Maybe," Levine whispered indecisively, "I don't know. You better prepare your emergent appellate brief on that one now. Maybe they'll hear it. Anyway, I don't think that we have any options open to us now in any event."

"Okay . . . are we agreed?" Ryan directed his gaze at the rabbi. "Okay with you, Rabbi? It's time we made our play. I'm afraid if we don't establish bail now, somebody like Dickson could have an excuse to take a potshot at you."

The early-morning sun was displaying its outer rim of blazing light as the final decision was made by the group. It appeared that the morning fog was going to burn off. The coldness of the night had changed into the warmth of a new day. At least that's what they all hoped.

CHAPTER FORTY

Mathias shepherded the rabbi through the rear entrance of the Larchmont Hills municipal police station. Depositing the suspicious arrestee in the cell at the end of the station closest to the municipal courtroom didn't allay the rabbi's distrust of the entire judicial system.

"The judge is on his way, Rabbi," Mathias said. "Ryan is in the courtroom and it'll be over in less than fifteen minutes. Don't worry, Ryan knows what has to be done."

The rabbi listlessly sat down on the cot against the wall of the cell, his watery eyes betraying the fear in his heart.

Judge Aaron Schwartz was a full-time lawyer first and a part-time municipal court judge second. It paid $10,000 per year and he convened the Larchmont Hills municipal court once a week. He was known to be fair but stubborn: hated to be told what to do by anyone including the Supreme Court of the State.

On several occasions he had ruled against clear Supreme Court decisions, cleverly interpreting the high court's decisions in such a manner as to allow Schwartz's ruling to become acceptable. Many times the Supreme Court didn't respond kindly to Judge Schwartz's clever manipulation of its judicial rulings. Yet because of the political influence of his uncle's Democratic party in Larchmont Hills, Schwartz was reappointed term after term.

At precisely 9:00 a.m., Judge Schwartz strode confidently into the sterile-white courtroom, his black robe fluttering around his ankles. Although small in physical stature, his regal bearing convinced the observer that a massive frame was hidden on the high bench Schwartz sat elevated behind. The court clerk sat to his left while a court reporter pounded into her machine every word uttered in the courtroom. Two Larchmont Hills policemen stood guard at the double entrance doors to the courtroom.

The courtroom was half filled, people still shuffling through rows of folding chairs. Judge Schwartz banged his gavel and commenced reading the mandatory legal disclaimers and conditions that he utilized in meting out justice in his courtroom. Silence was golden in Judge Schwartz's courtroom. He had held many an attorney in contempt for talking to his client while court was in session.

By prior arrangement with Sam Levine, who had been Aaron Schwartz's law professor at Rutgers two decades ago, the court clerk called *State v. Rubin* first on the list.

Mathias led the rabbi in from the cell block located behind the courtroom as Ryan stepped up to the podium in front of the court's bench. The rabbi stood alongside his lawyer as Ryan addressed the court.

"Your honor, my client, Rabbi Carl Rubin, has voluntarily surrendered himself to Lieutenant Mathias of the Larchmont Hills police department. It is my understanding that he has been indicted for the murder of Eleanore Rubin, his late wife. I have spoken to the municipal prosecutor, Mr. Banachi who is not here because of, I understand, a prior court appearance in the Superior Court and Mr. Banachi and I have agreed that bail should be set in this case. Because of my client's substantial financial and social ties to this community, Mr. Banachi and I agree that the bail should not exceed $50,000. I would ask this court to set a much lower bail, but of course, I have great respect for the experience and wisdom of this court in delicate matters such as this and I certainly would defer to the considered decision of your honor."

"Has the county prosecutor been notified that the defendant was appearing before me?" the judge barked at Ryan.

"One of his investigative troopers, a Sergeant Joseph Dickson, is aware of the defendant's presence in the county, your honor," Ryan replied.

"Lieutenant Mathias!" The judge called to the waiting Mathias. "Since you're the arresting officer in this matter, have you had a chance to corroborate, or dispute, the representations of counsel?"

Mathias walked slowly to the front of the court's bench and to the left side of Ryan.

"Your honor, I have been the investigating detective in the case of the murder of the defendant's wife and I can honestly say that the evidence against the defendant is so sparse as to warrant a limited bail amount to be set in this case. Further, during my investigation, I have learned that the defendant has an impeccable reputation in the community as well as long-term ties that would lead me to believe he would be present at trial."

A wisp of a smile crossed Schwartz's cherubic face, signifying his appreciation of the charade acted before him. Always protect the record, Schwartz's mentor would preach religiously in law school. Samuel Levine taught reality where others preached academic bullshit, Schwartz thought.

"I'm satisfied that reasonable bail should be set in this matter. I have also spoken to the municipal prosecutor who confirms Mr. Ryan's representations. Taking into account the favorable recommendation of the investigating police officer, Lieutenant Mathias, and the acknowledged permanent ties the defendant has with Larchmont Hills, I will set bail at $50,000."

"Your Honor," Ryan declared solemnly, "unfortunately we are not prepared to put up either cash or bond at this time. May I suggest the court accept the deed to the defendant's house, with a realtor's appraisal of its value, in lieu of cash or bond."

Schwartz smiled quickly at Sam Levine, who was seated in the front row of the courtroom. Many a night had been spent in Buzzies Tavern with the professor giving his tutorial to his law students, which included Aaron Schwartz. Levine's wisdom was fresh air blowing through the Socratic method of teaching principles of law. No answers, just questions that had ambivalent answers at best. Levine always gave an answer; both sides in any case had answers and he gave you both sides. Either side could be right if you argued the applicable legal precedents. Interpret the facts your way and the legal conclusions will follow.

"I will release the defendant in your custody, Mr. Ryan, pending submission of the deed to his home with an attached real estate appraisal warranting that the value of the equity in the home is $50,000 or above," Schwartz ordered.

"Thank you, Your Honor," Ryan said.

As Ryan was turning to leave the lectern with the rabbi, Roger Leary burst excitedly through the double doors to the courtroom followed by Dickson and another trooper, both dressed in full uniform and sidearms.

"Your Honor!" Leary yelled as he approached the lectern, Dickson and the other trooper right behind him.

"My name for the record is Roger Leary, prosecutor of Summit County. I have an objection to the granting of any bail to this defendant. He is a fugitive from justice and bail is certainly not acceptable in a capital case such as this. Further," the words rushed out of Leary's mouth as if he feared someone would cut him off, "the defendant's counsel, Joshua Ryan, is himself a defendant in an indictment for obstruction of justice and aiding and abetting a fugitive, his client."

"Good morning, Mr. Leary," Schwartz pronounced the Prosecutor's name with articulate relish. "Unfortunately for the state, Mr. Ryan has presented the investigating police officer, Lieutenant Mathias, to support his application for bail for the defendant."

Schwartz paused and extended his hand toward Leary. "Let me see that indictment. You say you indicted defendant's counsel? One of your own a few years ago, I remember, Mr. Leary," he added cynically.

"Here it is, Your Honor." Leary handed the indictment papers to Judge Schwartz.

Schwartz lowered his bifocals over his wide nose and read the document slowly. After completion of the reading, he raised his head, pushed his bifocals back against the base of his nose and said:

"It's an indictment, all right. Mr. Ryan, do you have anything to say?"

Levine raised himself from the folding chair in the first row and trudged painfully to the lectern.

"Judge, good morning, my name is Samuel Levine. Since there is an indictment pending against Rabbi Rubin's counsel, I will represent Mr. Ryan in this immediate matter."

"You can't represent Ryan!" Leary shouted.

"Why not, Mr. Leary?" Schwartz queried in an agitated voice.

"He hasn't appeared in court in over a decade, Judge. I don't even know if this man even holds a license to practice law in this state."

Levine smiled as if he was benignly arguing against an idiot child. "Judge, I can assure my worthy adversary, I am still licensed to practice law in this state. If he doubts my representation, he certainly can bring an indictment against me for practicing law without a license."

"Mr. Prosecutor," Schwartz pronounced, "do you really want me to believe that Mr. Levine, a prestigious member of this legal community for over three decades is a charlatan . . . a fake?"

"I don't care what you believe, Judge," Leary spewed out the words, sensing a conspiracy between the court and Levine, "You have no right to set bail in this case. I was never notified that this defendant was even arrested and I request . . . *no, I demand* . . . that you release this man into my custody until a proper bail hearing can be held on the county level!"

"Do you have any authority, Mr. Leary, which would preclude this court from setting bail at this time?" the pugnacious judge announced in a clear, even voice.

"I wasn't prepared to argue that issue, Your Honor," Leary replied, his body quivering noticeably.

"Then the point is moot, Mr. Prosecutor." Schwartz shuffled a stack of paper on his desk signifying that, as far as he was concerned, the matter was closed.

"Listen," Leary leaned over the lectern, his face close to the edge of the judge's bench, "I want you to know that this court does not have the authority to set bail in a capital case. Anyway, I want you to call the assignment judge, Judge King. He'll set you straight."

Schwartz's round, almost childlike face, flushed with dark red patches covering his cheeks. He stood up, his voice filled with anger, and leaned over his bench, nose to nose with Leary's outstretched face.

"You're not going to tell me how to run my courtroom, Mr. Leary. The Assignment Judge doesn't run my court. I run it. Until the Supreme Court tells me otherwise, I'm gonna run it my way. Is that understood, Mr. Prosecutor?"

Leary turned his head toward Dickson and the other trooper, both standing behind Leary.

The troopers unlatched their leather sidearm holsters and quickly drew their .45mm semi-automatic pistols from their leather jackets.

"Put your hands behind your backs, gentlemen," Dickson addressed his warnings to Ryan and the rabbi.

The court was filled to capacity and the silence in the packed courtroom was electric. Not a breath could be heard from the shocked throng of people sitting fixed in their folding chairs. The air seemed to cease flowing although the large windows of the council room.

Levine smiled in disbelief, reflecting his amazement at the stupidity of the county prosecutor.

"Mr. Leary," Levine's basso voice echoed through the bench area, "if you don't have your assistants holster their weapons immediately, I believe you will no longer be county prosecutor."

Schwartz recovered from the initial shock of Leary's Wild West show, and following the calmness of Levine, he nodded to the two armed Larchmont Hills policemen at the door. They unholstered their weapons, and aimed them at Leary as they walked quickly to the side of the judge's bench.

Mathias withdrew his .9mm Glock from his shoulder harness and also pointed it at Leary.

"Mr. Prosecutor," the judge declared in almost a whisper, "I think you just lost the last hand. I am instructing these three gentlemen to aim their weapons at you. If you don't have your . . . your . . . whatever they are . . . put their sidearms back in their holsters . . . well, this morning will make judicial history."

Leary nodded to Dickson and both troopers holstered their drawn weapons.

"Thank you, Sergeant." Judge Schwartz smiled at the taller of the two Larchmont Hills policemen. They holstered their guns and backpedaled to the double entrance doors of the courtroom. Mathias walked from the judge's side to the lectern. Levine addressed the court.

"Your honor, may I suggest that ROR* bail be set in Mr. Ryan's case. We certainly know that he will show up for his trial. But I honestly doubt that this matter will ever get that far."

"Yes, Mr. Levine, I agree. I think Mr. Leary's enthusiasm for his kind of justice makes one wary of zealous law enforcement officers. Further, I see no reason why Mr. Ryan cannot represent the defen-

---

*ROR—without money put up for bail (literally, Released on Own Recognizance)

dant, Rubin. Thank you gentlemen. This court is in recess until 9:45 a.m."

With his black robe furling in the breeze that suddenly appeared from the large back windows of the courtroom, the small compact body of the judge disappeared into the judge's chamber located on the side of the court's staging area.

Leary grimaced noticeably as he snarled at Ryan.

"Your ass is cooked, Mr. Ryan. You think you can bullshit your way out of this mess. By getting this Jew cocksucker," Leary nodded at the departing Judge, "Well . . . you don't know me. I just want to say . . . if you try to leave this county . . . I'll drag your ass back to the county jail. Do you read me, Mister?"

Ryan smiled. He turned his face toward Leary and almost nose to nose whispered gently into Leary's face. "Fuck you, Roger."

Leary turned petulantly away, followed by his two trooper henchmen as they hustled out of the courtroom.

Suddenly Leary reappeared at the doorway, and called out to Mathias. Mathias walked slowly over to Leary.

"Lieutenant, you know," Leary warned, his face flushed with unabated anger, "you're gone. I'm gonna make sure the chief knows what you did today.."

"Mr. Leary, do what you have to do," Mathias replied.

"I will. You bet your sweet ass I will. Just letting you know that you have to worry about something more than your job. That's the last time you fuck up my parade, Lieutenant. The last time!"

Leary turned, almost into a pivot, and marched noisily out of the courtroom to where his troopers were waiting for him.

A surge of fear rushed through Mathias's body. There was no doubt in Mathias's mind that Leary was capable of anything. Throughout Mathias's law enforcement career, he had seen men like Leary who knew no bounds to restrain them. Anything goes. The goal is only to win. Winning as they see it. Distorted or otherwise. Even killing. Murder is part of their personal arsenal. Leary had had his own way all of his life. It's that sense of invulnerability that is inherited in the young warrior. Until he is burdened by the smell and taste of failure, of defeat, he surges through life bowling over anything in his way.

And certainly Mathias was in Leary's way. Not ever knowing

defeat, Leary's fear was exponentially greater because of the unforseen future. He didn't know whether he could survive if he had to suffer defeat. Not being prosecutor would be the ultimate defeat. He would do anything not to taste the ugliness of being just one of the pack.

Ryan and company walked into the bright morning sunlight of Chester Avenue, the main business artery of Larchmont Hills. The town still maintained its rural character by continuing to have diagonal parking on Chester. The peach and apple orchards that surrounded Larchmont Hills were slowly disappearing under the bulldozer blades of the encroaching development. Township Council fought back by denying zoning changes to accommodate the construction onslaught, but the legal system aided and abetted the devil's progress. Decision by decision, the politically dominated judiciary reversed local decisions issued to maintain the status quo.

Larchmont Hills was changing in more ways than one. The immigration of cosmopolitan liberals from the urban centers of the Northeast formed a new majority. They now dictated the future of the town. And the future was growth. And growth meant more people. More people meant more crime. Until the previously settled residents took a step back and realized that the reasons that had motivated them to escape the towering chaos of Philadelphia and New York now appeared in Larchmont Hills. Suddenly the liberals become the conservatives and the recently arrived joined forces with the established residents to block the arrivals of the new hopefuls. And the cycle continued.

Everybody wanted a piece of the good life. For themselves and their kids. Clean air and the greenery of God's little acre were worth commuting the vast distances to the urban centers of work.

Mathias saw it coming. You can only take the chaos of the over-crowded cities so long and then most people want out. Like he did. And once the urban hamster found that there was life outside the revolving maze, he was hooked forever. As Mathias had been.

Now it started all over again. The lust for power never ends. It's all the same. City or country. The Learys were always out there. But now Mathias had nowhere to run. He had made his final bed and he had to stay and fight and survive.

"What now?" Levine said to no one in particular as they stood outside the municipal building on the path leading to Chester Avenue.

"Leary will run to the assignment judge to overturn the bail order," Ryan announced.

"I think I should call the AG's office," Mathias replied.

"If you do, Leary will crucify you," Olsham said.

"I'm already on his shitlist. I think I also have to find the captain. I can't believe he's involved in all this crap," Mathias said as his fingers grasped the ever present pipe from his shirt pocket.`

"Leary may already have disposed of him," Levine said.

"I don't think so. He knows too much," Ryan added.

"I'll have to file a change of venue motion," Ryan said as he observed Leary slam the door of the blue-and-white trooper vehicle parked on the sidewalk in front of the municipal building.

"King will deny it. You should expect that decision, Joshua," Levine announced.

"I have the interlocutory appeal and brief prepared along with the motion papers, Sam." Joshua paused as he stared into the face of his old friend Levine.

"Are you in, Sam?" Joshua added.

"I guess I am. I already stated for the record that I represent you. Which brings to mind that Leary will probably file the state's motion to preclude you from representing the rabbi."

"Well, Sam. I guess we'll be up tonight preparing a motion for dismissal of that indictment."

"Rarely given, my young friend. But I think in this case, our esteemed assignment judge may see the light of reason." Levine smiled displaying an irregular row of small teeth yellowed by the years of cigars that had passed by his lips.

"Can I go home, gentlemen?" The rabbi asked, his tired voice showing his built-up frustration.

"I think it'll be all right, Rabbi," Joshua opined. "Make sure we get the deed and the realtor's appraisal. I don't want Leary to overturn Schwartz's bail order on some foolish technicality."

"My daughter must be frantic," the rabbi mumbled.

"John," Ryan addressed Olsham, "Why don't you drive the rabbi home and then meet me at my office later this afternoon."

"Rabbi," Joshua paused and then continued in an emphatic voice, "Please, don't talk to anyone. Especially reporters. I'm sure Leary's going to leak everything he has to the media. And nothing favorable to you."

"I think, my friend," Sam interjected, "We have to arrange our own media campaign. Leaking information is a two-way street, y'know. And I know just the reporter to leak such tidbits."

Ryan smiled. Although ethically, counsel in a criminal case could not unduly flavor the information passed onto the media, it had always been done. Except when the court specifically orders it not to be done. And then it is done through "anonymous sources." The public sentiment on a heralded case sometimes is more important then the evidence presented at trial. Although juries can be sequestered, and be warned to wash their brains of all prejudices and predilections, they never do.

"Do we have a chance, Mr. Ryan?" The rabbi asked in a weak, lilting voice.

Ryan did not answer for several seconds. Each man looked at each other and then Ryan answered in a confident voice, "If we do all the right things, Rabbi, we're gonna win. I believe in your innocence."

From a distance, Mathias could hear the gargled noise of the VW Beetle starting up. He turned his head up the almost deserted main street of Larchmont Hills and observed nothing of the tiny vehicle. He did see Captain Crutchfield heading quickly up the path leading to where the group was standing.

Arriving at the group, Crutchfield asked Mathias if he would join him at the local luncheonette on Chester Avenue for a cup of coffee.

Mathias nodded and then said to Ryan, "I'll call you, Mr. Ryan. We may have something to discuss."

He followed Crutchfield out onto Chester Avenue toward the small restaurant across from the municipal building. The irritating sounds of the VW became louder as he crossed the street.

CHAPTER FORTY-ONE

"I had nothing to do with last night, Lew." Crutchfield rubbed his eyes as if the words caused shooting pains to course through his head.

"I didn't think you did, Captain," Mathias looked around the tiny near-empty luncheonette. His voice showed the fatigue of the endless night before.

"Leary is crazy. He told me to take a vacation. I've never seen him this bad."

Crutchfield pulled a filtered cigarette out of a pack. As he was puffing on the cigarette, his hand was shaking.

"He doesn't know what unemployment is, I guess," Mathias replied.

Two men walked into the luncheonette and sat by the counter. Crutchfield's eyes followed them to the counter.

"Dickson's taking over . . . my job. Everybody has to answer to him. You can't even see Roger until you get Dickson's permission."

"You ever hear the name *Elias Rubin*, Captain?" Mathias sipped on the coffee the waitress placed in front of him.

Crutchfield's face turned stony white. His eyes avoided peering at Mathias. He almost gulped the hot coffee down whole.

"Where did you hear that name, Lew?" he questioned in an almost inaudible voice.

"What's the difference, Captain?"

"It makes all the difference in the world, Lew."

"His name was on the cell wall of the old jail."

"It sounds familiar. It's been a long time, Lew."

"1970s, I guess."

"I wasn't on the job long."

"So you know the name, Captain?"

"Maybe. It's been a long time, Lew."

"You said that," Mathias replied in a steely tone.

"You're opening up a real can of worms, Lew."

Mathias stared at the backs of the two men at the counter. They appeared to be whispering to each other and the tall, stocky one occasionally stole a glance at the captain and Mathias.

"Need a can of worms to catch the big fish, Captain," Mathias answered.

"Nobody wanted it to go that far, Lew. It just happened."

"What happened?"

"I'll have to think about it, Lew. It's been so long ago."

"What did you want to talk to me about?" Mathias nodded to the waitress to bring another round of coffee. His head ached from the night's lack of sleep. "You should've stopped Dickson, Captain. I don't care what Leary does . . . but you're not Leary." Mathias, his face turned away from the cloud of smoke rushing from the Captain's twitching mouth.

"I just found out about last night. Leary's secretary told me. In fact, Ryan would be dead if she hadn't squealed. She likes Ryan. Believe me, Lew. I didn't know."

"Dickson's crazy, Captain. He's capable of anything."

"I'd go to the AG with you, Lew, except. Well, you know . . . I'm just shy of that pension."

"So you won't do anything?"

"Maybe I can help."

"How?" Mathias' voice surged out in bitterness.

"They're gonna slip some shit into the evidence locker . . . against the rabbi."

"When?"

"Probably already did. But I don't know. Leary and the county coroner's office work out of the same book."

"You know there's no statute of limitations on murder, Captain," Lew declared demandingly.

"What are you talking about?" Crutchfield's eyes stared down at his quivering hand.

"Elias Rubin. We have evidence he was murdered. You know what I'm talking about, Captain."

"I left, Lew. I left before anything happened. Believe me, I had nothing to do with that." the captain's voice rose almost to a frenzy.

"With what?" Mathias shot back.

Crutchfield's eyes focused on the two men who now got up from their stools, looked over at Crutchfield, smiled knowingly, and then left the luncheonette.

"Listen, Lew . . . I gotta go," the captain said as he rose hurriedly from the bench seat of the booth.

"You still haven't told me anything, Captain. I sure hate to see you sitting up there."

"Where?"

"You know what I mean, Captain."

"I'm trying to be helpful, Lew."

"No you're not. You're trying to save your ass. And you're not doing such a good job, Captain."

Crutchfield stood by the booth table as if he were trying to decide whether to leave or not. The two men could be seen standing on the sidewalk outside the luncheonette, their eyes darting from the street to the window of the luncheonette.

"We know each other a long time, Lew."

"I'm trying to help you, Captain."

"Let me sleep on it. There's a lot to think about."

"You're a good cop, Captain. I know you're gonna do the right thing."

"Whatever I did, Lew, I did for the senator. You understand that. You do, don't you?"

"That doesn't make it right . . . does it? You know that won't hold."

"Elias Rubin was a troublemaker, Lew."

"He didn't deserve to die."

"I only heard about it. After everything happened. You know, I never went in for the radical shit, Lew."

"Pensions make you do strange things, Captain." Mathias's face screwed up as he downed the bitter cold coffee.

"I fucking hate coffee," he pronounced in a sour voice.

"Lew, be careful . . ."

"Why?"

"You know why."

"Leary has the judges by the balls," Mathias said in a small voice as his eyes caught the two men still lounging nonchalantly on the corner outside the luncheonette.

"He has everybody by the balls, Lew. His father taught him well. Even you. He got enough on you to cause you some misery."

"Me?" Mathias blurted out.

"You . . . he knows about the charges against you in Brooklyn."

"They were dismissed."

"So what? How do you prove you're innocent of something that happened twenty five years ago?"

"I'm still going to the AG, Captain."

"They're still all Republicans up there, Lew. Just like Leary."

Mathias's face lifted up to stare at Crutchfield, who nervously shifted from one foot to the other.

"I gotta get home and get some sleep, Captain. I'll find somebody who'll listen."

"It's an election year for the governor, Lew. She won't want to get involved with some old bullshit."

"She's always been straight."

"You'll never get to her. A lot of her advisors are from the good ol'boys school. Just like the senator was. He may be dead but his influence is still up there."

"Rubin was burnt at the stake, Captain. Alive."

"Nobody can prove anything, Lew."

Mathias withdrew from the bench seat of the booth, and threw a couple of singles down on the table. As he rose to his feet, he said,

"Yes, we can. There's an old guy living out in the Pines who saw everything, Captain. An old trooper who drove the senator to the campsite. He saw the whole thing."

"You're really looking for trouble, Lew."

"What's right is right, Captain."

"I gotta go, Lew. Those guys outside are Dickson's men. I suddenly got a shadow."

"They don't look friendly, Captain."

Crutchfield smiled. His sallow face crinkled under the bloodshot eyes. He snuffed out his cigarette.

"I'm sorry about your wife, Dan," Mathias uttered the first name of the captain.

"It's been almost a year. She went so slowly, Lew."

"She was a good woman."

"The best. To take my shit and still laugh. That took something, Lew." Crutchfield smiled, his teeth barely showing between his lips. The two men stood face to face as if they hated to part but knew they must. Although on separate sides for the moment, they were both cops through and through. There was a fraternity bond that permeated law enforcement people throughout time.

"After all these years, it's tough to come home and not see her there," Crutchfield added solemnly.

"Get out now, Dan," Mathias warned as he placed his hand on Crutchfield's shoulder.

"I wish I could, Lew. I'm in so deep." He paused thoughtfully and then continued, "Anyway, it'll all work out . . . it always does."

He smiled broadly as if the smile would cover the fear in his eyes.

"You'll have to visit me down in Tampa, Lew. The fishing's great. Bluefish, pompano . . . whatever you like."

"Yeah, Dan. I'll see you around," Mathias replied as he watched Crutchfield leave the luncheonette into the waiting arms of his two shadows.

CHAPTER FORTY-TWO

The courtroom was built almost fifteen years ago. High ceilings, highly polished mahogany wood paneling on the walls, it gave one a feeling of spaciousness. Built along the lines of the federal courtrooms, Summit County wanted to appear to the world as if it wasn't just a county backwash dealing out inconsequential justice.

The interior of the courtroom was a stark contrast to the modern exterior of the county courthouse. This particular courtroom was the hallmark of the building. The assignment judge of the county, Alexander King, ministered selective justice out from the high bench. He never tried jury cases, but he insisted a jury box be in *his* courtroom. And whatever the assignment judge wanted, the county commissioners sanctioned.

There were a few reporters seated behind the wooden fence that separated the combat pit from the spectator gallery. Only lawyers, the court clerk, and the court reporter sat beyond the discriminating fence line.

The reverent gray-haired assignment judge, the Honorable Alexander King, sat back quietly in his high-backed leather chair waiting for the circus to commence.

Samuel Levine stood next to the seated Joshua Ryan on the defendant side of the courtroom. The county prosecutor himself appeared with a female assistant prosecutor in tow to argue against defendant's motion for dismissal of the indictment against Joshua Ryan, defendant.

Levine had donned an ancient tie and equally ancient sports jacket for his first appearance in Superior Court in almost ten years. He smiled wistfully to himself remembering the mortal battles he had fought in courtrooms all over the state, the inveterate desire for victory filling his head and body. Intellectually, he offered no reason why an old-fashioned liberal like himself would want to dominate the fellow on the other side of the courtroom. But he did.

He wanted to destroy his adversary, and then pick him up and take him out for a drink. Only few people understood the inconsistencies of it all. Only the warriors in the courtroom understood such insanity.

"Your Honor, as you know, the defendant has brought a motion for dismissal of the indictment number S2874-95. We have submitted required briefs and certifications to demonstrate to this court that the indictment was frivolously conceived and executed. There is no basis in fact or law that allowed the state to present this case before the grand jury. Most importantly, Your Honor," Levine's voice fumbled for the words for a moment, the phlegm in his throat mottling the words that came out of his mouth. He quickly then recovered and continued, "Your Honor, I have reviewed the grand jury transcript."

"Yes, Yes . . . I have also, Mr. Levine . . ." Judge King interjected impatiently, "Get on with it. I have a full day back in the office."

Levine smiled at the court's impatience, knowing how the Honorable Alexander King must be stewing in his own juices of indecision. Does he screw his padrone's son Roger Leary and dismiss the indictments or does he do the expected and possibly incur the wrath of the governor's office in an election year. Tough decisions for tough guys, Levine mused.

"Your Honor," Levine continued as if King had not interrupted him, "pursuant to R. 4-1(a) of our rules of court and *State v. Simon*, a Supreme Court case that I'm sure Your Honor has reviewed, an attorney cannot be prosecuted for exercising the lawyer-client privilege as Mr. Ryan did in the case before the court."

"Your Honor," Leary shot from his seat, "may I . . ."

"Your Honor," Levine's husky voice pronounced each word in an indignant tone, "may I be allowed to complete my argument before this court. I know my worthy adversary, Mr. Leary, thinks he has title to this courtroom. But as a matter of professional courtesy . . ."

"Your Honor. Mr. Levine has no standing in this court," Leary sputtered out.

"Why not?" King asked, with an annoying gaze at the prosecutor who was leaning over counsel table, his fists thumping the table nervously.

"Because he hasn't paid his attorney registration fee. That's why," Leary smugly replied.

"Has he been suspended, Mr. Leary? Do you have a notice of suspension for Mr. Levine?", the judge continued.

Levine thought that King, for some unknown reason, was attempting to be fair. He didn't expect fairness in the Summit County judicial system. The judges all went to lunch together almost every day, presided over by the assignment judge, at the Old American Inn, the only decent restaurant in Bristol. The judges' dining table was in the back of the old restaurant.

Levine remembered when he was first presented to the luncheon assemblage, his Jewishness hidden under his high-collared white shirt and black suit. They all suspected he was Jewish, because of his last name and his bulbous oversized nose but it appeared they all wished they were wrong. Minorities had not infiltrated into Summit County until the end of the sixties, early seventies, but here was the advance guard of the immigrants to come. He self-consciously ate lunch at a table far from the judicial head table, along with two other part-time assistant prosecutors recently hired by the newly appointed part-time county prosecutor Reggio Farbazzini, a native American Italian whose family had lived in Summit County for almost a century. He was a senior member of the ruling law firm in the county, the one that received all its blessings from the political chieftain, Senator Aloishus Leary, speaker of the state senate among other titles he held so possessively.

"If he's not suspended, he's allowed to practice law in this county, Mr. Prosecutor," King stated harshly.

"Judge," Leary declared, his beady eyes staring at the bench, his hands holding the corner of the table tightly, "the grand jury saw fit to indict Mr. Ryan and nobody can overturn the grand jury's decision."

"I can, Mr. Prosecutor," King bellowed back, startling the unexpected Leary.

King gazed demandingly over at Levine as the judge straightened his body into the leather chair, hands folded neatly on the table before him.

"Mr. Levine. Although I don't agree with Mr. Leary about the limits of the power of this court, he is somewhat correct in his argument that grand jury indictments are rarely, if ever, dismissed on summary judgement."

Leary smiled as if he sensed a turning of the judicial tide in his favor.

"I certainly would agree with the court that our motion is not commonplace, but extraordinary as it may be, the motion must be granted on technical grounds. May I, Your Honor . . . may I continue," Levine requested in a polite undertone. He continued after the judge nodded his head in the affirmative. "Under the stated rule and substantial case precedent, the prosecutor must give proper notice to the proposed defendant that the grand jury will hear testimony against him on a specific charge. The proposed defendant has the right to appear at the grand jury presentment and explain his side of the case. It is rarely done, Your Honor. But the rules clearly allow it. Well, as we know, Mr. Leary's office failed to serve Mr. Ryan with the accusation and his rights sheet. Further, nothing was served on Mr. Ryan informing him of the grand jury hearing and that it would involve a charge against him. Therefore, Your Honor, coupled with our belief that the attorney-client privilege would preclude Mr. Ryan from revealing his client's intentions to leave the jurisdiction, at least before Rabbi Rubin was indicted, the indictment fails to meet the Constitutional thresholds of the sixth and fourteenth amendments."

"Mr. Leary. What do you have to say in response?" Judge King nodded to Leary, who had remained standing during Levine's presentation.

"Hogwash!" Leary shouted as he turned his head to the crowd now filling the courtroom. "Levine here doesn't know what he is talking about, Your Honor. It is hornbook law that an attorney can not obscure a crime that his client has or will commit. He becomes an accessory before and after the fact. I cite *Pashnow*, the U.S. Supreme Court case that disallows lawyer-client privilege in the commission of a crime. And certainly fleeing the jurisdiction while you're under indictment is a crime, Your Honor."

Leary's face was flushed with exuberance, his voice reflecting his confidence that Judge King would never rule against Senator Leary's son.

Levine slowly raised himself from the wooden armchair as if he were tired of the whole dastardly mess but yet was forced to explain the inaccuracies of the prosecutor's argument.

"Your Honor, the prosecutor's reliance on *Pashnow* is misplaced. It's an old case that I argued on behalf of the defendant before the Supreme Court and lost. In *Pashnow*, the attorney actively conspired with his client to defraud an insurance company and the Court quite accurately said the lawyer-client privilege does not arise in such a situation. In fact, I think Mr. Leary's dear departed father, the senator, was prosecutor at that time. Anyway, it doesn't apply and Mr. Leary should accurately state what the case stands for."

"Conspiring to leave the jurisdiction is a crime, Your Honor." Leary bounced out of his chair knocking his knees noisily against counsel's table.

"Was the defendant Rubin indicted when he left the state, Mr. Prosecutor?" the judge asked in a loud voice.

King knew what Leary wanted and even what Leary would do if he didn't get his way. But King was almost 70 now and he was tired of the sullen threats of the Leary offspring. Judge King was alone now. For about ten years he had lived alone in the white house on top of the mount that surrounded Bristol. Twenty acres enveloped his Victorian house, stables still housing two horses that the judge would ride on the weekends. He was a vestige of an earlier age where everybody knew their place. Up to a few years ago, the judge still called his black butler, "boy" who wore white gloves when he served his master.

The Kings were lifelong Democrats but their political bent was right of George Wallace. They had come to the American coast just after the Mayflower had first docked in New England, armed with their King James Bible and their shotguns. They had always been administrators, judges, and the king's men. They settled outside of Philadelphia, alongside the Delaware River. Within two centuries they dominated the agricultural markets of the northeast. Cranberries became their golden carriage to wealth and power. With a confirmed reservoir of gold to their names, the Kings then turned back to manipulating the lives of their underlings, the common folk of Summit County. Judges, senators, administrators all, the Kings' power base became allied with Senator Aloishus Leary, a nouveau tyrant whose quest for raw power overwhelmed even his toughest critics.

And Summit County in the forties and fifties was ripe for a political tyrant. Homogenous in population, the base of the citizenry was white, protestant and Anglo-Saxon. Wide swaths of farmland crisscrossed the county making it the greatest and largest agricultural resource of the state. And the bogs of Summit County spewed gold out in the form of annual cranberry crops that nurtured and grew the King family fortune.

Alexander King strived not for wealth, he already had it; he wanted to interpret and execute the law as he saw it. His dream was to become a chief justice of the state supreme court, but even power couldn't compensate for his lack of human understanding. His bitterness over his failed dreams were often vented in decisions that the Dred Scott Supreme Court would think twice about. But he survived the criticism, the judicial ethics hearings that were held behind closed doors, the direct admonishments from governors themselves. All had failed to modify his traditional conservative views reflected in Summit County.

Occasionally the appellate courts would overturn his most outrageous decisions, but all in all the upper courts left Summit County to the Kings and their following. South of the Princeton line was alien country to the New York urban sophisticates who habitated in the horse country of the northern half of the state. There had even been scattered political movements organized to sever the state in half. They failed. How much the so-called cultured northern half of the state denigrated the rednecks of the south, they realized economically, anyway, the south was essential to the viability of the good life of the north. As long as the creatures of the south stayed in their bogs and pigpens, the north tolerated the naive shenanigans of their southern half-brothers.

Ryan sat disconsolately in the wooden armchair alongside the standing form of Levine. As the argument continued, Ryan's mind wandered to the other courtroom drama where he had also, unfortunately, been the star defendant. Déjà vu. Except here, today, he was innocent. But did it even matter? he thought.

Innocence or guilt is an excuse to punish the misbegotten. The depressed. The ones who dare to be different. It has always been like that. History is unrelenting. Even if the innocent found guilty are then to be found innocent, they are lifeless; they cannot recover the years of humiliation, of outright revulsion the public righteousness heaped upon them. Apologies do not bring back the years of torment. Ryan had wanted to be punished for his human misdeeds. The drunkenness, the failure to control his life, they all fell at his doorstep. He blamed no one else. Not even an abusive father. He was no longer a child. The abusive father rationale was dead. Maybe he grew up when he stopped blaming his father for all his faults.

"That's not the issue, Your Honor," Leary declared to the judge's question. "I don't know the exact date he left this jurisdiction, Your Honor, but it doesn't matter. He knew he was under the investigation for the murder of his wife. He knew it. Under *Sapio* and *Ulbrecht*, your Honor, the defendant Rubin was morally bound to stay. And Ryan knew it. There is no attorney-client privilege in the commission of a crime, Your Honor. We all know that."

"*Sapio* and *Ulbrecht* are cases where the defendant left the jurisdiction *after* the indictment, Your Honor," Levine interjected in a soft voice. He continued, "We don't have that situation here. In fact, the *Sapio* court even wondered whether fleeing *after indictment* should even be considered at the trial of the case itself. Anyway, Your Honor . . . I think Mr. Leary's reliance on *Pashnow* or any other case law is unfounded. There is no doubt that the indictment should be dismissed."

"Doesn't an attorney have the obligation, as an officer of this court, Mr. Levine," King's forehead lowered as his eyes blazed out at Levine, "to notify the authorities that his client plans to flee the jurisdiction, especially if he's under investigation as Mr. Ryan knew the defendant Rubin was?"

"I don't know what Mr. Ryan knew at that time, Your Honor," Levine responded quickly. "It's not important, Your Honor. The defendant was not under indictment, and even if he was, the attorney-client relationship precludes Mr. Ryan from revealing his client's intention to leave the jurisdiction."

"I don't think so, Mr. Levine. How much I disagree with the prosecutor, I think I would like to hear from Mr. Ryan, under oath, what he knew at the time as to the intent of his client."

"Your Honor," Levine replied in an aggravated voice, "the defendant Ryan testifying at this time is unprecedented. He would have to testify against his own client."

"That may be. But if you want me to consider dismissing the indictment against him, Mr. Levine, I want to hear from his lips what he knew. That's my ruling."

"May I have a few moments with my client, Your Honor?" Levine asked as his eyes shifted downward to Ryan's face.

"We'll recess for an hour. Give me your answer then, Mr. Levine." King bolted up from his chair, pivoted around his high-backed chair and exited noisily through the door behind the bench area.

Leary smiled. "I'd love to cross-examine your client, Mr. Levine. Are you going to chance it? Maybe I'll find out if Rubin did kill his wife from the mouth of his own lawyer?"

"Screw you, Leary," Levine whispered as his head leaned over toward Leary.

They met outside the courtroom. Levine shepherded Ryan to a corner of the corridor. Leary stood in the opposite corner laughing loudly with Dickson who had suddenly appeared at the break.

"He's setting you up, Joshua," Levine said, his eyes darting furtively at the group of the reporters gathering around Leary.

"Maybe. I thought he was trying to be fair."

"That's King for you. He always sounds fair. I've been before him a dozen times. On the record, he sounds like Oliver Wendell Holmes. But he's a devious old bastard."

"I'm not afraid of Leary in cross," Ryan admitted.

"It's not Leary I'm afraid of . . . that little girl assistant at his side. . . her name's Ambrosio . . . she's no dummy. Besides, King has the right to cross-examine also. All under oath, and I don't think he's going to allow you to claim lawyer-client privilege."

"What do you want me to do?" Ryan asked innocently.

"I don't know. You're damned if you do and damned if you don't. You know he's not going to dismiss the indictment without you testifying. And we certainly don't want to prolong the indictment till trial."

"What about an emergent appeal?"

"Premature. No appellate judge is going to consider the issue until after the hearing. Then it'll be too late."

"Then I don't think we have a choice, Sam."

Levine looked at the steely eyes of Ryan. He had been there when Ryan underwent his first emotional surgical procedure. Sam had stood by and could do nothing. Words meant nothing. Ryan, the boy, had to suffer the pain of the man as Levine had suffered years before. Personal trial by fire. An awful way to reach one's manhood.

Levine thought the savages of the Fijis had a better way to introduce boys to manhood. Circumcise them as teenagers without benefit of anaesthesia. One swipe and it was over. The pain was swift but over. What better way to feel your client's pain then to go through the same pain as a client, a defendant in the wondrous judicial system of America. You didn't even get the foreskin.

Levine led the way, past Leary and the media mob, into the courtroom. It was time to work your trade, he thought. You must have learned something in thirty years, he mused to himself, as he pushed the wooden gate leading into the combat pit, Ryan briskly followed behind him.

They waited for Judge King to enter the courtroom. Barely rising from their chairs when the extended bony hand of the wizened magistrate allowed them to regain their seats.

Leary and his assistant, Ambrosio, marched confidently to their table in the pit. Judge King's eyes cast over the capacity-filled courtroom. Nothing like putting a lawyer on trial to bring the termites out of the woodwork, he thought to himself as his lips opened slightly to a well-hidden smile. What to do? what to do? The Judge's mind echoed the words.

He looked down at Leary, who was beating his pen against the table nervously. Leary's face had developed a nervous twitch at the corner of his mouth. Never liked the boy, King thought. Second generation. Didn't like the senator either but at least he was the first. He was the original anyway. Common people. The worst comes out in the next generation. No class. Aggressive. Almost like those New York Jews.

King hadn't been confronted with Jews until he was in his teens. Heard about them from the whispers of his parents. Foreign element. Different sorts. The war had brought them to Summit County. Fort Dix and all. Now here they were. Levine. The ultimate Jew. Never liked Levine when he was with the prosecutor's office. Tried to block his appointment as assistant prosecutor but somehow he slipped through the political net.

"Are you ready, Counsel?" King asked in an authoritative bellow.

"My client will testify, Your Honor," Levine said.

"Swear him in, madam clerk," the judge instructed the middle aged women seated beneath his bench. Ryan walked to the clerk's desk, raised his right hand and put his left hand on the Bible and repeated the oath after the clerk's recitation. He then turned and walked to the witness box situated to the left of the judge's table. He sat down on the witness chair.

"Mr. Ryan, you know you're under oath," the judge said as if he thought Ryan didn't understand what the clerk had read to him.

"I understand, Your Honor," Ryan replied in a clear voice.

"Go on Mr. Levine, he's your witness," the judge said.

"Yes, Your Honor. Mr. Ryan, Joshua . . . what is your profession?"

"I know what his profession is, Mr. Levine. Let's stop playing footsie. here. Get on with it please," the judge shouted in an angry voice.

"I'm a lawyer, Mr. Levine," Ryan answered as if the judge had not spoken, further angering the court.

"How long have you been a lawyer?" Levine asked in a staccato tone.

"Ten years."

"What is your specialty?"

"I am a criminal defense lawyer . . . most of the time."

"Are you the defense counsel for one Rabbi Carl Rubin?"

"I am."

"How long have you represented Rabbi Rubin?"

"About one month."

"When were you first aware that the defendant Rubin had been indicted by the Summit County grand jury?"

"When I was informed by the chief of county detectives, Captain Crutchfield, about one week ago. When I was trying to bring the defendant back to the States."

"When did you learn that Rabbi Rubin had left Summit County?"

"About two weeks ago."

"How did you learn that he had left the jurisdiction?"

"From his daughter."

"Did you think that his leaving was unusual?"

"Not really. He had perfect right to go anywhere he chose. He was not under indictment at that time and no court order had been issued preventing him from leaving the county, the state, or the country."

"Did you in any way aid the defendant Rubin when he left Summit County?"

"No, I did not." He paused as if to collect his thoughts, and then continued, "Your honor . . . I still see no legal obstacle to him leaving the jurisdiction."

"Why not?"

"Because my understanding of the law, Mr. Levine, merely being under investigation by a police authority . . . and I assume that he was under investigation . . . does not manacle a possible suspect into any travel restraints. It was my understanding he had a long-term political commitment in Israel that he was fulfilling. If the prosecutor saw fit to restrain him, he certainly could have sought a court order . . . or an indictment . . . to prevent Rabbi Rubin from leaving. The prosecutor chose not to do so."

"Your witness, Mr. Prosecutor." Levine barked in a gruff voice as he sat down at the defense counsel table.

Leary jumped up from his chair and barely avoided hitting his knee on the wooden lip of the table. Advancing menacingly at Ryan, he stopped short of the witness box as he placed his hand on the wooden rim of the box.

"Good morning, Mr. Ryan," he announced jovially.

"Good morning, Mr. Leary," Ryan replied equally amicably.

"Did your client ever inform you that he killed his wife?" Leary blurted out, as his face leaned into the box almost touching Ryan's face.

"Objection, Your Honor," Levine shouted in a shocked voice. "Your Honor, Mr. Leary knows the lawyer-client privilege prevails in this proceeding. Mr. Ryan is not on trial for defending Rabbi Rubin. The rabbi certainly has the constitutional right to select counsel of his choice. What Mr. Leary is attempting to do is to elicit confidential and privileged information in a proceeding that has nothing to do with the guilt or innocence of Rabbi Rubin."

King's face lowered as a quixotic smile crossed his lips. For several moments he said nothing. All the spectators in that crowded courtroom heard were the sounds of the drumbeats of Judge King's fingers on the hard wooden table before him.

"Your Honor?" Levine persisted.

"I hear your objection, Mr. Levine . . . I may be old but I'm not deaf. I think . . . yes . . . I think I'll reserve decision on that objection. Let's see where the prosecution is going. Proceed Mr. Leary."

"Your Honor," Levine's voice was obviously agitated, "I don't think the court has the right to withhold its ruling on such an important issue."

"Mr. Levine," King thrust his face over the table, his body lifting up from the tall leather chair, "let me tell you how I run my courtroom. Nobody tells me what to do. How to do it. Maybe you're used to running over judges in your career. But not here. I just said I'm reserving decision. Whether you like it or not. Mr. Prosecutor?" King's monkish head came forward, indicating Leary to proceed.

Leary turned his back on Ryan and walked toward Levine at the defendant's table.

"Mr. Ryan, you knew Rubin was under investigation for the murder of his wife . . . and," Leary continued without catching a breath, causing his voice to rise, "You knew that his leaving Summit County would obstruct a lawful investigation into the murder of his wife?"

Ryan smiled briefly. He sat straight up in his chair and placed his hands on the wooden balustrade surrounding the witness box.

"Mr. Leary, in my many years as your first assistant, I have seen investigations of many people. Some are principal suspects, some are not. Until that person is indicted, the investigation goes on. For you to accuse me of obstruction of justice in allowing, and I've already testified I knew nothing of Rabbi Rubin leaving Summit County, an unindicted person to leave our county borders is ridiculous. The prosecutor's office investigates hundreds of people in any murder case."

"Yes, but you knew the husband of a murdered woman is always the primary suspect." Leary hopped toward Ryan as if his words needed physical support.

"So what?" Ryan replied acidly. "You can't depend on general statistics to prove that in this case the decedent's husband murdered her. That's ridiculous, Mr. Leary."

"You knew about the affairs. You knew about the insurance policies on the life of the decedent. That did tell you your client was the primary suspect. Didn't it?" Leary peered at Judge King to see what the court was going to do. King's face was a blank.

Levine laboriously raised his overweight body from his chair, his voice sharp and angry, "Your Honor . . . again I must protest. What Mr. Ryan knew or didn't know about his client's case, intentions . . . whatever . . . falls within the attorney-client privilege and there is no way in the world that testimony can be admissible."

Suddenly, Judge King's body stirred alive, his mouth nervously quivering as he spoke.

"Mr. Levine, you know as well as I do, the attorney-client privilege does not exist if the attorney and the client are conspiring to commit a crime, or even a civil tort such as fraud. What I conclude from the prosecutor's questions and what he is trying to show is that your client . . . Ryan here . . . and . . . what's his name?"

"Rubin, Your Honor," Leary chimed in.

"Rubin," the court continued, "I think it's permissible inquiry of Ryan here. An attorney who may have known that his client would be obstructing a lawful investigation into a murder by leaving Summit County. Of course, we don't know yet what Mr. Ryan was told or knew, but certainly *that* information is permissible interrogation."

"That would completely destroy any vestige of the attorney-client privilege, Your Honor," Levine replied in a voice he was attempting to control. His round belly extended over the counsel table, his hands palm down on the top of it.

"I never favored those technical exceptions anyway," King replied. "All it does is try and hide the truth, Mr. *LeVine*," King purposely mispronounced Levine's name, "and we are here to find the truth Mr. *LeVine*. Aren't we?"

King's wire-thin body sat back in the high-backed chair, his hands folded tent-like on his abdomen as he awaited Levine's response.

"The truth comes in different packages, Your Honor. To invade the attorney-client privilege is to destroy the air of confidentiality that is the cornerstone of our legal profession, Your Honor."

"Well . . . I've ruled, Mr. Levine. I'm instructing your client to answer the prosecutor's questions."

"Your Honor, respectfully," Ryan said in a low voice, his body turned toward the judge's bench, "I cannot, in anyway, reveal privileged information surrounding the defense of my client."

"Then, Mr. Ryan," the judge pushed forward in his seat and turned to face Ryan in the witness box, "I will have to hold you in contempt of court. I am *ordering* you to answer the questions put forth by the prosecutor."

"I'm sorry, Your Honor," Ryan repeated in a respectful tone.

The silence in the courtroom exploded into raucous murmuring. Nobody had *ever* refused to accede to the wishes of the assignment judge.

"Mr. Ryan, do you know what you are doing?" Judge King barked at Ryan. "If you proceed with the contempt of this court, I will have to put you in the lockup overnight or until whenever you come to your senses. And with your previous record before this bar . . . well . . . I think you know what I mean, Mr. Ryan."

Levine walked up to the judge's bench, Leary behind him.

"Your Honor, may I have a recess so we may petition the appellate division for an immediate stay of this proceeding," Levine said in a threatening undertone.

"No you may not, Mr. Levine. If your client will not answer the prosecutor's questions after I have ordered him to do so, then I have no other choice but to hold him in contempt."

The judge turned again to Ryan, who sat straight in his chair staring out into the sea of faces surrounding him.

"I'm sorry," Ryan repeated. "You have to do what you have to do. But I will not violate my confidence with a client."

There was no bravado in Ryan's voice as he respectfully uttered the words. He was tired, so tired. Not as much from the physical beating, more from the frustration of following the rules in a world where nobody seemed to care about the rules.

"Bailiff," the judge announced for all in the courtroom to hear, "I want you to handcuff Mr. Ryan here. Yes, handcuff him. Like you do any criminal suspect. And march him out of this courtroom to the jail. That's right, the county jail behind this courthouse. And you are to keep him alone in a cell. Until you hear from me. Do you understand those orders, Mr. Bailiff?" King's voice was hard and precise, his tone articulating each word as if he were talking to a deaf-mute.

"Yes, sir," the large, black bailiff said, his eyes displaying the confusion of his mind. "But sir, he's a lawyer. Mr. Ryan was a pros-ecutor . . . you know," the words came out in almost a stutter.

"Mr. Bailiff. I ordered you to take this prisoner to the jail. Like any other prisoner. Do you hear me!" The judge shouted, as his face turned beet red.

"Yes, sir. Sorry, Mr. Ryan," the bailiff led Ryan down from the witness box and handcuffed Ryan's wrists behind his back.

"Don't worry, Jonas," Ryan whispered with a smile. "You do what the judge ordered. I'll be fine."

Levine came up to Ryan and whispered in his ear for several moments. Ryan shook his head in the affirmative and then allowed himself to be led down the length of the courtroom. His eyes observed the shock and confusion of the spectators, many of them lawyers who had heard of the circus maximus being conducted before the assignment judge. Initially, most wished the worst to happen to Ryan. But now, their sentiments had changed. They hoped Ryan, the underdog, the valiant lawyer . . . would beat the old bastard at his own game. Ryan met the eyes of many of those lawyers he had dealt with in the past. From his powerful vantage point as first assistant prosecutor. He had always tried to be fair. Even if it meant incurring the wrath of his unreasonable prosecu-tor. Lawyers with a problem case came to Ryan. Not that he was a diehard-liberal, nor easy in his plea negotiation, but he admitted what had to be admitted. You could deal with Ryan, the undercur-rent opinion of the defense bar understood. Many young lawyers sympathized with Ryan's disastrous fall from grace. It could hap-pen to any lawyer. The five-year burnout they called it. Many never got past the five-year mark. Too much aggravation, too much loss of your own personal life and dignity. There were easier ways to make a living. Some even went so far as to put a gun to their heads and end it all. Many would have done just that to avoid a Ryan tragedy. Any day could be the next disaster. They all knew it.

As Ryan walked slowly past the last row of benches in the wide-open courtroom, it appeared to Levine, who trailed his handcuffed client, as if he were following Jesus on the Via Dolorosa to the cross. Levine laughed to himself. Visions of Biblical events rarely entered his mind. Guess I've seen too many Cecil B. DeMille movies, he mused lightly to himself.

Ryan turned slowly as he passed the last row of benches and searched the faces of the crowd. He smiled, not with humor, just smiled recognizing that he was the only one in this whole fucking county with any balls. Not that he was brave. Far from it. He recognized the many fears that he had but he had overcome those fears which, of course, is the real definition of a hero. Like anyone else trying to preserve his life. But he had taken too much. His mind had come to a point. Enough was enough. 'Damn the torpedoes,' roared through his head, bringing a faint smile to his lips.

The bailiff opened the tall doors of the courtroom and as Ryan started to leave, he heard the shotgun crack of two hands coming together in applause. Then another crack, and another. Until the young lawyers crowded in the backbenches of the courtroom were clapping their hands without restraint. It was as if a tidal wave had enveloped the massive courtroom and sprayed it with fresh water.

Judge King stood up from his bench and gaveled maniacally down on his table. His gaveling and shouts went unheard. Even after Ryan left the courtroom, the clapping continued for several minutes. Then it stopped suddenly. As if it had never happened.

The legal world had caught itself, naked, and upon realizing it, hurriedly dressed in its three-piece Brooks Brothers straight jackets again, as judicial control restored orderly silence.

It was just past noon. The sweet smell of grass bathed in the sun after a rainfall brought tranquility. Unless you were housed in the Lysol-drenched county jail. The guards of the jail knew Ryan from his law-and-order days and they liked him. As ordered, Ryan was placed in a lone cell but it had a wall filled with books and its own toilet. Sort of like the penthouse suite.

The lieutenant of the prison guards had testified in one of

Ryan's cases when he was first assistant prosecutor, one involving the lieutenant's sister. She had been raped by several drunken soldiers, off base, and Ryan had convicted all of them. Sent them to prison for twenty years. The lieutenant never forgot Ryan's diligent prosecution of his sister's attackers. Now it was payback time to Ryan.

Ryan thought how much the world turns in 360 degree circles. Maybe there is a God above, he thought. Maybe not. Anyway, he decided to sit in the soft lounge chair and read a book about retirement. That's what he needed, he thought, retirement. From what? He laughed.

Within four hours of Judge King's contempt order, Levine had prepared the necessary legal memorandum and attached certifications and had delivered it to the chief judge of the appellate division of the state. She was irascible and unforgiving in her judicial opinions. Although not the chief of the highest court in the state, her written decisions were summarily adopted by the state supreme court as if each justice had written the opinion himself. Jewish and female, she lost hope of ever reaching the highest judicial tribunal of the state. She had decided that even from her intermediate level, her brilliance could influence the entire judicial system. And it did. Many times her rulings had overruled Supreme Court precedents. The cognoscenti compared her to Oliver Wendell Holmes except for her wearing a dress under those unisex black robes.

Levine had met her at a legal seminar in Las Vegas. At the pool. They both realized the seminar was taught by lunkheads who didn't want to come out of their illusory clouds to the reality of the sodden legal world, so they sat by the pool of Caesar's Palace downing margaritas. She was divorced and Levine was long estranged from his wife. A natural fit. No sex, but great mental intercourse. She was fascinated with his stories of the old neighborhood. Both had been brought up in Brownsville, Brooklyn, and somehow both had migrated west of the New York City line. She came by marriage, he came by law school.

For three days they lounged mostly alone, an uncomely couple, but occasionally they allowed other recognized intellectual rebels to join and scoff at the world around their lounge chairs. Levine sun-burned his always extended stomach but he felt no pain till the tequila burnt off from his frazzled mind. She covered her pallid white body with large sheet towels. They laughed, criticized, mocked and then reconstructed their ideal world of justice for all, fully realizing that it would never happen. Egalitarianism was for the Keynesians, the pacifists, and the Greenpeace marchers. Neither wished to join the martyrs of change. They both realized they would go so far in their quixotic quest for the ideal world but withdraw when the personal heat became too intense.

They loved their three days. Promised to do it again, but never did. She remarried and Levine retired. They kept in touch by telephone but never saw each other again. Until this fateful day.

Levine arrived at her chambers about 3:00 p.m. Her court proceedings had just finished for the day and she greeted him warmly. After some small talk about remembrances, she reviewed the submitted documents from Levine. He added a verbal analysis, attempting to avoid sounding like an advocate. She wouldn't appreciate ex-parte advocacy he realized.

Peering over her bifocals at Levine, she picked up the phone, dialed a number and waited for the other party to pick up the receiver. "Yes," she finally said into the receiver, "Yes, is the good judge in? Yes, I know he may be busy, young lady, but I think he'll want to talk to me. This is Justice Friedholf. Yes, the *chief.*" She emphasized the word with relish. "Yes, chief of the appellate division, young lady. Listen. You tell that old sonofabitch if he's not on the line in ten seconds I'll tear his robes into shreds. Do you hear me? Yes . . . get his ass on the phone, young lady . . . now!"

She shouted into the phone, sounding more like the tequila-filled compadre of Las Vegas then a chief of the most respected appellate division in the nation.

"Hello, Judge King. Yes . . . you're excused for not picking up the goddamn phone when I call . . . the bathroom? Yes, I know about getting old, Alexander. Maybe you're too old to continue on as an assignment judge," she paused and then smiled at Levine and added, "maybe even as a judge, Alexander. Listen. I've just been handed some pretty persuasive legal documents. Something about putting a defense lawyer in jail because he wouldn't betray a client's confidence to that prick you call a prosecutor."

She paused and listened for a few moments and then continued in a loud, offensive voice, "I don't care whose son he is. How the hell in God's name did you jail a lawyer defending his client? A former prosecutor yet." She paused, listened and then continued, "I don't give a flying shit if he was suspended. So what. I know a lot of judges that *should* be suspended. And by the way, talking about suspensions. What the hell is this all about? I have a certification from a Lester Jones, a former state trooper, who says he saw you present when that anti-Vietnam war rebel was burnt. Am I correct, Mr. Levine, burnt at the stake?"

Her voice rose to a high lilting level of disbelief as she asked the question.

"I don't care if you were younger, Alexander. Maybe you should have quit then. Listen, I'm not going to rule on anything that happened twenty-five years ago. I'm sure the attorney general of this fine state might be interested, but I want you to let that young man go. Now. No further hearing. You hear . . . either you recuse yourself and let another judge . . . an impartial one I hope . . . to hold a proper hearing, or dismiss the goddamn indictment against Mr. Ryan. It's a bullshit indictment anyway, Alexander. You know it and I know it. Yes. Yes. I understand you were pressured by Leary but Alexander, you're the assignment judge in Summit County. You tell Leary what to do . . . not vice-versa. Listen I have to be in New York for the opening of a Neil Simon play. I don't have time for this shit. Do you understand me, Alexander. And by the way, your request for extension of your term has been denied. So get Ryan out of jail before they take your robes away now. No, I won't call the papers. But I can't stop Mr. Levine from doing so. He'll be down in 90 minutes to pick up his client. Nice talking to you again, Alexander. You, too."

Dropping the receiver on the cradle, she put her high-heeled foot on the corner of her partner's ancient desk, leaned back in her chair, removed a Dominican cigar from her robe pocket, chewed off the tip of the burly cigar, lit it with a gold lighter and blew a cascade of smoke out toward the standing Levine.

"I could use a margarita just about now, Sam," she said with a broad smile on her smooth face.

Levine marveled at the perfection of her teeth, straight as two parallel railroad tracks on a bed of red earth. She was a beautiful woman in an exotic ageless way, something you would think about if you were in the presence of Cleopatra. All she needed was a long gown wrapped around her reed-thin body and a diamond tiara on her head. Only her gravelly voice belied the womanly essence she emitted.

"I have to go, Your Honor, because I think my client would appreciate an early release. At least before he is forced to eat county jail food for dinner."

"I know, Sam. These black robes fool a lot of people." She paused, puffed heatedly on the cigar and then continued, drawing her feet off the desk. "I miss those three days, Sam. It was like back in the college dorm. . .shooting the shit with the guys. Are we getting so old, Sam, and so stodgy that we can't sit around and talk about nothing important? Everything here seems to be so important. Life and death. Money and power. God, I miss those days when the only important thing you worried about was where you were going to drink that weekend."

"We lived in a different age, Marilyn," Levine reluctantly said her first name, "the war was over and the world was saved. All we had to worry about was getting a job . . . and I guess for me . . . getting laid."

"Jewish girls didn't think about those mundane things, Sam." She laughed and then continued, "Maybe we did. Not about a job . . . but sex. I guess even if you didn't do it . . . or were not supposed to do it . . . you thought about it. God, what prudes we were, Sam. Anyway, you can pick up the order of release from my clerk outside. Let's get together, y'know, margarita and finger food. Let's do it soon, Sam"

He walked around the desk and kissed her affectionately on the cheek, startling the judge, but she regained her composure, stood up and startled Sam by kissing him full on the lips.

"Too bad I got married, Sam. I always had a hankering for an overweight aging liberal."

"Thanks again . . . Your Honor." Sam smiled, turned and walked out of the judge's chambers.

CHAPTER FORTY-THREE

"You made me look like a fool, Roger," Judge King said, his back to Leary, who was slouched in a chair situated in front of the judge's massive desk.

"They're all over the place, Judge," Leary replied as he proceeded to bite nervously at his fingernails.

"Who is?"

"Those mother-humping kikes, Judge. Friedholf. Your appellate friend. She had no right to overrule your order, Judge."

"Whether she had a right or not, she had the power to do it, Roger. And she's more powerful then you think she is. Her husband is the head of the Republicans in this state, Roger. And you know what that means as far as your hope for reappointment."

It was the morning after Ryan's release from the county jail. The local papers had played up the emerging drama on the front pages, and soon the urban media picked up on the fireworks. It was act one of the great religious murder trial soon to be enfolded before the American public.

The buzzer on Judge King's telephone intercom sounded. He picked up the receiver and then said, "Send him in, Louise."

The office door opened and Judge Sturmer walked in. He was dressed in his black judicial robes.

"I heard," Sturmer said abruptly, as he opened his robe and then sat in a chair next to Leary. His usual impeccable appearance seemed somewhat askew, almost careless for Sturmer.

"You're still trying the case, Albert," Leary pronounced in a confident voice.

"It's up to the AJ" Sturmer raised his hand toward King, who had turned around to face Sturmer.

"I see nothing wrong with Albert presiding over the Rubin case," King said.

"Captain Crutchfield mentioned . . . you know," Sturmer said in a quiet undertone as if he didn't want any reply.

"That looney tune Lester Jones." Leary grimaced, as he started to pick at the skin around his fingernails. "He knows shit. My father used him as a goddamn gofer. Even if he was there, who the hell is gonna believe a screwball like him?"

"The body has never been found," King said.

"What happens if Jones knows where the body is?" Sturmer's face was lined with abject fear.

"I thought it was burnt . . . gone . . . disappeared . . ." King interjected.

"Not all of it," Sturmer replied, as he rose to stand next to the window.

"Even if they find what's left of the body . . . it's been 25 years," Leary said in a snide voice.

"With DNA testimony. And carbon analysis. Goddamnit, Roger, you're the prosecutor, you should know what's happening out there," King almost shouted as he nervously swept the long thin hair on the side of his head over his bald spot.

"I'll send Dickson out to talk to Jones," Leary said.

"Maybe you should muzzle Dickson until after the Rubin trial," King ordered.

"He's a loose cannon, Roger," Sturmer added.

Leary jumped up from his chair and walked back and forth across the office in almost a straight line, his head down in seeming concentration.

"We have to get Rubin to trial, Judge," Leary said addressing Judge King.

"Are you ready?" King replied.

"I think we have enough. And if we don't, Albert here can provide the fuel that burns that Jew cocksucker."

"I think maybe, Roger . . . and I'm not telling you how to run your office. . ." Sturmer raised his hand to show Leary he was not really advising Leary how to run his office, "but the way you feel about the defendant. Well, I don't think an obviously partial prosecutor looks good in front of a jury. I was thinking maybe . . . what's her name . . . that nice little Italian girl that did such a good job in the double-murder trial last month."

"Ambrosio," Leary barked in a hateful tone. "She ain't trying this case. Over my dead body. She'll be second chair. *I'm gonna face that jury*. And all that good media shit that's gonna follow *me*, Albert . . . *me*. So forget about advising me how to run my office!"

Leary again sat down in the black leather chair in front of the judge's desk as his body slumped even lower into the chair.

King stood behind his chair, his hands planted firmly on the top of the chair.

"We go to trial Monday, gentlemen. I'll clear the calendar of any other trial that would interfere with Albert presiding over the trial or preventing him from picking a jury," King announced in a stentorian voice.

"What about . . . y'know . . . the body. Elias Rubin." Sturmer's mouth had difficulty pronouncing the name.

"Roger, send Captain Crutchfield out to talk to Jones," King ordered. "The captain can be discreet about delicate matters like this. Besides he was there also . . . he has as much to lose as we do."

"I don't know if we can trust him, Your Honor," Leary replied. "Ever since he came back. I don't know. And my guys have seen him palling around with Mathias. Y'know the Larchmont Hills cop who helped Ryan."

"Talk to the captain, Roger. Use the little common sense your late father gave you. Don't be such a hothead all the time," King criticized the little body crouched in a pathetic slump in front of him.

Sturmer's eyes roamed around the office filled with mementos of judicial honors heaped on the assignment judge who had presided over the lives of thousands for over a quarter of a century. His gaze stopped at the rows of handsomely embossed law books, their contents well known to Sturmer, who had graduated summa cum laude from Harvard Law School. Many New York law firms had beckoned to him after his law review year at Harvard but he chose to return to Summit County, his family's home for over a century. They had migrated from Germany in the late 1860's, farmers all, and they had built a family heritage from honesty and hard work over many years. He was the first to achieve the rewards of a profession. A lawyer, then a judge, his parents were ecstatic that he was so well respected by all. Yet he knew all the honors were hollow within. What his parents did not know, and would never know because they had died years ago, was that he had to do things that would have shamed them if they had known.

He was Senator Leary's bagman. Whatever the senator wanted, Sturmer delivered. Without question. When was enough enough, Sturmer thought scornfully to himself. New York looked pretty good to him now. He wondered what would come out of it all . . . with Roger Leary deciding his future. He was almost 65, retirement age, but he valued his judicial name more then anything else. He would rather die a horrible death then face dishonor and disgrace. And he knew not what to do. Fate had delivered his last few years on earth in the hands of a young madman who knew no bounds, nor honor. Just power.

"I will be ready Monday, AJ," Sturmer said in almost a whisper, as he turned from the assignment judge and walked slowly out of the room.

King stared at Leary's fetus-like body before him. Can it come down to this, he wondered almost aloud. A lifetime of work and honor all sucked down the drain by events he could not control. And control was the essence of the judge's life. He had controlled the lives of so many people who had appeared before him over these many years. Lives he knew nothing about. Nor cared for. His was to dispense justice. Alexander King's justice. As he saw it.

Now, he wondered, had the circle come around? Like Sturmer, his greatest desire was to leave this earth with his name and honor intact. Revered. He believed in a Presbyterian God; he believed in Heaven and Hell; he believed that he would ascend to Heaven and gaze down upon this Earth, a world that would not only remember his name but eulogize his works for all time.

Elias Rubin may be the only name they remember, he mused, as he motioned Leary out of his office. He had had enough for one day. Getting old wasn't as good as it was cracked up to be, he muttered to himself. He was alone now. Solitude had descended on the world he had known for these many years. But he knew the solitude was fleeting. The days ahead would not be lonely.

CHAPTER FORTY-FOUR

Captain Daniel Crutchfield had arrived early that evening at Lester Jones's cabin. Yehuda and Olsham had driven into town to pick up Ryan and Levine.

"What d'ya want, Captain?" Lester had asked suspiciously of his uninvited guest. Grabbing the spike collar of Lyndon Junior, Lester was tired of the whole mess. Everybody wanted something from him. Even the old captain. They'd never been friends when Lester was a state trooper chauffeur of the senator. The captain had looked down on Lester. And he never even hid his repugnancy toward the Piney trooper.

Now everything had changed. The captain was clearly afraid. He had aged dramatically in the last ten years. veins creeping along his jowls, the captain appeared frightened of the world around him.

"They sent me to tell you to keep your mouth shut, Lester," he warned the tobacco chewing, half-naked Lester who didn't appear threatened by the captain's warnings.

"About what?" he innocently replied to the captain.

"Y'know about what, Lester."

"Yeah I do, Captain. And you were there too. I saw you. along with those other fellows, Captain."

"I don't know what you're talking about, Lester."

"Yes you do, Captain. Yes, you do. You were with the senator. And them two judges. You stayed back when they put that nigger up at the stake. I saw you, Captain. Getting back into the pine grove. But, I guess, you felt sorry for that poor black fellow . . . because then I saw you run up . . . through the fire and try to untie him. But Dickson didn't let you. You remember all that, Captain?" Lester smiled his missing-tooth smile as if he had just finished the punch-line of a dirty joke.

"They could hurt you, Lester, if you don't keep your mouth shut . . . they . . . y'know who I mean, Lester."

"Sure I do. That's why they ain't been out here to kick me off the government's property. But I know what I know and I ain't keeping it all in my head just because you fellows are running scared." Lester knocked his head with a clenched fist.

"I'm trying to save your life, Lester . . . for old time's sake." The captain was noticeably shaken, his voice tremulous with fear and frustration.

"You better leave, Captain. I can't hold Lyndon forever. And he don't take kindly to strangers."

"I'm your friend, Lester. I just want to help you," the captain's voice pleaded.

Night was falling and stars were shining brightly through the open windows. Night sounds of the Pinelands filled the cabin with an eerie sensation.

"You better go, Captain. I got nothing to say to you fellows. What I saw is what I saw and nobody's gonna tell me to lie about it."

"You know Dickson, Lester. He's a mean fellow. I'm trying to save you from being hurt."

"You're trying to save your own skin, Captain. I ain't that dumb, y'know. The Senator was an evil man, Captain. He shouldn't of burnt that fellow. No matter he was a big-mouth nigger. He shouldn't burnt that fellow."

"I didn't burn anyone, Lester." Crutchfield's voice was quivering with fear echoed by his frenzied eyes.

"You didn't burn him, Captain. But you were there . . . with those other fellows."

"I'm trying to help you, Lester," the captain repeated.

"That's what you said, Captain. But nobody's gonna help me. Except maybe my nephew, John. Do you know John, Captain?"

"He's a friend of mine, Lester."

"Maybe so . . . but you better go, Captain. And tell those fellows . . . the ones who were there . . . they shouldn't of burned that fellow. No sirree, they shouldn't have burnt him."

Crutchfield left the cabin and walked slowly down to the campsite. He thought about his wife. He should've died first. He missed her. The last year she went through hell. He remembered how she suffered before she died of Lou Gehrig's disease. She was so brave

. . . never complained of the horrible pain . . . that wracked her body. 'Why couldn't I be so brave? he thought. And his son . . . a big-time lawyer in New York . . . had not spoken to him in the last year. 'She kept us together,' he murmured as he walked up to the charred remnants of the once fiery cross set in the middle of the infamous campsite.

She gave him love and respect, like nobody else in this world ever had. Not his son, anyway. He won't care if I live or die, he paused and smiled, his fear slowly dissipating. Getting old is the shits. The Eskimos have the right idea, he laughed to himself, put the old fellows out in the icy wasteland to die before they can feel the disrespect of the young ones.

The .45 was stuck in his belt. Just in case Lester wouldn't cooperate. And he won't. So what to do? No more retirement if Lester talks. The captain could never take prison. . .never.

Slowly he lifted the gun out of his belt, cocked the trigger mechanism, placed the muzzle of the square-shaped gun in his mouth and pulled the trigger. He was half smiling as his brains cascaded out of the back of his head onto the charred grounds of Elias Rubin's inferno.

Yehuda and Olsham found the half-decapitated body of the captain near midnight. They wondered if Dickson had murdered the captain.

CHAPTER FORTY-FIVE

"I love you, Moira," the rabbi whispered to the delicate, seemingly ageless woman lying next to him.

"I love you, Carl. I wish this was all over with already. So we could live our lives without . . . you know . . . this frightful uncertainty. That any minute our world is going to self-destruct. Even here, Carl, I'm so frightened that the police are going to crash through the front door." She started to cry softly, tears rolling down her childlike face.

"Soon . . . darling . . . soon." He smiled that charismatic, even smile that had comforted so many believers before Moira. "My lawyer doesn't believe that they have anything concrete. Just a lot of suspicious, circumstantial things that always occur in marriages."

She lifted her petite body onto her elbows and placed her head in the palm of her hand and stared directly into the rabbi's face.

"You didn't do it, Carl?" she asked in an accusatory voice.

"Moira," the rabbi smiled, his voice deep and ambiguous, "can you see me killing anything? Even an unfaithful wife?"

Moira rose from the bed and swiveled her body around to face the rabbi's prone body lying flat in the bed.

"What are you talking about, Carl?" she half shouted. "Eleanore . . . you never told me!"

"I still don't know for sure . . . and I don't know with whom . . . for sure. But, yes, Eleanore."

"Does anybody know? I mean the other side?"

"Maybe. I don't know what the prosecutor knows. My lawyer says they have to tell us what they know before trial. Unless they claim it's newly discovered just before trial. It's probably nothing, Moira," he added.

The Ritz Carlton suite was on the 31st floor overlooking Central Park.

"How can they blame you, Carl? You weren't even there," Moira declared.

"I know . . . they talk about contract killers. Like I was some kind of a gangster."

Moira sat cross-legged on the bed, her hands absentmindedly touching the rabbi's naked arms and chest.

"You do love me, Carl? I mean I'm the only one."

"Of course, Moira. There is no one else."

"You swear to it, Carl?" Her voice turned severe in her questioning.

"On the Old Testament, Moira."

"Because if there is somebody else, Carl . . . y'know I wouldn't stand for it." She paused and her liquid-green eyes narrowed "Not like Eleanore. I wouldn't stand for it, Carl."

"I know, Moira. Those days are gone forever. I'm too old to play around."

He smiled as he rose to wrap his arms around Moira's tiny body, his legs astride her crossed legs. The events of the past weeks had not diminished his appetite.

CHAPTER FORTYSIX

Selection of jurors have, and will always be, a crapshoot. The public relations side of a major capital case is often times more important than the events that occur at trial. Although both sides of the courtroom seek favorable jurors, they would easily settle for totally non-prejudiced jurors. Every prospective juror that sits so innocently on the panel waiting to be selected as a sitting juror harbors conscious or subconscious prejudices that come into play when he or she ultimately decides guilt or innocence of the defendant.

Being black, as a juror, might cause some black people to listen more to a black defendant's side than the prosecution. And maybe not. Being Jewish leads some lawyers to believe that a juror is too liberal, favorable toward the defendant's side. Of course, as most trial lawyers know, Jewish can also mean Republican conservative. And that means law and order. And that means believing in the state against the defendant.

In the case of Carl Rubin, rabbi extraordinaire, the state made a concerted effort to diffuse the general belief that religious men do not kill their wives.

Leary attempted to publicly demonize the good rabbi; to show the prospective jurors reading about the upcoming case that the rabbi was a lecherous, manipulative, all too greedy human being, just like many of the prospective jurors. Jurors tend to lose their lustful predilections when they enter the wooden corral of the jurors' world. A shroud of purist innocence descends on their minds and they expect the defendant to demonstrate the same Christian values as they have recently assumed.

Leak upon leak was distributed by Leary's office about the rabbi's indiscretions. Enough to force Carl Rubin to resign as head rabbi of Temple Beth Shalom. Not because of the indictment against him, but more because of the admitted violations of his rabbinical oath to comfort his parishioners through verbal ministrations only. The resignation was a public relations blow to the rabbi's public persona. The inviolate shield that had previously enveloped his image dissolved and the public eye suddenly realized that maybe defrocked rabbis *do* kill their wives for the same reason ordinary men kill their wives. Money, sex, and frustration over their marital relations.

Levine had counter-leaked news squibs to his female public voice at the local newspaper in an attempt to show the rabbi as his devout followers believed: a true man of God and the people. Levine also hired a publicity agent to create enough paid and unpaid literary distributions in the Philadelphia-area Jewish week-lies. Jew against redneck. The rabbi was being prosecuted not because the state had any hard evidence that he was the killer of Eleanore Rubin, but rather because he was a leader among the growing Judaic community reaching throughout Summit County.

Ryan, as promised, filed his motion to change venue out of Summit County with Judge King. It was summarily denied. Ryan opined that the appellate division would deny his motion for leave to appeal because it wasn't a final judgement in the case. The appellate division probably wouldn't accept the premise that a defendant couldn't get a fair trial anywhere in the most civilized state in the union.

Also as expected, Sturmer was selected as trial judge. Levine suggested a motion be filed by Ryan to request Sturmer to recuse himself, but they knew that the court rules allowed judges wide discretion in denying recusal motions.

After a week of blistering news announcements, motions, and impassioned arguments, both sides were ready for trial.

Monday, October 13 was cloudy and bitter cold. Indian summer had disappeared like a pleasant dream gone south. Golf shirts were replaced with sweaters and overcoats. The fertile trees of Summit County had begun to shed their leaves. Bristol braced itself for the onslaught of twenty-first century justice, as seen through the eyes of television legal color commentators.

Sturmer moved the trial to the old courthouse, unused for over a year, with high ceilings and a cavernous amphitheater that could reasonably house the abundant curious trial watchers. The media arrived in panel trucks and limousines, dressed in overalls and Versace suits, all vying for the inside story of the trial of the year.

It had everything modern soundbite Boswells crave; it was the Jewish Jimmy Swaggart soap opera with murder thrown in.

Ryan hadn't slept most of the previous night. No matter how much he meditated, how many Pepto-Bismol tablets he swallowed, or deep breaths he choked on, his eyes stared at the ceiling of his bedroom.

Recurring thoughts of failure overtook him. He had come so far in the last couple of years; far enough to stand the legal world on its mendacious ass, but he had to win to do it. The legal world only respected winners. Losers were dead people relegated to an unknown cemetery. He had been there. He didn't want to go back.

About 3:30 in the morning, he realized what he needed more than anything else in the world. Sosie. He couldn't tear her out of his mind. The face, the body, the supple hands, and her reassuring voice . . . all kept him awake.

At 4 a.m., he called her. It was mid-afternoon in Jerusalem and she was on her way to a soccer match with her then boyfriend. He stuttered at first, hoping she wasn't there. They talked small talk for over a minute. They both wondered what each wanted of each other.

"The trial starts this morning," he said.

"I know. Poppa called last night." She paused. There were several moments of silence before she continued.

"I've thought about you," she said.

"So have I."

"What about?"

"There are things that shouldn't be said over the phone."

"You're a strange man, Joshua Ryan."

Ryan could see the sun beginning to rise.

"I wish we had had more time, Sosie."

"Can you use an extra hand at your trial?" she said in a husky voice.

"Your hand?"

"Maybe. Shula is coming to New York with her senior class. I can always go along as a chaperone."

"Would you? What about your job?"

"I don't have a job. I'm an unemployed soldier. Maybe you can offer me a job." She laughed a throaty laugh.

He could imagine her face lighting up with that inner joy she revealed when she laughed.

"Tell me when, Sosie. I miss you."

"We have nothing in common, y'know, Joshua. You're not even a full-blooded Jew."

"Come anyway." He laughed for the first time in days.

"Go back to sleep, Joshua. I'll call when the plane leaves Tel Aviv. By the way, did I tell you, I've missed you. Ever since you left."

He fell asleep shortly after he hung up the receiver. His mind had somehow cleared, enough to allow the tranquil cloud of sleep to blot out the ugly images penetrating his aching racing brain.

The oldest working courthouse in the United States was overwhelmed with the detritus of national media coverage of the trial. That morning, Ryan and company had assembled in Ryan's office up the street from the courthouse. The rabbi was dressed in a conservative dark pinstriped suit. Ryan thought he appeared too successful for the Pineys of Summit County.

Yehuda, Olsham, and Levine were all in nondescript sport jackets while Ryan wore his funeral black single-breasted suit, barely revealing the shining spots near the shoulder areas. It was one of his two trial suits. Like all superstitious athletes, Ryan wore clothing, shoes, and other accessories that he had worn when he was a winner. Why tempt the fates, he thought. Litigation was a gamble at best.

Surrounding the rabbi, the four men walked into the courthouse with the rabbi in the center of the human umbrella. Microphones and video cameras were violently thrust into their faces by frenetic reporters and cameramen. They all smiled, as ordered by Ryan. It was 8:50 a.m. and the early rays of sunlight sprayed into the courthouse.

The courtroom was filled with rows of hardback wooden benches, surrounded by massive windows with paint peeling around the rims. A whirring fan was slowly revolving around the center of the courtroom. Old wall sconces inefficiently washed streams of light onto the walls.

Ryan and the defendant Rubin sat down at the counsel table located on the far left side of the trial pit, away from the jury box.

With great concentration, Ryan emptied the box-like briefcase onto the table. Olsham carried in two more boxes of files and placed them behind Ryan's chair.

At exactly 9:00 a.m Judge Albert Sturmer stormed in from behind the judge's bench onto the elevated judge's area. The clerk hammered a gavel loudly against his desk located to the right side of the Judge and demanded all persons in the courtroom to stand. Sturmer then waved the overflowing crowd to sit.

Sturmer's face appeared haggard. His eyes were bloodshot and his mouth quivered ever so slightly. Topped with a shock of ghostly white hair, he looked the part of the scholarly old respected judge.

Leary strode into the courtroom shortly after the judge had been seated. Followed by Ambrosio, the female assistant prosecutor, and a young male associate, Leary pushed open the gate to the pit area without holding it open for his two following associates who were loaded down with several cartons of files.

"Good morning, Your Honor," Leary said in a clear voice, noticeably ignoring Ryan's presence at defendant's counsel table.

"Good morning, Mr. Leary," Sturmer replied with his bushy eyebrows somewhat raised.

"Mr. Ryan," Sturmer announced as he turned his face toward Ryan.

"Your Honor," Ryan replied, as he respectfully stood as he spoke.

"Gentlemen, are we ready to pick a jury," Sturmer announced.

CHAPTER FORTY-SEVEN

The selection of the jury devoured a day and a half. Each side used nine of their alloted ten peremptory challenges before the jury was finally selected. Sturmer asked all the questions to the prospective jurors after requesting each side to submit questions that he would consider in the voir dire process. Usually, most prospective jurors attempted to avoid jury duty by vain and thinly-veiled excuses tendered to the judge. Job, medical appointments, disability, and the like were excuses that were usually sufficient to escape the timeless boredom of jury duty. Not in the case of *State v. Rubin*. Everybody wanted in. No matter what.

The potential jurors envisioned themselves on the Geraldo show voicing suddenly desired opinions requested from the television talk show hosts. The O.J. trial had forged a pandemic precedent. There was money to be made in being a juror. It suddenly became a sought-after position. Like being a doctor to a Jewish mother's kid. Now jurors became celebrities. Winners of an odd national lottery. And fourteen ordinary citizens were chosen. To decide the fate of one Carl Rubin.

And others . . . Joshua Ryan . . . and Roger Leary.

Prosecutor Leary opened to the jury. The state had the first word in every trial. Lawyers knew that the first twenty minutes could decide the outcome of any trial. Brevity was the mother's milk of favorable verdicts.

Give'em a show, as Levine had tutored to his neophyte warriors. Don't move too much, but move! Don't show too much because they will listen only to the way you act, and then forget your words. Treat them like children watching *Sesame Street*. Grab'em and hold'em. Tightly, he would preach.

Leary placed a legal pad full of written notes on the lectern in front of the jury. Glancing occasionally at the notes, Leary's voice climbed from its lowest strata to its highest tenor. Then he caught himself. As if he had been told what to do. Or not.

"Killers may come in strange garb," he pronounced as he wrapped his hands around the edges of the wooden lectern, "but they all have the same evil. Whether they be rabbi, priest or businessman, they all murder for the same reasons. And so did the defendant. Cold-blooded, premeditated, and with malice aforethought, defendant Carl Rubin, a once revered rabbi, arranged, for money and lust, to have his beloved wife of twenty-seven years eliminated. The State will show, ladies and gentlemen of the jury, that Carl Rubin arranged to have his wife, Eleanore, murdered. No, we don't have the actual perpetrator in hand, but the circumstantial and direct evidence are so strong to show that only Carl Rubin could have arranged to kill his wife."

"During this trial," he continued, "you will hear testimony that the defendant secured a one- millon-plus dollar policy on his wife's life while fornicating with members of his own church. Most importantly, the state will show that that one piece of tangible evidence, an envelope left at the scene of the crime by the probable murderer, contained the defendant's fingerprints on the outer cover."

Ryan was on his feet, his voice crying out his objection.

"Your Honor, the prosecution's allegations that the defendant's fingerprints were found on any envelope must be stricken. In fact, I must ask for a mistrial."

Sturmer motioned for counsel to approach the sidebar, on the witness box side and away from the jury.

"What's your objection, Counsel?" Sturmer pointedly demanded from Ryan.

"Your Honor, defense has never received any discovery about fingerprints on some envelope. Mr. Leary had an inviolate obligation to notify us about any envelope evidence relating to fingerprints. Especially if it is alleged to be the defendant's fingerprints."

"Mr. Leary?" Sturmer turned to face Leary, who had a stupid grin on his face.

"Your Honor, as Mr. Ryan knows, the state has the obligation to turn over evidence that it has in its possession before trial. Well, Your Honor, we have just come into possession of this envelope. And, of course, I was going to reveal our scientific findings to Mr. Ryan . . . right after my opening. I certainly would have no objection to Mr. Ryan securing an expert to examine the *clear, unmis-*

takable fingerprints of the defendant on the envelope left at the decedent's door by the actual perpetrator."

"Your Honor," Ryan could feel a wave of panic coming up through his stomach and surging to his throat, "the prosecutor cannot present such damning evidence at trial. He should have presented the evidence to the defense and then, if need be, ask for an adjournment of this trial. That's if he really only received the envelope and fingerprint analysis *just before trial.*"

Ryan articulated the words in a biting manner, his voice obviously disbelieving in tone.

"Is my worthy adversary calling me a liar?" Leary pronounced indignantly, the smile still blatant on his face.

"You know you are!" Ryan replied in a voice that could be heard beyond the sidebar area.

"Keep your voice down, Mr. Ryan," Sturmer warned. "From what I see, Mr. Ryan, the state has not presented its evidence yet, and if Mr. Leary represents to this court that he has just received this piece of evidence, I'm not going to call the prosecutor a liar. Unless you have proof of intentionally hidden evidence, I'm going to allow the representation in Mr. Leary's opening to stand. You certainly will have the opportunity to submit the envelope to your selected expert. If that will do any good."

"Your Honor," Ryan persisted, "I don't know if you know how strongly I feel about this. . . ."

"I know how strongly you feel, Mr. Ryan. But I have ruled . . . and there will be no further argument in this matter. Is that understood?"

The jurors were starting to squirm nervously in their seats, their faces denoting the irritation of being kept waiting for some ruling they knew nothing about.

"Let's carry on," Sturmer said in a loud voice, nodding his head toward the lawyers to return to their respective positions.

Ryan attempted to hide his churning emotions, knowing full well that this decision could already be the turning point in this case. What envelope? What fingerprints? He thought painfully to himself. How the hell did we miss such a vital piece of evidence?

"Continue, Mr. Prosecutor," Sturmer blared from the bench, smiling at the jurors.

"Thank you, Your Honor," Leary obsequiously replied. Slowly he turned to face the jury, his face a mask of dire concern.

"As I said, ladies and gentlemen of this jury, the state will not only present clear and convincing evidence in the form of the defendant's own fingerprints on an envelope left by the actual killer, but also will show that the defendant knew that he was going to be convicted of the murder of his wife."

Ryan almost jumped to his feet, waited in a painful half standing stance, waiting for Leary's next words.

"Why else would a defendant, Carl Rubin, flee Summit County *after* he was indicted for the murder of Eleanore Rubin."

Ryan leaped to his feet, his chair falling loudly behind his fast rising body.

"Your Honor," he declared in a patronizing voice, "Why does Mr. Leary continue on with such malignant contentions when he clearly knows he's lying to this jury."

Ryan knew now a mistrial must be declared if he openly accused the prosecutor of lying in front of the jury. Ryan had no other choice. No matter what Sturmer ruled as far as Leary's brazen lies, it could not cure the contention that the defendant had fled the jurisdiction.

"Counsel," Sturmer announced in an exasperated voice, then directed his attention to the jury, "ladies and gentlemen of the jury, I'm going to ask you to return to the jury room while we discuss the defense's objections. Please give your luncheon orders to the bailiff. Thank you for your patience."

They all waited for the jury to leave the box before anyone said anything further.

"Counselor," Sturmer declared, his finger pointing at Ryan, "in my thirty years on the bench, I have rarely seen such rudeness . . . to a brother counselor no less."

He paused and then interrupted Ryan as Ryan started to explain.

"Wait a second, Mr. Ryan . . . I haven't finished. It is customary, in this county anyway, to allow your adversary to finish his opening, without frivolous objections being thrown in and about . . . especially in front of the jury. What are you trying to do, Mr. Ryan? Have me call a mistrial? You don't want me to do that, or do you?"

Leary's grin returned to his pinched face. They all knew that's exactly what Ryan wanted. A mistrial . . . with the hope that Sturmer would be forced to recuse himself for the next trial.

"Your Honor," Ryan said in a voice less respectful than expected when addressing a judge of the Superior Court. He then waved his arms toward the spectator gallery of the courtroom, "*you know*, Leary here knows, the whole courtroom, they all know what Mr. Leary is doing. He is fabricating a prosecution by innuendo. The State has no case. None to overcome the burden of reasonable doubt. The issue of flight of the defendant is a non-issue because Mr. Leary knows full well that the indictment was returned *after* the defendant legally went to Israel for a preplanned speaking engagement. In fact, as the court knows, Mr. Leary indicted me . . . for obstruction of justice . . . and we all know what happened to that charge. He's grasping at straws, Your Honor."

"I've seen the briefs you filed, Mr. Ryan," Sturmer answered heartily. "I don't buy them. Your client knew he was under investigation. And I'm not conceding the probable fact that he could have been indicted before he fled Summit County. I think it's relevant comment by the state to show evidence or at least the mindset of the defendant at that time."

"Your honor," Ryan's fist pounded absentmindedly on the table, "then declare a mistrial. *You* certainly have not displayed the requisite impartiality to preside over this case."

Ryan paused and stared at Levine, seated to his side. Levine was scribbling on a yellow legal pad. *Yes, yes*, was the inscription.

"You're not going to force me into declaring a mistrial, Mr. Ryan. Before I do that I will hold you in contempt of court because you are obviously baiting me into granting your motion."

"You may have to, Judge," Ryan declared, knowing full well a mistrial would be the defendant's only chance of getting a fair trial.

Rubin sat on the other side of Ryan, his face cloaked in confusion. Was Ryan right in what he was doing? The rabbi wondered. Why bait the judge? The client as well as the jurors observe the judge as an impartial element in the deliverance of justice. We all believe in justice, the layman think.

It's only the very perceptive laymen who can sometimes realize that even the judge is human, with the usual prejudices, favorites, and predilections toward one side. Lawyers well know it. Most experienced litigators bank their entire case on who the trial judge will be. Judge shopping is the primary activity of most successful trial lawyers. In some states judges are elected, and many of the lawyers who appear before them are substantial contributors to their political campaigns. In states where judges are appointed by the politicians, they worry not about removal from their vaunted benches after their first term in office is ended. Tenure then kicks in and only catastrophic deviation from judicial ethical conduct can cause removal. Either procedure comes with latent defects but the bottom line is that judges come to a trial with injudicious baggage.

And, of course, Sturmer carried more baggage than most judges. He was afraid and that fear would carve his decisions in favor of the one he feared the most, Leary the prosecutor.

"I will not recuse myself, Mr. Ryan," Sturmer announced in a heated voice, "and further you are ordered to remain in your chair during the completion of Mr. Leary's opening. I will hear any objections *after* he has completed his opening, and not until then are you to voice your opinions to this jury. Am I clear, Mr. Ryan?"

Ryan stood on his feet, his hips cemented to the edge of counsel table. He wanted to vomit. He knew the case could be lost if he strictly followed Sturmer's orders. Yet, as an officer of the court, he was honor bound to follow the instructions of the court.

Where does the line end, he thought. Where does his allegiance to his client end and his duty to the court begin? Ryan knew that if he disobeyed the court's very clear instructions, and the appellate courts sided with Sturmer on appeal, Ryan could easily be disbarred. Forever this time. And he knew he couldn't take that. Not ever.

"Your honor," Ryan walked in front of counsel table, "with all due respect to this court, I must strenuously disagree with the court's instructions. There is no rule, nor case law, that requires defense counsel to sit still while the State maliciously and intentionally lies to a jury. To bind me to silence, this court is sealing the fate of my client. And I will not sit idly by and let that happen. I am asking this court for an adjournment of these proceedings so I may deliver an emergent appeal to the appellate judge assigned to Summit County."

"Denied, Mr. Ryan," Sturmer angrily replied. "You will follow my instructions to the T. If you violate these instructions, I will call a recess and then appoint other counsel to defend your client, *then* I'll call a mistrial and have you locked up for contempt of court. I will file a grievance complaint with the Summit County ethics committee against you and propose you be disbarred. You understand me, Mr. Ryan?"

Ambrosio, seated alongside Leary at the state's counsel table, pushed a torn page from a legal pad toward Leary. Leary waved her aside for a moment, obviously relishing in the rebuke heaped on Ryan, but she grabbed his hand and placed the note in it. With obvious anger, he looked at the note.

Leary then whispered into Ambrosio's ear. For several seconds it seemed Ambrosio and Leary were arguing in subdued whispers. Then with a wave of his hand, Leary pushed away from Ambrosio. But Leary had digested his second chair's advice as he rose to finish his opening. Ryan dejectedly took his seat.

The jury appeared frustrated, being shuffled into the courtroom every ten minutes. They couldn't understand why they should know less of what was going on than people outside the jury box.

Leary placed his hand on the jury balustrade surrounding the box. For a moment, he just peered at the jurors as if he were deciding what to say next. Then he spoke. In deliberate well-spaced sentences. Ambrosio had warned him that if he pushed Sturmer over the edge, and they all knew Sturmer would do whatever he thought Leary wanted, a mistrial might seal the state's case forever.

Certainly, Ambrosio had cautioned Leary that there was no guarantee that the appellate courts would disqualify Ryan from defending Rubin in the second trial, and the defendant would certainly raise the double-jeopardy defense. If the appellate court deemed Sturmer's and Leary's concerted actions were so egregious against the defendant and his counsel, they could sustain the defense motion that a second trial would place the defendant in a second "jeopardy" position, disallowed under our Constitution. They would have to decide whether the defendant Rubin had been placed in "jeopardy" during the first trial, and if so, that he could not be placed in "jeopardy" again, during a second trial.

Ambrosio was the ultimate technician and she feared Leary's unrestrained prosecutorial actions could nullify any chance the state might have in trying Carl Rubin again.

Leary, in a tired voice, defined to the jury the crime of first degree murder and that the defendant Rubin had perpetrated that heinous crime. For lust and money, premeditatedly and with malice aforethought, the defendant Rubin arranged the horrible execution of his loving wife of twenty-seven years.

"No doubt exists, ladies and gentlemen of the jury," Leary's voice rose in fervor. "You must punish the defendant for the most hated of all crimes, murder for money, for greed. And nothing else but a guilty verdict would ever suffice."

Leary stood by the jury box for several seconds looking innocently at every juror, something he picked up at a prosecutors seminar years ago. Leary the actor was always more acceptable then Leary the human being.

After Leary sat down, Ryan rose slowly from his table.

"Your Honor, ladies and gentlemen of the jury." Ryan stared at each juror as he walked over to the box, and after a few moments continued, "Your Honor, I reserve the defense opening until we present our case. Thank you."

Ryan walked slowly back to the defense counsel table.

CHAPTER FORTY-EIGHT

Nothing as celebrated as the Rubin trial had ever hit Bristol and Summit County before. The courtroom was overflowing with media and the excited ever-present trial watchers . . . except for the civil rights demonstrations twenty-five years ago. Suddenly, Summit County had become the Selma, Alabama of the sixties. Those liberal eastern commentators and reporters couldn't believe that there was an eastern enclave that still believed in George Wallace and yet was no more than eighty miles from the penultimate bastion of liberal democracy, New York City.

The young lawyers of Summit County occupied the last two rows of the courtroom. After each pitched battle between Ryan and Sturmer, their zeal for Ryan increased exponentially. They all hated Leary, and most of all, Sturmer. Repressed among the legal community was the blatant fact that Leary had Sturmer in his hip pocket, and maybe even the assignment judge. Why, nobody knew. They had little respect for Leary's ability as a lawyer and prosecutor, yet nobody would challenge him. They accepted the status quo. As most lawyers always do. Their inexorable fear was that if they raised their voice in rebellious protest, no one would believe them because they were lawyers.

Even the young, and uninitiated members of the bar caught on very quickly. They offered their time and their words but rarely any productive solutions. And they got paid for all that non-productive advice. Guilt pervaded the profession. Very few lawyers ever considered themselves worthy of being paid for their words. Words that often complicated the ultimate solution. So why stir the pot. Live with Leary, and Sturmer, and the whole crusty hierarchy that sustained their unwarranted livelihood. Or so they thought.

Ryan had come back. Nobody comes back from suspension. Whole anyway. The process eviscerates the young lawyer. Ryan never knew he could be despised by so many. His friends became his critics and nay-sayers. But here he was. In the most celebrated case in a quarter of a century in Summit County. Battling with the dynamic duo, Sturmer and Leary. You had to respect such obstinate stupidity. Bravo! Ryan, Bravo! They enjoyed the fracas but knew the knight in silver armor was going to lose. He had to. There was no recourse for modern knights in shining armor. Not in the legal profession, anyway. But the battle was great to watch, as long as you stood far away from the fireworks.

The state's first witness was Darryl Spencer, the county medical examiner. He had had a checkered career as a medical examiner that only the lawyers of Summit County knew about. Screwups were common in the medical examiner's office. Spencer had refused to take the certification course given by the state for medical examiners based upon his claim that he was being discriminated against because of his advanced age. Since he knew all the governing politicos in the county, no one insisted on Spencer taking the exam. Just be careful when you reviewed his autopsies, they knowingly warned.

After examining Dr. Spencer on his curriculum vitae, limited as it was, Leary emphasized that Dr. Spencer had been medical examiner in Summit County for over thirty years, even belonged to several national occupational organizations that, of course, required no testing to become a member.

"Did you have an opportunity to conduct an autopsy on one Eleanore Rubin?" Leary questioned in almost a drawl.

"Yes, sir, I have . . . or did." Spencer's voice was hoarse from the cheap cigars he chewed and smoked throughout the day. His suit showed the drippings of cigars gone by. But his mound of snow-white hair and wrinkled face gave him an aura of authenticity, of knowledge, which, of course, he did not have.

"And what was the result of that autopsy, Doctor?"

"Well, let me see, Mr. Leary." His speech had the undercurrent of a North Carolina mountain village. He shuffled through a manila file on his lap, "Yes siree. Yes, here it is. I noted that her neck had severe bruises covering most of the throat and . . . yes, I remember. The strangulation was so severe it nearly severed the head from the shoulders."

"Could you tell what time of day she died, Doctor?"

"Yes. Mostly because the watch on her wrist . . . well, it was almost 5:45 p.m. on the day in question, Mr. Leary."

"How did you conclude that she died as the result of strangulation, Doctor?"

"Well . . . what else could it have been?" Spencer asked as if he were replying to an idiot. "Sure, it was strangulation. God, the tire marks were there. The bruises around the back of her neck, the severing of the neck, partially from the shoulders. The marks were there, Mr. Leary, that's how I know."

Spencer's voice became slightly belligerent, as if he was bothered by even having to appear in court.

"Did you find anything in her hands?" Leary questioned.

"Yes. According to my report, she had an envelope crushed into the palm of her hand. Like she had crushed it in anger or something."

"Did you send the envelope to the FBI lab in Washington for analysis at my instruction, Doctor?"

"Sure I did. That's what you told me to do. And I did it. I gave you the report. Had those fingerprints on it. That fellow's fingerprints." Spencer pointed toward Rubin.

"You mean the defendant, Carl Rubin?" Leary turned and faced the jury as he also pointed accusingly at the defendant.

Ryan rose and his voice was filled with repressed anger. "Your honor, I again repeat my objection to any evidence, or testimony being presented as to the envelope. The court and Mr. Leary know . . ."

Sturmer cut him off before he could continue his argument.

"Mr. Ryan, I have already ruled on your motion and any further mention of it . . . will force me to issue sanctions. Do I make myself clear? Continue, Mr. Prosecutor."

The jurors heads swiveled back and forth between the judge and Ryan, their faces acknowledging that the court obviously did not favor defense counsel.

"Was there anything in the envelope?" Leary continued his questioning of the medical examiner.

"Nothing. That was the strange thing about it. There was nothing in it."

"Did your examination reveal any other relevant evidence, Dr. Spencer?"

Levine looked over at Ryan, whose face clearly showed his confusion at the question. The state's discovery had nothing about any other evidence found during the autopsy than the material concerning the strangulation. Ryan started to rise but Sturmer waved his arm in Ryan's direction, ordering him to remain seated. Ryan slumped back in his chair awaiting the medical examiner's reply.

"Yes, sir. I sure did. I found faint traces of blood on her scalp. Like she had been struck with a hand. Except it weren't her blood."

"Whose blood was it, Doctor?"

"Well, we sent it to the FBI lab. And the report said it . . . DNA and all . . . and the blood samples we sent along of the defendant . . . they said it was the defendant's blood, Mr. Leary."

"What type was the blood, Doctor?"

"Type O. The same type we found the defendant had."

Ryan had received nothing in discovery concerning blood tests of the defendant. In fact, his client had failed to inform him that blood had actually been drawn from him.

Without rising, Ryan voiced his objection.

Sturmer acknowledged it as if he were swatting a fly away with his hand, his head nodding toward Leary to continue.

"Anything else found in her scalp? Her hair?" Leary continued.

"Sure did. The FBI lab report found traces of skin. And it wasn't the victim's skin either."

"Whose skin was it?" Leary asked.

"The defendant. The one over there," the witness pointed accusingly at Rubin.

"Do you have an opinion, Doctor, within a degree of reasonable medical certainty, how the defendant's blood and skin could be found in the victim's hair and scalp?"

"Sure I do. I've seen it before. In victims who get beat up. It's not uncommon for the attacker's blood and skin to attach to the victim's body."

"And is it your opinion that that's what happened here? To the victim?"

"Sure. The guy . . . the defendant probably hit her with his fist or something. Broke some of his own skin in the beating. Bled over her head."

"Could you opine when this beating took place, Doctor?"

"Probably a day or so before the murder. Let me look at the evidence slide of blood recovered from the victim's scalp, Mr. Leary," the witness demanded.

Leary handed him the evidence slide that had a tape attached to it identifying the name of the blood donor, the date and time of the examination, and the case number.

"Sure. That's it. I removed it during the autopsy of the victim."

"How could you tell the age of the blood and skin samples, Doctor?"

"Simple. The drying of the blood can tell you an approximate date of when it happened. And the skin, well, I think the FBI lab said it was the day or so before the killing."

"Doctor, how can you be so sure it's the defendant's blood and skin?"

"Well, DNA results don't lie. It's his all right. I think the odds are one in a hundred million or so that it could be somebody else. It's his all right."

"And your opinion on how it got there. On her scalp and hair?"

"You already asked me that," Spencer replied in an agitated voice, "but like I said he . . . the defendant . . . had to have hit her. On the head. And probably over her face, too. We found some black-and-blue marks near her eyes that were a few days old. Can't positively say these contusions came from the same beating as the blood and skin we found. But it's mighty close, Mr. Leary."

"Did you find anything else near the scene of the crime, Doctor?"

Ryan peered over at Levine, whose face was contorted in pain.

"Well, strange thing. I saw a couple of butts . . . cigarette butts near the body. And something like a leaf. A small green thing, a sliver of green or something."

"What did you do with those? The butts and green thing?"

"Sent it over to the FBI lab. Along with the other stuff. They got one hell of a lab in Washington."

"And what were the results of the FBI lab, Doctor?"

Ryan bounded up from his chair in repressed frustration, his voice carrying boldly across the pit area.

"Your Honor. You can't allow this witness . . . a medical examiner . . . to offer an opinion. An opinion he certainly is not qualified to give to this jury, based on a hearsay report from some lab."

"Is that an objection, Mr. Ryan?" Sturmer bellowed back at Ryan.

"Yes it is, Your Honor."

"Then it's overruled. Please. Mr. Ryan. Just voice the objection. We don't need a long speech accompanying your objections."

"Your Honor," Ryan started to speak.

"I've already ruled, Mr. Ryan. It seems like you don't like any of my rulings. If you don't, you know where you can take your objections after this trial is over with, Mr. Ryan. Mr. Leary, please continue."

"Your honor," Ryan insisted, "What is the basis for overruling my objection? I'd like to have the record reflect your reason for overruling my objection."

"Mr. Leary," Sturmer addressed the prosecutor, "why do you think Mr. Ryan's objection was overruled?"

Ambrosio passed a note over to Leary, who read it quickly before he responded.

"The doctor has been qualified as a scientific expert. And we all know under our rules experts can render an opinion based on other scientific reports, lab reports . . . or even pure hearsay."

"I agree with you, Mr. Leary. Please proceed."

"Doctor. Can you answer the question?"

"Well, if I remember the question." Spencer lifted a pair of bifocals from his rumpled jacket and put them on, although when he looked at the reports in his file he seemed to read over the bifocals.

"The tobacco in the cigarette butts came from Turkey. And the experts in Washington . . . they got tobacco experts there also . . . they said that the tobacco is usually found in cigarettes sold in Turkey. Or Israel. Mostly in Israel. And the green thing must have fallen off the killer. Was a sliver of something from a mandrake herb bush. They also said that it most probably came from vegetation grown in Israel. Supposedly it has aphrodisiac properties. I guess it makes you more virile."

Levine and Ryan stared at each other, their gaze filled with disbelief. Murmurs of surprise emanated from the spectators, like a bubbling brook gorging into a fast-moving river.

Ryan whispered into the ear of defendant Rubin. Rubin whispered back, Ryan shaking his head in the affirmative.

The juror's faces turned toward the defense table, displaying their questioning minds as to the relevancy of the medical examiner's testimony.

"Thank you, Doctor," Leary said with a broad victorious grin on his face as he walked back to the prosecutor's table, his eyes dancing over the jury box.

"Mr. Ryan, any questions?" Sturmer asked of Ryan as if it would be a waste of time to even question the medical examiner.

"Yes, sir. I do have some questions," Ryan replied as he sprang to his feet and rushed at the witness box, his yellow pad thrust out in front of him like an attacking spear.

"Doctor, you have testified, as an expert, one trained in the medical sciences, is that correct?"

"Sure. That's what I am. For over thirty years. I've done over 1,000 autopsies."

"Doctor, please. Please only answer my question. *Your attorney*, Mr. Leary, will allow you to address the jury on re-direct."

"I object to the accusation of defense counsel, your honor," Leary bellowed, not rising from his chair.

"What's the objection, Your Honor?" Ryan interjected. "Is Mr. Leary saying the good doctor here is not his witness: not part of his team? That the good doctor is not trying his darndest to prove the state's case?"

"Enough, Mr. Ryan," Sturmer said with a raised hand. "Go on with your cross."

"Doctor, it is your expert opinion . . . within a degree of medical certainty that the decedent, Eleanore Rubin, died from strangulation. Is that correct?"

"Sure. That's what I said. There were ligations on her neck. Sure, that's what killed her."

"Did you find any other medical or physical evidence, besides the marks on her neck . . . and the half severed head . . . that caused you to conclude that she died from strangulation?"

"That's all I need, sir. What else did I need?"

"You're the doctor. You tell me."

"Nothing else. That's what I found. Whatever I said."

"Well, Doctor, won't you agree with me that it's the strangest phenomenon to only find marks on her neck. But yet your report suggests nothing was in her lungs . . . in her mouth and nostrils."

"What are you talking about, defense counsel?" Spencer's voice rose in anger and fear, not knowing where counsel was leading him.

"How many strangulations have you found in those 1,000 or so autopsies you've performed?"

"Maybe 50 or so. I don't keep score, Counselor."

"Well do you remember the details of any of those 50 or so strangulation autopsies? Any of them?"

"Where are you going with this line of questioning, Counselor?" Sturmer interjected to the irritation of Ryan.

"You'll see soon enough, Your Honor. May I please continue?"

"Your Honor," Leary rose to his feet as he spoke in quick sentences, "I don't see where Mr. Ryan's going. Is he representing to this jury that the decedent didn't die of strangulation?"

"Mr. Leary. I'm not representing anything. I'm not a medical examiner offering an opinion. Your witness is. Your honor, may I continue without Mr. Leary trying to also control my cross-examination?"

"Gentlemen, please. I feel a migraine coming on," Sturmer announced with his hand placed on his head to specify the location of his pain.

"Doctor, can you answer my question? Or don't you understand it? I can rephrase it if you feel it's too difficult to understand." Ryan offered in a solicitous voice.

"I understand your question, Counselor," Spencer replied in an acidic tone, a bitter grimace on his face.

"Yes. Usually we find marks on other parts of the body. Maybe the arms. Maybe in the front of the neck. Scratches. But they weren't found here."

"What about fluid in the lungs. Did you find any fluid in the lungs, Doctor?"

"No, I did not."

"Don't you think it strange, *Doctor*, not to find fluid in the lungs in a strangulation as gross and horrific as this strangulation? Don't you, Doctor?" Ryan's voice started in a quiet low bass and then increased in intensity and pitch as the words came rushing out of his mouth.

"I don't understand, Counselor." Spencer wanting to lash back at Ryan. "Why would there be fluid in the lungs from a strangulation?

I've seen it on other occasions but I don't think it's always there."

"You don't?" Ryan attacked with his words and body moving toward Spencer in the witness box. He repeated. "You don't?"

"Well," with a slight smile on his lips Ryan continued, "isn't it a medical fact that when the victim is strangled, obviously there is a shortage of oxygen being ingested into the lungs of the victim." He paused to stare at the witness, "You agree with that, *Doctor?*"

Ryan chewed on the name cynically. "You do, don't you?" He continued in a incredulous tone.

"Probably . . . it all depends on how quickly the victim dies. I haven't seen any scientific studies on it."

"But you would agree with me, Doctor, that one would expect an insufficiency of oxygen into the lungs of the victim, while she is being strangled. Her life's oxygen being sucked out of her body."

"Was that a question or a lecture?" Leary whined in a loud voice from his chair.

"Was there an objection, Mr. Leary?" Ryan shot back. He continued, "Anyway, Doctor, we agree, don't we, that the victim would be suffocating during strangulation because her oxygen supply is being terminated."

"I guess so. Also depends, as I said before."

"You would also agree, would you not, my good doctor, that because of the shortage of oxygen to the victim, her dying efforts to breathe would produce not only fluid in her lungs but also a froth would gather in her mouth and nostrils, coming from within her body."

"It could be. I don't know." Spencer answered in an almost inaudible whisper.

"You don't know, Doctor!" Ryan shouted as he wheeled and faced the jury.

"You don't know! A man of science like yourself. A reputed medical examiner for thirty years. A man who refuses to even consider taking a required certification test . . . for the very job you hold . . . you don't know, Doctor?" Ryan's voice rose to an almost tenor's pitch, his voice dripping with sarcastic fervor.

"You didn't find any fluid in the lungs, did you, Doctor?" Ryan asked in machine-gun fashion.

"No, I did not. I wasn't looking for any."

"You didn't find any froth. Or excess fluid in the mouth, around the mouth, in the victim's nostrils. Did you, Doctor?"

"I said I didn't, Counselor," Spencer replied hatefully.

"Doctor, do you consider the textbook on medical forensics written by Dr. Herbert Seltzer, one of the most respected medical examiners in America, authoritative. Do you, Doctor?" Ryan sharply asked.

"I've read his books. I don't know if I've read that book."

"But you would consider Dr. Seltzer an authoritative expert in medical forensics. Such as the forensics in this case?"

"I guess I do," the doctor answered without confidence.

"Well, Doctor, I have here in my hand," Ryan picked up a large textbook from the defense table, "do you see it, Doctor?"

Spencer shook his head forward.

"Okay, since we both agree that Dr. Seltzer's opinion would be authoritative in the field of medical forensics . . . in the science of murder . . . let me read to you a passage from his chapter on strangulation."

Spencer moved nervously in his chair, his hand wiping his mouth nervously, his eyes peering out to Leary, who sat with his pencil in his hand scribbling something on his legal pad.

"I'm reading from Chapter five. Page 118, 2nd paragraph. It says 'it is almost universally found during the act of strangulation, an increase in fluid in the lungs, mouth, and nostrils of the victim. As expected the victim's ingestion of oxygen has been terminated and in the victim's quest for air to breathe, produces a mixture of air and fluid arising from within the body resulting in a substantial increase of fluid to the lungs, mouth and nostrils of the victim.'"

Ryan raised his eyes from the book and searched the jurors' faces. Except for the occasional nod from a juror's head, the faces remained transfixed, nothing.

"Do you agree with that opinion? From one of the most respected medical examiners in America, Doctor?"

"I wouldn't disagree with Dr. Seltzer. But I think every case is different. Maybe Dr. Seltzer would have come up with my results in this case. I don't know." Spencer said in a recovering voice, his eyes now focused on the jury, as he had been instructed to do in preparation for trial by Ambrosio.

"You found no dominant scratches and bruises on the front of the victim's neck, is that correct, Doctor?"

"None to speak of. Mostly on the side and rear."

"You also found no bruises on the arms, legs? Or any other parts of her face and body?"

"Except for the old bruises under her right eye, no."

"Isn't it strange not to find bruises and scratches on the front of the neck, on her arms and legs?"

"Not if she was surprised by the attacker." Spencer's little smile denoted he thought he had won some points on that answer.

"We assume that the killer was a delivery man. The man that came to the door when the victim was on the phone with her daughter. Is that correct, Doctor?"

"We can assume that."

"So if she let in the deliveryman . . . presumably a stranger . . . we can also assume that she would not be led down the primrose path. As if it were her husband sneaking up behind her."

"I don't know what happened here, Mr. Ryan. He might have attacked her while her back was turned. I don't know."

"You're the medical examiner, Doctor, you're paid to find scientific evidence to show how the crime was committed, isn't that so?"

"I did my job in this case."

"Okay," Ryan agreed in a conciliatory wave of his hand, his body now facing the jury box, his back to the witness, "Let's say you did your job. You would then agree from what I read in Dr. Seltzer's authoritative text on strangulation, in your own experiences of maybe 50 or so autopsies of victims of strangulation, that if she was alive—the victim here . . . when she was strangled, there would have been a buildup of fluids in her lungs, mouth, and nostrils. There would have been marks and scratches on the *front of her neck*. Maybe on her arms. While she's thrashing around trying to fend off the attacker. Some physical residue on her body to show she was alive when she was being strangled. Wouldn't you agree with that scenario, Doctor?"

"I don't understand what you're getting at, Counselor. Are you asking me whether she was alive when she was being strangled?"

Ryan walked to the side of the witness box, his voice low and easy, as he replied, "Yes. That's exactly what I'm asking you, Doctor."

The silence had been electric in the courtroom until Ryan's last statement. A thunderclap of noise rose from the spectators in the gallery. Judge Sturmer banged his gavel hard on the table calling for immediate silence from the audience.

Spencer raised his head toward the judge as if to seek guidance in answering Ryan's statement.

"Was she alive when she was strangled?" Ryan asked sharply.

Spencer leafed through his manila folder as if he expected to find the answer to the question somewhere in the file. Hearing no reply from the witness, Ryan turned to the bench and said:

"Judge, could you please instruct the witness to answer my question."

"If he can," Sturmer replied, gazing at Spencer who still had his face down toward his file.

"Well, Mr. Ryan," Spencer replied, his eyes out of focus in an attempt to cover all the players in the courtroom, "I never considered strangulation of a person already dead. I see no reason . . ."

"You don't. I know you don't. But my client, the defendant is on trial for his life, because your boss, the county prosecutor believes that he arranged the strangulation of his wife. Isn't that the charge against my client, Doctor?"

"I'm not a lawyer, Mr. Ryan. I was asked to gather medical evidence, as I always do. As to the cause of death of the victim, and anything else I find. I did that. Nobody told me she was dead already."

"Well, isn't that your job to determine what killed the victim? And you must admit, Doctor, there is reasonable doubt on the scientific evidence you *didn't* find. That she may have been dead and *then* strangled, isn't that correct?"

"That's if we believe your theory, Mr. Ryan. I still say strangulation was the cause of death."

"No matter what, is that correct, Doctor?"

Spencer didn't answer. His eyes focused on the back of the courtroom, to the busy TV cameras whirring themselves into a frenzy.

"Doctor. You're not a tobacco expert, are you?" Ryan continued.

"No, I'm not. I don't claim to be. All I did was pass the cigarette butts up to the FBI lab. And they were the ones who concluded that the butts came from Turkey . . . or Israel."

"And you're not a botanist or any expert dealing with trees, bushes, and so on."

"Again, Mr. Ryan, I'm not. But often, as here, we use the FBI lab in Washington. They have all kinds of experts. Botanists. Whatever. They were the ones who came up with the origin of the green residue found at the scene of the crime. That it must have also come from Israel."

"And, I guess, Doctor, that your testimony is to show this jury," Ryan extended the palm of his hand toward the jury, "that the killer was also from Israel. Is that correct?"

"It shows that that might be the case. That the killer was Israeli, yes."

"Could he not have been a tourist who visited Israel and then came back to Larchmont Hills to kill the decedent?"

"He could have been. But I don't think so, Mr. Ryan. Tourists don't usually smoke Israeli cigarettes and walk around with parts of bushes *only* grown in Israel."

"Have you ever heard of a French cigarette called Gauloise? That also uses Turkish tobacco. The same tobacco that was contained in the cigarette butts found at the scene of the crime. And Gauloise are usually sold in France, not Israel."

Leary rose from his chair and voiced an objection to Ryan's questions as being too speculative.

"Yes. Mr. Ryan, I think we're getting into an area where no relevant information can be gleaned from this witness," Sturmer decided.

"Your Honor, the state has put forth this . . . this . . . medical examiner, whose credentials in the field of forensic medicine are quite dubious. And speculative. But yet Mr. Leary has the gall to have Dr. Spencer opine on the origins of tobacco, botany, and God knows what else. I should be allowed some leeway to rebut that line of testimony."

"You've already done it, Mr. Ryan. Go on please," Sturmer ordered.

"Did you look for traces of drugs, toxic residues, anything else that could have caused her death, Doctor?"

"We usually do. Let me look at the autopsy report." Spencer shuffled through his file and selected a ten-page report from the pile and started to speed read it.

"Yes, here it is," Spencer lifted the report up from the file as if to show the world that there really was an autopsy report.

"I don't see any reference to any finding of any drugs, toxic substance. No. Nothing like that."

"Does that mean, Doctor, that you didn't search for drugs or that you searched for them but didn't find any?"

"Look, Mr. Ryan. We did a thorough autopsy on this victim."

"Wouldn't you affirmatively state in that so-called thorough report that you did not find drugs, toxic residues, and the like? That's if you really looked for them."

"We don't put everything down on the report."

"Let me see that report, Doctor." Spencer handed the report over to Ryan who turned to the last page.

"Doctor. I have the strangest feeling. I'm looking at the signature page of the report. And it seems that a Doctor Fielding . . . Horace Fielding signed the report."

Ryan thrust the report at Spencer, who grabbed it as he pushed his bifocals back against his nose.

"That's his signature, Mr. Ryan. So what?" Spencer replied in a bellicose voice.

"Doesn't the medical examiner who actually conducts the autopsy sign the report, Doctor?"

"I was there. I supervised the autopsy."

"Did you sign the report?"

"I didn't see where I did. But so what? Many times I supervise the autopsy and let my assistant sign off on the report. Doesn't mean anything, Mr. Ryan."

"How long were you actually at the autopsy of Eleanore Rubin, Doctor Spencer?"

"I don't know. Probably during the important parts. I don't know. I do hundreds of autopsies every year. I don't put everything down."

"You didn't do this autopsy, Doctor, did you?" Ryan shouted at the witness.

"Your Honor," Leary shouted as loud as Ryan's voice, "he is harassing the witness. There's no doubt in anybody's mind that Dr. Spencer did the autopsy. He says he did."

"That's what cross-examination is all about, Your Honor," Ryan addressed to Sturmer.

Sturmer peered down at Spencer and asked, "Did you do the autopsy, Doctor?"

"Yes, Your Honor. I don't know to what extent I was there. But yes, I supervised the autopsy."

"How long were you there?" Ryan persisted.

"I said already, Counselor, I don't know how long I was there. But I guarantee you Dr. Fielding performed the autopsy under my supervision."

"Where is Dr. Fielding?"

"He left the office almost six months ago. I don't know where he is."

"Your honor," Ryan said, "I'm asking for an adjournment of this trial until the state produces Dr. Horace Fielding, the examiner who actually performed the autopsy on Eleanore Rubin."

"Denied, Mr. Ryan. You should have addressed your motion to the Court during the discovery period. We're not going to adjourn this trial because you were careless in your discovery."

Sturmer paused and looked over at the state's table. Leary sat there, smiling openly.

"Do you have any further questions of this witness, Mr. Ryan?" Sturmer stated.

Ryan returned to his seat at the defense table.

"One second, your honor. I'd like to look through my notes."

"Hurry up, please. The lunch hour is approaching and I don't want to keep our jurors sitting beyond the lunch hour."

Ryan sat down at defense counsel table. Levine and Rubin pressed toward him and Rubin spoke quietly as the other two listened.

After a minute or so, Judge Sturmer's anxious voice bellowed from the bench, "Mr. Ryan . . . please. You may have an iron stomach but I'm sure these wonderful people, who kindly sit here as jurors, would like to go to lunch. Do you have any further questions of this witness?"

Ryan rose from his chair and slowly walked in front of the witness box. "Doctor, did you know the decedent was an insulin-dependent diabetic?"

Spencer listened to the question and then briskly leafed through his file. After finding nothing, he replied, "No. I didn't know. It wouldn't have made any difference in the cause of death. Even if she were a diabetic."

"I thought you said you analyzed her blood. If you did, wouldn't the analysis reveal an inordinately low blood sugar level?"

"Maybe. But we weren't looking for cause of death relating to natural causes, Mr. Ryan. It was an open-and-shut case of strangulation. That's all there is to it."

"Well, isn't it true she could have died from an overdose of insulin?"

"I don't believe so, Mr. Ryan."

"You didn't look. You stopped at strangulation. That's it, isn't it?"

Spencer didn't reply.

"Time of death," Ryan announced in more of a statement than a question. "You say she died about 5:40 p.m. Give or take a few minutes. Is that correct, Doctor?"

"Yes . . ."

"The body wasn't found until 7:30 p.m. that night, is that correct, Doctor?"

"I guess so. That's what the police report says. I got there around 8:00 p.m. or so."

"And I think your report says that the time of death was based on the broken wristwatch. That's what the watch said. Is that correct?"

"Not only that. We took the body's temperature. I analyzed the state of rigor mortis. And, of course the watch."

"Did you examine the contents of the stomach?"

"Probably. But I didn't note it in my report."

"I don't even see any note about examining the pancreas, Doctor. The pancreas produces insulin, is that correct?"

"I don't know what you are getting at, Counselor. No, I didn't examine the pancreas. No need to."

"Could she have died from, let's say, an overdose of insulin?"

"She could have, but she didn't. It was strangulation as plain as the nose on my face, Mr. Ryan."

"Of course, Doctor. If she had died of an overdose of insulin . . . or a drug . . . something other than strangulation, the state's case is out the window, is it not?"

Ryan's voice was low and steely.

"I don't know about speculation, Mr. Ryan. I guess if it was something other than strangulation, you could be right. But I'm damn sure it was strangulation so all the other causes you rattled off are to mislead this jury. That's all I have to say."

"Isn't it a fact that you were instructed to dispose of the decedent's body through cremation above the objection of the decedent's family, Doctor?"

"I was instructed to dispose of the body by Mr. Leary. I knew nothing of any objections."

"I don't have anything further, your honor," Ryan sweetly intoned. Then added with a bright smile on his face, "I think the jury deserves a good lunch, your honor."

CHAPTER FORTY-NINE

After re-direct by Leary that rehashed the head notes of his direct, Dr. Spencer slowly walked out of the witness box.

Ryan had scored his crucial points on cross and with a denigrating wave of his hand he told the court he had no re-cross of the medical examiner.

During the long lunch hour, Ryan, Levine, and Rubin just talked instead of eating. Olsham brought a thermos of black coffee to Ryan's office.

"Did you ever abuse her?" Ryan bluntly asked of his client. The rabbi sat low in the cumbersome black leather armchair, looking more like a small boy being questioned by a suspicious parent then the famous rabbi of Temple Beth Shalom. His smooth face appeared lined, as if some crazed plastic surgeon had beveled wrinkles in the formerly unlined skin. His eyes were rheumy from lack of sleep. The immaculate appearance he normally put forth was gone. The rabbi appeared almost disheveled, lost and confused.

"We had had our fights," the rabbi replied, paused and then continued in a low voice. "Yes, I struck her. She did me, also. The last few years were filled with distrust. There was no love left for either of us. But . . . I didn't kill her, Mr. Ryan. I swear to you."

"I wished you had told me about the fights before the trial," Ryan replied soulfully.

"Is there anything else I should know, Rabbi?" Ryan added while sipping the paper cup of black coffee. He needed the caffeine to open his mind. Pull his gut up to the offensive line of battle.

"Was your wife having an affair, Rabbi?" Levine asked, while munching on a brownie that seemed to fall more on his rotund belly than into this mouth.

The rabbi paused, his eyes averting the three other people in the room. He rose from the armchair. Slowly he removed his handkerchief from his back pocket and brushed it against his face.

"I think so," he mumbled.

"You never said anything!" Ryan's voice stopped in mid-sentence.

"I didn't think it was important, Mr. Ryan."

"You didn't think it was important?" Ryan shouted as he rose from his chair, knocking over a half cup of coffee onto the floor.

"Easy, Joshua," Olsham said, as he picked the fallen cup up from the floor.

Recovering his calm, Ryan spoke to his client, who had resumed his place in the armchair.

"Rabbi. Please. We go back to that pit in less than thirty minutes. Tell me everything. Please. Who was your wife having an affair with? And more importantly does the prosecutor know about it?"

During the same lunch hour, Leary and Ambrosio discussed the next witness over delivered tuna fish sandwiches on pita bread. Leary sat at his mammoth desk, his feet up on the corner of the wide overhang, his hands thrust behind his head, listening to Ambrosio outlining the next witness's testimony.

"Mr. Leary," she said in a husky voice, "I think Mathias could hurt us."

"Son of a bitch is all we got, Ambrosio. That asshole Crutchfield had to blow his brains out. Couldn't the sonofabitch wait until after he testified at least. Some people have no sense of timing." He smiled at his attempt at sarcasm.

"Mathias was the investigating officer," she continued. "Normally he would be the center of our case. But his relationship with this office has not been . . ."

"He's a fucking traitor, that's what he is, Ambrosio," Leary shouted, cutting off his assistant in mid-sentence.

"We have no one else, Mr. Leary."

"Then we put him on the stand. He has to be talked to . . . not just prepared . . . maybe I should have Dickson talk to him."

"Dickson would be a mistake, Mr. Prosecutor."

"Dickson is okay. Don't worry about Dickson, Ambrosio."

"I do worry about Dickson, Mr. Prosecutor. Anyway, his relationship with Mathias is a troubling one. I don't think Mathias is afraid of anyone at this office. He'll tell it like it is, Mr. Prosecutor."

"Then put him on . . . this afternoon."

"Do you want to talk to him before he takes the witness stand? I can get him up here."

"The hell with him. I don't want to talk to that scumbag. If he fucks me on the stand . . . he'll wish he was back at Brooklyn vice."

Mathias took the stand about 2:00 p.m. that afternoon. He was clean-shaven, his back straight as he strode to the witness box. He appeared as if he were advancing toward the front of a firing squad.

Leary went through Mathias's extensive police experience at the beginning of the direct examination. Mathias, the professional witness that he was, answered in short, succinct sentences, only elaborating when an explanation beyond brevity was required.

His demeanor was bland and noncommittal, his face rarely expressing any emotion.

"You were the investigating officer on the Rubin murder, were you not?" Leary rattled the question off as if he wanted the witness to do his thing and get off the stand as quickly as possible.

"Yes, sir, I was."

"Did you find any unusual circumstances at the scene of the murder, Lieutenant?"

"Several things, sir. Firstly, the glass in the outside door to the laundry room was shattered."

"What was unusual about that finding, Lieutenant?"

"At first we thought the glass was broken from the inside of the room. But the lab boys determined that the glass was actually broken from the outside . . . Just like you find in any breaking and entering scenario."

"Anything else, Lieutenant?"

"The empty envelope in the victim's hand."

"What else, Lieutenant?"

"In examining her face, I failed to notice pectic markings in her eyes. You usually find tiny veins that are broken in the eyes after a strangulation. Also, the kitchen was upset. It looked like somebody fell and crashed into the kitchen table."

"Did you question the defendant Rubin after the discovery of the body, Lieutenant?"

"Yes, I did. He came in voluntarily and gave us a statement. Also allowed the nurse to take a sample of his blood. Also voluntarily."

"What else did you discover during your investigation, Lieutenant?" Leary was surprised at Mathias's cooperation on the stand.

"That the defendant had had affairs with several women who were members of his synagogue. One particularly . . . Moira Harbinger . . . a fashion designer from Philadelphia. He admitted the affair but wouldn't give us any information about his relationship with Ms. Harbinger except to say he had an affair with her."

"Anything else, Lieutenant?"

"We discovered two life insurance policies in the master bedroom of the victim's house. Each . . . the decedent and the defendant Rubin had taken out large insurance polices on each other's life about a year before the murder. Something over a million dollars a piece."

"Who was the beneficiary on the decedent's policy, Lieutenant?"

"The defendant."

"Did you find anything else about the relationship between the defendant and the decedent before her murder?"

"Just rumors, Mr. Prosecutor."

"Please tell the jury what you found out," Leary insisted as he rose from his chair and approached quickly to the side of the witness box closest to the jury.

Ryan objected.

"Your honor, rumors about the relationship between the defendant and the decedent are pure speculation."

"Maybe . . . and maybe not, Mr. Ryan," Sturmer opined.

"Well, if the court's going to allow rumors to creep into this case, I'd like to have an in-camera hearing, out of the presence of the jury, and hear those rumors."

"Mr. Ryan," Sturmer spoke directly to the jurors, "I think these fine jurors, using their collective intelligence, should be allowed to hear all relevant testimony concerning the relationship between the defendant and his departed wife. Why don't we allow them that courtesy, Mr. Ryan."

"With all due respect for the intelligence of this jury, your honor, the rules of evidence particularly exclude speculation or rumor to rise to the level of admissible evidence."

"Well, we'll wait and see, Mr. Ryan. Proceed to answer the question, Lieutenant," Sturmer instructed the witness.

"Your Honor, may we have a sidebar discussion about my objection before the witness is compelled to answer," Ryan insisted in a strong, clear voice.

"No, we may not. These jurors have withstood enough of the defense's grandstanding. Answer the question, Lieutenant," Sturmer ordered forcefully, his face staring down on Mathias.

Mathias looked over at Ryan and then said in a soft voice. "The rumor was that the defendant and his wife, the decedent, had had a stormy marital relationship."

"You mean physical abuse by the defendant?" Leary shot back at the witness.

"Something like that. It was only rumors, sir. There was no direct evidence that I discovered that corroborated any physical abuse by the defendant."

"What about the bruise under her right eye, Lieutenant?" Leary questioned his own witness as if he were cross-examining him.

"I didn't see any, Mr. Leary. Except a small discoloration near her scalp. Like she had hit her head while falling and crashing into something . . . maybe the kitchen table."

"Weren't you here when the medical examiner said there was a bruise under the right eye?"

"I was here, Mr. Leary. But other than him saying it, I found what I just said."

Leary paced back and forth in front of the witness box. He realized that Mathias was not going to be bullied into corroborating the State's testimony.

"Didn't you take a statement from the defendant?"

"Yes, I did. He denied ever abusing his wife, Mr. Leary. And during my investigation I found no evidence of marital abuse by the defendant."

"It could have happened but you didn't discover it, is that correct, Lieutenant?"

Ryan objected to the question as being purely speculative. Sturmer surprisingly sustained his objection.

"Didn't you warn the defendant during your interrogation of

him at the Larchmont Hills police station that he couldn't leave the country?"

"I had no power to restrain him from leaving the country, Mr. Leary. I suggested he be available for further questioning. That's all the authority I had."

"But he did leave the country, did he not, Lieutenant?"

"I presume he did. No one at your office advised me that the defendant had left the country. I had to read about it in the newspaper, Mr. Leary."

"After he was indicted?"

"Are you asking me whether he left the country after he was indicted? Again, I can't say either way. After the initial investigation was completed by my office, the county detectives from your office took over the case, Mr. Leary."

"Were you aware that the defendant's blood was found on the hair and scalp of the victim, Lieutenant?"

"Only by reading the medical examiners report of the autopsy. I found no blood in her hair or scalp."

"Did you ever look to see whether there was blood in her scalp, Lieutenant?"

Ryan objected on the grounds that the prosecutor was leading his own witness. Sturmer overruled the objection.

"No, I didn't. That wasn't my job, Mr. Leary. The medical examiner had the obligation to examine the body, not me."

"But you were in charge of the investigation, weren't you, Lieutenant?"

Ryan again objected.

"Your Honor, it seems that the prosecutor is harassing his own witness."

Leary pointed his forefinger at the witness.

"Your Honor," he shouted at the bench, "this witness has consorted with defense counsel to undermine the state's case. I'm demanding that he be declared a hostile witness so I may indeed cross-examine him."

Ryan smiled.

"Your honor, Mr. Leary doesn't like the lieutenant's candid answers to his questions so he wants to declare him a hostile witness for telling the truth. He should have requested that the court rule on the witness's hostility at the commencement of the lieutenant's testimony. Not after he's received answers that don't fit into the state's game plan."

"I'm going to allow the state some leeway on examining this witness, gentlemen. Whether he's hostile or not is in the eyes of the beholder. Go on, Mr. Leary," Sturmer ordered.

"You found that the defendant was having a series of affairs with female members of his church, did you not, Lieutenant?"

"From your office, Mr. Leary. I was told that you had wire-tapped defense counsel's office and had found out about the extra-marital affairs."

"That's my business, Lieutenant, how we gathered the truth about the defendant's *illegal conduct*!" Leary whined in a loud voice.

Ryan bolted up from his chair and shouted, "Your Honor! I not only want to object to Mr. Leary's outburst and misrepresentation about any illegal activities allegedly conducted by the defendant, I must again ask for a mistrial. Nothing this court can say to this jury can remedy the egregious statements and conduct of this prosecutor!"

Sturmer ran his hand through his hair, then allowed his fingers to rub along his forehead. His face clearly showed indecision, the lines around his eyes seemed to grow in depth.

"I would ask both counsel to confine their objections to just that. We don't need lectures supporting every objection." He paused, reached under his robe for a handkerchief and wiped his brow. "Motion for mistrial denied. Continue, Mr. Leary."

"Did you know the defendant was sleeping with members of his congregation?" Leary announced, as he stood no more than two feet in front of the witness box, his legs spread-eagled, his arms akimbo at his sides.

"Like I said, Mr. Leary, what I was told by your office, and what was admitted by the defendant."

"You didn't even interview those people? Did you, Lieutenant?"

"Again. Your office asked me to withdraw from any further investigation. It was in your hands, they told me."

"You were once accused of taking bribes, weren't you, Lieutenant?"

On his feet, Ryan again shouted his objection. "Your Honor. I don't think this court can allow any more outrageous conduct from Mr. Leary. His zeal to convict this defendant without any foundation . . . Your Honor . . . here we have the prosecution attacking the honesty of its own witness. The investigating officer in this case . . ."

Ryan's hands flew out toward the bench as he spoke.

"Approach the bench, Counsel," Sturmer said in a low, aggravated tone, his hands outstretched in a pleading stance. Sturmer clenched his teeth as he spoke in a hurried whisper, "Listen. You too, Mr. Leary, I'm not going to watch this trial become a circus. Mr. Leary, *he is your witness*! Although Mr. Ryan and I are not seeing eye to eye in this trial, that last question may have gone beyond the bounds of propriety."

"Listen," Leary repeated, waving away the court reporter, "I'm not going to stand by here while you let this case go down the tubes. *Your Honor*."

Leary spat the honorarium out as if he were addressing a homeless bum. "I'm going to continue the way I see fit!"

Sturmer wiped his forehead, the beads of sweat evident.

"Just calm down, Roger." Sturmer said in an acquiescent voice. "You're not doing your case any good if you lose on appeal."

"*Fuck the appeal*. I want to win here!" Leary blared in reply.

"Your Honor, you must recuse yourself *now* and call a mistrial," Ryan insisted. "I don't know what's happening between the court and the prosecutor. But I can't see how the defendant could possibly receive a fair trial."

"We'll proceed, Mr. Ryan." Sturmer nodded his head, and then announced to the courtroom; "Let's proceed, gentlemen."

Ryan sat down in his chair, leaned over to Levine, and said, "Sturmer is scared out of his gourd, Sam. He won't call a mistrial. But yet, I think he knows things are getting out of hand."

Levine smiled an irreverent smile, as he leaned over to whisper in Ryan's ear. "Leary will commit hari-kari. He's so stupid. Let him go, Joshua, the more Leary attacks his own witnesses, the more the jury will see what it's all about."

"Can you answer the question?" Leary bellowed at Mathias.

"Yes, I was. But I was fully exonerated, Mr. Leary." Mathias looked at the jury as he spoke. Eye to eye. His gaze never faltered.

"I don't have any further questions of this witness." Leary turned his back on Mathias, his hands thrown up in disgust, as he walked back to his chair at the counsel table for the state.

Ryan sat back in his chair and waited.

The eyes of everyone in the courtroom slowly turned toward Ryan. His hands were clasped under his chin, his body half slumped on the wooden chair. His eyes were half-closed, but still focused on the jury box. The jurors started to squirm in their chairs. Then their faces turned to each other in a questioning manner. Slowly their heads, almost in unison, turned toward Ryan. He sat immobile, his head turning from the jury to the court bench. Levine placed his hand on Ryan's arm as if to see if Ryan was still breathing. Ryan mechanically turned his head toward Levine and smiled innocently.

The murmurs in the courtroom grew louder as Ryan waited; the court finally addressed Ryan.

"Mr. Ryan, I presume you have some questions for the Lieutenant."

Ryan rose slowly from his chair, peered at the jury, then walked behind Leary's chair. Leary turned his head as if he were afraid of Ryan striking him from behind, then Leary turned toward the judge.

"Thank you, Your Honor," Ryan said, his arms crossed at his chest.

"Lieutenant, how long have you been a police officer? Not just in Summit County. But anywhere through your lifetime?"

"About thirty years or so, Counselor," he answered in an even, well-modulated voice.

"How many murder cases have you investigated during that lengthy career?"

"Maybe about ten or so. I was mostly in vice and drugs when I worked out of the city."

"How many were deemed to have been caused by strangulation?"

"Maybe two or three."

"You examined the victim's body. In this case, I mean."

"Sure. Not extensively because the medical examiner was there and that's mostly his job."

"Did you look at the victim's eyes, Lieutenant?"

Leary objected in a lurching voice and manner as if he had suddenly been awakened from a sound sleep.

"Relevancy, your honor. This witness isn't medical examiner and besides the questions are beyond the scope of direct examination."

"Where are you going, Mr. Ryan?" Sturmer demanded.

"The prosecution directed its questions to this witness relevant to his observation at the scene of the crime, Your Honor."

"Just a few more, Mr. Ryan. Let's get on with it," Sturmer reluctantly added.

Ryan nodded toward Mathias to continue his answer.

"Her eyes were still open. I noticed that the eyes were clear. Unusually clear for a strangulation," Mathias replied.

"What do you mean, Lieutenant?"

Ambrosio rapidly wrote onto the legal pad and shoved a note over to Leary, who impatiently waved her aside.

"Usually . . . anyway . . . I'm not a doctor, you know, but the victims I've seen who are strangled. Usually they have little broken veins . . . red marks in the whites of the victim's eyes."

"And do you know why that's so, Lieutenant?" Ryan quickly added.

Leary had gazed at Ambrosio's note and then suddenly jumped to his feet, his hand raised toward the ceiling as if he were asking the teacher in the class room permission to speak.

"Your Honor. This has gone far enough. This witness is certainly not qualified as a medical expert. How can he testify what the significance of physical signs on the victim mean?"

"Yes, Mr. Ryan. I presume the prosecutor is voicing an objection. I must agree with him. This witness is the investigating police officer. And by the way, not even qualified as an expert in *any* field. So I'm not going to allow him to render an opinion. Objection sustained. Go on, Mr. Ryan."

"Officer," Ryan's face remained unflinching, "in your long years of police investigation, have you ever experienced an investigation where the defendant's attorney's office phone was wiretapped by the state."

Again Leary jumped to his feet, this time knocking his chair back against the rail.

"Hogwash!" he yelled, the faces of the jurors showing signs of confusion, "This court cannot allow the defense to question this witness about legal matters. That's the court's decision to make, Your Honor!"

Sturmer's face evidenced his concern about the topic of wiretapping the defense counsel's phone. He had signed the order, concealed it from even the assignment judge and knew he had, at least, spiritually violated the rules.

"What does this witness's opinion on this issue have to do with relevant testimony, Mr. Ryan?" Sturmer rhetorically asked, and without waiting for a response, Sturmer ordered the witness not to answer the question.

"Lieutenant," Ryan continued, "did you find anything at the scene of the crime even remotely linking the defendant with the murder of his wife?"

Mathias placed his hand to his chin in a questioning pose. He looked at Levine and then Ryan as if seeking guidance.

None came so he replied in a soft, almost inaudible voice, "I don't know, Counselor. The medical examiner found a bruise under the eye of the victim. And I did find out through my investigation that the defendant and the victim had had a stormy marital relationship. There probably was some physical abuse. I don't know, counselor. I don't know whether that contributed to the defendant's guilt in committing this crime. It could"

He paused and released a deep gasp of air, "And then maybe it couldn't."

Ryan didn't like the answer. He thought, from previous discussions about his investigation at the scene, Mathias found nothing to relate the crime to Rubin. But Ryan knew Mathias would hold nothing back when he testified. Neither for the prosecution nor the defense.

"The defendant voluntarily gave you a statement, did he not, Lieutenant?"

"Yes . . . yes, he did."

"Was there anything in his statement that you considered linked him to the murder of his wife?"

"The defendant briefly mentioned an affair with a woman but after that," he paused to reflect and then added as an afterthought, "he told me about the life insurance policies."

"But you found nothing at the scene of the crime linking this defendant to the murder of Eleanore Rubin?"

"Just what I said, Counselor. Nothing tangible."

"Thank you, Lieutenant."

Leary conferred with Ambrosio at the state's table. After a few moments had passed, he turned his head toward the witness.

"What you mean, Lieutenant . . . when you said you found nothing linking the defendant to the murder is that you didn't find a smoking gun, is that correct?"

"No smoking gun, Mr. Leary."

"Do you usually find a smoking gun during the initial investigation at the scene?"

"Not usually."

"So your answer that you didn't link the defendant to the crime . . . well, that's what you normally discover. Nothing of any consequence until the investigation is completed. Is that correct?"

"Most of the time. That's correct. But I wasn't allowed to complete . . ."

"Nothing further, Lieutenant," Leary shot at the witness, cutting the answer off in mid-sentence.

Ryan slowly drawled, as he walked over the side of Mathias, "Lieutenant . . . that bruise near the victim's scalp . . . could it have been caused by her crashing into the kitchen table . . . the one you said had been damaged?"

Mathias responded slowly. "Maybe . . . that's what I originally thought . . . but I couldn't prove it."

Ryan smiled and said, "Thank you, Lieutenant. That's all, Your Honor."

"You're excused, Lieutenant," Sturmer addressed the witness.

As Mathias walked off the witness stand, Ryan felt a sinking feeling in the pit of his stomach. He wanted to ask more, but he was afraid of the honesty of Mathias.

Leary called Moira Harbinger to the stand. The defendant was noticeably shaken when her name was called by the clerk. He whispered over to Ryan, who attempted to mask any appearance of surprise on his face.

Ryan followed her small steps to the witness stand where the clerk swore her in. Tiny, middle-aged, yet everything about her was in place. Her face was fragile and without lines that could be seen by the naked eye. She settled into the chair, hands folded neatly on her lap, her eyes staring at the rabbi.

"Ms. Harbinger," Leary started in a soft voice, as he roamed in front of the jury box, "I presume you know the defendant in this case."

"Yes . . . yes, I do," she replied in a small, unsure voice. Her hand stroked the side of her head.

"How well do you know the defendant?"

"Intimately. We have been lovers for over three years," she admitted without shame.

"How did you first meet the defendant?" Leary's voice got stronger as the answers he sought from the witness rolled from her lips.

"I was a member of Temple Beth Shalom. My husband and I were, I mean. My husband passed away a little over three years ago. And . . . well, anyway. . .we had been married for over twenty-five years. I was devastated when Joel died. That was his given name. He was a wonderful man."

"He was the weatherman on a Philadelphia TV station, wasn't he?" Leary offered.

"Yes. He also was on National Public Radio. Everybody loved Joel." She withdrew a lacy handkerchief from her sleeve and dabbed her eyes gently.

"I'm sorry," she said.

"How did you meet the defendant?" Leary repeated, disregarding the emotional display of the witness.

"Well, after Joel, the synagogue provided grief counseling. The rabbi . . . Carl Rubin . . . well, he was wonderful to me. I don't know what I would have done without him."

"I see," Leary said, although he obviously didn't care. "Well," he impatiently added, "when did you first become his lover?"

"A few months later. I don't really know when the first time was." Her voice had developed a hard edge as she answered Leary's pointed questions.

"Did you know he was married?"

"I knew," her face slackened along the mouth, "it happened so quickly. I'm sorry. I needed someone. He was . . . well, Carl provided the tender care I needed."

"But he was your rabbi!" Leary exclaimed in a shocked voice. He wheeled dramatically around to face the defendant, his arm extended to the defense table.

"He was. But even if he wasn't . . . He just is a kind, caring man. And he was unhappy."

"Unhappy! You say he was unhappy," Leary repeated. "So because he was unhappy he had an affair with a grieving member of his church. Is that it?"

Leary was shouting by this point.

Ryan objected, rising from his chair.

"Your Honor, Mr. Leary has a tendency to call witnesses that he attacks on direct examination. He also knows he can't lead his witnesses."

Sturmer waved his hand at the witness and asked Leary to ask another question. The judge seemed to have reached the wall also, his lips tightening as he heard Leary's voice.

"Are you still the defendant's lover?" Leary asked.

"Yes . . . we still are."

"Did his wife know of your affair?"

"I don't know what she knew."

"Did you know the victim?"

"I met her on occasion at synagogue functions. I didn't really call her my friend."

"Did you know if the defendant ever physically abused his wife?"

Ryan was going to object but thought it would be futile to object anyway.

"I can't imagine Carl physically abusing anyone, sir," she replied.

"But they obviously were having marital problems. That's right, isn't it?"

"He was unhappy. He had been unhappy well before he met me."

"You mean he had had other affairs?"

"I don't know what he had. He never told me about any other affairs," she angrily answered.

"Did you know he was sleeping with other women . . . while he was sleeping with you?" Leary's voice lashed out callously across the courtroom.

The witness's face froze in shock. Her mouth quivered slightly, her round eyes narrowed.

"I don't know what you mean, sir. I know of no other women. He never told me he was seeing anyone else."

"Would you be surprised if I told you he was? Many other women. Women like yourself. Grieving widows. Taking advantage of all of you."

Leary's body braced in the middle of the pit, his face extended out toward the witness.

Ryan bolted to his feet. Sturmer waved him down and said to the witness not to answer. He motioned both counsel to the bench. Ryan arrived just after Leary.

"Roger. I'm ready to call a mistrial if you persist. I've been contacted by the chief of the appellate division. She is not happy. Please . . . try the case the right way . . . unless you do . . ." Sturmer warned.

"Bullshit! Don't put that in there," Leary motioned to the court reporter who was standing by the side of the trio.

With a wave of his hand toward the bench, Leary turned and sat down in his chair. Ryan looked at Sturmer who seemed dazed at the prosecutor's action. Ryan returned to his chair.

"Any further questions, Mr. Leary?" Sturmer announced.

Leary shook his head petulantly without saying anything.

Ryan rose from his chair and stood alongside the witness box near the jury side.

"Ms. Harbinger. Did the defendant ever strike you?" Ryan said in a clear voice.

"No. He never did. I just can't see Carl hitting anyone."

"You have no knowledge of Rabbi Rubin, in anyway, abusing his wife, do you?"

"No, I do not."

"You said that the rabbi . . . the defendant . . . gave you . . . compassion . . . counseling. Months before you and he became intimate, is that correct?"

"Yes. Yes. We never thought. I never thought I could ever fall in love again. Not after Joel. We had a wonderful marriage."

"Did the rabbi make any overtures? Sexual overtures to you . . . at anytime before you became intimate with him?"

"He wasn't the one who made the first move." She smiled brightly. "He refused to even acknowledge the physical attraction between us. For months. I was the one who sought the physical relationship."

"Was it because of your emotional state at that time?"

"No," she replied quickly, "not at all. He's such a . . . the rabbi . . . he's such a charismatic man. Everything about him. I guess beneath it all . . . over the many years we were associated at the synagogue. I never admitted there was anything . . . mind you . . . not as long as Joel was alive. But I guess there was. And we were working so close. Well, it happened. And I'll tell you . . . I'm glad it did."

Ryan paused for several moments. His mind raced through the evidence of the case. What more could he glean from this witness without harming his client's case? When to let go of a witness is always a trial lawyer's eternal dilemma. The next answer could lead your case into hell.

"Your Honor," Ryan addressed the court, "I see the hour is getting late. Could we adjourn court for today and I can finish my cross-examination of the witness tomorrow."

Sturmer directed his gaze at Leary, who didn't seem to mind.

"Yes. We'll adjourn to 9:30 a.m. tomorrow."

Sturmer banged his gavel on the table and quickly disappeared into his chambers.

CHAPTER FIFTY

Sosie arrived that night. Yehuda picked her up in New York and drove her to Bristol.

Meanwhile, Ryan, Levine, and Olsham were seated around the fireplace in Ryan's rented Victorian house located on the outskirts of Bristol. The mini-estate backed up to an Italian sporting club's hundred acres of roaming, semi-wild animal reserve. Deer, raccoons, groundhogs, and rabbits inhabited the untouched forest, half wet and preserved by government fiat.

Ryan always wondered how half the world could be homeless and starving, yet preserve the enormous marshlands for its four legged inhabitants who had acres to roam and enjoy.

"You've really become a recluse in your middle age," Levine said to Ryan while sucking on a lime between sips of his Corona beer.

"I learned to live with myself when all that shit hit the fan, Sam," Ryan replied. He was buried in the leather reclining chair, his eyes buried deep into the glowing orange flames of the roaring fire.

"That's the hardest part of getting old. You start to like being with yourself. You just withdraw from the rest of the world," Sam replied.

"Women ain't like that," Olsham said. He was sprawled out on the sheepskin rug in front of the fireplace slugging down a glass jar full of margaritas. He added, "They get friendlier as they get older."

"You like your women, John," Levine stated.

"Always have. Something about them that brings out the kid in me. I always wondered how a man could turn away a soft-skinned woman."

"Some men do," Ryan said.

"I know they do. The army was full of them. They preyed on the young recruits."

"The rabbi sure likes his women," Levine interjected.

"They like him," Ryan said.

"He's a powerful little guy," Olsham said.

"He listens to them," Levine replied. "They need somebody to listen to them."

"Do you think he killed her, Joshua?" Olsham asked.

"Maybe," Ryan replied. "Sometimes you get to the point where you want to kill somebody. Maybe even yourself."

"Too bad about Crutchfield. I liked the captain," Olsham said. The warmth of the hot flames from the fireplace covered the trio in a tranquil blanket of camaraderie.

"He got in too deep," Levine said. His jowly face was flushed from the beer and the heat of the fireplace. "He wanted to get out of it too badly. Leary knew that. He got boxed in. We all do sometimes."

"Sometimes," Ryan's voice choked for a moment, then he continued, "dying ain't so bad. You get there and you think there isn't any way back. Maybe instead of killing yourself, you kill a thing that's murdering you. Maybe that's how the rabbi felt."

"His wife?" Olsham asked.

"Who knows. We all have our threshold," Levine said in a throaty voice filled with the foamy residue of the beer. "Life gets unbearable . . . and you think there's a better way."

"Then it's good to have a friend," Ryan said.

"There are friends and there are friends, my young friend. When you got real trouble, then you know what *friend* means."

"You think Leary is alone?" Olsham queried.

"He always has the ghost of Senator Leary to keep him warm," Levine said.

"I tried to be his friend . . . once," Ryan said, "Nobody liked him in law school. He never seemed to mind except when he was drunk. Then he would cry in his beer how lonely he was. Tough life with all that money. Hated his father for giving him everything he ever wanted. I never figured out why he hated his father so much."

"The senator was a tough act to follow," Olsham said. "Strong. You never said no to the senator."

"Roger did. I never understood why the senator would take so much crap from Roger," Ryan said. "I remember when the senator came up to Carlisle. Roger would humiliate him in front of the other students. And the old man took it."

"We all have our weak spots," Levine said. "Maybe the senator felt guilty about the boy. . . no mother and all."

"Fathers do strange things," Ryan mused in a low voice. "My pop died in my arms. Down in the Bowery in New York. At the men's welfare shelter. He had been beaten up by a few bums robbing him for the few dollars he had on him."

"I remember," Ryan's voice halted as he seemed to gasp for air, regained his composure and then continued, "he looked up at me. His shining face all blotched with blood. And he asked me to forgive him. I asked him for what? He said he should have been a better father. He was sorry. He wanted my forgiveness."

"Did you?" Levine asked.

"I wanted to. But I couldn't give him the satisfaction.I hated him so much. It was like all I felt . . . overwhelmed by it. That's what drove me every day. That hate."

"And now?" Levine asked.

"Now it's too late. Too late for anything. If you carry hate around all your life, it eats you up, not anybody else. Besides," he paused sullenly and then added, "He's dead now . . . my pop . . . it's too late to console him . . . no matter how much I want to."

"You sometimes wonder if anybody is that bad," Levine declared.

Sosie walked into the darkened living room, the trio never hearing her entering footfalls.

Ryan suddenly raised his head from the chair as he saw Sosie standing above him.

"Sosie!" he half-yelled as he rose from the chair.

"You have room for her?" Yehuda shouted from the kitchen as he removed a beer from the refrigerator. Her lusty laugh filled Ryan with joy.

"Hello, Joshua Ryan," she declared as she knelt by his chair and kissed him on his flushed cheek.

"You came at the right time. Joshua was wallowing in his horrible childhood," Olsham remarked as he left the room to get another margarita from the kitchen.

"I'm Sam Levine," Levine announced without leaving his overstuffed chair.

"I'm Sosie." She extended her hand to Levine who gently grasped and kissed the back of it.

"He needs a friend about now," Levine said. With great effort, he lifted himself from the chair.

"I think I've had enough for an old man. I'll see you tomorrow bright and early, Joshua. Don't stay up too late." He smiled as he left the room.

Joshua heard very little as he sat up in the chair and stared at Sosie's face beside him. He remembered feeling like this many years ago at Carlisle when he met a beautiful young girl at a college dance whom he fell in love with at first sight. Although he was a football hero and all, she spurned him, left him sitting in his car one wintry night wondering what was wrong with him.

"I never thought you'd actually come," Ryan said as his hand touched Sosie's head.

"I had nothing else to do." Her smile lit up her high cheekboned face. The hate vanished from his body as he stared at her, replaced by a yearning so deep that he could feel his heart pounding in his chest as he looked at her.

"I missed you," he said.

"Me too," she replied.

"Will you marry me?"

"You're drunk, Joshua Ryan."

"I'm a recovering alcoholic. I can't drink. But I still love you. Very much."

"Maybe you're just looking for a shoulder to cry on, Joshua."

"That too," he paused as his eyes brightened and he held her face between his hands.

"Do you hear the music?" He declared, his eyes raised toward the ceiling.

"Ravel's *Bolero*," she replied.

"I miss music in my life and someone to share it with," he said sadly and sincerely.

"You're an old romantic, Mr. Ryan."

He laughed. The pain that had been filling his head vanished. For some reason he suddenly felt safe.

"Will you sit next to me at the concerts?" he asked.

"If you want me to."

"I want you to."

She rose from her half kneeling position and walked to the fireplace, placing her hand on the mantelpiece.

"I broke off my engagement to the doctor in Jerusalem," she said in a low voice.

"A doctor?" He laughed.

"A doctor. My mother thought I was crazy! You don't really know each other!. You're strangers! She warned me about you."

"We must be crazy," he declared as he rose from his chair and walked to her. He wrapped his arms around her waist and kissed her. Slowly. Tenderly . . . lips barely touching. Then they kissed with passion.

"You're a good kisser," she said in an out-of-breath voice.

"So are you," he replied, equally out of breath.

They stood side by side staring into the flames reaching up from the fireplace opening.

"You make me feel like a kid again," he remarked as he reached for her hand.

"You are a kid, Joshua."

"Not anymore."

The lights in the house went out. Except the natural glow of the fireplace before them.

"Everybody's gone to sleep, Sosie."

"Even my father. I guess he trusts you."

"My bedroom is the only one left in the house."

"I guess that's where I sleep," she replied.

"Is that what you want?"

"That's what I want, Joshua."

They walked slowly up the stairs to the third level loft of the old house, hand in hand, to the only bedroom left in the house.

CHAPTER FIFTY-ONE

"Do you have any questions for this witness, Mr. Ryan?" Sturmer asked in a stern unbending tone.

Morning had arrived so quickly and the court started promptly at 9:30 a.m.

"None, Your Honor," Ryan said quietly.

Moira Harbinger walked from the stand, momentarily stopping at the defense table, her hand reaching out and almost touching the rabbi. The rabbi never looked up.

"Next witness, Mr. Leary?" Sturmer asked.

"Norman Goldstein, Your Honor," Leary announced as he stared over at Ryan.

Ryan rose and asked, "May we approach the bench, Your Honor?"

Sturmer motioned them forward.

"Your Honor," Ryan said in an agitated voice, "Mr. Leary never listed his next witness on the discovery sheet."

Leary grinned knowingly.

"Mr. Ryan should realize by now he had to request newly discovered witnesses thirty days before trial. It's not my obligation to do his work for him, Your Honor."

"Mr. Ryan?" Sturmer's eyes seemed to brighten as he spoke.

"It's not an affirmative action that's required of defendant, your honor. Mr. Leary well knows the rules call for an automatic release of newly discovered evidence or witnesses."

"We just discovered Mr. Goldstein in the last day or so, your honor. It seems that Mr. Ryan's buddy Mathias withheld his notes about his interview with Mr. Goldstein, who will prove to be the straw that broke the camel's back in this case, your honor." Leary's grin grew into a malicious smirk.

"Mathias is the state's witness, your honor," Ryan replied in a loud voice.

"Quiet, please, Mr. Ryan. Your voice carries and I don't want your case prejudiced by the jury hearing this colloquy," Sturmer warned. He continued, "I don't think the state is bound by Mathias's failure to disclose the witness, Mr. Ryan."

"Who would be then, Your Honor," Ryan persisted, "Mathias is the state's agent. The state is responsible for any withheld information of its agents, Your Honor."

"I don't see it that way, Mr. Ryan. I'm going to allow the state to present Mr. Goldstein. Proceed, Mr. Leary."

Goldstein wore a conservative Brooks Brothers suit as he walked from the spectator area into the combat gallery. He looked the part of the corporate lawyer.

After being sworn in, Goldstein settled comfortably into the witness chair and focused his eyes on the jury.

Leary rose from his seat and walked to the side of the jury box and the witness chair. He smiled affably at the witness who returned the smile. Ryan's stomach churned noisily as he watched the friendly exchange between Leary and the witness.

Mathias passed a note from his gallery seat to Ryan. Ryan quickly looked at it and then crumbled it in his hand.

"Mr. Goldstein, what is your occupation?" Leary started in a whispery monotone.

"I'm corporate counsel for Loftus Corporation. Head of their litigation department."

"Do you hold any honorary positions with Temple Beth Shalom?"

In a deep, proud voice, his face glowing with pride, he replied, "Yes. I'm president of the board of directors of the synagogue. Have been for ten years."

"Do you know the defendant?"

"Yes. Yes, I do. We have been associated at the temple for as long as I've been president."

"What is your relationship with the defendant?"

"How do I get along with him? We have a good working relationship."

"Did you know the decedent, Eleanore Rubin?" Leary's voice appeared to gain momentum as he fired off the questions. As if his questions were leading somewhere. Ryan's stomach gurgled with anxiety. Who the hell is Goldstein in this case he thought? Why is he here? He knew Goldstein's appearance wasn't supposed to be helpful to the rabbi. Not in a long shot.

"Yes. I knew her. And I knew the rabbi. Saw them together many times at temple functions. She was a lovely person. Loved by all of us."

"Especially you." Leary declared in a piercing voice, his body leaning over the jury box.

"I don't understand," Goldstein replied in a confusing tone.

"Where the hell is he going?" Ryan whispered over to Levine.

"We'll know soon enough," Levine replied, his eyes narrowed onto the two characters in front of him.

"Sure you do, Mr. Goldstein," Leary declared loudly.

"Your Honor. I don't know where Mr. Leary is taking us," Ryan said. "This witness was called by the state and it seems Mr. Leary is questioning the witness in a threatening manner."

"Your Honor," Leary announced, "the way I handle the state's witness is my business. Mr. Ryan wants to run both sides of the courtroom."

"Gentlemen. Please. Mr. Ryan. I haven't heard anything that is improper by Mr. Leary. Can we proceed in an expeditious manner? I don't want to keep these kind people," Sturmer extended his hand toward the jury, "a minute longer then they have to. . .okay, Mr. Ryan?"

Ryan wondered if the jury sensed the court's partiality toward the state. Or worse, its disfavor toward the defense. Ryan knew that it would take an atomic bomb to destroy the jury's belief in the judge's godlike image. The judge even explains to the jury, during his jury instructions at the close of the case "that lawyers cannot be believed. Instead, *you must listen to me*. Because I am the fountain of your knowledge. I will guide you to the promised land."

"Answer the question, Mr. Goldstein," Sturmer barked at the witness.

"I didn't know Mr. Leary had posed a question," Ryan stated.

"Did you love her?" Leary shot out.

"We all did," Goldstein repeated.

"Come now, Mr. Goldstein. You're an attorney who is under oath. You have an obligation to tell the truth."

"I don't know what to say," Goldstein replied, his hands grasping the edge of the wooden rail of the witness box. His eyes stared down at his hands.

"Did you love her?" Leary reiterated in a louder voice now tainted with anger.

"Yes. Yes, I did. But not like . . . well, it wasn't as if we were intimate. . .she was the rabbi's wife. And yes, she was a wonderfully warm person."

"Come now, sir," Leary strode in front of him, blocking Ryan's vision of the witness.

"Look, Mr. Goldstein. We have concrete evidence that you were the paramour of the decedent. Her lover!" Leary shouted as he wheeled around toward the spectator gallery to emphasize the accusation.

Ryan and Levine turned toward the defendant, who continued to face forward, his body slightly lowered into the wooden armchair. Ryan put his hand on the rabbi's arm. The rabbi turned his face toward Ryan, his eyes clouded. The rabbi said nothing. After a few moments he again turned toward the witness box.

The jurors seemed to be waiting for the question and answer that could link the witness and the decedent. It was almost there. . .but the linchpin was still missing.

"I don't know what you're talking about," the witness replied in a dramatically changed tone of voice. The loquacious cooperative witness was now defending against the enemy. Leary.

"Your Honor, again, Mr. Leary is attacking his own witness. Attacks against the credibility of a witness are reserved for cross-examination by the other party. Not by the state who calls the witness," Ryan said pedantically.

Sturmer's face tightened. His mouth quivered noticeably.

He motioned again for counsel to approach the bench. The faces of the jurors were noticeably agitated, their body movements clearly signifying their growing impatience. The noise of the gallery increased to the high-pitched level of a discordant buzz.

"What the hell are you doing, Roger?" Sturmer half-shouted, waving away the court reporter.

"I'm questioning my witness, Your Honor," Leary replied in a noncommittal voice.

"No, you're not. You're making me look like an ass. Sometimes you can win the battle but lose the war, Roger."

"Those are my sentiments," Ryan agreed, as a glimmer of a smile crossed his face. *Maybe Sturmer is finally seeing the light,* Ryan thought.

"Judge, listen," Roger Leary lectured, "if you're going to fuck up my case. Well . . ." He paused for a moment as if he was really thinking about his next words and then continued in a rapid-fire manner, "Well. Anyway . . . it's my case. And nobody tries my case for me. Not even you, Albert. *Now get the fuck out of my face or else!*"

Leary turned on his heels and walked back to his counsel table. Ryan continued to stare at the judge and then, when Sturmer did nothing, Ryan slowly walked back to his chair shaking his head from side to side. The jurors appeared totally befuddled as they looked quizzically at each other and then back to the judge.

Leary continued as if nothing had happened to interrupt his direct examination of the witness.

"Did you ever stay at the Ramada Inn in Philadelphia?" Leary paused dramatically and then continued, "With the decedent as your roommate?"

"I don't," the witness replied as his eyes focused on Leary's hands pulling papers out of his file.

"You don't what?" Leary demanded as he approached the witness with a disorderly sheaf of papers that appeared to be receipts of some kind.

"I guess I did," the witness admitted in a whisper.

"Sure you did," Leary repeated, "You stayed there many times, Mr. Goldstein. With Eleanore Rubin. Didn't you?"

The witness remained silent. Leary shoved the receipts toward the witness.

"Take them," Leary ordered. "I want you to look these hotel receipts over. Carefully, Mr. Goldstein. You're under oath and anything you say could lead to a perjury indictment against you. Do you understand me, *Mr. Goldstein?*"

Leary stepped back from the witness box to allow the jury to watch the witness shuffle the receipts between his hands as if they were a deck of cards.

"Did you stay at the Ramada Inn on the dates signified on the receipts? Look at them, Mr. Goldstein. Did you?"

The witness continued to stare at his hands, which were over the papers on his lap.

"I did."

"You what?" Leary shouted. "Please speak up, Mr. Goldstein," Leary's eyes stared pointedly at the jury.

"Your Honor," Ryan stood on the balls of his feet. "What does all this have to do with the defendant and the charge against him. So what if the witness had an affair with the decedent? Where is it relevant to the guilt or innocence of the defendant, Carl Rubin? I just don't see where the prosecutor is leading us. Except to a diversionary dead end."

Leary smiled as he leaned against the jury box, his back to the jury. The noise level of the court spectators was at a fever pitch. Sturmer gaveled the courtroom to silence. No one seemed to listen.

"Your honor. The state will show . . . through the lips of the defendant himself that he knew of this illicit affair between his wife . . . the victim . . . and Mr. Goldstein. And with that knowledge, and the hatred that rose out of that knowledge, motivated him . . . along with the other reasons clearly shown by the state . . . to cold-bloodedly arrange to have his wife killed."

"Ridiculous!" Ryan shouted.

"Your Honor," Ryan continued, "I have never heard such . . . such . . . drivel. Your honor," Ryan waited a few moments for the noise of the gallery to subside and then continued, "Your Honor. I don't think we have any choice anymore. You must call a mistrial. The prosecutor's comments in open court . . . in front of this jury . . . has so tainted this trial that the defendant cannot possibly get a fair trial."

Sturmer peered over his bifocals at the jury and said in a low, tremulous voice, "Ladies and gentlemen. Will you kindly take a short coffee break in the deliberation room. Counsel . . . I want to see you all in my chambers. Now!"

Confusion reigned in the courtroom and increased substantially as the judge left the bench and the courtroom. There was the redundant sound of clicking cameras.

Leary opposed the presence of Levine in chambers. Ryan insisted. Sturmer didn't want to face any more issues then he had to, so Levine stayed.

They sat around the judge's desk, books lining the walls of the room along with the plaques of honors awarded to Judge Sturmer by local and state bar organizations.

"Gentlemen, you're all making it very difficult for me to continue with this trial." Sturmer announced.

""I've moved for a mistrial on several occasions, Your Honor," Ryan insisted.

"So you have, Mr. Ryan." Sturmer admitted in a sullen voice. "It seems that's all you're ever doing, Mr. Ryan, is trying to get this trial aborted."

"Because Your Honor should recuse himself in this case," Levine interjected.

"On what grounds, Counselor?" Sturmer replied cautiously.

Levine knew he had to play his ace now. The way this trial was proceeding, Levine knew the defendant could only be found guilty. Not because he was, merely because the circumstantial evidence allowed in by Sturmer was overwhelmingly prejudicial against the rabbi.

"We were never notified of the testimony of Norman Goldstein, Your Honor," Ryan interjected.

"Why do you think I have to recuse myself?" Sturmer bitingly addressed his question to Levine, whose hands sat tentlike on his extended abdomen.

"Because I think Mr. Leary has you in his pocket, Your Honor," Levine replied blandly, his narrow slit eyes staring directly at the judge.

"That's a serious accusation, Mr. Levine. Especially from a member of the bar. You know if you can't prove it . . . you could lose your license for such an unfounded accusation against a sitting judge."

"I know what I hear and see, Your Honor," Levine said in a staunch no-give position.

Sturmer rose from his high-backed chair and leaned over his desk. Both of his hands were placed as supports for his leaning body.

"You do what you have to do, Mr. Levine. I'm not declaring a mistrial or recusing myself from this trial . . . unless you have damn sure evidence for any reason I should recuse myself. What I'm going to do is continue this trial. At least until I see the defense side of the case. At that time I will entertain any motions by the parties. As of now . . . Mr. Leary . . . are you finished with the state's case?"

"After Goldstein, your honor, I have just one minor matter, and then the state rests," Leary pronounced, that ever-present smirk fashioned on his face.

"And you, Mr. Ryan, what can we expect from the defense?"

"We have a Dr. Seltzer, Your Honor," Ryan replied. "Maybe the defendant. Also I want to present my opening to this jury at the beginning of the defense case, Your Honor."

"Of course, you reserved that right at the beginning of the trial. I would hope to get this case to the jury in the next couple of days, gentlemen. Am I correct?"

"After conviction, your honor, we still have the death penalty phase of the trial," Leary said in a confident voice.

"You already have him strapped to the gurney, Roger," Levine said in smiling voice.

"I knew that it would happen from the beginning, Mr. Levine," Leary retorted.

Goldstein testified to the affair with Eleanore Rubin. It had continued for over a year, then it ended suddenly about a month before her death. Goldstein did not know if the defendant's husband knew about his wife's infidelity. The witness left the stand after perfunctory cross-examination by Ryan. He didn't want to prolong the witness's presence in the box nor elicit answers he did not know what they would be before the questions were asked. Trials invariably led to failure when the questioner didn't know the answer. Surprise! Surprise! Surprise! Three reasons not to ask dumb questions in cross-examination, especially of an unexpected witness.

Leary's "minor matter" involved the submission of a taped telephone conversation between the defendant and Moira. Without advance notice to the defendant, Leary's technician began to set up the recording machine in the courtroom.

Ryan and Levine wondered what surprises Leary had to offer.

After a few minutes of waiting and watching the technician set up the device near the jury box, Ryan requested a bench conference with the court.

"Your honor. I thought the state had rested after the last witness. Unless the state has a musical recording of *Phantom* to entertain us all, I'm completely in the dark as to what Mr. Leary is doing."

"Looks like the state is going to offer a recording into evidence, Mr. Ryan," Sturmer brightly revealed.

"We have not been apprised of any recording, Your Honor. May I know of what we are going to hear?"

"A taped phone conversation of your client and his lover, Mr. Ryan," Leary said.

Ryan's face twisted in abject pain as his chest pounded with anxiety.

"Your Honor. Nothing has been revealed in discovery."

"We don't have to reveal a telephone intercept if it's done by private parties, Mr. Ryan," Leary answered smugly.

"What private parties, Your Honor? No one has revealed a telephone intercept by private parties." Ryan's voice was insistent.

"A recording perpetrated by a private investigator hired by your client's wife, Mr. Ryan," Leary admitted proudly.

"Your Honor . . ." Ryan started to protest.

"Mr. Ryan . . . a telephone intercept by the victim's agent does not have to be revealed," Sturmer pronounced.

"Your Honor, under *Brady*, everything is discoverable. We all know that. It would be an irreparable error to allow this recording into evidence, Your Honor," Ryan announced.

"Enough. I've ruled, Mr. Ryan. Mr. Leary, proceed."

The telephone recording revealed the defendant Carl Rubin informing his lover Moira about his wife's affair with Goldstein. The rabbi apparently knew of the affair *before* his wife was murdered.

"What are you going to do," Moira had replied in a confused voice.

"I don't know."

"Maybe she did it to get back at you?" Moira had offered.

"It's been going on for years. Right under my very nose. I was livid when I found out. Everybody seemed to know. She's made a laughingstock out of me!" The rabbi's voice was noticeably angry.

"Have you told her. That you know?"

"No . . . I was so . . . so . . . I can't even say it. *I felt like killing her!*"

"You're just upset, Carl. Please."

The rabbi's voice was silent, the recording sending out heavy breathing noises for almost a minute.

"I'll take care of it, Moira. Go to sleep. I'll take care of it," the rabbi repeated in a low-threatening tone.

"Don't do anything foolish, Carl. Please."

And then the recording went dead.

"Your Honor," Ryan stood up from his chair, his voice strained with accumulated anger and frustration.

"Yes, Mr. Ryan," Judge Sturmer said.

"I renew my motion for a mistrial," Ryan said without feeling.

"Denied! Mr. Leary. Is that the state's case?"

"Yes, Your Honor," Leary replied, his face aglow with a sense of victory.

Ryan sat down in abject resignation. Levine whispered to him but Ryan's head seemed to be frozen in place. He had difficulty masking his sense of defeat.

"Mr. Ryan?" Sturmer said loudly. "I thought you wished to open to the jury?"

"Yes. In a moment. May I have a moment, Your Honor," Ryan replied.

"Take as long as you need, Mr. Ryan," Sturmer declared, a smile evident on his face.

Sosie and Yehuda were seated in the first row of the gallery, not ten feet from where Ryan was seated. Ryan was stonefaced. Only his hand moved onto the legal pad, nervous movements that resembled involuntary responses to a frenzied thought process.

The night before had been blissful and scary. He was exhausted physically but his mind raced maniacally from headnote to headnote, face to face, problem to problem. He had counted too much on winning. On an acquittal. But it *now* seemed far away. At one time, it was so close he could taste it.

Then that fucking tapped phone call! Leary had found the linchpin. Even though the state couldn't produce the actual killer, they could show the motive and desire that destroyed Eleanore Rubin. By her husband, the good rabbi. And all of it came as a surprise to Ryan.

No way to prepare for it. No way at all. It was one of those electric moments in a trial when the sense of defeat crystallized perceptibly.

Sosie consoled Ryan in every tender way. They both knew no matter what, he had to return to that courtroom the next day.

No one else would or could bear the weight of the outcome. Only Ryan, the lawyer for the defendant.

She felt his pain. His confinement. His total lack of hope. Reality had set in. The rabbi could be convicted and executed for a death they all believed he did not cause.

Ryan jumped up from his seat, dropped the pen angrily on the table and walked quickly to the middle of the jury box. He said nothing for several moments, his hands clasped in front of him. His eyes resting on each face of the jury. Boldly, he stared until some of the jurors looked away.

"Never again, ladies and gentlemen of the jury, will you have the power to decide whether another human being will live or die." His voice was low and the words flowed in a deep current of repressed emotions. As if he were going to explode at any moment.

"Beyond a reasonable doubt. You have heard the words time and time again. They are the most important words you will hear in this trial. Words that you must remember before you can render a verdict that may cause the murder of an innocent man. The defendant, without any doubt, is innocent of the vile crime of murder. Simply said, he did not murder, arrange to murder, or in any barbaric fashion, destroy the life of his wife of over a quarter century, one Eleanore Rubin.

"Marital problems? Sure. We all have them. Infidelity? Certainly. Many marriages survive the ravages of time, of boredom, of the sameness of seeing the same face everyday. Who among us can say we don't feel those emotions? Daily. Obviously, there are civilized remedies that spouses can use to separate themselves from their marital bonds. Murder isn't one of them. And it certainly wasn't the remedy arranged to destroy the life of Eleanore Rubin."

"You heard the defendant declare in anger, on the telephone, that he would 'kill her.' His wife, who he had recently discovered was having an affair with another man. 'I felt like killing her,' those were the words you heard.

"How many civilized human beings, in anger have uttered the same threatening phrase, but do not mean nor execute that damnable threat. I must admit to being one. Certainly in the depths of despair, of blinding anger, *we all* involuntarily feel the urge to kill. For that moment only. It passes. As it has for all of us. It passes.

"Nowhere in this case has the state shown, *beyond a reasonable doubt*—those are magical words, ladies and gentlemen—nowhere has the state shown you that level of incontrovertible evidence that would give rise to your decision to execute Carl Rubin.

"The State will not, and has not, displayed a shred of evidence worth considering by you, that the defendant Carl Rubin strangled his wife. Their contention is that he arranged, unmercifully arranged, the destruction of another human being. A rabbi. A man of God. It is just not true!

"Lastly we will show you, in the defense case, that the cause of death itself is in serious question. Was it strangulation? Or was it some other cause not even explored by the state? And certainly not caused, in any way, by the defendant. Ladies and gentlemen, Carl Rubin is innocent. Thank you."

Ryan turned slowly and walked back to his chair and sat down, his hands folded on the table, his face a mask of unconcern.

Dr. Herbert Seltzer was a short block of a man, trudging to the witness box. He wore an old wool sports jacket, patches on the elbows, and a tie that was left open at the neck of the faded white shirt he was wearing. He either looked like a homeless bum getting dressed up for court or an academician who never thought about his dress appearance.

After Ryan meticulously questioned the noted forensic professor on his credentials, Leary agreed to his qualifications as an expert on forensic medicine and pathology.

"Doctor," Ryan started his direct examination in a voice filled with respect for the eminent pathologist, "did you have an occasion to examine the victim's body in this case?"

"No, I did not. By the time I was called, the body had been cremated."

"Is it unusual for a murder victim's body to be cremated within one year of her death?"

"Yes, it is. When I asked the county medical examiner why the body had been removed and destroyed, he informed me that those were the orders he received from the county prosecutor's office. It is very unusual especially in this case."

"Why so, Doctor?"

"Because cremation would be against the restrictions of the Jewish religion. That's why I thought it was strange, Mr. Ryan. The decedent's family would never have approved cremation of the body."

"Did you have an occasion to receive the medical reports of the county medical examiner as a result of his autopsy of the decedent's body?"

"Yes. I did."

"And what, in your opinion, within a degree of reasonable medical certainty, was the cause of the victim's death?"

Dr. Seltzer rustled through his file, the papers falling to his feet. He stooped to pick them up, knocking his head against the wooden box surrounding the witness chair. Ryan expected more of Wally Cox to emerge from the bottom of that witness box than the unruly head of Dr. Seltzer.

Sitting upright in his chair, the witness smiled benignly, ran his rough-hewn hand through the furrows of salt-and-pepper hair, and then said in a husky, articulate voice, "The victim here had to either have been poisoned . . . drugged . . . or over insulined. Whatever, it was difficult to find traces of any drugs in her system."

The words were said in such a modulated voice that the meaning of the witness's statement took almost a half minute to sink in. Then the buzzing undercurrent started to rise from the gallery of onlookers. Even Sturmer, who occasionally seemed to fall asleep during a witness's testimony, jerked his head toward the witness.

"Doctor," Sturmer addressed the witness in a shocked voice, "did I hear what you just said?"

"Which statement, Your Honor?" The witness smiled as he replied to the judge.

"The one . . . the one about the cause of death?"

"Well . . . yes. What is so surprising? I, of course, didn't examine the body, which I would have loved to do. But, yes, from the reports I have seen . . . and I would have to say they were shoddily prepared . . . anyway, those reports show me that the county examiner's conclusion that the cause of death was strangulation is totally wrong. She couldn't have died from strangulation. So, I surmised that since she was a diabetic and her blood-sugar reading at the autopsy was unmercifully low. She either died of an overdose of insulin, putting her in a diabetic coma, a heart attack or what have you. Or, as I have seen many a time, injected with a drug perhaps put into her insulin. Like curare. Or even cyanide. Small amounts. Cyanide in larger doses would have been detected if . . . that's only if the medical examiner had looked for it. And the way this autopsy was performed, I highly doubt it would have been found. Anyway, I think in further thought, she probably . . . for whatever reason, probably accidentally . . . and you know it happens often . . . over insulined herself . . . maybe even doing it twice in a short period of time. That's why the blood sugar level was so low. It was probably thirteen . . . one hundred is normal   . . . She probably went into hypoglycemic shock within minutes of the second injection. And probably also fell . . . fainted . . . whatever . . . like crashing into the kitchen table. That's probably where the bruise on her head came from . . . she probably expired within minutes of the last injection and the fall. Certainly she was dead before the strangulation. That's my opinion."

Ryan knew Seltzer's opinion all along. Whether it would fly in court was another story. Maybe Leary would now call for a mistrial.

Leary suddenly jumped up from his chair as if shot from a cannon, with the note from Ambrosio in front of him, and then in a voice filled with fear and confusion said, "Your Honor. The state has never been apprised of Dr. Seltzer's opinion. Not like this. It's totally inconceivable that this kind of opinion should be allowed in. And besides, this witness never even examined the corpse. How can he now say that the doctor who did the examination was wrong? How can he say that!"

Ryan rose slowly from his chair. Levine was smiling, trying to keep his lips from parting.

"Your Honor," Ryan intoned haltingly, "the defense has provided the state with the name of Dr. Seltzer as a witness. Unfortunately, the state failed to request Dr. Seltzer's opinion. As Mr. Leary has said so often in this trial . . . it is the affirmative duty of the party seeking the information to, at least, ask for it."

Leary would not be denied. He rushed toward the bench as if he were going to attack Judge Sturmer.

"Albert," he shouted. Sturmer's head raised toward the ceiling as if he were looking for divine intervention.

"Your Honor," Leary shouted, "I move that this witness's testimony be stricken. The defense has hidden his preposterous opinion from the state. Besides how can he now testify as to any reasonable medical conclusion and differ with the medical examiner who saw the body? *He didn't* see the body!" Leary repeated loudly.

Ryan, in a quiet, understated tone remarked, "Your honor, how can the state try and exclude Dr. Seltzer's opinion now, based upon the fact that he did not view the autopsy or see the body. The state had ensured that the body could not be seen by the defense by destroying the only evidence in this case of any value. But even so, Dr. Seltzer has testified that strangulation was not the cause of death of Eleanore Rubin. And if it's not strangulation then the state's case must fail. Because they have not shown any other possible cause of death. Nothing to link the defendant with the death of the victim."

Sturmer turned to the witness and said, "Doctor, why do you conclude that the victim wasn't strangled?"

Dr. Seltzer smiled, almost like a reflex action, and spoke in a voice filled with pedantic frustration.

"Your Honor. It's really very simple. I didn't say the victim wasn't strangled. She was. But it didn't cause her death. Listen," the witness leaned sideways toward the higher judge's bench, his hands extended as if physically offering the explanation with his hands, " . . . if she had been alive when she was strangled, then the whites of the eyes would have contained little red spots, broken blood vessels . . . caused by the lack of oxygen to the eyes. Also, there would have been foam around the mouth, sputum in her mouth and water in her lungs. The good medical examiner found none of this sympathology. She was dead when she was strangled. Why I don't know. But she probably had been dead for over an hour. Note—I'm presuming that the time of death was just before 7:00 p.m. That is my reading of the autopsy report. Certainly, not at 5:45 p.m. as stated by the medical examiner. And definitely before the daughter of the victim discovered the body. Anyway . . . most probably . . . within the degree of medical probability . . . the death occurred from the over insulined injection that the decedent did to herself . . . and probably the fall accelerated her expiration as well. So there . . . have I explained myself?"

The doctor appeared relieved that, at last, he had explained to the world the secret of life and death. In simple, uncomplicated terms.

Ryan leaned against his table, arms crossed, his face tranquil and pleased.

Leary suddenly walked out of the courtroom through the door leading to the judge's chambers.

The jurors sat transfixed, their eyes moving between the witness, the judge and counsels' varied physical movements.

Sturmer left his chair and walked slowly out of the courtroom toward his chambers. He said nothing. The clerk sent the jury into the deliberation room on her own volition. The crowded gallery loudly questioned each other, nobody understanding the sudden turn of events.

"I'm going to ask for a mistrial, Your Honor," Leary shouted at Sturmer in the judge's chambers. Levine and Ryan were standing against the book-lined walls saying nothing.

"On what grounds, Roger?" Sturmer replied.

"Why? What grounds? Goddamn it, Albert, what grounds? A deaf man could see what grounds. Don't be such a goddamn fool. I'm not going to let the bastard witness throw my case out the window. Listen. You grant a mistrial now . . . or else!" Leary warned with his forefinger extended toward the judge.

Sturmer peered over at Ryan and Levine in a hopeful gesture. As if Ryan would agree to the prosecutor's belated motion for a mistrial.

The room seemed to close in around Sturmer. He thought of peaceful retirement in the Smoky Mountains of North Carolina where he owned a mini-estate full of birds, maples, and tranquility. Right by the side of a mountain stream that appeared from nowhere and ran along side his hundred acres of land.

"I'm going to exclude the testimony of this witness, Mr. Ryan," Sturmer blurted out.

Levine jumped forward as far as Sturmer's desk. Standing over the extended edge of the desk, Levine in an apparent rage, shouted, "You goddamn coward. You goddamn coward! You have no right to make your own rules up just because this little piece of shit scares the hell out of you!"

Levine turned toward Leary who withdrew back toward the entrance of the room.

Sturmer quickly punched in a number on his phone, and two bailiffs suddenly appeared at his chamber door.

"Mr. Levine," Sturmer spoke in a fear-laden voice, his eyes avoiding Levine who seemed unafraid of the bailiffs, "these men will put you in jail for the rest of the trial if you ever . . ."

Ryan moved between the bailiff and Levine, his arm extended, "Judge. You can't exclude Dr. Seltzer's testimony. Mr. Levine is as shocked as I am. If you do, your honor, I must ask for an immediate adjournment to appeal this decision."

Sturmer almost appeared relieved at Ryan's request.

"I'll grant you till 4:00 p.m. this afternoon to appeal my decision and if the appellate division refuses to hear your request we proceed to a verdict. That's final, gentlemen!"

Leary stepped toward Sturmer, whose eyes avoided Leary's approach. The prosecutor's face was beet-red, his mouth twitching hysterically.

"You can't!" Leary shouted. The bailiffs moved between the approaching Leary and the judge, the tall bailiff holding Leary at the chest.

"That's my order," Sturmer repeated.

The frenzied reaction by the spectators to the ruling of the Court was volcanic. Voices erupted in surprise, anger and support by the milling lawyers and media people.

Without hesitation, Ryan and Levine walked through the

courtroom, stopping briefly to instruct Olsham what to tell Rubin.

Sosie sidled next to Ryan, as he kissed her on the cheek and whispered into her ear.

At Ryan's office, the phone rang incessantly. Ryan's newly hired part-time secretary, Dawn, kept switching from one line to the other attempting feverishly to record the messages on the memo.

"Dawn," Ryan said, "get me an open line. Now!"

Ryan and Levine walked into his inner office. Ryan picked up the telephone and dialed the number for the chief justice of the appellate division.

CHAPTER FIFTY-TWO

They all congregated in the conference room outside the assignment judge's office. Justice Marilyn Friedholf, chief of the appellate division, sat demurely at the head of the conference table, saying nothing as the characters in this ongoing drama sat themselves around the large oval table.

Alexander King's face was wreathed in lines of apparent concern. He sat next to the chief justice, who failed to even acknowledge his presence. Judge Sturmer sat alongside the assignment judge, his eyes staring at his feet. Ryan and Levine sat at the other end of the table, two chairs away from Leary and Ambrosio.

"Do you want coffee, Chief?" King said in a plaintive voice.

"The hell with the coffee, Alexander!" she replied angrily, her voice gruff and yet clear as a bell in winter.

"You," the Chief announced as she pointed her face toward King and Sturmer, "you . . . idiots have made a laughingstock of the entire state's judiciary. With one ruling, Sturmer, we are going to be the main joke on the talk shows tonight. This morning I was awakened at 6:00 a.m. by the governor. She couldn't understand why her administration, in one fell swoop, in an election year yet, was being humiliated by not only the state's press but the national media as well. I, of course, couldn't explain to her except to say that was what one expected from the comedians running Summit County."

"Chief," King interjected in a weak voice, "I don't know . . ."

"Shut up Alexander," she replied harshly. "You better retire to that campground I've been hearing so much about."

She paused and stared angrily at Ryan and Levine.

"Well, gentlemen," addressing Ryan and Levine, "you really stirred up one hell of a mess."

"Your Honor," Levine said, "unfortunately you were in Europe during the first few days of this trial. We would have filed the appeal earlier."

"I'm here now. My trip was cut short because nobody expects the chief justice of this idiot state to enjoy herself. Now tell me . . . in simple terms . . ."

Ryan described the events that led up to the emergency call to the appellate division late yesterday afternoon. The chief had been in conference with the judicial committee that runs the administration of justice in the state. Nobody could reach her or even knew whether she, personally, wanted to intercede in the war in Summit County.

"So . . . Judge Sturmer. You have selected to exclude the well respected scientific opinion of one of the leading forensic pathologists in the country based upon . . . what?" Her voice rose to almost a disbelieving whine, her seamless face crinkled with ridges under her eyes.

"Your Honor, Chief . . ." Sturmer replied in a halting voice, "the defense had failed to submit the expert's report before trial."

"So what? Did the state ask for it? Even so . . . Judge . . . we're here to mete out justice. Not to railroad an innocent defendant to the death house." She paused and raised her hands toward the ceiling. "Where the hell are we? In Hitler's Germany?"

Leary stood up at his place at the table. Ryan thought he appeared shorter than he had normally appeared in the past.

"Your Honor," he started in a stuttering voice, "I. . .I."

"You what, Mr. Prosecutor," the chief shouted an angry retort, "you did what?"

"Well . . . you can't expect the state to proceed with this trial."

"I can expect the prosecutor . . . the people's lawyer . . . to act like a human being. Not as if you were an executioner from the Inquisition. That's all I expect, Mr. Leary."

"Your Honor, I have a job . . ."

"No, you don't, Mr. Leary. Your re-appointment is dead. You know what that means, Mr. Leary. It means you may have to work for a living."

"That's not fair, Your Honor." Leary spoke with a garbled mouth, his words almost unclear.

"Okay, gentlemen, here's where it's at. Obviously the cause of death is in serious question. Dr. Seltzer . . . whom I know personally, is the final authority, in my mind, on forensic pathology. He says that strangulation was not the cause of death. And, as I understand it, Mr. Leary, that's the only potential link . . . or should I say thread . . . you have to tie the defendant with his wife's murder."

Leary searched the room for support. Not even tiny Ambrosio offered any notes of authoritative support to Leary. He looked at her with childlike eyes hoping that she would again pull Leary's rabbit out of the hat. She offered nothing.

"We have the county medical examiner's opinion," Leary blurted out.

"That old drunk," the chief replied. "He couldn't find a watermelon in a dead body. Besides, from what I read in Seltzer's testimony, she was dead before strangulation occurred. If that's so . . . then you must dismiss the case against the defendant. Does that ring any bells, Judge Sturmer?"

Her soft blue eyes hardened into marble aggies, forming laser beams focused at the deflated jurist.

"I'll do whatever you say," Sturmer whispered.

"Now. . ." the chief's face brightened into a smile, "what about this murder that happened twenty-five years ago . . ."

CHAPTER FIFTY-THREE

"Didn't you hear, Lew?" the Larchmont Hills police chief blared into Mathias' telephone receiver.

"Hear what, Chief?", he replied as he munched on a liverwurst and onion sandwich his wife had packed for him that day. He loved liverwurst.

"About the Rubin trial?" the chief said in an agitated voice.

"It's still going on. What's new about that?"

"Not anymore. Sturmer dismissed all charges against Rubin. On orders of the chief justice of the appellate division. And that ain't all. She ordered an immediate investigation into the disappearance of an Elias Rubin over twenty-five years ago. Got some Oakie in the woods who supposedly saw our great assignment judge and Sturmer witness the cremation of this rebel. You ever hear of Elias Rubin, Lew?"

"Yeah . . . I did. It must have been Uncle Lester. He was there all right."

"Did you call the AG's office?"

Mathias smiled as he finished off the sandwich and devoured a can of Sprite.

"Maybe," he answered in a garbled voice.

"Well, you better watch your ass, Lew. Leary is finished. He has about three months to his term. But he's one to watch out for. Him and Dickson, Lew."

"I'll watch out, Chief."

"Dickson may be indicted by the state grand jury. Something about kicking the shit out of Joshua Ryan, the defendant's attorney. Where the hell have I been when all this is happening? Did you know all this shit, Lew?"

"I knew, Chief."

"Don't you think your superiors should know also, Lew?" Mathias could hear the twinge of resentment in the chief's voice.

"You told me you didn't want to know, Chief."

"Yeah . . . but y'know. . .things like this I should know."

"I'm sorry . . . next time I'll bring you into all this crap, Chief."

"Anyway, Lew . . . Dickson has been suspended from the troopers and he's looking for somebody to blame."

"I can handle myself, Chief."

"I know you can, Lew."

"Come over to the house for dinner Saturday night, Chief, Joanne is making a pot roast and we'll break open a half-keg of beer"

"Okay . . . but be careful."

The phone clicked dead as Mathias finished off the can of Sprite. He wiped his mouth with the cuff of his beat-up sport jacket and rose to stare out his office window.

Dickson, he thought. Watch out for Dickson, the chief had warned. What the fuck could he do? Mathias mumbled to himself.

It was past 5:00 p.m. and it was Friday. Mathias looked forward to a weekend with Joanne and the boys who were returning home from the reserves tonight. Should be a hell of a weekend. He missed his sons. They'd been gone for almost a year. Joined the army the same time. Shipped out to Germany in the same outfit. He had missed them. Things were going to be great again, he thought. Another couple of years and he would be out. Retired. Maybe go to Colorado to live. He'd always wanted to live near the mountains. He skied there as a kid. Before it became popular with the stars. No more shit. No more responsibilities. No more guys aiming for his head. It had been a long haul. He was approaching sixty. He felt good physically but this case had taken a lot out of him. Any case with Leary would take a lot out of an honest cop.

Leary had threatened that if he ever went to the AG with inside information about the prosecutor's office he'd be sorry. Well, he had. Leary knew about it. He had a mole in the AG's office who told Leary every bit of dirt that came his way. Especially about Summit County.

Mathias walked down the steps to the first level of the Larchmont Hills police station. He waved to the desk sergeant as they exchanged insulting farewells. It would be a good weekend.

Stepping to the sidewalk outside of the police station, Mathias heard the cacophony of the VW engine starting up. It was the same car. The old Beetle. And finally he saw it. Slowly moving down the main street of Larchmont Hills.

He waited on the curb. The vehicle stopped five feet up from where Mathias was standing. Then it crawled in front of Mathias. The sunroof opened up and Dickson's head popped out. He had a malevolent smirk on his day-old bearded face. His eyes were watery and red as if Dickson had downed too many beers that day.

"Hello, lieutenant asshole," Dickson blurted out in a slurring voice.

"You shouldn't drink and drive, Sergeant," Mathias replied as he reached down toward the hip holster under his jacket.

"Fuck you, squealer," Dickson yelled.

Dickson was standing full height through the sunroof, the flat-top of his head turning side to side as if he were sizing up the area.

"You better go back to your boss, Dickson. Or else I'll arrest you for drunken driving."

"Fuck you too, you ain't getting away with what you did, fuck-head." With that battery of obscenities, Dickson raised his hidden arm through the sunroof opening and aimed the massive .45 pistol at Mathias's chest.

Before Mathias could unholster his gun, Dickson had pumped three hollowed-out bullets into the chest of Mathias. He fell to the cold hard sidewalk, his mind still thinking about the weekend with his boys. Then his mind went dead. And so did Lieutenant Lew Mathias.

EPILOGUE

It was near the end of May. Almost a year after the trial of Rabbi Carl Rubin. Paris was beautiful in late spring. The chestnut trees lining the boulevards made Ryan's heart jump for joy. Just like in the movies, where Leslie Caron and Louis Jourdan and Maurice Chevalier strolled down the Champs Elysees singing "Gigi" to celebrate the magnificent essence of living in Gay Paree.

Since the dismissal of the murder charges against the rabbi, Ryan had been paid over $200,000 by the the grateful defendant who had now secured the million or so bucks from the life insurance policy on his wife's life . . . or death.

All the participants had taken different paths. Some illuminated with glory, other's blackened by shame and disappointment, even death.

NEW YORK TIMES, FEBRUARY 5, 1996

Front page:

Today the grand jury of Summit County has indicted the former Assignment Judge Alexander King and the associate judge of the Superior Court Albert Sturmer on the charge of being accessories to the murder of Elias Rubin over twenty-five years ago. Bolstered by the telephone tapes secured from the home of the former prosecutor, Roger Leary, the F.B.I. also introduced the testimony of Lester Jones, an eyewitness to the fiery murder of Elias Rubin, a 1960s rebel of the Vietnam War. Both judges, if convicted, face long term incarceration, loss of their pensions, and disbarment.

The attorneys for both defendants have no comment.

Front page:

Summit County detectives found the former prosecutor of Summit County, Roger Leary, hanging from a rafter in the loft of his Bristol estate home.

Mr. Leary had virtually disappeared from public notice when his term in office had expired in November, 1995.

Neighbors of Mr. Leary had commented that the former prosecutor was extremely despondent after his wife and seven children had left him. Mr. Leary had been unable to secure gainful employment as an attorney and was relegated to the role of a volunteer at the local Republican Club.

Jennifer Leary, the decedent's wife, when reached, had no comment.

The foursome sat side by side around two marble-topped café tables at the Deux Magots Cafe watching the people passing on the Boulevard St. German de Pres. Sosie was pregnant with her first child, the fruit of the union with Joshua Ryan, the celebrated former defense attorney of Summit County, U.S.A. Ryan sat next to her, his face glazed with serenity, his mouth opened idiotically as his eyes traveled along the boulevard devouring the sights and sounds of Sunday in Paris.

Yehuda and Zeppi sat at the table adjacent to Ryan and Sosie. They were seated on the front line of the sidewalk cafe, all drinking Pernod or champagne or hot chocolate made with milk (Ryan's favorite).

"Sam called last night," Ryan said in a whispering undertone.

"How's his book coming?" Yehuda asked as he drained the last drops of champagne from his glass.

"Finished. His agent says he's putting it up for auction," Ryan replied.

"You'll become a star, Joshua," Zeppi said in a laughing voice.

"I'm going to hold out for the movie role."

He paused, smiled and then added, "With my luck, they'll want me to play Leary."

His hand covered the warm mug of hot chocolate as he lifted it absentmindedly toward his lips.

It was just past noon. They had eaten breakfast alfresco on the Ryan's fifth floor veranda outside the apartment Josh and Sosie rented on the Place Von Furstenberg. The apartment overlooked a park bench under a broad chestnut tree.

Eight months of heaven. Fresh baguettes and charcuterie and heavy cream and sweet fruits from Provence, as Ryan and Sosie luxuriated in the daily life of Paris.

Ryan took French language classes at the Alliance and Sosie learned to play the saxophone. In between, they made love.

"Have you heard from John?" Yehuda asked.

"He's traveling back and forth to Israel and Europe as head steward on El Al," Ryan laughed.

"With Triana, I bet," Sosie added.

"He broke up with her. She became too confining for Olsham. He needed his space, he told me," Ryan said.

"A man with that kind of sexual appetite should be preserved in a museum," Yehuda said.

Sosie placed Ryan's hand on her belly as the baby started to noticeably kick.

"Who'd ever think we'd be in Paris. Together. Sosie pregnant . . . who'd ever think?" Ryan said wistfully.

"You never asked about Dickson?" Yehuda declared.

"I thought you would tell me when you wanted to," Ryan replied.

"Osham called me. Right after Dickson had shot Mathias. Lester thought he saw somebody sneaking around his cabin."

"Was he?" Ryan queried.

"Lester said he found him tied to the cross at the campsite."

"That's it!" Zeppi exclaimed.

"There were dog bites all over Dickson's body," Yehuda said.

"Olsham told you all this?" Ryan questioned.

"Yes . . . Olsham found Dickson's body out there . . . On the cross . . . Bitten into hanging pieces.

"So who did it?" Sosie asked impatiently.

"Olsham is sure Dickson came out to finish off Lester. Right after he shot Mathias. Well . . . Dickson didn't figure on Lyndon .

. . a mean sonofabitch . . . that dog . . . Lyndon almost tore Dickson's arm off . . . and then mauled him to death. Lester somehow got that body up on that cross.

"He hated Dickson," Ryan interjected. "Dickson made fun of Lester when Lester was a trooper. Lester never forgot it."

"Lester was a sensitive fellow," Yehuda replied with a broad grin on his face. "I always thought Lester was creative. The cross?" He paused. "A religious fellow Lester always was . . . just like the rabbi . . . "

"And Elias Rubin. Did they ever find his bones?" Sosie asked. Her face was cherubic and radiant, highlighting her flashing smile. Pregnancy made her more beautiful than ever.

"Never," Ryan answered quickly and then continued, "You want to go to lunch?"

"You just ate, Joshua," Sosie chided good-naturedly.

"I can eat all day in Paris."

"Judge King would love to be sitting here," Yehuda stated absentmindedly.

"He wanted Sam to defend him," Ryan said.

"And what did Sam say?" Sosie asked.

"He said he was retired. He writes novels now."

"And you can also write novels," Sosie answered.

"So," Zeppi said, looking around at Yehuda and Ryan.

"So what?" Yehuda replied.

"Come now, my beloved husband. And you too, Joshua Ryan. You all talk around the only topic worth talking about. Did he do it or didn't he?"

"Do what, who did what?" Yehuda playfully replied.

"You idiot, Yehuda," Zeppi castigated Yehuda with a jovial slap of her hand on Yehuda's head.

"I received a letter shortly after we arrived in Paris," Ryan declared cryptically.

"From the rabbi?" Zeppi asked quickly.

"From the rabbi," Ryan replied.

"And what did he say?" Sosie joined into her mother's clamorous interrogation.

"He wished me well. Said he had married Moira. They were moving back to Israel. He had become an advisor to Netanyahu's government and then he ended with a few lines. Like a poem or sonnet. Biblical in nature."

"So . . . tell us already?" Zeppi shouted, her hand gently touching Joshua's face.

Joshua recited:

> *And Ruth came to lie with Moab. . .although she was the wife of Boaz . . . and Boaz was told by his kinsman of his wife's adultery . . . all of them knew of her betrayal of Boaz . . . and she was stoned . . . by all . . . she was stoned until she was dead . . .*

"What does it mean?" Sosie said, her face dumbfounded.

Ryan smiled, his palms raised up toward the sky.

"Yehuda?" Ryan motioned toward the stone face of his friend.

"It's nothing I know from the Bible," Yehuda replied.

"The rabbi makes up his own Biblical declarations," Ryan added. "I think . . . well, anyway. It doesn't matter what I think."

Sosie demanded, "Yes, it does, Joshua Ryan. We know *what didn't* kill Mrs. Rubin. What we don't know is what did kill her . . . and why?"

Ryan smiled enigmatically. He stared at Yehuda who said nothing. For almost a minute there was complete silence between the tables.

Ryan stood up from his chair. He walked back to the bar inside the massive café. He ordered another hot chocolate. He then walked back to the table sipping on the hot chocolate. Pedestrian traffic was building up as the Sunday lunch hour approached. He sat down next to Sosie; leaned over and kissed her on the cheek. He placed his hand on her stomach, laughing when the baby kicked out as if to touch him. He looked over at Yehuda who was gazing out at the sidewalk acrobats putting on their show.

"We should leave well enough alone," Joshua finally murmured. His voice was laced with the foam of the milk hot chocolate.

"We want to know," Zeppi insisted as she punched Yehuda on his shoulder to garner his attention.

"Beating me up won't get you any answers," Yehuda said with a sly grin crossing his sunburned, craggy face.

"You start, Joshua . . . and I'll jump in when I think you're going astray."

"We know she wasn't killed by strangulation," Ryan slowly started. "After the trial . . . right after . . . I had dinner with Seltzer . . . we all remember Seltzer, I presume."

"Stop beating around the bush, Joshua Ryan," Sosie declared in a laughing voice.

"You have to let me tell it my way, my love."

"Who strangled her?" Zeppi insisted

"Seltzer told me . . . our forensic guy . . . he told me . . . and that's after he had reviewed *all* the autopsy reports, the police reports, and Lilli O'Malley's statements of what she saw when she entered her mother's house on that fateful day . . . Well, anyway . . . Seltzer said that day, the daughter arrived just after 7:00 p.m. He concluded that the person at the door . . . the so-called delivery man . . . the one the victim mentioned to her daughter on the phone . . . well, Mrs. Rubin most likely didn't let him in. I don't know why, except that he did hand her an empty envelope. The one presented at the trial . . . with the rabbi's fingerprints on it. Mathias . . . I spoke to him after he testified . . . both he and Seltzer concluded that the delivery man . . . the strangler . . . came back to the house just before 7:00 p.m.

"But he didn't kill her, did he?" Zeppi half shouted in an anxious voice.

"No," Ryan continued, "he didn't kill her . . . because she was already dead when he returned to kill her. There's no doubt he was a contract killer . . . probably from Israel . . . and most probably from the Russian mafia that infests Tel Aviv. But," Ryan stopped to drink his hot chocolate, "Mrs. Rubin . . . the victim . . . and Seltzer was pretty sure about the scenario that led to her death . . . she was so aggravated about something . . . maybe that her husband was nowhere to be found, on their anniversary, no less. Maybe she knew about his affairs. We do not know what aggravated her. So much that she either overdosed on her insulin injection . . . you know she was an insulin dependant diabetic . . . or she might have forgotten that she had injected insulin into her arm once already, and then injected herself again. We do know that she fainted and

- 352 -

then died of hypoglycemic shock . . . her blood sugar count was thirteen or less and normal is 100. Seltzer concluded from the tests done on the blood, the tissues, the state of rigor mortis, her body temperature, and the organs at the autopsy that the time of death was a good hour *after* the medical examiner's conclusion that 5:45 p.m. was the time of death. Certainly it was before the arrival of Lilli O'Malley, her daughter, at about 7:15 p.m. and the contract killer at minutes before 7:00 p.m. Well, anyway," Josh paused with a smile, "I'm not boring you, am I?" Ryan emitted a dramatic sigh accompanied by a chuckle. "Anyway . . . we . . . Mathias and I and probably Seltzer . . . we think that the contract killer came back shortly after Mrs. Rubin fainted . . . and then fell forward hitting her head on the kitchen table. That's probably what caused the bruise near her scalp. Remember the kitchen table and chairs were damaged. She probably died shortly after the fall. Our friend probably knocked on the front door . . . of course, no one answered. And he knew that if he didn't complete the contract, he couldn't collect the fee . . . and most probably incur the wrath of his bosses for screwing up the job. I understand that they are an unforgiving group of people. So . . . faced with his dilemma, Mathias figured the killer went around the back . . . by the laundry room . . . and using the only quick way to enter the house . . . he busted the laundry room window . . . from the outside. Not as originally deduced that it was from the inside. It actually was a breaking and entering. So there he was, inside the house looking for his contract victim. . . and guess what . . . Surprise! Surprise! . . . She's already dead on the floor. Right on the kitchen floor. But what is there to do? If she died by accident, as she did, he's out . . . his bosses . . . they're out a lot of money. And believe me . . . as I will show you . . . a real lot of money. So . . . in order to collect his contract fee for killing Mrs. Rubin, he strangled her. Probably with a metallic wire or cable. With all his strength. To make sure that the whole world knew she had been strangled and died because of it. He probably left the scene just seconds before Lilli O'Malley arrived . . . out the laundry room door . . . "

"So Leary wasn't far off when he told the jury that the tobacco and the leaf found at the scene were probably left by someone from Israel . . . the killer . . . the one Leary tried to impress upon the jury who had been hired by the rabbi to kill his wife," Sosie said.

"He was right on the mark," Joshua responded. "More so than Leary could have ever imagined."

"But . . . ," Zeppi hurriedly stammered, her hand motioning to the waiter to bring her another glass of Pernod, "So what? How does the rabbi . . . what is the rabbi's connection to all this?"

Yehuda's soft voice murmured in almost a whisper, "Follow the money . . . somebody once said that in a movie . . . well, it's true . . . somebody got paid and somebody paid it."

"For what?" Zeppi questioned in a frustrated voice as she took the glass of Pernod from the waiter and eagerly sipped down half the liquor in the glass.

"Should I take over, Joshua?" Yehuda said.

"You might as well . . . it was in your ballpark, Yehuda."

"Well . . . Joshua . . . probably a month after the trial was over, called and asked me to check on an account with Bank Leumi. At their main office in Tel Aviv. He sent me a copy of a check that the rabbi had written to him in payment of his fee . . . drawn on Bank Leumi in New York."

"Why?" Sosie interrupted.

"You'll see," Joshua replied. "Go on, Yehuda . . . we have such an impatient audience."

"I had my friends at Shin Bet get a copy of the rabbi's checking account records."

"For what?" Zeppi demanded.

"Well," Joshua said, "I always knew there was a contract killer hidden in the wood pile. Where did he come from and who hired him? That was the mystery . . . so . . . and I reluctantly suspected the rabbi . . . I asked Yehuda. Go on, Yehuda . . . you have the floor."

"The checking account records show that the rabbi had written a $50,000.00 check after his wife's death, when he was in Israel. Made out to cash . . . and he endorsed it, collected $50,000.00 in cash, in American dollars."

"For what?" Zeppi demanded an answer.

"Of course, Joshua answered, "we don't know exactly what he did with the $50,000.00 U. S. dollars . . . but the assumption is he paid the fee over to the contract killer."

"Pinny . . . he's one of my associates . . . in the Shin Bet . . . Pinny checked around Tel Aviv . . . he has all sorts of friends in the Russian immigrant community. Well, Pinny heard that a large sum of money was paid to a certain group of Russian mafia . . . for a killing in the United States," Yehuda said.

Zeppi exclaimed in a loud, disbelieving voice, "How do you know it was the rabbi? Maybe it was something else . . . ."

Joshua and Yehuda both smiled. Pedestrian traffic on the sidewalk in front of the café had increased substantially as the acrobats and fire-eaters near the café were exciting the Sunday crowd.

"We don't know for sure," Joshua said in a matter-of-fact voice.

"Maybe it was some other deal . . . we'll never know . . . but don't you think it is strange for the rabbi to cash a $50,000.00 check in Israel, take the cash and then disappear . . . until we finally discover him in Mea Shearim . . . without the cash on him." Josh stared out into the traffic-filled Boulevard St. Germain noticing that Brasserie Lipp across the boulevard was getting crowded with American tourists. The hot summer sun beat deliciously down on his face. He certainly liked Paris, he thought.

"I always wondered why he would chance being convicted of his wife's murder by running off to Israel . . . especially after I definitely told him it could damage his defense."

Sosie's pale porcelain skin crinkled around her nose in a puzzled visage.

"I don't understand . . . I know I'm not a lawyer . . . Joshua . . . but you told me the the rabbi had to go to Israel . . . on behalf of the Rebbe . . . the elections . . . whatever. You told me he had a perfect right to leave the U.S. Now you are wondering why he left? Something is not kosher." Sosie paused and reached out to touch Joshua's arm. "I am your wife . . . Joshua . . . please explain . . . " Sosie's face ignited in a blaze of white teeth as her laughter bubbled out from her pixieish face.

"The Rebbe was part of the excuse to leave. It was essential that the rabbi pay off the killer . . . the group did not wait for its money very long . . . paid in Israel . . . in cash. Check or Visa was not acceptable."

Zeppi was now getting high from the mixture of too many Pernods and the hot afternoon sun beating down upon her head. She asked, "So . . . Joshua . . . how do you feel? The rabbi's wife is dead . . . the rabbi is runnng around . . . free as a bird . . . married to his mistress . . . .It just seems that all is not right with the world."

Joshua's face turned into stone. You could barely hear him breathe as his eyes hypnotically stared out onto the clogged, noisy boulevard. "Now," he thought, "I could use a drink."

Joshua rose from his chair and faced Yehuda and Zeppi. He then sat down again as if he had forgotten the words he was going to speak. Turning to Sosie, he said in a hushed tone, "I don't know how I feel. I did my job. I defended a man who was charged with murder . . . capital murder. His life was in my hands. I don't think I had the choice. If I was going to defend him, I couldn't judge him. That wasn't my job." He stopped breathing for a moment as if his whole body was consumed with thought.

"In all honesty, I don't feel good about it. That's why I am here . . . sitting with my friends . . . my love," he directed his head to Sosie, "you give everything you have for the client. You are his only life support. And you win. He wins."

"But that's all you wanted, Joshua," Sosie stated as her hand lovingly touched his face. "To win . . . to be respected again as a winner . . . as a trial lawyer." Joshua smiled and moved her hand to his lips and kissed her gently. "I thought so . . . that winning was everything. But sometimes it's not . . . I felt empty . . . Hollow inside . . . It was different than what I had thought it would be. You realize you never really win." Joshua paused as if to gulp in fresh air and then continued slowly. "And . . . well . . . it may not be right that he's free and took another's life . . . or wanted to anyway. That's not for me to decide. But I won't do it again . . . no matter what I do . . . it won't be me."

Joshua Ryan laughed. With all his body and soul he laughed. His knees did not pain anymore. His heart was light. His eyes were clear. And most of all the great overwhelming fear that had engulfed his life since his abusive childhood through disbarment and until today was gone. He could actually feel joy in his body and head. Touch it. Feel it. Chew on it. And he would never go back. Not to the law. Not to Summit County.

"I have to make a living somehow," Joshua declared as he rose from his chair. "Besides . . . there's lunch at the Bistro de Vagenennes. I hear their coq au vin is exquisite. And the sauce . . ."

He laughed. They all laughed. It was sure good to be alive.